T0245616

THE BALLAD OF MARY KEARNEY

A Tragedy of '98

Katherine Mezzacappa

THE BALLAD OF MARY KEARNEY

A Tragedy of '98

**HISTRIA
ROMANCE**

Histria Romance

Las Vegas ◊ Chicago ◊ Palm Beach

Published in the United States of America by
Histria Books
7181 N. Hualapai Way, Ste. 130-86
Las Vegas, NV 89166 USA
HistriaBooks.com

Histria Romance is an imprint of Histria Books dedicated to outstanding books in the romance genre. Titles published under the imprints of Histria Books are distributed worldwide.

Certain characters in this work are historical figures, and certain events portrayed did take place. However, this is a work of fiction. Names, characters, places, and incidents are either the product of the author's imagination or are used fictitiously. Any resemblance to actual persons, living or dead, is entirely coincidental.

Library of Congress Control Number: 2024944040

ISBN 978-1-59211-509-9 (softbound)
ISBN 978-1-59211-524-2 (eBook)

For Carmine Mezzacappa
'How do I love thee?
Let me count the ways.'

PART ONE

VOICES

Charity

"My name is Thomas Kearney, eldest son of Patrick Kearney of Tullaree Townland in this county. I farm twenty-two acres of land belonging to my Lord Goward in the Big House there, and for this I pay two shillings every quarter day. But my father he did tell me that this land was mine and he gave me a document the priest gave him to say so but that no Englishman will look at it for the priest wrote it. Do you get this down, sir? My father had his letters from a hedge school-master and he did try to learn me them but I could not be kept at them as my hands were needed from when I was seven years old.

"As you are a learned man sir you could tell me what is writ here but the priest tells me that for as long as my Lord is there in the Big House then I must pay him to farm the land that is mine own. I have five childer that live and two buried and my wife is in her seventh month and it is hard for me to pay my Lord sometimes, but it is not my Lord I fear but his man Blanch who tells me always that if I do not pay it is because I am idle and I will be turned off and how will my own live then? It is not one time that I have gone to the Offices round the back of the Big House—you will know sir that the horse-whip is there for any tenant who takes that there path where Lord and Lady can see us from the windows—and my Lady has put the coins into this my hand or I do not know how I should be here yet.

"Before Mr. Blanch it was better. My mother may perpetual light shine upon her said in the old Lord's day when the Quality danced in the Big House the tenants came to the windows and seen all the fine people leaping and all the candles burning. No, we have no money for tallow but rushes are plentiful.

"My age, sir? I believe I am about forty years of age. My father built this cabin himself. I have two cows in the byre here and we sleep on this wood above for to get the heat of the beasts. Potatoes and milk we have and some flax. The year there is a calf then more seed potatoes I have and sometimes a herring but only if there is money for to pay for the bull, if you understand me.

"Bridget my eldest is in the kitchen at the Big House and my boy Patrick goes the messages for them. If they take my daughter Mary too then it would not be so hard for us but I fear my Lord Goward's son and that lady who is there with him when he came back all dark from foreign places the priest said Rome. They say her husband is an old gentleman from down the country and for me it is not right and I know from Father O'Dowd this is so and their punishment will come he says."

The family of Thomas Kearney from my visitation I would judge better-situated than many by the possession of his two cows and the two children already in service. I have inspected their dwelling and it is of the usual two rooms, the byre to one side with a sleeping loft above, the other being where the family cooks at the peat fire. Their belongings number one hanging cooking pot, one griddle, two rush-seated chairs of peasant make and two or three farm implements, no ornament save their Bridget cross nailed above the fire. There is little light and air in the cabin and what there is reeks of peat smoke so I must confess I remained but a short time within, but I will say the room was swept though whether in honour of my visit I cannot say. Their windows are as usual small, and stuffed with rags. In the sleeping loft is an ancient straw-filled palliasse. The father tells me that he and his wife sleep in the centre, with the youngest child next the parent of the same sex, and thus lying outwards in order of age—this arrangement we have often seen. Thomas would not accept our offer of help willingly, for he feared that we would take his children from him and send them to the Charter School, and, he says, he cannot put in danger their immortal souls. After some reasoning he accepted of the Society clothing for the children of the most rude cut and stuff. The entire family goes barefoot but he would not permit me to speak of any shoes for he said this would arouse too much suspicion especially from my Lord Goward's man Blanch, of whom we have already heard speak and little of it good especially when that gentleman have drink taken as he do often. The presence of Lady Mitchelstown at the Big House is of scandal to us all that even his lowliest tenants should know of it though it is said that Lord Goward tolerates this as it keeps his son from the servants and Lady Goward will hear nor see no ill of her boy.

The deed Thomas shew'd me is in the form of a last will and testament of Patrick Kearney inheriting his only surviving son Thomas against the day when this land be returned to its owners, but this document have no legal worth though Thomas set great store by it.

We are grateful to our brother Edwin Chittleborough for bringing this family to our notice. Our brother warns that the House is not a fit place for girls without protection though he and our sister Janet do what is possible that the girl Bridget not be ruined nor her sister Mary if she is to follow her there.

I have sought to put down Thomas's words faithfully to shew that he be worthy of our charity. This is the deposition of Brother Samuel Ingham, Chandler, of the Religious Society of Friends, Moyallan Meeting House, in the county of Down the eighteenth day of the first month of the year seventeen hundred and sixty-five.

Slievenalargy

"Almost there…" Fr O'Dowd whispered, though had he spoken aloud there would have been no risk of them hearing him above the tearing of the wind. And again he thought, "Is this to be my martyrdom, then?" as his sodden alb whipped and slapped cruelly against the back of his knees, "To die of an ague on this mountain amongst these poor wretches, and not on an English gibbet?" He lifted his head and filled his lungs and called the Latin into the rain: "*Ecce Agnus Dei, ecce qui tollit peccata mundi*" as he raised the Host.

Behind him the ragged response battled wind and wet:

"*Dómine, non sum dignus, ut intres sub tectum meum: sed tantum dic verbo, et sanábitur ánima mea.*"

Few of those grey shapes, huddled, inert and immutable as standing stones, could have told him what those words meant, yet they repeated them as they would a long-remembered spell, and would not question doing so anymore than they would their pagan circlets of Bridget crosses or the healing powers of the dank waters of Struell.

"I'll look after your vestments today, Father", said Thomas Kearney, taking the soaking garments from the hands of the shivering priest and rolling them up into a dirty canvas bag. "Sure I'll have to put straw on the top in case they're after stopping me".

The priest pushed back a memory of the slanting sharp shadows of July in the Via degl'Ibernesi, of cool tiled rooms and the vast oak cupboards, built *in situ*, in which vestments hung in dry and reverent silence. These were places he would never see again. He turned to look at Thomas, hunched against the rain, his greying hair slick to his head.

"I do not know will Sarah get through this time", he was saying. "What will I do?"

It was barely a question, more a statement of despair. The priest despised himself for falling back on the old formulary: "She is in God's hands". Yes, but what did God intend to do? Leave this bone-thin man to somehow struggle on alone, with those old-weary, hollow faces of his children looking to him? "Dadda, I'm hungry". Of course they were, God love them!

"I shall come. Send Robert. Send the child as soon as you know… as soon as Sarah knows."

"I will so. Thank you Father. I'll see to the ould vestments."

Moneyscalp Clergy House
15th March 1765
Feast of St. Menignus, Martyr

Thomas Kearney's wife was brought to bed of a daughter this wretched night. Robert the boy still at home came for me, which was well for me and they, for otherwise no baptism—the child is puny and fretful, and for her, tiny Christian soul, I fear the worst. But might it indeed be better for this innocent to be gathered in than to turn her face to the wind in this life that awaits her? Without my hand on Robert's bony shoulder I should not have found my way across that bog—as it is I stumbled above three times and I still feel the cold of that peaty water in my knees. Thankfully a pale dawn saw me home again or I should have had to ask that poor child to guide me once again, sure-footed even in darkness. His younger brother is the new bog-trotter for the Big House, and we must be grateful for this for Revd. Samuels would have him sent to Downpatrick to the Charter School where the price of scant food and clothing would be the loss of that poor child's soul, for a Protestant they would make him.

Feast of St. Patrick
17th March 1765

"Come away now, Mary," murmured the priest to the girl kneeling by the bed. He laid a hand on her thin shoulder.

"I'll not leave her, so I won't."

The girl's eyes were large and glittering in her pale face. *Could she be feverish?*, the priest wondered—no, the cap of her shoulder had been cool to his touch.

"She'll not be alone." He had learned in Rome that what he'd assumed was the Church's teaching, that a body should never be left until it was safely in the ground or a devil would steal the soul, was nothing but a superstition of his native country—and probably a pagan one at that. Yet the knowledge changed nothing.

"Your mother is beyond all harm. Tis you we must think of now." He held her arm, easing her up from where she knelt amongst the shawled, droning women.

"She sleeps in Christ, Mary."

The girl gazed down at her mother's face, looking for the woman she had known. This hollowed face was not hers, nor the rosary-chained fingers. The child that had uselessly claimed her life lay alongside her mother's corpse, a crumple-faced doll swaddled in a piece of old altar cloth.

The priest lead the girl outside. The wavering candlelight through the half-door haloed Mary's tangled head, but her face was in shadow. *She'll need to be made decent before she's let go to the Big House,* he thought. *Sure Bridgie can take her in hand.*

"I can get you a place at Goward Hall, Mary." He heard her intake of breath.

"This is no surprise, surely?"

"So soon?" she whispered.

"You'll eat there. And be clothed. Shoes even."

"They say it's not a place for a Christian child—that the squireen is back and another man's wife with him."

"True. But Bridgie must also have told you that for as long as that lady is there, there can be no danger to any other female. The boy has lost his head to her, God help him."

"How can he have? Has he no fear for his immortal soul, Father?"

"That you have is what'll save you, child. That and your sister being along of you, and the good Quaker lady that serves Lady Goward. You'll be well guarded."

Poor child to worry herself so. Sure his Lordship will not be looking at a half-starved sparrow like yourself. He thought of Letty Mitchelstown's opulent flesh and bold eye and shivered. A vision to tempt a saint, never mind a threadbare, bone-tired mountainy priest.

"Who'll look after Dadda and Robert and Kate?"

"Kate herself. Sure isn't she ten years old already?"

William Blanch

The innkeeper eyed the two drinkers covertly from behind the high counter. The speaker had his back to him, but his story was familiar; William Blanch was in the habit of regaling it to any Englishman he succeeded in cornering for long enough. Rather than listening to it again, Mulholland watched the face of the other man.

"I've been Lord Goward's land agent for these past seven years after I was cashiered from the Dragoons. That matter I do not wish to dwell upon, suffice to say that I was treated very sorely and had I had the means to defend my name I should most assuredly have done so and been victorious."

"Certainly—"

"I was born in Middle Hambleton in the county of Rutland in 1721, the second son of the vicar of Normanton. Doubtless you have heard of the place."

"I must confess, being of the north country—"

"It matters not. My brother distinguished himself in the East India Company before succumbing to cholera in Calcutta at the age of thirty-two. I have failed to satisfy my father's expectations in almost every way, and my brother, being dead, thus has the advantage of me in my father's eyes. Two sisters remain alive, one condemn'd to genteel poverty as the wife of a curate without a permanent living, the other unmarried and trying to make up for the itch that no one will scratch, in tireless work for the Dorcas society. She will expect in due course to be supported in her meaningless existence by *me*."

Hargreaves glanced in desperation at Mulholland but got no more than a nod.

"Father expected me to follow him into the Church and so sent me up to Cambridge as a gentleman-commoner. I do not know how my two years of parsing and gambling were to fit me for such a role, though it did nothing to prevent my fellows from seeking preferment in whatever way possible. My closest companion at the dogs now dons lawn sleeves and suffers from gout. When it was clear I would not perjure myself to take Holy Orders my father then got me a commission."

"An honourable undertaking, I am sure—"

"The proudest moment of my military career was the subduing of the Scotch rebels in '45. What I learned then has I believe stood me in good stead for the task I face now. It is necessary to take no prisoners if one is to impose order. In those northern wastes I found it necessary to act on that principle to the letter—naught else would suffice. The rebels were dealt with insufficiently in the Old Pretender's day, and what Cumberland's men had to do after was the result of there not having been greater resolve in an earlier time."

Hargreaves squirmed.

"My health is sometimes indifferent," Blanch went on. "I suffer periodically from a stricture, the result, I believe of scratching the itch of my commanding officer's wife, which feat I managed periodically by the simple expedient of shutting my eyes or by turning her over; the lady was pock-marked but persuasive, and had I not obliged her (as did I believe a number of others) then it would have gone ill for me—which it did in any case, but not because of the lady."

Hargreaves struggled to his feet. "You must excuse me, sir, I am somewhat fatigued—"

"You will take another drink, sir? I do not bore you? It is not often I may speak with an Englishman though what you find to trade with here I do not know and I doubt you will come here again."

"I will not, sir, thanking you for your kindness. I—"

"Then at least keep me company until I finish this one."

Supressing a sigh, Hargreaves subsided onto the wooden form.

"My Lord Goward spoke to me in rapturous tones of his Irish estates, the picturesque aspect of his fine house, his deer park, his demesne. I will confess that his offer was welcome to me for it suited me well to leave England for a time. His London house was very well-appointed—one of those fine new houses in Berkeley Square, you know—and so raised my hopes as to what I should find here. But for all his talk of Charterhouse and Tom Tower, he is little more than an Irishman himself, though his family be here but for three generations. He will drink in what he is pleased to call his library with a popish priest, but not with an Englishman and a gentleman born! And what, pray, am I to do? I take my meals in what was the head footman's pantry; did he expect me to eat in the servants' hall with that canting Aminadab of a Quaker manservant and his plain-faced dame and those scrubbed-up Irish peasants pretending to the role of loyal retainers, who if their intelligence was not so slow would be plotting to murder us in our beds? The estate itself is of fine aspect, well-wooded and with a sweeping drive—you should take the time to see it—yet it is not graced with a house worthy of a gentleman, but more a crazed hotch-potch of castle-barracks and oh-my-lady's-chamber, no more a noble seat than a chap-book is a mezzotint. Yet of this my Lord is inordinately proud. Englishman he might claim to be, but half of what he calls his house is merely a tower-house with asymmetrical masonry thrown against it seemingly without plan or apparent purpose, other than to make it larger. A part of it is an enormous bawn, as they call it here, an ancient fortress which gunpowder would not shift, and this he tells me with all the pride of a decayed Irish noble (one of the scores descended from Brian Boru were you to give their stories any credence) is the work of one De Courcy, some Norman robber baron, I believe, who made penance for his bloody excesses by setting up houses of monks to pray for him and thus buy his way into the Empyrean. This brutish structure rubs up against a long three-storeyed building of austere aspect of the Lord Protector's Day, dominated within by a vast oak staircase of frightful aspect which creaks and groans when it do thunder and up which a carriage and four could pass. I will not suggest such a feat to my Lord or he would I am sure have McNamara saddle up his favourite hunter and expect me to make action of the thought."

"I doubt I shall have the opportunity to see the place, as the pressure of business permits me so little time, but I thank you for your suggestion. I must retire, sir, begging your pardon."

Lord Goward

"Pass me that stool, there, my good fellow. If I can just raise this leg up so – *no!* Damn you to blazes man, not like that… oh… oh, how is this to be borne— *CHITTLEBOROUGH!* Where is that wretch when he's needed?"

"My Lord?"

"Edwin, raise this confounded leg, man, before the Reverend here decides he can no longer call on his patron or risk his immortal soul…. oh… ow… did anyone ever have to suffer as I do… oh, that's better, man."

"Perhaps the salt bath after supper, my Lord, and fresh bandages?"

"Has my Lady company this evening?"

"No, my Lord."

"And my boy?"

"Viscount Kilkeel is now gone to Gormanscourt with Lady Mitchelstown."

"Ah, Chittleborough, best not name that excellent female, for we upset the parson. Can't you see how he fidgets? Fill the fellow's glass will you, and ignore his protestations, or I declare I shall ask his papist colleague to call on me instead. O'Dowd is a decent man, likes his port and to talk to me of Rome. Reverend, you look pale; this will fortify your blood. What's that you say? That cob of yours has enough sense to get you home, as long as Chittleborough here and McNamara can get you into the saddle.

"Chittleborough knows me better than my own wife. He came to me when he was not more than fifteen years old, and I a fine young gallant shaving for a beard. Found him on my cousin's estate in Norfolk, sharp-witted for a stable boy and with a fine enough leg for both here and my London house. He has been everywhere with me and when we got him his letters he did all that parsing for me at Charterhouse and none of the masters the wiser! His only fault is his religion, sir, for he will not take a glass with me, no matter how often I have pressed him— how many masters would do that, Reverend? Yes, yes, I know he sits quiet beneath your pew Sundays, and makes you believe he listens to your sermons more than any man in the place, but Chittleborough is an obstinate Quaker—oh fie, you have spilt your port, sir, let me remedy that. And damn his eyes, but did he not turn our maidservant too when he wed her. But a better servant I could not find."

Edwin Chittleborough and the Reverend Samuels

"Now Sir, the steps here are somewhat worn away and thou must mind thy poor head, for it has problems enough without breaking it on this stone, though I fancy thee might not notice if 'ee were to take a tumble, sir. Hold steady, sir, and hold to Chittleborough here, for he hath much practice in helping gentlemen who be in a merry state, if thee understand me sir.

"No sir, with respect, thy horse can wait. Some of my wife's camomile and ginger will help thee, and then the fresh air will quite clear the cloudiness and Mrs. Samuels be none the wiser.

"Here sir, sit 'ee here close to the fire. Lift your feet, just so, rest them on the fender. Try not to sleep just yet, not till 'ee have this brew drunk down. No, it is no witch's potion, sir, my own wife has prepared it here before thine eyes. My Lord has had the better of 'ee sir, as he has many good men. Ye came here to speak to him of Lady Mitchelstown, I believe, but thee'll not turn him, sir. See, my Lord, her father and Lord Mitchelstown were the closest of friends from when they boxed each other's ears at Charterhouse. Mitchelstown knew what he was about when he took my lady at the altar, for she and the Duke of York had as you might say, an understanding, one that the Duchess did not care for but about which she could do nothing. 'Twas an advantage for Mitchelstown, for that is how some sees this world—not thee and I sir, no, thou art quite right sir, no, for 'tis not God's plan that marriage be used in such a fashion. I too know it well. But, Mitchelstown's debts were paid, and the old gentleman was always happier at Newmarket than in his marriage bed. His Highness the Duke of course took his eye elsewhere, and not to his Duchess neither, and it is young Goward who protects Lady Mitchelstown since he come back from his Tour. I fear he may not do so long, for the poor lady doth cough so, though perhaps that brightness of eye and feverish cheek do please some, sir.

"Half-naked thee say she was, when thee called. Well, sir, Edwin Chittleborough has learned to look down or look away. 'Tis what a good servant does, sir, sees all, says nothing, hears nothing… I speak only to thee sir, so that thee may know what 'ee do go against, sir, and because I do not like to see my master in an ill-humour."

From the Diary of Revd. Dr. George Samuels, Rector of Kilcoo Parish

17th March 1765

This being the feast of that good man that did bring the light of Christ to this miserable island, and as the Papists would have it drew out also the snakes, I was today at the service of my Lord Bishop in the cathedral church in Downpatrick. As this was a Wednesday no large numbers of papists have congregated at the wells, though I understand spies have been sent to Struell to ascertain what transpired there today; if the magistrates were not so idle then those who indulge in this idolatry would be whipped as the law provides.

Though much fatigued by the journey, the roads being not improved nor my horse either, I was obliged to call afterwards upon my Lord Goward at the behest of my Lord Bishop. What is a man to do to honestly obtain preferment or even in this benighted place to keep his living? Word has reached his Lordship the Bishop of the return of Lord Goward's boy from his Tour—a journey that had been de-layed by the late hostilities with France and thus by his mother's unwillingness to let him go near danger—a delay which has been to his benefit as he was older than is customary when he set off. I must confess to some admiration of this young man and hope that he may do his class and religion honour, for we do stand in sore need of it. He has an openness, a directness of eye and a straightforwardness of speech—without his father's habitual profanities—which I do appreciate. And he seems free of that vice which corrupts so many young gentleman, as well as older ones who should be wiser, that of the gaming-tables. It appears he limits himself to the occasional wager on the nags, but for the fun of the thing. I see that he is returned quite the gallant, that English uprightness of his now given some elegance of pose and bearing, of what they will call *ton* in the circles to which I cannot quite aspire, helped by a cut velvet coat and frothings of Brussels lace—he is undoubt-edly what women are pleased to call handsome. With the ardour of youth and the help of some treatises he has ordered from England, he do make noise about im-provements to the lands he will one day inherit. Such youthful zeal is perhaps to be recommended, but will he find in his father's tenants the wit to carry out his desires? And what of my Lord Goward's man Blanch? Merely disagreeable when sober, irascible when not, which is oft the case, he will not look kindly on a younger man interfering in his domain, not least as young Kilkeel is sure to discover Blanch's methods. But the state of Goward's tenantry is not my Lord Bishop's concern, anymore than he gives much thought to the state of his own. Nay, the brake upon young Kilkeel's reforming appetite is of a different sort. He has come back to Ireland in the company of Lady Mitchelstown and she lives at the House and is waited on by all as though his wife and not that of that old fool Mitchelstown. So as my poor bones were rattled still further on the road into Goward's demesne, I was obliged to cudgel my feeble brains with some stratagem to both voice my displeasure (or rather, my Lord Bishop's) without incurring the same from Lord Goward. Without his support I shall not long stand in my pulpit and look down on his pew. My Lord Bishop refuses to see the difficulty in which I am placed.

In my Lord Goward's company I had no choice but to fortify myself in the Irish fashion, though I would fain do this alone, even if his claret be infinitely better than mine, but it gave me no courage to voice what I went there to say. I am late home and here only thanks to my faithful cob and the ministrations of my Lord's servant Chittleborough, a Quaker betimes but a good man who with his wife did what he could to restore me to my proper senses and get me homewards as a decent Christian. I owe thanks to him for knowing the magnitude of the task that faces me. Today I have seen Lady Mitchelstown with my own eyes, seen rather more of her person than I would have wished, she delighting in my discomfort. What an example to the servants! Yet them I cannot speak ill of, though wish that I could for they are papists all of them save Blanch, the young Viscount's dandy of a Swiss valet, and this man Chittleborough and his wife. This I may never express to his Lordship the Bishop but 'tis their popery that saves their souls whilst they dismiss our Protestantism for the lack of morals their betters show them. The maid they call Bridgie with a mutinous stare answered my pull of the bell (Goward no doubt for the London season has a fine liveried footman with an elegant turn of calf, but Ireland has its way of setting a different standard for all of us. My old friend now Dean of Worcester would blench at what I could tell him, so I write but little to him now). And well she might stare at me and not elsewhere, for as I was removing my hat and handing her my cane, who should I see but Mitchelstown's lady skipping down the stairs in her petticoats and stays and nothing to shield her bosom, whilst barefoot young Kilkeel in his shirt came tumbling after, laughing and shouting betimes. The sight of Lady Mitchelstown's snowy orbs perched high above her stays, displayed as fruit on a platter ready to be grasped and eaten is an image I must pray to forget, though I fear I never shall. My own wife's dry and pendent dugs were once thus, but their promise was not to be realised, for poor Meg is barren and all do know it, though some may choose to blame me for our childless home. Unfortunate lady, she sleeps as I write this, her little dog in a trug by her bed. She talks to that pug as if it were our longed-for child. She will kill it with kindness for it eats twice what will any normal beast, and then what will comfort her?

Lady Goward

"So, Bridget, this is your sister Mary? Come here, child, do not shuffle so. Look up! I am merely an old lady and cannot bite you, though there may be others under this roof who would wish to try. Do you be schooled by your sister, child, who knows our ways here."

In terror of stepping out of the unaccustomed clogs, and still in awe of the noise they made on the flagged floor, for bare feet no matter how hardened make little sound, Mary stepped forward. Bridget's gentle nudge propelled her onto the Turkey rug and relative safety (at least from the noise made by her own feet). But it was more than she could manage to raise her burning face to the old lady's gaze. All of this was so new: the rough fustian of her dress, the marvellous feel of worsted stockings over her feet and toes (her calloused soles felt nothing yet), the sleeping in a bed high up in a building that felt as vast as a mountain with no one alongside her but her sister and with no sounds nor scent of the cows shifting and lowing in the byre beneath. The vast size of the rooms overawed her and the furniture seemed to stare at her. Deep windows let in so much light but so little cold, their sashes tight, draped with curtains in which if she were to hide herself she would be as muffled as in her grave. The cleanliness of it all… and the expectation that it should always be so, and herself also.

"Look up, child. I want to see your face, not the top of that mob-cap."

Obedient, Mary raised her eyes, tried to look at the old lady but eventually rested her gaze in confusion on her left shoulder. What she had glimpsed was the most beautiful face she thought she had ever seen. It was true, the Quality were different. She did not know then that simply having enough to eat, a warm bed of one's own whatever the weather, and freedom from the relentless grubbing in earth or at teat to survive, was enough to make of another human being a different species entirely. Lady Goward wore no whitener, no spots, no rouge, yet there was a powdery softness to her cheeks, a comfortableness about the flesh of the neck (if Mary noticed the incipient goitre, then she did not recognise it for what it was, for it was simply part of the marvel that was the whole). Unlike young Lady Mitchelstown, of whom Mary was already heart-thumpingly afraid, and not from any unkindness shown her, but from the knowledge that that lady was damned to hell and could take others with her, Lady Goward wore her own hair, pinned beneath what looked to Mary like a large handkerchief of a whiteness never before seen. She sat by the marble fireplace in an old wrapping gown of faded brocade which to Mary looked like cloth of fabulous richness, a frilled lace tucker folded demurely into her bodice. One hand was hidden in the folds of her dress, whilst the other rested on the embroidered firescreen. Mary already knew that she would one day soon have the handling of the marvels of Lady Goward's clothes ("though you'll not find them so marvellous after you have had the laundering of them a few times", her sister said later).

"You are to take your orders from me alone, child, and from Mrs. Chittleborough, but not from the men of this household—apart from Chittleborough of course. You know Mr. Blanch, I believe? Regrettably my husband has not been here often enough to manage things to our liking, thus need we a Blanch though I would lief have any other but him. I know the day your father comes to pay his rent and mark him that he must not change it whatever he is told by Blanch in case I should not be there. I think he will understand me.

"My boy has his Swiss valet. I believe you have met Mr. Niederer, though I think you will find he is little in the kitchen quarters, that gentleman being a little too refined perhaps for our simpler Irish ways."

Mary had met Niederer, but Niederer had in effect declined to meet her. The valet had simply raised an eyebrow but had refused even to look her directly in the face. Now Lady Goward *was* looking at her, smiling, and there was patience and kindness in her smile, but some sternness too, the face of someone long accustomed to have her own way.

"I believe you will see little of my son the Viscount Kilkeel. I do not know how long he will remain with us. He and my lady Mitchelstown do lead a rather gay existence."

Mary trembled. What confusion was this? An outright acceptance of this flaunting of God's law? These Protestants were strange people.

"You can do what my husband asks you, of course, but he will not ask you much. Chittleborough is his man; he and Janet you may trust to protect your good character—no need to blush, child. In fact I would urge you and so does your sister I am sure, to put your faith in them both, for they are good people even if they do not conform in their hearts—but those hearts are loyal to *us*.

"You will find my Lord Goward likes to amuse himself in the Irish way, but there is no real harm in that, though the Gout do make him irritable at times. His interests are his port and the nags, and I do not complain of these, for there are worse things some wives have to bear. Sometimes you will see your priest here—I believe my husband finds him better company than poor, solemn Mr. Samuels— but do not, child, meet with him for the purposes of your religion under my roof. You will have one Sunday in four free, and if you choose to spend it walking up to Slievenalargy you are free to do so, though you must endeavour to keep your clothing free of the mud. When you are here, you are part of this household and so will accompany the other servants to their pew in the parish church of Sundays, and pay reverent attention to Mr. Samuels's words."

James, Viscount Kilkeel, to Letitia, Countess Mitchelstown

Goward Hall,
20ᵗʰ April 1765

My beloved Letty,

You are cruel indeed to one who cannot live without you. You are kindness itself to think of the health of your old aunt at Ardglass, but in being so you cause suffering to me. I hope the old beldam knows the honour that is done to her. But perhaps you think not of her but of how you may inflame my ardour still further. In fact, my lady, I am on fire, as you well know, and I would lief give you proof of it if you will send me line of when you return to my arms that I may hold up your coach and tup you within before your dainty foot crosses my door and sets all the viperish tongues in the county wagging again. How is my pego to keep warm without the tight snugness of your little burrow? How is your poor servant to rest his weary head without your pretty diddeys for a pillow? I press my fevered face into your linen by night; I cannot live without you, d--n you!

I have been to Church as a dutiful son should, and to set an example to the servants, as my mother insists I must (though why I know not, for she will turn neither the Chittleboroughs from their quaking nor the rest from Rome). It took all my power not to laugh in the face of poor Samuels, for I heard not a word he spake but saw again only his horror when he espied you all tumbled and disarrayed that day he came to call on my father. I am certain too that he will not forget what he saw, much as he may wear out his worsted knees in prayers for deliverance!

I send this letter by the little bog-trotter-grease-boots you thought so picturesque. He tells me that he will take it barefoot, "for to run the faster, sorr!" In the house he is made to wear shoes, but outdoors where he needs their protection he will have none. Ah, but this is a mad country. The child, as you know, is brother to my mother's little maid Bridget, and has lately been joined by a sister, who if she pleases you shall be moulded for your use. She is a puny thing of not above fifteen years of age, and when she can be prevailed upon to raise her head, has the most charming pair of dark blue eyes—but she is painfully shy. Take you her in hand, and you will make something of her I am sure. Should you do so, you will have my mother's undying gratitude, for these are the children of that tenant my mother protects for having saved her darling boy from the duck pond when years ago his tutor was distracted by the dimpled rear of one of the dairy maids.

To please my mother though I shall attempt to make all well with Samuels. I shall take as my subject the sobering matter of turnips, and seek his view on whether we should essay some changes to agricultural methods on this estate. I have seen some interesting theories at work on my cousin's lands in Norfolk—but my love, let us not talk of turnips! Tell your aunt that you leave me at death's door without you—for if one can die of love I am surely moribund and there is but one cure—the touch of your soft lips on mine and all that follows. I am prostrate before you, so please make haste and join me where I lie—but expect not to rise up again quickly. All the rising shall be mine! My love, my life, come quickly—and come and come again with me!

Your obt. Slave,

James Kilkeel

Lady Mitchelstown's Chamber

"Is Lady Mitchelstown down yet, Mary?"

"She is so, Mrs. Chittleborough. I seen her go into the dining-room."

"I *saw* her, child. Do thee go and see to her room then, before she has done with her breakfast. Thou hast not had the doing of that chamber yet, but thou know'st which it is and I have taught thee what to do."

Mary gathered her tools and ran up the back stairs, then slowed her pace along the landing, pattering on tiptoe as she had been taught. Though she had seen its occupant downstairs, she knocked softly at the bedchamber door; the sound felt less loud to her than the pounding of her own heart. No answer. She grasped the porcelain handle, but it rattled and further jarred her nerves; a tied bundle of feathers slipped through her fingers. She picked it up, tiptoed in and at once retreated a step; so strong was Lady Mitchelstown's scent that Mary had again to tell herself that Lord James's lover was downstairs. She remembered Mrs. Chittleborough's instructions: "Start with the bed but as a God-fearing child avert thine eyes!" But on closing the door, Mary was at once distracted by the silk peignoir huddled on the floor. The finest material Mary had until then handled had been Fr. O'Dowd's lawn alb, when it was the turn of the Kearneys to slap and scrub and throw fistfuls of ash into the laundry-barrel. That fine Italian weave from the workshop near the Via degl'Ibernesi had seemed to her fit covering for an angel. But here was a stuff the colour of pale butter, that when she picked it up slipped over her fingers like warm water, that made a sound like wind in the reeds as she reverently returned it to its hook on the back of the door. She marvelled at the fineness and regularity of the drawn-thread work... ah, the bed!

Mary thought she would never cease to be surprised at the height at which the Quality must sleep. It was as though even the shape of the furniture reflected their station in life. Here the young Viscount climbed up to his sinful embrace of Lord Mitchelstown's wife, whilst she and Bridgie had to huddle together in their low truckle bed. She took a deep breath and tied back the heavy bed-curtains.

So vast a bed, and so many pillows! Did they play hide and seek here, lose each other in this tangle of linen? Mary's face burned. She extricated the satin embroidered counterpane, marvelling at the patience and uniformity of its workmanship, the tendrils of flowers and foliage so near to the life, but which would never fade nor have thorns to scratch. Mary knew how and by whom every article in her father's cabin had been made; she wondered if it ever entered the heads of the occupants of this bed to consider the labour of whoever had stitched this, when they tumbled it aside in their feverish need?

"Air the room!" Mrs. Chittleborough's instructions dinned in her head as though that good lady stood at her elbow. Mary crossed to the window, nearly tripping over a delicately embroidered shoe. She picked up this other marvel reverently, running her finger over the encrusted satin, the little waisted wooden heel. This was a shoe that could only be worn on polished boards, on carpet or marble, a shoe to dance in whilst the likes of herself, with her bare soles pewter-grey and hardened like saddle leather, gazed in at the window. Mary looked at it as it lay light in her hand. She was still getting accustomed to the stockings and serviceable boots that Janet Chittleborough had provided as an alternative to the cacophonous clogs, never having been shod in her entire life before coming to the Big House. Surely her own small foot… Never in her life had she possessed anything simply for its beauty, and precious little of her own even for practicalities. Mary dropped to her knees and scrambled around for the shoe's partner, then placed them decorously together by the side of the bed.

Below the window stood a dressing table with Lady Mitchelstown's pink and white complexion contained in demure little porcelain pots. Mary hurriedly dusted up scattered powder, then reached behind and lifted the sash, pausing to look down on the sweep of the park which none of the servants excepting the gardeners and McNamara the ostler were allowed to cross and McNamara only if he was leading the horses. She turned back towards the bed and cried aloud. Facing her was a thin, pale-faced girl with dark hair gathered under a mob cap, wearing a servant's grey garb with a clean white handkerchief at the neck, her sleeves rolled to the elbow and a too large apron tied twice round. Only when the girl put her hand against the tester for support did Mary realise it was herself she saw. Taller, straighter and thanks be to God a little fuller in the face than the little girl she had last seen reflected in the still, dark water at Struell.

Mary pulled the linen sheets tight, pushed the bolster back into position and gathered up the pillows, one of which had fallen to the floor. *Why do they need so many? Sure to God they don't have four heads.* Pounding the goose-down back into shape, she caught sight of two long golden hairs. She plucked them up and walking back to the window saw them sail out on the breeze. Then looking over her shoulder as though fearful of being observed, she furtively searched the other pillows for shorter, darker hairs.

"I wonder how he looks when he sleeps?" she asked herself.

Letitia, Lady Mitchelstown,
to Her Sister Anne Peveril

Tyrella House
Ardglass
22nd May 1765

Dearest Anny,

I have stolen a few days rest from the arms of my adorable boy Kilkeel, and am passing them in what you might term good works by the side of Aunt Evans. My little Viscount must sometimes rest from me to keep him ardent, in my view! I promised to tell you something of Goward Hall, the oddest, tumbliest place you ever saw, with a rare cast of charming rustics to add to the picturesque confusion.

Mine host Lord Goward is an amiable old fellow, who spends most of his time in his library not reading but drinking his claret and sending the boy to place his gold on the horses. He is an old friend of my husband, but for all their friendship does not look askance at my bedding his son, for dearest James in the eyes of papa and mamma can do no evil. The old lady loves me because her son does, and that is enough for her. She is a gentle old dame, who feeds all the cats in what they call here in Ireland the Offices— the Home Farm we would have it—embroiders fire screens and cushions as much as she can still see, and carries out furtive acts of charity to save the tenants from ruin, for my Lord's estates are managed by a hard and bitter Englishman by the name of Blanch, who regards me (for all I take notice of him) with grey disapproval. It is as well that he is firm with the peasantry, mayhap, for without him I fear confusion would reign. My dear boy has some dilettante ideas as to improving his lands, but for me I see little point to this for the ground is stony and inhospitable, the fields the size of pocket handkerchiefs and fit for nothing but sheep and potatoes. But he has his dull moments when he must pore over agricultural treatises and speak of new-fangled machinery—why, heaven alone knows when the people here are so cheap and plentiful, for poor as they are they have no limits to their fecundity. What a world it must be, Anny, if after dark there is no light and nothing to do but grope at each other in the blackness, when we the Quality can work ourselves up to a fever pitch of anticipation by forcing ourselves to the card table or the harpsichord before lighting our way to our beds and keeping the candle lit to have the pleasure of seeing what we do there.

There is no footman for me to marvel over a fine turn of calf, and Lord Goward makes do with a lumbering Norfolk manservant who is a veritable Hodge, sturdy as a beer barrel in fustian breeches and impeccable linen. His wife heads the maid servants and as to her dress is merely a female edition of her lord with a preposterous bonnet atop—replaced only when she goes forth to her quaking meetings, when she dons a black silk cap with lappets and an apron of a most unbecoming green—altogether a garb which would not tempt anyone to assail Mistress Chittleborough's virtue. These are the only English servants at Goward Hall, the others all being Papists of varying ill-grace and manners, who will never look one in the face for fear of some contagion to their religion, it seems. James has a Swiss valet brought back with him from the Tour, but I would swear his interests lie in the backgammon line, though Kilkeel seems not to see this. I am to have the gift of one scrawny little girl, says my Viscount, so that I may have the making of her, though she does nothing but blush and tremble in my presence. What I am to do with such a hoyden I know not, as she is sure to cause me more trouble than she is worth, but the faithful Janet Chittleborough can see if anything can be made of her. Dear James seems to regard her as he does his stony fields—capable of improvement. She is a "natural human" he says, whatever that may mean, and he will observe her with his head to one side which makes the girl more clumsy and awkward than she already is. He tries to coax her out of her uncouth gabble, telling me that this is all that is wanting to make her dignified and noble. Anny, what am I to do with this boy's enthusiasms? Does he have no understanding of what it means to be a lady? Were he not so devoted I should take offence, as though all a lady's arts and her learning of them were as naught against the "natural" charms of an unlettered barefoot Irish peasant.

The most amusement I have had with these people has been at the expense of the parson, whose living is in the gift of old Goward. He called some days ago when James and I were more than usually active, and it is thanks to him I had the best sport I have had in days. There is no pleasure in scandalising an Irish servant as one would an English one, because the English servant will enter into the game willingly; though he pretend to be shocked to his marrow—he will look! An Irish one will turn his eyes away in horror, convinced that he risks his immortal soul. Nor, even if any of them were comely enough, which they are not, is there to be any congress between servant and served. No story like Lady Mowbray's with her handsome footman—we are of different races entirely! But I was telling you of our sport—me in my petticoat and stays all undone, and James in his shirt—along the upper gallery and up and down that high-way of a staircase, all for nought until Revd. Samuels was announced. The PARSON looked horrified, but the MAN looked on my déshabillée just a little longer than was needful! What sweet amusement did I find the following Sunday sitting beneath his pulpit and watching him blush and stutter when I loosened my kerchief so that he might the better look upon my bosom from his point of vantage, smiling and fanning myself the whiles against the heat—of which there was none in that tomb of a church but what my heart and mischief supplied.

Mitchelstown does not trouble us; he and Goward meet at the races and he and I will of course be together when I travel to Queen's County in three weeks, a small matter I have not yet shared with my lovelorn Viscount. I shall have to betray him with my husband but it is not worth it that I tell him so now and suffer days of long faces and recriminations. Were he to know the true nature of my husband's beery fumblings he would pity me. The poor old wretch takes his pleasure merely from my nakedness; he looks, he sniffs, he paddles in my neck, my bosom and my privy parts but he is by now beyond performance. But his doing so raises me to such a pitch, dear sister, that I am merely inflamed for the embraces of my straight, true and indefatigable boy—if only my dear James would understand the service this cuckold renders him.

You had noted my cough, dear sister, when last we met, and I have it still. I am hoping that the sea air here at Ardglass may serve to shake it from me. For the rest, I am well, and I do my utmost to make hay wherever I can for as long as the sun may shine on me.

Your loving sister,
Letty Mitchelstown

Mary and Bridgie

"Move your feet over, ye wee hoor, they're frozen."

"Bridgie!"

"Ye've went with him, so you have. I heard him come in. You've been hours."

"You were sleeping."

"I was not."

"Lady Mitchelstown's dead."

'What!" Bridgie sat up in bed, crossing herself and muttering the prayer for the dead. "Light that candle, will ye?"

Mary did so.

"It wanted only time," said Bridgie, "dear love her. Pretending that cough was only from living a rackety life and too much rum-shrub with the oul' Lord. If I was in such a way I know I'd've prayed for forgiveness and hoped for a better life in the world to come, but not she."

"Dr. Benson saw her two days since. She knew. I heard Lady Goward saying to Mrs Chittleborough that she feared the scandal of her dying under this roof and not her husband's down the country, but 'twas too late by then."

"So that's why Lord James came for you."

Mary didn't miss the tinge of jealousy in Bridgie's voice.

"Only because I've been waitin' on her ladyship. I've laid her out, so I have." Mary trembled. "It was a terrible thing, Bridgie."

"Come closer, or ye'll catch your death as well," said Bridgie, mollified. "Tell Bridgie, now."

"When we got out on the landing I saw he was all over blood—his shirt, his hand that was shaking my shoulder to wake me was sticky with it."

"I'll put salt on your linen for ye. Ye're not to do it."

"He was weeping. He put a cloak on me and made me carry my shoes so's not to rouse the house. Oh Bridgie, to see my Lady Mitchelstown when I had known her so gay was a shock, her poor face all sunken in and her jaw lying slack-like all bloodied from her last fight with her poor lungs. He had come away so fast from her death-bed that he had not even closed her eyes and they stared up at the bedhangings as if she was angry with them. I never told him he was wrong for letting her alone like that."

"They maybe don't believe it, the Protestants, that the devil can take a soul when there be no one to pray for it to our Blessed Lady who comes between us and all harm and most at the moment we die."

"Then *we* must pray to her, Bridgie. Lady Mitchelstown was kind to me, though she frightened me with the way she lived. I said to my Lord James that I should fetch Mrs. Chittleborough but he would not hear of it. "I will not have others look upon her thus, she would not want it so. You had the washing and dressing of her and you shall have them now, Mary." "We will need clean rags, and water" I said, and he says, "Whatever is needed, Mary, tell me and I shall help you." I was loath to leave him but I had to draw the water from the barrel below stairs more than one time for what remained on the wash-stand was all bloodied. You know what must be done to make a poor body decent—we both saw it at home too often. It was a strange and shocking thing for me to handle her poor nakedness and to ask him to help me move her back and forth to do what I had to do to make of her a decent corpse." Mary hesitated, and her sister squeezed her hand.

"That wasn't all, Bridgie. When I'd finished he plumped her cheeks with rags so that she might seem as she had been in life before illness took her. And then he rummaged with her pots and powders there before her looking glass "for I would have her anew as she was in life" he said, and he went about—honest to God, Bridgie—powdering and colouring her so that she looked as though the hue of life was still in her though I had needed to tie a handkerchief about her head to stop her jaw from falling by. Then he made me bring her finest gown and put it on her with the best lace about her neck to hide that tied-up handkerchief, and a wig too, to hide the knot above. He put the wig on by himself and it is well that he did for I had no stomach for lifting that poor head more, but he did it with all gentleness as though he feared to wake her. I had to tell him to put pennies on her eyelids for otherwise they would open again even though she already grew cold.

"I asked him about getting Mr. Samuels, thinking as how I'd want Fr O'Dowd to my deathbed. He looked at me with wild eyes but then bade me rouse our brother and send him to the rectory. Only Samuels sent him away for a superstitious fool saying that no Protestant would want such a thing and that he would call at a more seemly time to do what was necessary for the conveyance of my Lady's remains to her husband's house in a decorous manner.

"When Packy came back with this message my Lord raged and I was feared first that he would strike our poor brother, but then Lord James did what I would never have dreamed of—he sent him for Fr. O'Dowd—"for she must have someone, and if parson Protestant will not stir himself then begod she will have a Papist priest say prayers o'er her instead."

"Is Fr. O'Dowd there the now?"

"I think so. Lord James sent me back up. Otherwise he's with her alone."

Edwin and Janet Chittleborough Discuss a Morning After

14th June 1766

"There was Docherty, that horse dealer from Kilkeel, my Lord Gorman and his brother, and Parson Samuels,' said Edwin. "The others I did not know—they came with Gorman. Lord Goward looked in early but did not remain with them. His Lordship likes his glass, but a gathering is not for him. Two friends at most in his library peering at those French prints together is more his way."

"Did Parson Samuels shame himself again?"

"Yes, though I did get him away just after midnight chimed but not before he had fouled the Sabbath. McNamara got him into the trap and home to Mrs. Samuels."

"Poor lady."

"Poor lady, indeed, and not only her. Here, help me to get this table back upright. Ah, careful, Janet, there be more broken glass behind there, mind thee not step in it."

"This Turkey carpet be quite ruined."

"So that's where the stench was coming from. Let us lift it carefully, Janet, and take it outside. I'll get Patrick to put it under the pump and if the colours stay true then we may save it yet. But this cloth is burned to holes, 'twill do only for rags."

"Edwin, I did hope for better of the young Viscount."

"Hush! Think who may hear thee, Janet."

"Nay, he sleeps yet, he who have kept the entire house awake."

"He grieves still, though he have no right to it. He is not happy in drink—it makes him more melancholy than he is even when sober. His father is good-humoured always and the drink make him more so, but we have never found him unmanageable. Our Lord James is not all wicked, my woman, even in his cups. He did aid little Mary this night, when one of those sots would molest her, and Blanch looking on as if waiting his turn."

"And well he might. Lord James is sweet on her himself, Edwin."

"*Sshh!* He is kind to her because she did help him with the laying-out."

"A pretty work that was too. Not decent Lady Mitchelstown was, not even in death, but all tricked out as if she were on the stage—and to have the child help him in that."

"She had no choice in the matter."

"I blame him, Edwin, not her. And then sending for the priest… Edwin, would life not be kinder to us in England?"

"My woman, know that I cannot desert my Lord after all this time! And my Lady Goward is a decent body, and thee know'st it well. They fear for their boy in his unhappiness, both of 'em. No, they are not to be abandoned now."

Mary and Lord James

Later that day.

"Mary!" he called, stopping her just as she was about to disappear down the servants' stair to safety.

"Come here, I must speak with you."

Mary rested her brushes against the stair rail, turned round and bobbed a swift curtsey, keeping her eyes lowered.

"What is it you are afraid of, Mary?" he asked, more gently.

"I would not say, sir."

"Me, then?"

"No, no, sir, not exactly, not *you* sir…"

"Well, look at me then. Look me in the eye."

"Mrs Chittleborough told me not…"

"Ah, Dame Chittleborough. Between you papists and that tribe I am well caught."

He placed a finger lightly against her jaw, felt the tiny shiver and recoil this provoked, and turned her face towards him.

"Now look up." he commanded.

She looked up and finally held his gaze, steadily.

"Fine eyes, Mary, very fine eyes. You are under orders now to always turn them towards me."

"Sir."

"You shiver, girl, do you feel cold?" he asked, deliberately misunderstanding her. Unbidden, an image of an inn at Susa came to him, and a servant girl who made it her business to stare at him, with saucy, laughing eyes devoid of innocence. The eyes of the girl before him were not knowing, but they were frank, alert. Fine eyes indeed, he thought, dark-lashed, of the deepest blue. He noted the ivory skin of her neck against her white linen, which it rendered by the contrast more roughly woven than it really was, and the dark hair tucked under a mob cap. With Janet Chittleborough's plain but nourishing fare, the girl was no longer stick-scrawny, indistinguishable from so many of her kind; he wondered was it because of that and his grief that he had never really noticed her? Yet Gorman had taken notice of her last night, and that wretch Blanch, though he had been too devious to act on it, but in one of those illuminating moments of utter, pellucid sobriety that force their way through drunkenness, James Kilkeel had seen their intent, and stalled them. But he also remembered the words he had hurled at Viscount Gorman to stop him: "Take your hands away, sir! That one is mine!" The girl could have interpreted those words in only one way. Blanch had jeered, "*Droit de seigneur* to his Lordship, Gorman, but she'll be ours once she's ruined." James had tried to recall when he had asked that wretch to his gathering and couldn't. Chittleborough had come in at that moment with another jug of claret; he didn't know if the manservant had heard those words or if he had only seen young Gorman pushed aside, Blanch silenced with an oath and himself shoving a frightened Mary at the manservant, with the words "Take the girl out of it and see she gets safely to bed" No wonder Mary trembled now. Would warmth, food put regularly before her, a warm bed be adequate price for her virtue? Of course it would. None of his friends would say otherwise. But something else stirred besides his lust—pity, pity! And her father had saved him from the duck-pond and his mother treated her kindly. Looking down at her, he saw some substance there. Yes, perhaps there was another way.

"Do you have your letters, Mary?"

"I have not, sir, I have no need of them, I am told, though Mrs. Janet she have taught me some sums with the peas, sir."

"With the peas, Mary?"

"Yes indeed, how to add, take away, and to count how many are left, sir."

"And what happens to the peas after these calculations, Mary?"

"We eat them sir."

"Of course!" He was laughing now but Mary didn't drop her guard. He stood silent for a moment, still gazing at her.

"Mary, I have an idea, and I wish you would humour me in it."

"Sir?"

"What opinion have you of Mr. Samuels?"

"I, sir? What opinion should I have? I am sure he is a gentleman."

"And I am not, Mary—I mean I am not sure he is the gentleman you take him for, but learned he is. I am going to demand of Samuels that he teach you your letters. You will go to the Rectory for them so that I do not have to see his melancholy face here. He has, I believe, a lonely addiction to his poor claret, but Mrs. Samuels will be on the premises so I see no risk to you there. Will you do this, Mary? And will you put far from your mind the events of last night?"

Mary's eyes widened, and a flush crept up from her collar-bone. Nervously, her hand went to her neck.

"I will do as you please, sir."

In the darkness of the turn of the stair down to the kitchen, Mary paused and listened. Head bowed, she had heard Viscount Kilkeel pass through the front door. Sure that she was alone, she lifted a finger to her chin and gently touched the spot where his had rested earlier. Then she shook herself, picked up her brushes and went down.

How Mary Became a Scholar

"I will not have this! I am humiliated beyond endurance! Is this what an Oxford man is worth? Bought and sold on the whim of my young Lord so I have no choice but to waste my gifts on some rude peasant who simpered at him when he was in his cups. His little whore, younger and cheaper than the last one. I cannot *bear* this! I shall tell him I have tried, God alone knows I have tried, but with anyone less tractable, more bone-headed, less lacking in native intelligence, I might have succeeded, but *this!*"

Mary's face lay on the table against the flurry of paper, the spattered ink, as she nursed her bruised fingers in her lap. She wept now not for the pain in her knuckles where Samuels had struck them repeatedly with his riding crop every time she failed to recognise in that swirling step the word "dog", or saw in those stippled waves what he said read "mouse", but from humiliation and fear, not only of Samuels's rage but of Kilkeel's disappointment. No letters certainly, but the clarity of native wit that Samuels denied her, had told her that Kilkeel had hesitated at a cross-roads between educating her or ruining her when he sent her here, and that it was probably only the shadow of Lady Mitchelstown that had blocked the other path. Her fear was what Kilkeel would do now, since this attempt to educate her had proved a failure.

"George... George..." Meg's timid but insistent voice could not be heard immediately above the hubbub.

"What do you want in here, Meg? Do you come to laugh at me too, woman?"

"No George, I would not do such a thing. If you will permit me, I would have a suggestion to make." Meg Samuels continued to wring her hands but her voice grew stronger with each word. "Let me try, George, to teach her. I still have those little chap-books I bought when...when we both hoped...' She tailed off and looked at him with the air of a spaniel who has been kicked for a fault he does not know to be one.

"No one need know that it is I who teaches her. You would not say, Mary, would you?"

Mary lifted her blotched face and tried to smile.

"No, Mrs. Samuels, I would not."

Mary and Bridget in Bed in their Attic Room

20th June 1766

"So how did you get on with your man Samuels?"

"Hush, Bridgie, don't talk of him that way!"

"So who will hear me? *Parson* Samuels, then."

"*He* was horrible. He didn't want the learning of me, Bridget, that's for sure. Twas only Lord James insisted on it. The parson put me at his kitchen table for he would not have me in the rooms of his house and called me names he had no call to give me, and spoke bad things of Lord Kilkeel. I am only his servant and should not hear such things spoken for Our Lady knows they are not true."

"No, he should not say such things but be careful, my sister. A female in this house with one like Kilkeel after his doings with her ladyship is not safe."

"Bridgie... has he ever... have you—"

"Don't be an eejit, Mary. 'Tis you as has the best face."

"No Bridgie, it is that he loved that lady. I am sure he would have no other."

"He's a *man,* you child, and your master. Never drop your guard. Go on, though, tell me about this lesson."

"Parson Samuels showed me this paper writ all over, a page in a great book— all these horses and carts of all sizes moving across the page in rows like the way into Newry was when we went with Dadda on market day–looking as if they'd kick me if they could. He pointed to a short one and said it meant dog, though it looked not like dog to me but a chair that would fall over if you sat in it. Then he told me to copy them but he said it so fierce that I could barely hold the pen though I know how to do that for Mrs. Chittleborough showed me for to do the figures with her. I tried and he told me I was stupid, that all I had done was scrawl, though these were words from the Bible, he said. He put his finger to other words and told me to write them too but he frightened me so that I wrote wrong, though Bridgie I could see no difference. He rapped my hands—see what he did? No, don't touch, they sting me still though Mrs. Chittleborough washed them in sage water—and when I started to cry he hit the table so hard with his crop that I tipped over the inkwell. In the middle of all that stramash comes Mrs. Samuels and she managed to quiet him poor lady, though I know not how she did for he was awful angry with me. So now it is not Revd. Samuels who learns me but his wife. She said to take away the book he said was the Bible to save it from harm, but the way he picked it up it was as if he cared nothing for it but even so I was glad the ink went on me and on my papers and not on it.

"She took me first to the back scullery and we washed away what we could, rubbing away the stains on my finger-ends with a rough stone she had though she tried to be gentle. They were the only part of my hands that did not pain me but the rough stone was not so rough when in her hand. My apron she said to turn about when it was dry so that I could try the cleaning of it with vinegar myself and none would be wiser for it.

"She had this wee book with pictures in it and the words were bigger so I could see each one wonderful clear after looking in that Bible, and she showed me how to take apart the words like unpicking an old petticoat for to see the pieces. The pictures were of the words and so I had no fear of forgetting what they said when she asked, though once I said ass instead of donkey which was written there, and she laughed but not as to mock me. I was glad when she laughed for when she first showed me the wee book I could see tears on her face but perhaps 'twas her husband who put them there. Bridget, I have the alphabet, so I do! Mrs. Samuels says it's like having a lot of good strong bricks you never run out of. When I've the bricks learned, she says I can do anything with words I want."

There was a short pause. Mary wondered if Bridget was already asleep, and was disappointed because she had wanted to recite at last to her sister the cadence of those letters that had run through her head all afternoon, spoken into the laundry vat, over the milk churn, over the wooden board where she chopped the vegetables, something magical. Then Bridget spoke again, in an altered tone.

"Sure, what would the likes of you and me be doing with an alphabet. Out of bed so, on our knees, let's be saying our prayers. They'll not be teaching you them at that Protestant table."

The Revd. Samuels Regrets Much but Tells Only his Diary

20th June 1766

I have this day done myself much harm, more than at other times, and the good Lord knows that I do not use His gifts as I should, but in truth I am much tried. If I survive what I have done today, I must take this as a lesson and mend my ways.

The little bog-trotter called today with a message from Viscount Kilkeel, which he delivered to Meg as I had said I did not wish to be disturbed. She knows well enough that my company is the decanter and not the preparation of next Sunday's sermon but as a good wife and obedient to me in all things she says nothing. But this time she taps the study door, and waits so that I may go through the pretence of putting by the claret, opening my books and dipping my quill in the inkstand. The note, which I hope has not been read by those of the servants who can (which means the Chittleboroughs and that Swiss valet), bids me to receive one of his housemaids and please to instruct her in what is necessary that she should read, write and know her numbers as a good Christian child. Would that I were not the third son I am, and my father a plain English squire in ever reducing circumstances, for he did sire many without the wherewithal to provide elegantly for them. Thus my scholarship was hard-won, long years a servitor waiting at the Tufts' table. The only living being on this island to know the extent of my humiliations is my poor Meg. Often has she asked me in trembling accents to give her leave to run a little school. Other parsons' wives do this profitably and wisely, she says. But I have never wished my wife to serve anyone for that to me is too near what I was obliged to do to pay my way. And then comes this missive dashed off by his Lordship that I should letter some hoyden that he drops his breeches for now that there is no Lady Mitchelstown to tail!

So after our meal comes this child, scrubbed to the point of decency, I must say, dropping eyes and curtseys and 'if it please you, sir' and all coy manners. "No!" I hurl at her, "it pleases me not, but I must do as I am bid." Meg comes at the noise but I shoo her away, though I know she stood trembling behind the door throughout. But I did wrong. I visited on that child all my rage and frustration. She merely stood in my path though she did not choose to be there. Does he tup her? I know not. It is none of my business to know. If he does, I should pity her, for no man of her class will want her after, and she shall be consigned to the Magdalen or given up for worse. I do not know how much native wit she might have that would permit her to learn from me, for in truth I gave her no opportunity, railing at her as I did. Nor can she have missed the reek of the claret. If he have ruined her she is sure to tell him all of this. His Lordship may be laughing at my expense even now. And yet, perhaps I have no justification for thinking ill of her. There was none of that tawdry pride of the fallen, none of the base cunning of those who think they have the upper hand for a brief time and so must make much of it. Nay, she cowered before me and took the blows I gave with tears but no protestations. Could she know that as she felt the sting of that crop that it was myself I really wished to punish? If she dissembled she did it so well—no, I believe she did not.

Bless my Meg for coming in as she did. I took myself to the yard and put my head under the pump. The fresh air and sunlight worked on my rage and self-loathing, and with the shock of that cold water I found I could no longer contain myself but spewed all I held within over the cobbles. I took the pail and washed it away, and by my exertion, the expulsion of what was poisoning me, and copious draughts of that spring water, I came more or less to myself again, and so am face to face with my foolishness. The realisation that I cannot even hold my drink is itself merely another confirmation of the fact that I am not a gentleman and should not pass for such. And my actions in drink today were those of a lunatic. To think that I was so proud to have obtained this living.

My hope lies now only in poor Meg and her good offices with this child. Later, I went into the parlour and asked her as gently as I was able how she had found her pupil. She needed some encouragement, but I got out of her that the girl was biddable, quick in her wits once her tears were dried, and most desirous of coming here again. And the poor lady's eyes I saw fill with tears of happiness when I heard myself say to her: "If it pleases you to instruct this girl, then let us consider also your little school." She deserves some joy after so many years of disappointment that no child of our own ever came to stand at her knee. It seems it may take so little, if today I have really learned to be less proud.

In which Meg Samuels Speaks as a Mother

9th July 1766

"Mary, before we look at your lessons I must talk with you. Neither I nor Janet Chittleborough can take the place of your poor mother, though you know we love and care for you. You blush, child, why?"

Mary looked down at her books.

"I will take this as a sign of your conscience, Mary, and thus of your better nature. I attach no blame to you but I must give you a warning. Any girl risks much when she leaves her father's house if it is not to go under a husband's roof."

Mary looked up. "Mrs. Samuels, I never did want to leave my father nor my brother and sister. But he could not manage the feeding and clothing of all of us, though the Quaker man was very good to us. And I'd be with Bridgie and all."

"Mary, listen to me carefully. Your sister Bridget has come to me, and so has Mrs. Chittleborough. I have even had a report of a kind from McNamara. Here, take this and dry your eyes—no one wants to betray you or talk behind your back. But you are without defence or protection there unless you listen to those who love you."

"My sister has lived there without blame for near three years."

"Your sister is made of different stuff, Mary. How can I put this... Bridget does not have your natural advantages—no, don't dismiss this—and furthermore, she is, let us say, a little rough in her manner. As that is no attractive quality, it does mean that the girl defends herself. A quick tongue and a scowling face will keep away all but the most persistent of men. Your sister loves you, but she is not immune to the fault of jealousy. I could have dismissed her speech to me on those grounds were it not for Janet Chittleborough who like me has outlived that emotion."

"I do not like the way Mr. Blanch looks at me."

"Nor I, Mary, but he is not your greatest danger, I think. You do not like him and provided you are not left alone with him, as you should not be with any man, then that is your greatest defence. Happily Lord James has gone to London but only in answer to his mother's entreaties, from what my husband tells me... oh, Mary, Mary, you will never make a coquette for I see what you feel... 'tis writ all over your face! You will probably dislike me for this but I pray he is distracted in London for I would not have him distracted by you to your own ruin. Oh, this is worse than I feared—your little heart is taken."

"I... I felt sorry for him, Mrs. Samuels."

"Oh Mary, what have you done?"

"I have done nothing! I would swear on Our Lady's name."

"Well, I shan't insist that you do that... let us pray that his head is turned in London and that all you must do is nurse a broken heart. You will survive that, even though you might not believe it now. The other you would not—that way lies misery, destitution, disease. Oh cry, dear Mary, it is better that you should."

"He was so unhappy when Lady Mitchelstown died. I know it was wrong but she was such a pretty lady and she was kind to me I think because he wanted her to be."

"What do you mean?"

"I mean that when he was there she would fuss and pet and give me things. She had such pretty things the like of which I have never seen... ribbons, handker-chiefs. I have them in my box for I do not dare to use them for fear I ruin them, and I have no occasion for them anyway. When he was not there, well, she was not unkind but she noticed me less. Then I was afeared of her, Mrs. Samuels, though she did me no harm. She would sit before her glass and pull her face this way and that, and put on more powder, and she would cough so and rub her cheeks. When she was doing that I had to keep the door locked. He was not to see her that way."

"My Lady Mitchelstown was certainly astute," muttered Mrs. Samuels.

"Astew?"

"I mean, Mary, that Lady Mitchelstown had arts and stratagems that you can-not run to. She was a lady experienced in the ways of the world and the ways of men above all. I think she saw before I did, before Janet Chittleborough did, and certainly before you did, child, that your sweet face appealed to Lord James. She knew she was ill, she knew she was older than him and knew more of the world than he. You were a threat to her but to criticise you would put her in no good light with him. So she was kind to you, but did not love you, Mary."

"But *he* was taken so bad when she died."

"Of course he was. Guilt, regret, genuine kindness and affection… that confusion the young have between the satisfaction of fleshly pleasures and true long-lasting esteem. For Lord James *is* kind and affectionate—but thoughtless. He has been spoiled, Mary, though his natural disposition is a gentle one and that has saved him from outright wickedness. His mother will wink at anything he does rather than guide him, and Lord Goward is too interested in the port bottle, and now too caught up in illness to be the father his son needs. Mary, say nothing of this to anyone, for Mr. Samuels's post depends on Lord Goward's generosity as much as your father's right to live in his cabin.

"And when I say thoughtless, consider his view of the matter. You are under his roof, you are biddable, you are fair of face and figure. You shared with him that sad task of preparing Lady Mitchelstown's poor corpse—preparing her I might say that she might lie blamelessly in her husband's family vault. He is more disposed to your religion than is fit for someone in his position."

"Fr. O'Dowd is often with him at the house—not only with Lord Goward. They talk of Rome, I mean as a place they both know."

"There is talking of Rome and talking of Rome, child. No doubt they talk of my Lord's Tour, or as much as he would share with a priest. Let your religion protect you and do not yield to him even if he says he wishes only a chaste kiss from you—for between a man of his class and a girl of yours there is no such thing. You say you pity him, Mary, and pity is a most dangerous emotion in your position for it holds the door open to love, and that you cannot afford though he can always. Be warned: the more you resist him the more ardent he will become, but do not yield. Do not let him kiss you, Mary… do you blush because he has or because you wish he would, Mary?"

"He has not,'"said Mary in a small voice. "He does take my hand whenever he speaks to me."

"What does he speak to you of?"

"He asks how I do in my lessons. He asks how my father and Robert and Kate do. How it was to grow up in our cabin. Whether I miss my poor mother. What my father grows and how, and how he manages the beasts. He asks has anyone come asking for me, if I have a sweetheart. And he looks at me directly, Mrs. Samuels, with his head a bit to the side, and he smiles, and says I must look directly at him. I do not know sometimes that he does not mock me."

"He knows to be correct, and this is something. Mary, try not to be alone with him. About this I will speak to Mrs. Chittleborough. Know that you always have a confidante in me and in her. And now we should look at your lesson."

Mary opened her book and reached for her slate. That she was quieter and sometimes distracted did not alarm Mrs. Samuels; on the contrary, she was pleased that her words had found their mark.

But had they? Though she fixed her eyes on the primer, what Mary saw was the cool interior of the dairy, with Viscount Kilkeel blocking the doorway, smiling and saying, "Let me kiss you just once, Mary, and you shall pass", his head tilted as he looked down into her face. A slow clop sounded on the cobbles outside, with McNamara's cry, "Your horse, sir, I have her ready", and he slipped away. But the words that fluttered in Mary's head, beating against her thoughts like an imprisoned bird, were Mrs. Samuels's: "The more you resist him, the more ardent he will become."

Lord Wickmere to James Kilkeel

42 Grosvenor Square
17th July 1766

My dear James,

 I was so heartily pleased to see you again in town yesterday that I did not comment overly on what you told me, but now after sound sleep and a clear head I feel impelled to marshall my thoughts onto paper before I should see you next. Let us arrange that meeting soon, and not in the hurly-burly of Vauxhall but better in some quiet snuggery where we may talk without interruption.

 Please remember that I love you as I always did. The memories of our shared school-days and then our time in France and Italy can never for me be cancelled. And because of our friendship, it grieves me to think that you may be taking leave of your senses. James, it must take time to get over the loss of our darling Letty; her memory deserves that as no less than its due. I was more than happy to hear that you are once again in love, when you never expected to be. But you tell me that she is a servant girl, and that you have scruples. I gib not at the first fact but do not comprehend the second. Why have you not made her your mistress, and have done with it, for as long as it might please you? This is not the devil-may-care James that I knew in Rome. The girl resists, does she, and would protect her virtue? A pretty ruse and one calculated to raise your ardour. You tell me that her father is one of your father's tenants, but with pretensions to restitution of land that is not his? Well, it is in your power to turn him off that land for we should see then if virtue is to be priced above a cabin roof and a fistful of potatoes and filial devotion. Now, I know you well enough to know that you would not countenance such an action; I merely want to point out the strength of your position. It is entirely in your kind and impulsive nature to want to educate this girl, but to what end? Is it indeed a kindness to her to thus single her out and place her above the companions of her class? Her station destines her to be the wife of a cottager or at most a footman with pretensions one day to run a tavern. If the last of these then her learning may have some use, but you would do better to give her companions in her studies from amongst her fellow-servants so that your action may be taken as benevolent eccentricity but not as a design that gives others cause to mock you. I say this to you as your friend.

Women find you loveable, James, so let them love you and do not lose your head in this way. I shall be in a private room at the back of The Ensign this evening at eight o'clock, if you would join me for ale and a simple chop. But you must promise that tomorrow you will follow me into the most amusing society—Vauxhall in the afternoon, then the pit of the Theatre Royal—the talents of the delightful Mrs. Bellamy lately arrived from Dublin I am sure will distract you from your distraction. It is unlike me to say this, James, but think also of your future, for it would not be so early (given that you show signs of desiring domesticity) to consider what quality of wife could grace your table and fill the Goward cradle. Even here in London where all is not what it often seems, (for many practise to deceive and not only in Drury Lane), a young and biddable heiress of good character could be found for you, one whose fairness of face is matched by a fair fortune to bring lustre to your father's estates. If it is too early yet for that, then there are many respectable ladies of livelier aspect and maturer years who are not, shall we say, fully appreciated by their husbands. There are of course risks to run: young Portland, as you know, is the object of a suit for damages from Captain Penston for his crim. con. with that gentleman's lady. Yes, we must speak soon, dear friend. Let the boy who brings this let me know if you will meet me this evening.

Yr. aff. Friend,

Jack Wickmere

Lord and Lady Goward

14 Berkeley Square,
20th July 1766

"Goward! We must speak."

"Certainly, my dear."

'Would you put down the *Gazetteer* for a moment and hear me, sir. I am concerned about our son."

Lord Goward reluctantly placed the paper on the side table, with the article he had been reading uppermost.

"James? Looks all right to me. He's out again this evening with young Wickmere. Thought about going with them—Wickmere was full of some actress or other—but don't imagine they wanted this old cove to slow their steps. Pity!"

"Goward, the boy is not himself. He is smitten again, and in quite the wrong place."

"Young man—it's normal. Good for him."

"One of the servants."

"That pretty one, is it? The one that came as a little scrawny thing 'till Mother Chittleborough had the feeding of her? I'd have chosen her myself."

"I wish you could be serious, sir! She's one of Kearney's daughters; a pretty pass if the man saved our son only to have him ruin his child."

"He's a boy. I am sure he means no harm." Then he added reluctantly, "I suppose you wish me to talk to him, to direct his attentions elsewhere."

"This is what I had hoped when persuading him to accompany us to the London season; for the first time, you will recall, he was singularly unwilling. It strikes me as strange that one who had his eyes opened to the world on his Tour should suddenly wish to bury himself in an Irish estate of no great aspect when—"

"*I* for one am very happy there."

"And it is right that you should be so, but you, dear husband, are not a young man in want of a wife. Lord Wickmere has already been to see *me,* sir, in the hope that a mother's counsel may help him see sense. He has himself already tried."

"Ah."

"Goward, he talks of *marrying* the child."

At this Goward started up in his chair, knocking over the little table where he had put down his newspaper.

"But that's preposterous! He'd do better to marry some actress, like that fool Norton. He *cannot,* no more than I could marry my favourite hunter! Why, O'Dowd would thrash the air beneath the nearest bridge for marrying them, and find his fine head on a spike outside the court-house for his pains, were it not that thankfully the justices in our part of the country are too idle to enforce that law. And dammit, I *like* the fellow; a better companion than that miserable parson. Can't the boy just make her his mistress as would any other prudent young man? I mean, she is clean, she has that sweet face. And those blue eyes of hers when she can be persuaded to look at one…"

"*Goward!*"

"I am sorry, my dear, but I lose reason when I consider this foolishness. Anyway, he can't marry her without breaking the law, so there's an end on it."

"Is it? Do you not recall that he had O'Dowd come to the house when Lady Mitchelstown died? Samuels would not come."

"Of course not. Samuels is a son of his church—our church—and as you know we have no mummery over corpses as the papists do. The boy was distracted with grief; it was all he could think of to do."

"But if he should turn, sir?"

"No, *no,* unthinkable. To lose his position, his estates, his name. I am damned if I will leave a penny to Cousin Timothy."

"He must be made aware of what we expect of him, for the first time in his life. We have always let him have his way in all things; I would be the first to admit this. Yet he must not feel that we pressure him, for he would only resist us more. He must do his duty, sir, and we ours. He must be found a wife. And we must find a situation for the girl elsewhere. I shall speak to Chittleborough that he may write his wife."

"It's Blanch who knows the other agents, and so who is in want of a servant. A pity, though, such a pretty little thing to have about the place. Were she only his mistress I would not mind. Think, dear, how well she might look in silks in place of that old paskeen."

"Goward, you do exasperate. Her father deserves better, and so does she. To Blanch I will not write, for you know I do not trust the man."

"You have always had a down on Blanch, but you know the receipts have increased since he came."

"I do, but he have done this by turning off, as you well know. He wished also to serve the Kearneys so—sheep would be cheaper, he said. Had Bridget not come to me all tears I would not have known this, for he neglected to tell you and I had to have sharp words with him. I hope he remembers his lesson, for I fear what he does there whenever we are here."

"Mrs. Cracklethwaite" Writes in *The London Spy*

26*th* *July 1766*

We had predicted in these pages an Engagement between Viscount K_____l, only son of Lord G____d and heir to considerable estates in an Irish county and Lady A_____a B_____s, whose lineage is not so long-established but which K_____l is prepared to overlook to the tune of £15,000 per annum. Certainly, the Lady's fortune make palatable her celebrated Nose and Teeth which are the envy of the best of the Newmarket Stables.

The Viscount is indeed known for his Gallantry, which he shewed to its full advantage in his Kindness to the late lamented Lady M_____n, being constantly at her side since his return from the Tour eighteen months ago, thus undoubtedly providing a great service to her Husband Lord M_____n, (he being much advanced in years) by sparing that Gentleman much of the Effort required to satisfy the Needs of a much Younger Wife. A decent interval having followed the demise of that amiable Lady her cicesbeo, doubtless in need of defraying the costs of his unselfish Chivalry towards Lord M_____n's dashing lady, has now been paying assiduous court to his new Amour at Vauxhall, at the Theatre Royal and in all the finest salons of the season. Lady A_____a may lack some of the Spirit of the dear deceased, and the unkind may say that she does not compare well from the point of view of face and figure to her dead rival, but her plainness has without doubt assured her Virtue. Viscount K_____l, though he has no military experience is as we write positioning his battering ram in the vicinity of Bushey Heath for his imminent assault on Maidenhead, for he would be right to expect some Resistance as he takes possession of his Conquest and inundates the long-defended fortress (though there are some would say that Lady A_____a let down her drawers-bridge a long time since in desperation at not seeing any action, but none have as yet had the courage to venture in). His Lordship's earlier manoeuvres have not provided him with experience for such a long siege for by contrast the portcullis of Lady M_____n's castle was always raised and the gates thrown open wide to all comers to partake of the festivities within. We wish Lord K_____l every success in his matrimonial endeavours from which we expect him to emerge bloodied, but victorious.

"Good God, Jack, how can they write this farrago?"

"With the greatest of ease—it is what makes a scandal sheet sell, James. *We* bought it. But did you give the Bellows female any encouragement?"

"What do *you* think? I can't stomach the woman. She has a face that reminds me of a horse I failed to back when I should have, and a voice like a cat clawing at a window pane. Some old tabby, a friend of Mamma's, insisted that I dance a minuet with Arabella at Lady Bowles', and did so within the wretched girl's hearing, so a refusal was out of the question. I brought her a glass afterwards, but that is all. It is not as if the lady showed any great interest in *me*, but I have encountered her at Mamma's At Homes twice in the last ten days, when Mamma herself has expressly asked me to be present. I'm fond of my mother, dammit, so I can hardly avoid her drawing-room, can I?"

"I wonder—forgive me for this question, as I am merely thinking aloud—but could your mother have spoken to *The Spy?*"

"Mamma? I don't think she even knows of its existence. She frowns enough at my father for reading the *Gazette*—and he only does that for the nags—and she would never have said all that about poor Letty, let alone go as far as describing my imminent assault on Arabella's chastity. Horrible thought."

"That part is just Madam Cracklethwaite's invention, whoever she, or he, may be. But perhaps some old beldam in her circle might have seen some advantage in putting this word about."

"Or the woman's mother."

"Precisely. Arabella has been thrown at many heads before now, but most have been able to duck before the blow landed. So this is a new stratagem, a more desperate one but one which in its boldness risks being successful. We must consider how to counter-attack, with the risk of course that all that does is fan the flames."

"I have a better idea, Jack. It has everything to recommend it except the loss of your society. I shall go home. I shall go back to Ireland."

"To your pretty maid-servant."

"Yes, to my Mary. But for the pleasure of your company, Jack, I wish I had not come to London this season. I have had nothing but vexation from it saving when I was in your company or your dear Peg's. But I came to please my mother. She reassured me all the while that if my love was true then it would withstand that test, and it has, but strengthened it too, whilst, poor woman, she hoped that she might see me caught in a snare more to her liking. I would that you would know my Mary, for you would know then how wearisome these weeks have been: these endless levées, at homes, promenades that have little to do with walking but much to do with being seen... those cackling powdered girls employing all their arts in appearing artless or shredding the characters of those they call their friends the moment those friends have left the room, and calling this wit. You know, Jack, I could not convince Mary to look me in the face until I ordered her to do so. I would talk to her in *profil perdu,* though this did give me ample opportunity to study the curve of her lovely neck and the contrast of those dark tendrils escaping her mob-cap against the whiteness of her skin. I must confess when I first saw her, Jack, all I saw was an ungainly, spindly child and that pretty neck was so exceedingly grimy that the fine grain of what lay beneath the dirt could not have been imagined. But now she obediently looks straight at me, and the directness of her gaze sometimes near unmans me, for she knows no art nor boldness. Unlike the lady, whose figure is dictated by the strength of her stays or padded out where Nature has failed to oblige, that coarse homespun of Mary's servant's garb only whets the desire to know what it hides, like a fine statue wrapped in jute."

"Have you forgiven me, though, James, for speaking to your mother?"

"You have asked me that already, and I again say, yes, and yes. I know you love me and feared this was another of my foolishnesses. You must meet Mary and then you will know otherwise."

Blanch Loses his Head and Loses his Place

17th August 1766

"Ah, so here she is, the skivvy that apes her betters!"

"Please, Mr. Blanch, I must finish turning this room out today, or Mrs. Chittleborough says we will be behind before the family comes back."

"Want me to get out of your way, do you, wench? Well, can you not ask me nicely? Has that damned parson not taught you manners?"

"Mr. Blanch, I don't know what you do up here, but I beg you to let me pass."

Blanch had crept up on her soundlessly in stockinged feet, swinging his shoes from his left hand. It was merely a sense that the air in the shuttered room had been displaced, followed quickly by the smell of him—horses, sweat, and whiskey—that alerted Mary to the fact that she was not alone. And now he had her hemmed in between the bed and the wall, the door open behind him but beyond her reach, unless she were to hitch up her skirts and scramble over the counterpane.

"I see you, you little witch, already casting your eyes on the bed. Get up there now, for you know what I am about, and I will not be satisfied until I have you. Too good for a gentleman, think you, now that Kilkeel paws you? Come! Climb up, and lift your skirts, for I have little time! And cease that snivelling."

"Sir, please, leave me in peace! And you do Lord James ill speaking so of him, for he has never touched me."

Blanch seized Mary by the shoulders and pushed her back against the side of the bed.

"Hasn't touched you, you liar? You must show me proof of that. But, if you do not lie, when he does know you I will make sure he finds you a whore. If you will not climb up, then I shall have you here against the bed, dirty little peasant!" She felt his hot, wet mouth in her neck, his stubble scouring her skin. With his weight he pushed her backwards against the high bed, one hand scrabbling for her breasts, the other blindly attempting to pull up her skirts. Mary opened her mouth to scream, but nothing came out—only the soundless cry of nightmare. In his impatience Blanch ground her against the bed so that she was half-propped against it, half-inclined back over the mattress, and it was the pain in her back that finally woke her from her shock, enough to move a knee in the tangle of her skirts and upwards—hard.

"Harlot!" shouted Blanch, and doubled over, releasing Mary long enough for her to scramble up onto the bed and attempt to get over the other side. She heard the tearing of the bed curtain and then it enveloped her. Blanch seized the wriggling mass, as if trying to contain a struggling cat, but by now Mary was shouting for help, though muffled by the velvet. Blanch, shirt hanging out and breeches half-unbuttoned, made mad with pain, continued to hurl insults at her, until suddenly his arms gave way, though Mary continued to struggle inside the curtain.

"Mary, stop! 'Tis I." Mary eventually emerged from the nest of dusty velvet, tear stained and bruised around the chin and neck, to look up into the anxious face of Janet Chittleborough. Through the open door came the sound of shouts and the thump of struggling men banging into wainscoting.

"Your brother and McNamara have him fast. Now I must write to Lady Goward, but if Blanch sees sense then perhaps there will be no need."

Goward Hall
18th August 1766

My dear Niederer,

I will be quit of this Godforsaken place in the morning, and though I have no situation to go to I believe I have willed this outcome myself.

That young fool James Kilkeel has persisted in his idiocy towards that simpering girl. Not content with sending her to be lettered by the Parson's wife (I understand the Parson was to have had the teaching of her but as an Englishman and a man of the Church he had enough pride to stand his ground and refuse such humiliation), he must believe himself in his calf-eyed fashion to be in love with the girl. Nor is he content to honestly want her and make her his mistress so that she may take the place of Lady Mitchelstown until he should tire of her and cast her off to one of his friends—as is the normal way of things—but he would treat her as though she were a lady with an honour worth defending.

Your humble servant yesterday afternoon, being weary with trying to dunn these whining peasants for their Master's dues (a task for which as you know I get precious little thanks, never mind fair recompense) spent some time with Docherty the horse-

dealer and came back to the offices in fighting mood——the fight in mind being to break down the defences (if defences she still pretends to have) of her ladyship Mary the house-maid. I was in that state of drink that I do pride myself that I had the courage of the lion but nevertheless the capability of carrying out my purpose. Of the latter I will furnish you not much detail for I know it interests you little, but having cornered my quarry in an upstairs chamber, made piquant by being that which Lord James himself usually occupies when he is at home, the wench fought me like a cat. First she begged me prettily and tearfully to leave her be, and cried that she was no whore of Lord James—which urged me still more to my purpose, for the satisfaction of deflowering her to his disappointment once he comes to his senses and decides at last to tup her. Alas, I cannot say whether she be chaste or nay, for though I was in a good way to overcoming her scruples and had her laid down ready, the bed curtains fell all of a tangle, and as I attempted to extricate her we were interrupted by her brother (who is grown stronger for here he is fed more than is good for him), that female Quaker and the ostler McNamara.

The nymph wept and exclaimed and defended her injured innocence, as if innocent indeed she be. Mother Chittleborough threatened the constable but I know him as a good Protestant who would accept the word of a gentleman and not some scheming girl whose head has been turned by the compliments of my pretty Lord. However the threat the Chittleborough woman made of writing to my Lady Goward is one I cannot discount and so I must take myself away of my own accord and make shift elsewhere, anywhere but on this benighted island.

I send this ahead of me as tomorrow I will arrange the transport of my box and myself to Belfast where I shall take the earliest passage for Liverpool if I am fortunate, Scotland if I am not, but either will satisfy me if I am gone from here. Then I shall seek you at the London address you gave me. I hardly need to remind you of the obligation you are under to me, for I cannot not see what I have already seen.

I would have satisfaction for the treatment I have had here that puts uncouth peasantry above a freeborn Englishman. I believe that together we may find some means of bringing pressure to bear on this family that has not given either of us our due; you hinted something to me of an incident in Rome that Kilkeel would not want noised abroad. Should you also have any knowledge of a suitable opening for a man of my parts and experience I shall be forever in your debt.

Yours respectfully,

William Blanch

Kiss Me

Kilkeel stood in the doorway of the wash-house, watching the rhythmic swaying of the girl's slender body as she moved the wooden dolly back and forth in the steaming barrel. Her neckerchief lay on the table used for ironing; her bare arms and nape were damp and pink with heat. A strand of dark hair had escaped her cap and clung like seaweed to her neck. He approached her stealthily. She did not hear him against the slap and suck of the water and the pounding of the dolly; she was humming softly. He stood behind her without speaking, without touching. She stopped moving the dolly; alert as a cat she lifted her head.

"Mary," he whispered, and saw her start.

"Oh, tis you, sir," she said, and turned to face him. He smiled at her flushed face, at the smudge of ash on her cheek. He twitched off the cap and took her in his arms. "Oh Mary," he murmured into her loosened hair. "I missed you so much. I should never have left you here, exposed you to that man's insults."

Mary stroked his hair timidly, thrilled and scared at his size, the warmth and smell of him.

"You hold me too tight, sir!"

"Don't turn your face away, Mary. For heaven's sake, let me kiss you."

"I daren't."

"Yet you want me to, dear girl. The rise and fall of your breath tells me so, and this pretty pinking in your neck."

"Tis warm in here, so it is."

He looked over her shoulder into the barrel.

"This is *my* linen."

"I asked for to do it."

"You did? But I only returned late last night."

"I've been up these three hours. I came into your chamber for to get it."

"I never knew you were there."

"You were sleeping, sir."

"You were tempted to look behind the curtains, then?"

"I did not look. But I heard you breathing."

"And I knew nothing! Will my pretty laundress kiss me now?"

Mary pressed herself back against the barrel, restraining hands on his arms, but he pulled her against him.

"You know what that is, surely?" he murmured, his mouth seeking hers. She craned her head away, but she did know what "that" was, and realised with astonishment that she was standing on tiptoe to meet him, that she was roused.

"I am in an utter stew for you. They paraded all these fine ladies before me and all I could see was your sweet face."

He drew back, releasing her.

"Not in a wash-house, or a scullery. I want you for other than my washer-woman."

Breathless, Mary reached for the mob cap and lifted her hands to gather up her hair.

"Oh God, Mary, do you have any idea of how you look to me now, with your elbows raised and these dear diddies pointing at me?" He placed his palms over her breasts.

"Oh, don't," she cried, pulling at his hands. "'Tis what Mr. Blanch did to me—you frighten me more than him!"

"Oh God, don't cry. I'm sorry." He fumbled for a handkerchief. "I'm a clumsy fool, Mary, but please tell me you like me a little more than Blanch."

"There is a world, sir, between you and Mr. Blanch."

"Then why be fearful of me?" He put his hands on her waist.

"Because he was your servant and I could fight him off. I cannot be let fight you."

"And fight you did, by all accounts. I'm proud of you."

"I must go away, sir. Those that love me warned me of this."

"*I* love you, Mary."

"You can't love me."

"Well, I do. The question is whether you can love me."

"It is impossible I should, and you mock me to talk like this. It is unkind." She started to cry again. "I've been so happy here, and I get on grand with my lessons, so I do. Mrs. Samuels says so. But you—you are more danger to me than Mr. Blanch ever was."

"I want only to protect you, to cherish you. I wish you would allow me."

"That is why you are the greater danger. Because I do like you, sir. You could ruin me, and I would not cry out for help."

"My God, you blessed innocent. There is no fine lady would ever risk herself by such candid talk. I won't ruin you. If I'd wanted that, I'd have dispensed with all the niceties long ago. I am no Blanch, Mary, except that I go on two legs as does he."

'You smell much sweeter, sir.'

"I do?" He laughed. "Not so sweet as you to me, dear Mary," and he leaned forward and nuzzled beneath her left ear. "I may be mad, my beloved, and you may think me so, but I have a suggestion to make. Hear me out and if it pleases you, for heaven's sake kiss me after."

Threshold

"Who might ye be at this hour?"

"I am Viscount Kilkeel. Will you let me in, Thomas?"

"Viscount Kilkeel, is it? Then I'll be his Holiness himself. Will it be Blanch has sent you, whoever you are?"

"Blanch is no longer in our employ."

"Thanks be to God for what is no small mercy. So who is it you are? My Lord's new man?"

"I'm my Lord's own son, Thomas. Now will you let me in or won't you? Father O'Dowd and I will catch our death out here."

There was a pause in which the men outside could hear the muttered command within to "clear away out of it," then the scrape of boot nails on stone and fumbling with a wooden catch before the top half of the door swung inwards. Kearney appeared in the gap, holding aloft a rush-light in a crude pewter holder, but its intermittent flickering was not adequate to the task of illuminating the faces of his visitors. O'Dowd stepped forward and lifted the lamp he carried.

"You can let us in, Thomas, there is nothing to fear," he said.

Wordlessly, Thomas unlatched the bottom half of the door and his visitors' bootnails rang on the cobbles of what the country people called the street, though it led nowhere, being but the forecourt of the cabin. O'Dowd held back, holding up the lamp to light the way for a younger, slenderer figure who had to stoop beneath the lintel, then followed him inside.

Kilkeel shivered, and pulled his cloak more closely around him. "Little better than a cave," he thought, "and barely warmer."

Mary's father had placed the rush-light above the cavernous darkness of a dead fireplace. Here, away from the air at the doorway, it burned more confidently. O'Dowd fastened the two halves of the doorway. There was a tang of peat in the air, something Kilkeel had never smelt, for in Goward Hall heat came from good coal, or wood. He was glad of its earthy sharpness, for it masked, in part, an almost palpable smell of unwashed flesh, and the reek of the animals he could hear shifting in a space somewhere to his left. He was thankful there was no fire or the stench heated might have been worse, and then reproached himself for that thought, as by the flickering light he made out, crouched against the wall behind Thomas, the pinched faces of a stunted boy of about sixteen and a little girl.

Thomas stood waiting, furtively studying his visitor. Kilkeel, for his part, saw hollowed cheeks, dark, sunken eyes etched around with grimy wrinkles, scant hair beneath a shapeless hat, worn indoors against the cold. This man had nothing in common with the ragged but rosy peasants he had met in his journey down to Italy, picturesque in their impoverishment. Here was utter desperation, yet he had never met it face to face though it was a mere two miles from his own door. His errand struck him now as vainglorious, preposterous, impossible. He remembered Wickmere seated opposite him in the warm fug of *The Ensign*. What would he, or any of his friends, say if they saw him here, now?

"Have you a chair, Thomas?" said O'Dowd at Kilkeel's shoulder.

"I have Father, begging your pardon."

"Give it to Lord Kilkeel, so."

"This is...?"

"Yes, Thomas. This is the child you pulled from the duck pond."

Thomas turned away, reaching for a rickety rush-seated chair to one side of the fireplace.

"Thank you, Thomas." The chair creaked beneath him, and Kilkeel lent slightly forward, trying to concentrate his weight on his feet. If he should break this man's one miserable chair...

"Father, will you have this stool?"

The priest sat himself next to Kilkeel, but so low was the stool that he seemed crouched close to the ground, in his dark clothes a raven with feathers fluffed up against the cold.

"I cannot sit whilst you stand, Thomas," said Kilkeel.

His tenant stared back at him in astonishment, then recollecting himself said: "Sure won't the tatie sack do for me," and dragging this article forward lowered himself onto it, never taking his eyes off his guest.

"I have nothing to offer your Honour," he said.

"Indeed but you have," said Kilkeel, "I have something to ask of you."

Thomas glanced at the priest, as though Kilkeel spoke a language he did not know, and expected O'Dowd to interpret for him. The boy and girl edged closer, wide-eyed. The rounded vowels of the fine young man in the cloak sounded in their ears like those of Blanch, yet he had been brought here by the priest. Father O'Dowd's accents to them were familiar—refined, yes, for priests must be learned men although obliged to live like their flocks—but recognisably an Irishman. All three men had been born within five miles of each other, but it was as if each inhabited different worlds.

"Mr. Kearney," began Kilkeel, and stopped, as Thomas stiffened at the shift to his surname.

"'Twould be best if the children were not present," murmured the priest.

"Yous go to bed now. Say your prayers and I'll come later. Kiss your father good-night."

As each child moved into the light Kilkeel observed that they were better clothed than fed, no shoes or stockings on their grimy feet but simple rough-spun garments to their backs, though too large for them. As though reading his thoughts, Thomas said: "Tis the Quaker gentleman brings their clothes, or they were as ragged as myself."

"And Parson Samuels? Does he ever come here?"

"No, sir, but his lady did come once along of my Mary, for to see would I send the other childer to the school she was getting up—a kind lady but I could not spare them. Since their mother died I need them here or I would not have the rent to pay your father. Your mother, sir, have saved us from being turned off often enough as it is."

"Mr. Kearney, I will have it that you do not pay rent again. No one need know this and no one *must* know it. Your dues will come to you by means of Father O'Dowd and then you must bring them to Goward Hall in the usual way."

"Tis a bargain ye make with me, sir, but the advantage is all to ye," muttered Thomas, turning his head towards the darkness of the fireplace.

"I do not understand you."

"I speak plain, sir, for you are plain with me. For you to say these things makes clear as day, and I should be grateful to ye, surely. It is certain sure to me now that you have made a hoor of my child, sir." There was no anger in Kearney's tone, only resignation.

"Thomas," interposed the priest, but Kearney went on.

"I feared this when she went to the Big House but 'twas that or sending her to the Charter School for them to turn her for sure. I thought for to send her to your father's house was best, to be with her sister and her brother too and the Quaker gentleman of your father and his lady, which Mr. Ingham who helps us did vouch for. But what is a poor father to do? There are plenty fine gentleman who would hold the honour of a child of mine of no account, nay, would turn out one such as me for to not hear his reproaches, so now you call me Mr. Kearney and give me my rent and I should thank you. But tis a poor thing," he added sadly, turning to Fr. O'Dowd, "that even a priest of God must wink at such things."

"She is not my mistress, Kearney, and nor would I have her so. Do you know why Blanch is turned away? He tried to violate her, and if others had not intervened, would likely have succeeded. I am not here to buy your daughter's virtue. I come to request of you that as her father you give her to me."

'Does he mock us, then?' cried Kearney, appealing to the priest.

"No, Thomas, he is in deadly earnest. And so am I. If this came out then a zealous magistrate could have me dance in the air beneath the nearest bridge for my disobedience to their laws. And *he* would earn the scorn of the world at the very least, and likely the loss of all he has. My Lord Viscount comes quietly to my cottage, just as Nicodemus came at night under cover of darkness, and I have the turning of him. When that is complete then I will join them before God. But before the world, he can appear as no more than the man who keeps her."

4th October 1766
Moneyscalp Clergy House
Feast of St. Francis

The first step is taken and I see no going back. I will have need of courage for this may lead to my death, and thoughts of martyrdom may be signs of pride, deadliest of all the sins. Lord James was silent for some time after we left, but he had need to take his steps carefully for he does not know the land in the dark as I do now. Thomas will be his good-father in the New Year—he who has clung so fast to his belief that the land he toils over and pays for would one day be his own again.

That Mary should be for the world no more than Kilkeel's innamorata pleases neither man, no more than it does me, but they see the necessity for it. Thomas is thought well of by his neighbours, and will be pitied more than reviled for his daughter's fall. There may even be some who will praise him for his perspicacity and hers, though that he would hate more than their derision. Yet it may protect her even, for though one day this marriage might be able to proclaim itself to all the world without fear, yet she may never go among those of her husband's class though she be worth any of them many times over.

"So those half-starved urchins are to be my brother and sister?" says my Lord at last. I feared then he might be thinking better of it, but with his next words I understood that his thoughts were taking another turn. "My Mary grew up in that place, in that want, and I knew nothing of it, nor wanted to know. When I was whiling my time away at school, wasting it further at Oxford and strolling around the continent, she laboured here as they do daily.

"The children must go to Mrs. Samuels," he then declared, as though determined in his impulsive manner to at once address their wrongs. "I will impress on her that she is not to proselytise, merely to instruct them in reading, writing, arithmetic, for they are to have another station in life. What that is, I do not know as yet, but they must be ready. I must convince Thomas, I mean Mr. Kearney, of the merit of this. A man, or men must be found to do the work they do. There are enough who would be glad of it. And he must have a better house to live in."

I marvelled at the ease with which enthusiasm comes to he who has the means to advance his plans. But I also saw their wisdom and told him so, for all this made sense as the actions of the keeper of a favoured mistress, though some others in his position might see no call for such benevolence. At this he was momentarily discomfited but saw that this argument was right for its purpose also.

"My father is in search of a new agent as you know. There is a Mr. Andrews of whom I have had good reports who was lately with a gentleman in Waterford, whose estates are to be broken up for he was less fond of his fields than of the gaming table. I will go no more to England and the season, for I am sorely bored with the whole proceeding, and my mother's machinations to find me a wife."

"You must not tell her," I said.

"I have no intention of it," says he, "but nevertheless I am sorry it must be so. She likes my Mary though, as she loves anyone who is dear to me. I was indiscreet in London, O'Dowd, and told a friend that I wanted Mary as my wife and he alerted Mamma. If she sees Mary as my mistress before all the world I believe she will be happier with that, though it pains me not to tell her the truth."

Kilkeel is attentive in our closeted talks, an able Nicodemus indeed though inclined at times to rush off at a tangent or to ask questions which one who is brought up in the Faith does not think to ask. I would also have been failing in my duty as a man let alone as a priest if I were not to have warned him of what he goes to meet with open arms. Secure in the Big House with his mother and father, and in the rightness of his love for this girl, he did not realise that if it were known that he was a Catholic he would never again be able to acquire more land, that he must leave his wealth to all his children equally, so that the estate be broken up, or that a child of his becoming a Protestant could deprive his brothers of their inheritance and turn him out—a not impossible chance for if his children are to go to school at all, I tell him, it must perforce be a Protestant one. I see him stare at me, and wonder if he is about to say "It cannot be so!" as good men do who are not in the habit of looking over their demesne walls. But he does not, and I go on to tell him that a political or military career would be closed to him, and he could not serve on the magistrates' bench, nor even as a lowly constable. He would not even have the right to own so good a horse as the one he now rides so proudly. To finish, I tell him that what passes for polite society would of course shun him. He went pale and quiet a while (I held back from telling him of the disabilities and indignities under which a priest must labour; that there was even within this very century a suggestion made by the Irish Privy Council that those priests who laboured in secret to avoid penalties be subjected to the gelding knife! Their English colleagues rejected such butchery, in their mercy favouring branding in the cheek). But the more I warn him the more I see in the obstinate set of his jaw not only the zeal of the convert but also the young man's determination to battle injustice, before he becomes either too old or too wise to do other than bend his neck beneath the yoke. I see also his determination that no man shall deprive him of having Mary Kearney on the only terms he believes his respect for her deserves. So there is to be no triumph or declaration of his salvation. I will receive him in my own house. None of them at Slievenalargy can ever know of it, save Thomas, and this is for their safety as well as his and mine. The Lord alone knows where tonight's events will lead us.

Thomas Kearney Accompanies Mary
to Moneyscalp Clergy House

10ᵗʰ January 1767

"That's a good warm cloak you have there, child. You need it for a day this cold."

"Lady Goward gave it me, Dadda. She has always been kind to me."

For some minutes the only sound they made was the dull crunch of their boots on the frozen packed earth of the lane, and all they heard was the twittering of birds. Mary smiled at a memory: James telling her that the birds were not singing but warning others away from their territory. She'd laughed: "Everything here is about the land you have, or do not have." She pulled the cloak closer around her. The dawning day was crisp and clear, the drystone walls either side of them sharper in outline as the sun rose higher.

"Well, it will not rain on me today, so." she said.

"Might be her Ladyship would not be so kind if she knew," said Thomas, as though she hadn't spoken.

"Dadda." Mary tightened her grip on his arm.

"Do you still want this, child?"

"Oh, I want it."

Thomas sighed. "We must put our trust in God and do what Father O'Dowd says is right,' he murmured.

The long low profile of the cabin came into view as the lane curved, as if it had crouched down in the hollow and was now rising up to meet them. In truth, though his parishioners knew it as the clergy house, the priest's home was little different from their own. It did not nestle alongside a church, for O'Dowd had only the altar high up on Slievenalargy. Thomas half-wished that Kilkeel might have thought better of this rash step, but one sideways look at his daughter, trying to rub life into her frozen nose with her sleeve, made him push the thought away. So it was with relief instead that Thomas saw Kilkeel's charger snorting and champing before the priest's door; despite the cold morning the horse had not been taken into the byre, for they would not be here long.

Mary knocked softly at the cabin door, then opened the upper part and un-latched the lower, and stepped inside. The cabin's flagged floor was swept and clean, and two armed oak chairs were drawn up either side of the peat fire. Candles in pewter sconces stood on a rustic but solid dresser and Mary smiled as she re-membered Mrs. Chittleborough complaining of the number of candles the young Lord needed for his chamber ("he reads overmuch," she had said); James must have brought them here. Father O'Dowd, already robed, stood with his back to the fire. The hem of his cassock was not long enough to hide his countryman's boots. He reached both hands to Mary and said, "God bless you my child on your wedding morning." She stepped up to him and looking into his face, saw his eyes were wet.

"Your bridegroom is here," he said.

The door to the left of the fireplace opened and James Kilkeel moved out of the shadows. His hair was unpowdered, and he wore plain brown fustian but with spotless white linen at his throat; Mary had laundered it herself. *He's pale, God love him,* she thought, but he smiled gently at her. She trembled, and muttered some-thing about a cold morning, but in her belly and breasts flickered fire and fear.

"Would you both kneel here," said the priest.

"Where are you going, Mary? You must come by the front, with me. Humour me in this, for though I have stabled the horse myself I believe McNamara is still awake. I see a light up in his window there."

"Sure could we not just go in through the kitchen?' she asked as he took her hand and led her round the house, walking on the grass verge to avoid the crackling of the gravel path.

James laughed. "Dearest girl, you are my wife and my wife does not work in the kitchen now. And were you my mistress you would not work there either."

"My sister does."

"She is my sister too now. I must consider how to manage this. But for now, let us think of other matters. Your bridal bed awaits you."

"Let me do that. Sit down here."

Mary looked down at his dark cropped head as he knelt by the bed to unlace her boots. His wig sat forgotten on its stand on the dressing table, and seemed to Mary to belong to another man; she liked him better without it. The neckcloth she had so carefully washed and ironed lay carelessly crumpled beside it. His coat hung on a hook inside the press where she had insisted on putting it before he had stopped her nervous sally around the cheerful disorder of the room and told her to see to her own toilette.

"My twoy, sir?"

"In plain language, I want you to undress, wash and climb into my bed—our bed. And before all that, I must hear you call me James. You called me so when you made your promises before O'Dowd, remember."

"James" she murmured, more to herself than him, then "James" more loudly, attempting to dispel the fantastic sense of unreality that engulfed every gesture she made.

"I must find you new clothes. We shall go to Belfast and have you measured there, and get a last made for those pretty feet."

They are pretty, she thought, looking down. Warmth, stockings and first clogs and then the roughest of boots had already transformed them. She remembered the day she had gathered up Letty Mitchelstown's slippers and promised herself that she would try them on. She never had, afraid of being caught or of leaving some sign of her presence. Instead she said, timidly, "Something quite plain."

He looked up, holding her naked feet in both hands, weighing them.

"You know what the world is to think. You are to be my mistress and I shall dress you as such. This means that you will not mix with the wives of those friends of mine who are married, but with their lovers. Look not so shocked, dearest. I fancy you may find the company of those ladies more congenial than you would have that of the wives. They are handsome and sophisticated women, actresses some, chosen for love and not by negotiation."

"I think I may be feared of them. I would not know what to say to them."

"You need fear no one, for you have the best of native wit. There is only one quality in you I would have you change, and that is your speech—and only because I want others to understand you. Nor will I have you crop your pretty hair for one of those wretched wigs. For your speech my friend Wickmere's lady will help you, for she was an actress for a time. Between Dame Chittleborough and Mrs. Samuels I see that you already make progress."

"Am I to continue at Mrs. Samuels?" she asked, half in disbelief, half in hope.

"I wish it, Mary, and as long as you do too, so you shall."

"But what will she say, about this?"

"Meg Samuels is no fool, and knows how her husband's bread is buttered. She may look her regrets but will not say anything. And *you* must say nothing, though I see from your face you would lief do otherwise. Not a word to her, nor to Bridget, nor to Dame Chittleborough, nor to anyone. If they do not know, they cannot speak, even accidentally. Remember that O'Dowd's life may depend on it. If they truly love you, they will love you still. If they do not, know that I will."

Mary sat silent. She had never felt so alone in the world, her life in this man's hands. He was standing now, his back towards her, lifting something from a drawer. He turned. Smiling, he held out to her a white garment.

"This must be your trousseau, Mary. I will go and wash in another chamber, just this night. I will come back in a quarter of an hour, so please be wearing this, and be ready behind the curtains."

She looked down at the embroidered white linen and saw all its story: the harvesting of the flax, the scutching, beetling, hackling, the clack and throw of the loom, the bleaching green, the peering eyes and deft fingers that did this fine stitching. Another world awaited her, one in which she took rather than gave for the first time. But what was it she must give for this?

Will I snuff the candle? No, how'll he see his way back? He has his own candle, so he does. Finally, Mary set the candlestick on the little chest by the bed and enveloped in the nightgown, the first garment she had ever worn that had never belonged to anyone else, she parted the heavy bedcurtains that she and Mrs. Chittleborough had repaired after the struggle with Blanch, and climbed up. She lay on her back, just able to distinguish by the filtered light of the candle the knot in the gathered drapery at the centre of the bed canopy. She closed her eyes and listened to the tiny creaks and groans of the old house settling in its sleep, the same sounds that she heard in bed with Bridgie up above. *Bridgie!* Would another girl be found? Or would Bridgie be made to do all Mary's work herself, as she had done before her sister came? "Another reason to hate me" she murmured. "How am I to look at her again, or her at me?" Now came a new sound, the padding of confident feet along the landing, the rattle of the door-handle. Mary murmured a swift prayer.

He pulled back the curtain, the light of the candle sharpening the grey, cavernous shadows within the tester bed. He stood in his shirt looking down at her.

"I shall not snuff the candle, Mary. I want to look on you."

She felt the shift of the mattress as it took his weight, the smell, the warmth of him as he stretched alongside her, supporting himself on an elbow.

"What is this, your arms crossed so? Do you defend yourself from me?"

"Tis how my mother taught us. That if in the night we were taken then we were ready for our coffins."

"Did your mother, did anyone, Mrs. Samuels, tell you about what a husband does?" he asked, as he put back her arms.

"No, Mrs. Samuels told me not to yield—to you. She asked me had you kissed me, and if you had not, did I wish you to."

"And what did you say?"

She stared at him, but he was no longer looking at her but at his own fingers unbuttoning the neck of the nightgown.

"I said, then, that you had not kissed me. I did not say whether I wished it or no."

"I have kissed you since. Did you wish it?"

"Oh yes."

"And this yielding you were not to do. Do you know what she meant?"

"She didn't say, but I think she meant like the bull to the cows, that Dadda would not let me see, but I came round by the back field with Bridgie. It was the way you pressed on me that day in the wash-house."

The fingers tracing the line of her collar-bone halted and he laughed.

"I shall be kinder than that bull, I promise. Now, help me and pull this over your head, dear child."

"But I am just after putting it on."

"I gave it to you for the pleasure of seeing you take it off, Mary."

"Oh! But surely I shall catch my death!"

"You shall not, and nor shall I. We shall be warm enough, you'll see. Come now… oh, Mary, how beautiful you are. No, don't cover yourself. This too you promised me this morning." He sat up and pulled his shirt over his head. Mary covered her face with her hands. James laughed.

"I may not be so gifted as friend bull, but I promise you I am gentler."

He loomed above her, lifted her hands away and began softly to kiss her face, her mouth, tentatively, until he felt her timid response.

"Oh Mary, all mine!" he murmured. "Close your eyes."

He began to kiss her body with infinite gentleness. She felt his breath on her skin before his mouth landed. She shivered, wondering where the next touch would come, as he moved downwards from her neck to her shoulders, his hands in stealthy advance of his mouth. She felt the soft tickle of his hair in her neck, and lifted her hand to his nape, caressing him instinctively.

"Mary," he murmured, and then she felt the gentlest tug on her nipple, and heard herself groan, and a pleasure she thought she could not bear, nor could not bear that it should stop. But remorselessly his kisses moved downwards until he nuzzled into the most secret parts of her. Startled, she tried to push him away, but he held back her hands and persisted. Here, deep in her body, was something live, roused from sleep and demanding satisfaction. When it came Mary cried aloud and willed the waves not to recede from the shore. But it was not over.

"Now, my love… I will try not to hurt you, and it will be only this once I do. Hold me, Mary."

It did hurt, and it felt impossible that her narrow hips should contain him, but they did, and she held him close and felt him move in her, so deep that he would reach her beating heart out of her. And she understood that when she had knelt before Fr. O'Dowd that morning she was pausing on the threshold of a different life, and in these few moments had passed through a door which had forever closed behind her. Now, hearing her husband's strange lost cry, she uttered words of comfort as to a child.

Goward Hall
11ᵗʰ January 1767

My dear Wickmere,

I have taken your advice, and wished you swiftly to know it. My little maid-servant is now my mistress, and well worth the trouble I had in wooing her. I will return to London after all, once the season opens, for I want to bring her to make your acquaintance, and your Peggy's, though in my guise as new husband I would in this moment be as happy beneath my own roof here in Ireland as in any salon of the capital. I say guise, for yesterday I joined hands with this trusting little maid in a sham marriage. No buttock ball was to be had otherwise, Jack, for our Irish peasantry have morals of a standard far above those in which they are obliged to live. I do love her Jack, and would that no harm would come to her more than that which I have already done her in order to fulfil my love for her. I shall have no other, whatever machinations my worthy mother makes on my behalf. It grieves me to have had to hoodwink her so, and to presume upon her trustfulness, but it is her artlessness that drew me to her, assisted by the glossiest of black hair and the bluest of eyes—and other qualities of her person that have been revealed to me this night and in which she shewed herself the most diligent of apprentices, but of which I will not be so ingentlemanly as to—

"What are you doing, husband?"

"Ah, you are awake, my love. I am covering our traces. I shall have coffee brought, and then, after we have breakfasted and lain awhile, we may take a walk across the demesne."

"Who will bring us coffee?"

"You may stay behind the curtains this morning, Mary, but they will all know. Look not so sad, but make space for your husband. Coffee can wait, can it not?"

"I do not know. I have never drunk it."

"You have prepared it often enough."

"Below we have tay, and small beer."

"Had, Mary, had—in your case. Now, do this for me. Tip your pretty posteriors up onto this pillow—"

"Ah, so that's why yous have all them pillows."

"You, Mary, you. There is no 'yous.' And it's *those* pillows—that's right—your knees just so my darling… Does this hurt you still?"

"A little, not like before."

"Wrap your legs around me, hold to me, yes, your arms too. Mary, I am well caught and the happiest of men."

Edwin and Janet Chittleborough
Discuss another Morning After

11th January 1767

"Janet, what troubles thee? Put that linen down directly and sit thee down here."

Janet dropped the white bundle she was carrying and burst into tears.

"Oh Edwin, Edwin! A motherless child who looked to me for protection and I failed her!"

Chittleborough crossed to his wife, and it was only whilst his foot was shifting the laundry to one side to reach her, that he wondered what Janet was doing with bed linen when it wasn't wash-day. She sobbed into her hands but between gasps he made out the incoherent words, "Salt. Need salt before it's too old.' He looked down and saw the blood on the sheet.

'From young Kilkeel's chamber?' he murmured, and putting his arms around Janet felt her nodding against his shoulder.

"I let her have her day's holiday yesterday for she did say she wanted very much to see her father. I objected none for she said she would lay the fires before she left and indeed she did, too early for me to see her go. But young Lord James brought her back; McNamara told me this morning when I was looking for her that he saw them come after darkness, her bundled before him on his horse with one arm firm around her and the other on the reins.

"She looked me full in the face when she asked for leave to visit her father and I have always taken her for an honest girl in all things and though she did colour some I thought it only for the oddness of asking a day other than Sunday.

"I see'd them this morning, out in the park, going towards the pond. He was laughing and pulling her along by the hand, pointing out the deer. But she, poor ruined maid, was looking down as though she would find her lost honour there in the wet grass, and coming along of him all reluctant like, as though she'd not wished to be out there where all might see her, till he put his arm around her waist and pulled her close and then when he bent to kiss her face and I saw her look up and smile at him all happy—I could not look no more for shame. Early I found Bridget in the scullery crying with her apron thrown over her face saying she had slept alone and no one to lay the fires this morning with her and was she now to attend her own sister the way Mary had attended Lady Mitchelstown for she said it was not right and indeed it is not."

"Ah, Janet, if he could have only taken another fine lady to him such as had nothing precious to lose. I tremble to think what her destiny is now. This makes clear what Mr. Andrews told me—the new agent that knows so much about turnips. The bantlings that are still at home with Mary's father are to be educated by Mrs. Samuels and a man is to be hired to take on their work alongside of Kearney. Packy and Bridget are also to go to Mrs. Samuels. Mr. Andrews did say this was monstrous enlightened of Viscount Kilkeel and he hoped that all landlords in Ireland might follow his example."

"When all he wanted was to dishonour the poor maidy, and his way to it was to bribe her poor father through those hungry children," wept Mrs. Chittleborough. "That humble man who had saved him from the pond when he was barely out of leading strings. And we who have known the young Master since a babe and loved him too in our way—to know our kind young man is no better than those toping friends of his we did not care for and thought he'd grown away from."

"Janet, try not to weep. We must make the best of it. She will need us more than ever, and so will Bridget, though she is made of tougher stuff than poor Mary. We can give no blame to Kearney, for he is a decent man who strives to be a good father in the hardest of times. What choice did he really have? The Gowards own him as they do all their tenants. Who knows; her influence on Lord James may be a positive one though I wish it had been by some other means. I do believe that he loves her in his way, Janet, and let us hope he does not tire of her soon, for we have seen what he wanted these past months in all his looks and deeds—"

"And feared where it would lead."

"Remember his rage over Blanch? Yet he could have—forgive my indelicacy, wife—he could have had her long before now, and much easier, with threats to her, not bribes to a poor father."

"But will he love her still now that she has yielded?"

"We can only pray for them both."

Lady Goward Demands an Explanation

"Kilkeel, you grieve me! I find Mrs. Chittleborough crying as she serves me break-fast—at the table you chose not to grace this morning—this house at sixes and sevens. It's January but we must freeze for fires have not been laid, because you, sir, insist on bedding that motherless girl whose father must rue the day he fished you from that pond."

"You wouldn't let me marry her, mother, so I must have her this way."

"Impudent, unnatural son! We had all this out last London season, but I find you do not learn sense. You know such a connexion was impossible—treasonous indeed. Goward, speak up! You are his father, act as one."

"Great-uncle Edgar in Suffolk married his ostler's daughter. Fine looking girl by all accounts, a splendid brood mare."

"*Goward!*"

"Mother, you had no objection to poor Letty, even when she upset the parson. The Kearney children are to be lettered by Mrs. Samuels at my expense, her father's comfort ensured—"

"So you at least feel some guilt at having made a whore of his daughter and him derided by the entire county. And is it *wise* of you to letter the children of the tenantry? Who knows where *that* will lead? Unless of course your aim is to have all our tenants bring their marriageable girls here to await your pleasure so that you may make them *unmarriageable* at your leisure."

"Ha! Capital idea!" barked Lord Goward, "And it rhymes."

"Goward, you do vex so. Please be silent if you will not be useful. James, what is to become of this poor girl now?"

"Become of her? I intend to make a lady of her as far as I am able. She has a natural grace and native wit; Mrs. Samuels finds her a capable and diligent pupil. I will dress her, teach her to dance, to make music, put Italian or French in her mouth."

"Like a poor little doll, a plaything you will tire of. Her mother must weep, wherever she is now."

"No, Mother. I love her."

"Oh, *love.*"

"You must love her too, for me. You said you did."

"Yes, as my maid-servant, not as my son's little drab."

"She is no drab, mother!"

"Don't shout, Kilkeel. It is you that makes her so."

"Mother, I wish that she may dine with us today. Now, until I can get her to Belfast and into clothing that does her justice, have you anything I can put on her back that is not a servant's garb?"

"Oh sir, consider what you are asking. To think that instead of this madness you could have offered for Lady Arabella last season, a fine girl with all the right accomplishments and a tidy fifteen thousand—ample for all those agricultural experiments you are so keen on."

"And horse teeth and a neighing laugh to go with them—Arabella Bellows be blowed. Mention her again and I shall marry Mary, and there's an end of it. Now have you anything to clothe her?"

"Oh Kilkeel, Kilkeel, what am I to do? Where is the poor child now?"

"In my chamber, trembling at the thought of meeting you and all in this house."

"Very well, you leave me no choice. I will speak to Mrs. Chittleborough and see what we have that she can be tied into today and altered for later. And how I wonder does such a person comport herself at table?"

"With their pewter downstairs they do pretty much as we do with our silver."

In which Lady Goward Unburthens Herself to an Old Friend

To the Dowager Lady Wickmere
16th January 1767

Dearest Susan,

I beg your forgiveness for troubling you again so soon in this affair of my son. Nothing is to be done regarding Lady Arabella though I shall be ever in your debt for your part in trying to bring off that match. James is adamant that he will not consider her nor none other, yet he seems to have overcome his determination to marry the little maid-servant and has settled instead for dishonouring her. Two things have contributed to that better outcome: the girl herself has refused to recant and so be married honestly by our Parson Samuels, and yet in contradiction to her Papistry has yielded to James's pleadings, and is now under his protection, under our roof. I am grieved at this turn of events for as you know I hold the child in some affection and have a debt to her father that deserves better repayment than this. Now that the poor girl has no cards left to play it may be that she will not remain his plaything for too long, and in that event I shall do all I can to spare her the Magdalen or worse. So, I think you will counsel patience once more, dear Susan, until such time as the boy sees sense and understands his duty to his father and I. There is no reason why he should not make an advantageous and honourable marriage, and continue to keep the girl; thus do hundreds. Indeed such an arrangement is pleasing to some wives.

It pains me to say that Goward's behaviour in this affair has been disappointing but not surprising. He twinkles at the girl and pets her and tries to make her laugh. It must be said that sometimes he succeeds, and in those moments she becomes less awkward and shows signs of some native grace. James of course tells me that she is a "natural human" which is something he finds in the tracts of this Russo he learned to admire when he made his Tour, though he says he is no Russian but a Swiss but of doubtful religion from what he tells me, little better than that Folltair he had such a youthful enthusiasm for. He says the girl's natural wit and capacity for reason is the same as ours but he has nevertheless sent her to be schooled by the parson's lady and I am sure <u>she</u> does not know of Russo but relies upon a chapbook. He is at great pains to change the girl's way of speaking for it is exceedingly uncouth as it is in these parts and jars upon *the ear of an Englishwoman, yet Goward with all his English education seems not to find it so. Today my son has put the girl in the carriage and taken her to a mantua-maker in Belfast, after which I am convinced the girl will bear no resemblance to any "natural human," but it is unlikely either that she will be made a lady of. He insists that she join us at our table but to my mind imposes unnecessary suffering on the girl for she is so awkward in her handling of knife and fork and does blush so and drops things and then is unable to eat for fright and gulps her wine. But James will have his enthusiasms, for when he is not seeking to better a humble servant girl by ruining her he is reading tracts about the planting of turnips and is full of ideas as to how to trans-form Goward's barren acres into model farms that none of the peasantry here will be capable of managing. Her fellow servants, or former fellow servants (I know not what she do call them now) are naturally in uproar—her own sister and younger brother who are in our service now avoid her assiduously. My own woman, the good Mrs. Chittleborough, treats her kindly but has tears in her eyes as have I. McNamara the ostler, long in our service, chaffed her this morning as he handed her into the coach, with "Yew have seen off Blanch only to bag yourself the greater prize" which upset the girl greatly though from what I saw he spoke in jest and also in admiration, but he angered Kilkeel so that he would have sent the man off there and then but that he would have been forced to drive his own carriage and not sit within by his lady love's side. McNamara is a good servant and I won't have it that he goes.*

Susan, it is your fortune that your Jack keeps his establishment with his actress for she has all the airs of a lady without the pretensions of one and is safe for him for as long as her husband be alive.

We have the big canvas of James that Mr. Battoney did in Rome now framed and hung in the entrance hall; I prefer the little pastel done of him in Venice wearing a domino. I think it a better likeness and I am sure it cost but a small sum in comparison to that grand picture. But the painting looks very fine with him gesturing at all those ruins as if he had discovered them himself. Indeed though I am his mother I believe my son has the intelligence to do many things if he could leave alone his theories about natural humans and growing vegetables and have the sense to act the gentleman he has been brought up to be.

I thank you for your patience in reading thus far and know that you will understand my fears as a Mother and for this I will always be in your debt.

Your affectionate friend,

Emma Goward

Of Matters of Fashion

"Two small hoops, three pairs of stays, one cream figured satin sack, blue silk gros-grain petticoat and jacket, black woollen cloak, ten pair silk stockings, four garters, five neckerchiefs in white muslin… "

"What is this litany, Mary? I don't hear you well above the hooves."

"I'm trying to remember all them clothes. How will I ever be wearing them all?"

"All *those* clothes, dearest. Actually I thought you were very restrained. If you were my mistress, I would believe I had got you cheap."

"The lady says I shoulda had more, so she did."

"Indeed? Pressing you for custom already?"

"She said I would do well to get as much as I could, for as long as I could. She asked me did you give me stones—brilliants—for that would be best, for me to get stones from you."

"Well, I'm damned! The impudence of the woman. I am minded to make her wait for her bill. And from a mantua-maker too—not a class of woman famed for her virtue." James leaned back in his seat, frowning.

A moment later he added, "But I suppose she thought she gave you good counsel. You can have all the stones you wish, Mary. Sapphires to match the blue of your eyes, sewn onto your dresses and hung around your neck. We will go to London for them."

"London? Would that be the size of Belfast?"

"Ah, much greater," he laughed. "But you dazzle, with or without the damned stones."

"Would you leave off the swearing, husband?"

"To please you I shall leave off anything you wish, as long as it is not your neat little person. I was quite jealous of the old cordwainer when he got his hands on your pretty feet. And I'll not forget quickly the look on your face when he covered them in plaster. What a picture you made sitting there getting up your lessons whilst those clay bootees dried on you."

Mary looked away then, out of the coach window at the dank, jogging land-scape. It had been so bewildering, the sheer din of the city, buildings of an unim-aginable height all pushed together, the sparking rhythm of hooves on cobbles, the rattle of harness, the shouting, the stinking puddles, the hardened, cunning faces of the beggars thronging the carriage until McNamara drove them away, first by waving his horse-whip and finally by dragging a pile of coins from a pocket and flinging them far so that they were fought over in the gutter. "Tis Mrs. Chittle-borough with the hens!" Mary had exclaimed, longing in that instant to be home and in the next remembering that with her altered station it no longer felt like home. To her astonishment she discovered she missed the daily drudgery for the shape it gave to her life. Then one of the beggars, unsuccessful in the scramble for coins, came up to the carriage and looked straight in on her; Mary screamed and clung to James. She heard McNamara shouting, "Get out of it there now!"

She had seen a vision from a charnel house, a face where in place of a nose was a gaping hole in which bone and gristle faintly glowed, a face where open, suppu-rating sores sought to join across the remaining patches of dirty grey skin, where what had been the mouth had retreated from the long yellow teeth and greenish gums, the skull beneath gradually revealing itself as the flesh rotted away. Yet this putrescent mass was alive and recognisably female, with oily dark strands of hair straggling from beneath a filthy cotton cap, and protruding eyes shiny as black marbles.

"What was that?" she cried into his waistcoat.

"You know what that is, surely?"

She did not look up but moved her head from side to side, remembering Mrs. Samuels's warning, words spoken an an eternity ago, before everything had changed: "That way lies misery, destitution, disease." She heard James speaking, felt the words in the rise and fall of his chest.

"The pox. The poor wretch has little time now by the look of her. It would be a mercy were she to be taken to the bedlam, had anyone the courage to lay hands on her."

It was some time before Mary was recovered enough to be got down and through the mantua-maker's door. The frontage of Mrs. McKenna's atelier loomed above Mary as high as a cliff. Here she discovered another threat in the superior smiles of the seamstresses. She stood nodding in mute bewilderment as bolt after bolt was lifted down and unfurled before her onto long tables, but it was

Kilkeel who chose. In a smaller room the women divested her of Mrs. Chittleborough's valiant attempt at taking in an old sackdress of Lady Goward's. As she stood
in her shift silently obeying their commands to raise her arms, to drop them, to
bend her elbow, to turn around, she heard one of them stifle a snigger at her plain
servant's underclothes. Only later in the cordwainer's workshop had there been a
moment of comfort and that at a price. The old man first examined her naked feet.
Bending closer, so that she strained to hear him, he had whispered, "You have
good feet, young lady, that have been let grow as nature intended. No pinching or
cramping here." The blood had rushed to her face as she looked down at him but
the smile he gave her had been kind. "A wee drop of almond oil will soften them
faster," he had added. "That's what the ladies use." The man had found her out;
the feet that had gone unshod for most of her life had betrayed her as surely as the
speech Kilkeel strove to correct. Then she had heard the two discussing the lasts
that were to be made for her. "Now, I can make them of beech, your Honour, or
of hornbeam. Most ask for beech, but I do find it doesn't endure so well as the
hornbeam and will split or lose its shape sooner though the working of it is easier
and for that it suits the pocket better."

"Then they shall be of hornbeam,' answered James, and turning to her smiling
said, "Lasts to last."

So Much to Get Used To

Mary woke to the cawing of the rooks and for a moment didn't know where she was. She had been a very small child, too puny to work, when those birds had last roused her. For years a human hand or voice had pulled her from sleep, and she had accepted that such would always be the case. Yet the night of Lady Mitchelstown's death all those uncertainties had begun to unravel.

So much to get used to. Wearing her ring only when their chamber door was closed. The sound of a man using a pisspot in the night. Strange people the Quality, with all that fine park outside and no ditches to fall into, that they should not stir themselves from their bedchambers. Up in the attic Bridget had had to stop Mary from tiptoeing down the service stairs herself that first strange, sleepless night in the vast and creaking house.

Birdsong outside, and indoors no shuffling and lowing sounds from the byre alongside. Now Mary slept between linen sheets beaten and pummelled in a barrel and then blown to crispness in the wind, a task she had so often done herself, with Mrs. Chittleborough giving her goose grease afterwards to rub into her chapped hands. The ewer on the wash-stand was filled with rose-water. No sleep disturbed by the kick and thrash of a dreaming Bridget, or as it had been under her father's roof with the squirming of a younger child complaining of cold, of the scratching of straw through the mattress. That little girl now cold forever.

And here the strangest thing, to turn her head and see his sleeping face, the lips gently parted, the tufts of dark hair, the serene line of his brows. And then his eyes opening and his face in their shadowy world behind the bed-drapes awaking and with it his smile, the stretching of his limbs in readiness.

"Mary."

"Husband?" she whispered.

"My fortune indeed. Let me relieve you again of this. No, stay like that, your arms above your head... such sweet submission. See how your darling diddeys point at me when you do that? They demand to be kissed, and so they shall be... and now this one that it not feel lonely. See how they stand to attention now? And so sweet these little dark furze bushes," and he traced a finger down her armpit, "nearly as lovely as this dear little furred quim. Turn over Mary till I see you both sides. Oh lovely girl," he murmured, lifting her hair to let it fall over her right shoulder, kissing her nape and gently working down her spine.

"Lift yourself up here, Mary."

"Tis what the beasts do."

"You would compare me to friend bull again, would you? But I will acquit myself better than he... oh Mary... but he does not do this, nor this... does he? Squeeze your dear little hotbox my Mary—no, you cannot hurt me. Tight as you can. Ah let us make those diddeys swing back and forth like the bells in Parson Samuels's belfry."

"See how we fit to each other so neatly, Mary? I was made to lie in your arms. Our friend the bull has none of this after-joy, nor even the joy of anticipation. There he stands lonely in his field, not thinking of his cow, but at most of a passing peasant he can pitch by the breeks."

His head on her breasts, Kilkeel did not see the shadow cross her face.

"Only when he is brought to her does he remember what he must do, whereas I pass every day, every hour, in a stew of anticipation to be here with you beside me, beneath me, riding me rantipole—ah yes, we are yet to try that one. Does not the word itself sound joyous?"

"Rantipole, husband?"

"Astride me, my dear."

"And after the stride one, what will you do?"

"Well, we shall all the pleasures prove, as the poem goes, and when we have done all of them we will do them again, and again, so long as the good Lord gives us health and energy."

"Will it be always like this? I do not see others so happy as we. Not Parson Samuels and Mrs. Samuels. Mr. and Mrs. Chittleborough are kind but not joyful with each other. Your mother and father do not lie together. I mean they do not sleep in the same chamber."

"My father I believe is genuinely fond of Mother, whilst she tolerates him and would defend him, but I don't know that they were ever really lovers, Mary, not as we are. She brought him several thousands and a capable if untutored brain, and she was the third of four daughters for whom a suitable match had to be found. Affection but not love was in it. As for Samuels, he is a thwarted man, and such unhappy souls risk poisoning all around them with their bitterness. Had that parsonage been filled with numerous children he would have struggled to maintain, I believe it would have gone easier for him. A battle, yes, but perhaps a better man would have emerged in place of one who has too much leisure to dwell on his failings. The Chittleboroughs are Philemon and Baucis in Quaker fustian, devoted to one another as an expression of God's love, yet, dear Mary, I believe they have never asked God's permission to see each other unclothed."

"Ah, tis wicked of you," Mary hid her smiles in the sheet.

"Look at me," he said, suddenly serious. "You do well to ask me these questions. We may not always be as we are now. Your poor bull may tire, for he is merely mortal, but he will always love you. Had I not I would not have gone to see your father and all that came after. I would have bought you in the end with food in Kate and Robert's mouths and clothes on their backs. Or still easier, I would have threatened your father with turning off and used you as Blanch would have done. I feel you tremble, Mary, but you will never see him again."

"You will not tire of me, so? I don't have all my letters yet and I am slow to know what to do with them there forks and spoons and I don't know how to walk or talk like a lady."

"*Those* forks and spoons. Let my mother help you in these matters, for she will. She is angry with me for ruining you, and I cannot tell her you are not. I wonder how angry she might be if she knew what I *really* have done. But she loves you, Mary. She urged me not to cast you off. Nothing could be further from my thoughts; it is a measure of how well she thinks of you that she will not have you ill-used. No, I will not tire of you, but will you of me?"

"I could not even if I would. I promised you when we went before Fr. O'Dowd."

"You see? I have had this from no other woman. If I had done what was expected of me and married a fine lady with a marriage settlement I could not have had so sincere a promise; the bargain thus struck would have been a very different one."

"But that night you came to wake me, when poor Lady Mitchelstown—"

"You would compare this to what I had with poor Letty? I did care deeply for her, the more perhaps because I know she did not love me. Don't look so startled. Letty knew she was dying but she loved life and her liking for me was part of that clinging on. She was bored with old Mitchelstown, and bored with her children…"

"Mother of God, she had childer?"

"Four of them, pretty children all. The last one at least was certainly not Mitchelstown's—nor mine either, Mary, but fruit of a London adventure, so do not frown so. I do not see you do so but know that you do. Yet old Mitchelstown dotes on the little girl all the same, though he surely knows."

"Tis hard though for the poor bairns to have no mother."

"Don't cry Mary, though your tears do you honour. They hold their nursemaid and governess in greater affection, for they see of them than they ever did of their distracted mother."

Struell Wells

St. John's Eve
23rd June 1767

"Are you quite sure, Mary, that you want to make this journey? An hour's jolting in the trap on a warm day and you say there will be a great throng at the place. At least let me take you there in the carriage."

Mary stood apparently irresolute, but then looked James full in the face. "No, husband, I may not make another such pilgrimage, and I want to do it for the babby's sake. I will go with Bridgie and Packy and McNamara will drive us though he does not mean to make the pilgrimage himself."

"You do not want me with you?"

"It is not that. It is that the Wells are for simple people."

"And I would be too obviously not that?"

"Yes. They would not know you for one of them, one of us."

"So I would have you join my world but I may not join yours?"

"Husband, you have always counselled caution and I have followed your direction. Not even my sister knows the truth of it. But, believe me, you do not want to be part of what is my father's and Robert's and Kate's world though it is a much better one than it was before you—"

"Before they took the profits of sin, you mean."

'We know it is not so, but it is what my father's neighbours say—those that do not wish him well—though some of them envy him and would have given you their daughters without there was Fr. O'Dowd. Those that do respect him pity him and perhaps for him this is harder to bear." Mary spoke without resentment. "If you came 'twould make it harder for him."

"Your father will be there too?"

"No. He cannot leave the land and he has not wanted to go since Mammy died. But if you came you'd be noticed and the people would talk of nothing else for months, and he would hear it."

"Then for him I shall not come. But remember me there in your prayers."

"I'll be waiting for yous here under the trees," said McNamara, unhitching the horse and leading him into the shade. He watched the three figures moving away into the hollow where the wells and the church stood, Mary dressed simply and demurely as if the wife of a respectable shop-keeper. "And so she could have been," muttered McNamara, rummaging in his pockets for his pipe, "Great girl that she is. Good luck to her, so, and to hell with that cant about her immortal soul. 'Tis a marvel he let her come, and I wonder how does she want to be here when she's put herself beyond the sacraments." He shrugged, but something still nagged him. McNamara had witnessed Kilkeel as protective of Mary as of a wife, when it would have been so easy for him to have had her when he wished without all that trouble of making her a lady. *A very good lady she makes too, but even so.* And when Mary's lacings were loosened as her belly gently swelled they had watched breathlessly from below stairs to see would he send her away. *The divil he did!* Himself had clapped him, McNamara, on the shoulder, and demanded his congratulations for he was to be a father, "And I hope many times over, McNamara. This rambling old pile would be all the better if it had as many children in it as there are kittens in the stables." He'd wanted her to take a maid, but she would have none of it. The new girl was in the kitchen instead, for Miss Mary (for that was how McNamara thought of her now, and called her so) had insisted that she would have no one wait on her. So she laid the fire and ordered their room like any peasant's wife, but lay with my Lord behind brocade curtains just as had Mitchelstown's lady, but had the grace to stay there and not go trolloping up and down the stairs and frightening the parson. *Yes, Miss Mary is the lady.*

McNamara tapped out his pipe, checked the horse was tethered firmly, and went to climb up into the trap. It was a warm, quiet spring afternoon and just the occasion for a nap.

He didn't know how long he had been drowsing before he was roused by shouts, a babble of hostile but excited voices in which a woman's shrill tones could be distinguished. *Mother of God, to be saying such a thing in a holy place!* McNamara was not pious; thirty years ago he had buried his young wife, putting their stillborn son into her arms himself, and no priest had ever explained the justice of his tragedy in a way that made sense to him. He made his way up to the Mass rock at

Slievenalargy from time to time in an unconvinced attempt to find the faith he had lost, yet as a practical man didn't hold with all this getting yourself wet on an open hillside. *Sure wouldn't you be catching the cold?* But for some harridan to be shrieking "Hoor! Hoor!" in such a place was no way to behave. Another woman was giving back as good. *Sweet Lord, but that's Bridget!* McNamara jumped down from the trap with all the agility of a twenty year-old and then cursed the twinges in his knees that reminded him of his actual fifty-odd summers. He ran in the bow-legged way of the habitual horseman down past the half-built chapel, and picking up speed skirted the little conical Eye Well where those who had been queuing to bathe their faces had abandoned their wait, to stare at the spectacle unfolding on the crushed grass in front of the bath houses. *Nothing wrong with their eyes then.* A semi-circle of barefoot people stood behind the little group, some of them only half-dressed as they had hurriedly left the antechambers of the baths to witness the spectacle. A drenched and trembling Mary, her hair hanging in rats-tails about her face, her clothing clinging to a still-damp body, attempted with stumbling fingers to tie her bodice, whilst Patrick tried to comfort her with ineffectual little pattings. Before them circled and jabbed two women, for all the world like a cock-fight McNamara had once seen in a field behind a horse fair.

Bridget's opponent was a squat, greasy, middle-aged woman, her head lowered like a bull about to charge. The younger woman held her head high, eyes flashing indignation. McNamara halted in admiration, muttering to himself, "Ah, Bridgie, I'd marry you meself if you weren't sweet on that pink-faced Andrews, and him not even knowing it."

"Keep out of it yourself, ye oul' hag that you are! Lay a finger on my sister again and I'll tear the tongue and eyes out of your head, so I will."

"She's the hoor of the Goward squireen and has no business in this holy place with respectable people, strutting her shame for all to see! God love her poor mother who'll be turning in her grave."

"You leave our mother out of this, you witch," hurled back Bridget, and rushing at the woman pushed her so hard in the chest that the other staggered back. Some of the crowd cheered; the entertainment was improving by the minute.

Come now, McNamara, you'll have to stop this, he said to himself. *Just get them all away home*, and he moved between them just as Bridget's opponent pushed her sleeves up her meaty forearms and made to go back at her.

"Ladies—"

"What is the meaning of this? A tavern brawl in a place of pilgrimage!" A lividly pale Father O'Dowd was striding over from the direction of the chapel, vestments flapping.

"Ask that hoor what she's doing here," said the woman, unabashed, "Flaunting her shame with Lord high and mighty, him that gave scandal with another man's wife and soon enough will have someone else. Who'll look to you and your babby then, hoor? Make her do the penance, Father, the penance!" The woman smiled in triumph at the prospect of a humbled Mary, dragging herself on her knees seven times over the sharp circle of stones around St. Patrick's chair.

"Shut your mouth, Molly, and get back in the bath-house. Sure it'll never be yourself the young Lord would go troubling."

The smile congealed on the woman's face, and before she could think of a reply O'Dowd started issuing orders. "McNamara, get them away home as quickly as you can," and to the crowd, "Let him who is without sin cast the first stone. Now be out of my sight and remember what you came here for twasn't this. Quick or you'll have the penance to do yourselves until I get tired of watching ye's. Bridgie, with a voice as carrying as that 'tis a shame you cannot preach yourself. Get away out of it all of you and don't bring your sister back here."

He followed the chastened little group back to the trap, gently drawing Mary away from her brother. "It's over now. Stop crying for you'll make your baby weep too. But don't come back to the Wells, not next year, not ever. I warned you what you'd be letting yourself in for, and you're a good courageous girl and have brought your husband to God, but there's much will have to change before you're able to tell it to the world. The constables could have every soul in this place whipped just for being here today. That they don't is only because they're idle or not wanting trouble if people will only be discreet, so let's not be making the trouble for them. There are sure to be spies here as it is. I'll tell you of some quiet wee places you and he can go where you won't be known, where you can both make a pilgrimage in peace, and if anyone finds you there you were just taking the air."

"I'd wanted here, Father, for my mother brought us. I wanted her blessing."

"You have it, believe me. But now think about what you'll tell your husband."

Mary stared at the grass. "He wanted to come. I didn't let him."

"You have sense in that, at least. We'll go on with the Mass in your chamber and no one the wiser. Home, now. Be thankful tis a warm day or you'd be dead of the cold all wet as you are."

"She started in on me Father when I was under the water!"

"I am thinking we want another bath attendant than Molly Doyle."

"Mary, drink this and calm yourself. You are safe now, but I believe you owe me an explanation for this foolishness."

"I so wanted to go, husband. 'Twas something I looked forward to, so I did, when Mammy was still with us and we would work and plan as to how we would have the day to go to Downpatrick and who would give us space on their cart if we could find the pennies for to pay him. I was only a child the last time but it was the happiest day of my life. I wanted for to go to be closer to her there. I thought no one would know me."

"This Doyle woman did. Had you not considered that your story might have got about? How could it not, for people have little enough to talk about except ill of others. Mary, when you accepted me you knew that some would relish this scandal and not spare you. You told me yourself why your father chose not to accompany you. I would not have let you go myself, but that I thought all you did was wash your face and pray. I am no Catholic born, but I have seen pilgrims thronging at places considered holy in France and Italy, not half-starved people naked and shivering under icy water in a country that struggles to keep warm."

James shivered himself, imagining naked Mary and the gentle swell of her helpless maternity beneath the drenching shower in that underground bath. What if she had slipped on the wet flagstones, broken her poor head? And the baby? He frowned as he imagined the satisfaction of that grim bath attendant when by the light of her lamp she recognised Thomas Kearney's daughter and saw proof with her own eyes of her shame.

"Did Fr. O'Dowd know you were going?"

"He did not; indeed I didn't know he would be there. I begged Packy and Bridgie to take me and then I told you. 'Tis not their fault."

"He was right to tell you not to go again. He has told me there are other less frequented places where we may go. I confess though to some astonishment, for they formed no part of my instruction from him. These dark wells strike me as some pagan rite."

"St. Patrick himself called out those wells."

"Well, no doubt he did and I would never question the piety of anyone who went there, with the exception of course of the Doyle woman, but Mary, those three-legged reed crosses you and Bridget have—our Lord surely never hung on one of those?"

"It was St. Bridget who gave us that cross, for to tell us about the Trinity."

"But some have four legs."

"The Trinity and Our Lady. St. Bridget is a miracle worker if you will but call on her."

"I shall leave my card with her footman, then."

"Husband!"

'Forgive me. I'm afraid Fr. O'Dowd had some difficulty with me when it came to miracles performed outside the Holy Family. What wonders does she perform?"

"She turned water into beer."

"A true Irishwoman. All the same I think I will persevere with St. Augustine instead."

Mary went into his arms and hid her face in his neck that he might not see how little she cared for being mocked.

Lying within the bed curtains later, he stroked the gentle swell of her pregnancy, feeling beneath his hand the furtive wriggling of the life within. Mary turned his words over again and again. *But hadn't Fr. O'Dowd had the turning of him, and would he not be saved, even if he said some of the most fearful things?*

"I met him, you know, the Vicar of Rome," James said.

"You met His Holiness?"

"Many gentlemen of quality did so. Jack Wickmere and I went with our bear-leader—our tutor—just as we went to visit the antiquities or to spy on the courtesans of Venice, or to see Lake Nemi."

"Corty sans?"

"Ladies of pleasure. No, don't stiffen so, Mary. That sisterhood means nothing to me now. What need of such as they has a new-made husband happy in his choice? You should ask me instead about His Holiness. I met an urbane and astute Venetian, a politician who to advance the standing of Catholics in these islands had chosen to accept the German Georges as kings in the place of the Catholic Stuarts. I remember his plump but watchful face. Do not bridle, Mary, I speak well of him, believe me. He asked Jack and I the most searching questions on what we considered to be the commonality of belief between the professed Protestant and the Catholic, which merely flummoxed us. I fancy he was better informed in principles of Protestantism than would be poor Mr. Samuels. Of course we did not acquit ourselves well and had to be rescued by Mr. Abercrombie, our tutor. The moral, that relentless pedant impressed on us afterwards, was that we would never appear as gentlemen were we unprepared for intelligent discourse with a head of state, for such is a pope. Certainly he looked entirely the emperor in all that ermine and scarlet, seated upon his throne. What I saw in Rome was as far from those massings on Slievenalargy as it's possible to imagine, and from the quiet little meetings you and I have with O'Dowd. The grandiosity, the marble, the gilding, the finest stuffs, brocade and lace with which they bedeck themselves, and the cruelty. I saw grown men with faces as smooth as yours and great swollen hands singing with the sweetest of women's voices in the pope's choir; they were gelded, Mary."

"No!"

"Then there was the day Jack and I saw a girl of no more than fifteen taken forever into the Ursulines. She came tricked out as for a wedding—"

"Well that is so, for she was to wed our Lord."

"Indeed, it was not a wedding I saw but a sacrifice."

"Do not say so!"

"First she was shorn of all her hair. Pretty hair it was, red-gold ringlets and when unpinned, long to her waist. The Mother Superior wielded those shears gleefully, heaping all the richness of those tresses upon the altar. The girl was hung about with jewels and these were plucked roughly from her as though in punishment. It reminded me most of a shamed officer having his rank torn from his tunic. An Englishman at my shoulder had to be restrained by his companions from drawing his sword and striding forward to rescue her; indeed the poor girl did look close to a faint more than once. Then her beautiful dress was cut from her as if it were nothing but a muddle of miserable rags."

"Mrs. Chittleborough took my clothes from me when I came here, before she put me in the hip bath and scrubbed me, but they were the clothes from the Quaker gentleman and she said they would cover another needy soul."

"Ah, but we have not made a nun of you."

"No, but I know now that poor Dadda stinks sometimes like the beasts in the byre. So must I and Bridgie and Patrick have done before we came here."

"Mary, those who stink are the fine ladies who drench themselves in scent against the decay of their flesh, and eat peppermint against their foetid breath, who powder and rouge their faces until they make of themselves the most grotesque of painted marionettes."

Mary shifted in his embrace, thinking of Lady Mitchelstown's rouged corpse.

"All that Mrs. Chittleborough's hip bath has done is to reveal the beauties that your station in life had disguised," he went on, "your sweet secret skin all the whiter for the patina that covered it so long . But, Mary, what I wanted to tell you is that with all that pomp and vainglory I saw in Rome I could not see how any thinking man could subscribe to flummery and superstition and call it religion. Scratch me, you may say, and you might expect to find still the Protestant beneath the Catholic gentleman. Yet I also saw the patched friars tending to the most loathsome of wretched beggars. Not only. On our way towards Italy Mr. Abercrombie persuaded Jack and I, though we were most unwilling, to make a detour through the most terrifying and inhospitable mountains to visit the silent inmates of a remote French Charterhouse. So ignorant were we that we thought he merely wanted to show us a school, like our own of that name. The place, Mary, was such as only Mr. Walpole could have dreamt of—I would give you that gentleman to read but that I don't think that Mrs. Samuels would consider him edifying or instructive— a vast echoing warren of horrid and thrilling aspect, full of mysterious cowled figures living in silence. The cawing of rooks and the mewling of their kitchen cats were the only animate sounds to be heard. Each man there had his own door leading to his humble cell and beyond that his little vegetable plot. I looked into as much as I could see of their faces beneath those cowls and longed to ask them their stories, for Mary, I envied them though their lives frightened me too, but they were permitted to utter no word to me nor to each other. It was my fancy that some rich idlers like ourselves who came to gaze on those men as we did, never made the journey back through the pass, instead casting their wigs and wealth aside and bending their heads for the tonsure. Yet these men made us a sumptuous meal—one such as they would never themselves eat, said old Abercrumbly—and didn't demand of us that we exhaust ourselves in what passes for wit at the finest of tables but which is so often merely the chatter of starlings. We ate and were grateful. I am grateful still that even at this moment in that vast place—more fortress than cloister—they pray for those beyond their walls. The grandeur of Rome enraged me; less that worldly pope looking down on us from his throne than the splendour of those Cardinals. The Pretender's brother the Cardinal at Frascati is as much a crowned head in his palace as his brother has failed to be. Charles Edward Stuart himself we glimpsed too; he reeks of drink and disappointment and derides his wife for the fact he has no heir. It is said that when in drink he beats her. I marvelled then that any man who professed himself Catholic could remain so in such a place; only later did I think that he must do so despite it. Rome could never have had the turning of me. It was those silent men, and you and O'Dowd who succeeded, though you didn't even try. You, for your steadfastness the night poor Letty died, he for coming here when the parson would not stir. Such simple things, worth more than all the wealth of a papal court."

"Do you sleep, Mary?"

"No."

"I thought not. Listen, my love, there is a way to stop their tongues."

"You'd send me away from here?"

"How could I? No, quite the opposite. We go before Parson Samuels. You swear yourself a Protestant—hear me out—just for the look of the thing, no more. Then he marries us."

"We *are* married, or do you not see it so?"

"You know I do. This would just be for the world, not for us."

"I will not. I cannot swear to a falsehood. I can never be a Protestant."

"No one expects that of you, least of all me. But it would mean I could give our child my name."

"Oh... "

"Consider it, Mary."

"No. I cannot. It would be like telling untruths to the child, and I cannot do that. Sure is it not the law that is wrong, and should be changed, not us that should pretend?"

"If that law changed then the whole house of cards that is this island would come tumbling down. You're obstinate," he said, smiling into the dark, 'but I cannot fault your reasoning. Kiss me, would you?"

Lying-In

15th September 1767
Moneyscalp Clergy House

Mary was today taken to the Sisters. Only Mother Catherine is to know the full state of affairs but such is the respect in which the Sisters hold her and their obedience to her government that I am fully confident that they will treat Mary as they would any expectant wife. Though these holy women do not know Kilkeel it grieved me to give them a false name for him. I encouraged him to dress plainly and say little. They believe he is simply a Catholic Englishman hired as a gentleman's man to a Big House who practises his faith in secret.

He turned to me in astonishment when first he saw the ladies of the convent and I had need to press his arm to say no more. I believe he does not yet fully comprehend the ways in which we are constrained to live. He sees me dressed only in sober black like any layman, and that I appear to the world as a priest only upon the mountain where indeed there is precious little of the world to see me, but, says he, as we walked away (him all unwilling the same to leave her), "They are not like the religious I saw in Rome." It was upon my tongue to say that they are probably of rather better stuff than their Roman sisters, for in that city some nuns live a life of well-endowed ease and choose the convent as preferable to domestic toil. Then it broke upon me that what he expected to see was the garb of a nun where here in Ireland they may not wear the veil, for he did go on to say "They looked to me like Mistress Chittleborough" and it is true, our nuns do look like the soberest of Quaker wives.

The chamber they have put aside for Mary is as simple as the cells the sisters occupy. I fancy this reassured her for she smiled at the sight of it and said it reminded her of the room she had shared with Bridgie and I do wonder at how Mary settles to the finery of a bedchamber such as Goward Hall provides; Lord James tells me that she finds this hard sometimes though Lord and Lady Goward treat her kindly as the beloved of their son. I know though that she feels the separation from the other servants. Mrs. Chittleborough still loves her, for that woman is a true Christian. But it weighs grievously upon Mary that she may not share her secret with Bridget and it has been so arranged that Bridget does not serve her as Mary will have it no other way. When they chance to meet Bridget bobs a curtsey and gives her the coldest of looks, treating her with the most insolent of good manners and I see how much this hurts Mary.

Mother Catherine drew me aside as she bid them go into the chamber for their last words together. "She is slender but strong" were Reverend Mother's words. I hope and pray to St. Margaret Holy Helper that this chamber witness not her death nor that of her child. I will call on her there tomorrow without her husband and hear her confession and then we must trust all of us in God's mercy.

Afterbirth

10th October 1767
Siena Sisters

Reverend Father,

The child known as Edward Kearney thrives. He is small but cries stoutly yet I would have you come on receipt of this letter and baptise him that his salvation be assured. The condition of his mother causes me some anguish. This night she sweated so feverishly that all the bedlinen had to be changed yet she complains so of cold. Her travail was a long one and she suffered much but so it is laid down in Scripture that such is to be Eve's punishment. I crave your permission to engage a wet nurse for I do not know that Mary can persevere in suckling her babe though when she is lucid she tries; to this nurse once found I will say no more than that this is a child of a gentleman and that her reward will fit her task. The father of Mary's babe must know that his son will have no brother or sister of his mother, for even if she be spared such was the state of her after burthen that in my opinion she will never again be with child. I beg that you will be circumspect in what you say to him and urge him not to come here again though he may plead to see his son and his wife for the risk of this sisterhood being discovered would be too great. We nourish her with drink of warm spices and white wine as you have said that no expense is to be spared.

I remain most humbly yours,

Mrs. Janet Crilly

In Christ Mother Catherine Bernard

12th October

I beg you Father come on receipt of this message and bring him with you; circumstances demand that we sacrifice caution. The child thrives but we despair of his mother. Dr. Benson has been sent for.

+Janet Crilly

They made the journey in pale silence. Without being told, McNamara urged the horses to their utmost. "Tell my sister I love her! Beg her forgiveness of me for treating her so ill," Bridget had cried.

'Mother Catherine says the child does well," O'Dowd eventually said. "The rest is in God's hands."

"It is all my fault."

O'Dowd said nothing to this. He had heard comments like it so often that he was saddened only when he did not.

Kilkeel saw his son for the first time at the breast of the wet nurse sitting by Mother Catherine's hearth. At her feet was a basket where a larger infant slumbered. "There is plenty here for the both of them, sir" said the woman. She did not smile, even when she added, "You've a handsome boy," for Kilkeel's tense face did not invite it. He touched his fingers to the extraordinary softness of the dark down of his son's head, noted the determined fingers pressing the breast and with a lurch of his heart recognised in the shape of the baby's hand a miniature version of his own.

Mother Catherine appeared and silently led him into a larger room than the one where he had left Mary for her lying-in. Shutters were closed against the daylight and the room lit only by two or three candles. Mary appeared tiny and deathly pale amongst the pillows build up behind her. With a glimmer of sickly hope Kilkeel noted that the nuns had not crossed her hands on her breast.

"Benson," he greeted the doctor, who nodded in response. The doctor showed his recognition only in a momentary lift of the eyebrows; he had been wondering by whose orders it was he had been called to this odd little community of women and who was paying his fee. The oldest of them, who had proved herself a formidably competent midwife, had merely described the other three as her daughters.

"Mary," Kilkeel whispered, and kneeling by the bed took her unresponsive hand. Behind him he could hear the chink of glass and metal as O'Dowd prepared the oils and water on a little table made ready by Mother Catherine.

"She has lost a lot of blood," murmured the doctor. "She was in fever though that has thankfully abated, but her breathing is too shallow for health. She is full of milk though and it'll have to be drawn off before it curdles on her and sends her fever high again," and Kilkeel flinched as the doctor reached across and pressed on her breast through her nightgown with flattened fingers. He recognised that garment as the one he had taken off her on their wedding night and quietly started to weep. The gentle pressure of O'Dowd's fingers on his shoulder roused him. Mother Catherine was folding back the sheet so that Mary's feet were exposed. *How small and thin she looks,* Kilkeel thought, *just as when she came into Mother's service.*

He stood back with the doctor as the anointing of Mary's forehead, breast, hands and feet proceeded. Remembering Letty's deathbed and Mary's silent presence beside him as O'Dowd had lent over the dead woman murmuring prayers she had never heard in life, Kilkeel dug his nails into his palms and prayed silently. As the priest intoned the "Glory be" he raised his right hand and crossed himself, and heard the sharp intake of Benson's breath.

"It is done. If she leaves us now her path to heaven is assured," said O'Dowd.

Benson coughed and said, 'As she is yet with us, then this might be the moment for her milk to be pressed away." His voice sounded loud, clumsy and for a moment there was a stunned silence. Mother Catherine broke it.

"If I may suggest sir, might we try the child against her breast?"

Benson grunted. "I do not believe she is strong enough to bear it."

"With respect sir, would she be strong enough to bear the pressing off of her milk?"

Benson shrugged. "There is logic in that. We can try." With a finality that turned Kilkeel's heart to ice he added, "I do not think we have anything to lose."

"I shall ask Mrs. O'Keeffe to join us, so," said Mother Catherine.

"I will fetch her, Mrs. Crilly," said O'Dowd, grateful for the opportunity to discreetly withdraw before this intimate scene was played out. He found McNamara standing by the hearth wringing his hat in his hands and asking for news.

Edward Kearney had of course feasted already at Mrs. O'Keeffe and now slept soundly in the basket alongside his nurse's child.

"We should wake him. If he is not hungry he may still drink but will go more gently with her," said Mother Catherine.

Kilkeel watched in awed silence as the nun undid the remaining buttons on Mary's nightgown and gently freed her turgid right breast. The mark of the oils on her skin gleamed in the candle-light.

"I shall hold him,' said the nun, and sitting on the bed expertly manoeuvred the sleeping infant to the breast. He woke fully now and let out a thin cry of annoyance but being presented with the nipple muffled his protests in grunts and murmurs of satisfaction.

"Look to her," whispered Kilkeel to the doctor. "She knows he is there."

At the sound of her baby's cry the smallest tremor had gone through Mary. Then for the first time since he had entered the room, Kilkeel saw Mary's eyes open. Their expression was exhausted and far off, but he moved closer to the bed and cried, "Mary! Mary!" The eyes searched, focused, and she smiled. "Husband," she whispered.

A Family Christmas, 1767

"We are grateful to you, Dr. Benson, for attending so quickly," said Lady Goward. "The welfare of Miss Kearney is of some considerable concern to all three of us."

Dr. Benson bowed low in turn to each of the ladies in order of rank: Lady Goward, Mrs. Samuels and Mrs. Chittleborough. He had never in his experience come across anything like this degree of concern for a seduced maidservant. Lady Goward he considered magnificent, as he always had. She was putting a bold front on a situation most mothers would have sought to keep hushed. The parson's wife and the Quaker lady looked as anxious as any doting aunts could be.

"And how did you find our patient?" asked Lady Goward.

"Physically I would say she makes progress, but were she in a better frame of mind then that progress would be quicker. You indicated to me beforehand, my Lady, that you believed Miss Mary's normally equable spirits are considerably depressed, and this I have observed in her ceaseless weeping and desolation. She cries over her child's head and says she doesn't know how to love him and that he deserves better than she for a mother, yet her every look and action speaks of that love. But when I asked her if it would take some burden from her were we to employ a wet-nurse—there is, Madam, a most respectable person briefly retained when we feared to lose Miss Mary—she started up in horror and begged me not to deprive her of the only means she had of being of service to her child. "Oh do not take that from me, for it is the only thing I can do for him and do well," she cried. Indeed, her milk is plentiful and the boy thrives, though she weeps continuously even as he sucks. I would furthermore counsel, though I say this with some diffidence, that she be let alone more. She is sensible of the great kindness that all of you ladies show her, and of the love that you bear her. It is my view however that the actions of so many to relieve her anxiety by doing things for her, even while she appreciates them from her heart, will cause her to become even more listless, for she is all the more likely to feel that she does not have purpose, or that others may accomplish the tasks of a mother better than she. In time I believe her distress will pass, but we must tread carefully. I have seen cases where this melancholy descends into complete disorientation and ultimately madness. So the best advice I can give to you, ladies, is to show her your affection as a mother does to her older child: a kiss and a gentle embrace. To be ever about her when she is in this current anxiety she may see as a criticism of her failings, though she will never say this and would be mortified that you should think she does not welcome you. Lord Kilkeel I see has already assumed the role of bodyguard and seems poised to repel all comers. I observe she does seem most anxious to keep him in her company and hangs on every look and word of his."

"Poor little maidy," sobbed Mrs. Chittleborough. Meg Samuels reached over and took her hand.

"My son could have avoided all of this had he listened to a mother's counsel," said Lady Goward. "I am quite vexed with him, not with her."

"He is not the first young man to ignore a mother's advice, nor will he be the last, but if I may venture to speak boldly, Madam, that he has not abandoned this girl nor had her turned out of doors, is to his credit—and yours, my Lady."

Hope in a New Year

"Mary?"

"Yes, husband?"

"You look well. I came to watch you sleeping and I think you slept well. Did you?"

"Yes. Edward woke only twice and fell asleep as soon as he'd had his fill."

"Our boy is three months old in a few days. Benson gave me a warning that I should leave you in peace for that time so that I did not interrupt Nature's healing work."

"He told you that?"

"Certainly he did. Had I not said so before? Mary, why do you cry? Would my caresses cause you so much sorrow?'

"I didn't know. I feared you didn't love me anymore."

"Oh Mary. I've been so lonely at night without you. You have another, of course, and though he is mightily small, he is mightily powerful, but I miss my wife and must tell him to lend her to me from time to time. I asked Benson could I not lie nightly with you but not molest you, but he looked at me from under those fierce eyebrows and said he would not trust any man with a young and comely mistress to lie still at her back, and I was not to mock him. I assured him I meant nothing of the sort."

"I'd have been so happy for you to have been with me. I only hope you don't find me much changed."

"I do not, only that your face is rounder and softer; it has a mother's gentleness. But for three months I have seen no more of your person than I may spy when you feed that ravenous rascal, and this makes *me* hungry for you. Let me look on you, Mary, and I promise I will do no more but that, and will treasure what I see until I can avail myself of you this night or any when you permit me. Ah, these ties are fiddly and impatience makes me clumsy. Will you help me? Oh Mary, you are even lovelier than I remember you. This I like, the softness of your little tum now its tenant has packed his effects and quit his lodging. You were lovely before as a maiden, but are more beautiful now as a woman. Mary, I fear I shall struggle to keep that promise to leave you in peace till bedtime, but if you hold me to it I will, though with great effort. You are smiling so I think you won't. Edward sleeps soundly, does he not? We can be quiet, I think. Forgive my impatience… "

"How did you this first?"

"Mm?"

"When did you first do this, what we just did? What husbands and wives do."

"Well, I wasn't a husband, and the lady was no one's wife. She was a widow. Why do you ask?"

"I want to know more of you—now you're mine again."

"I have always been, I think from when I woke you the night Letty died. Perhaps before but I didn't admit it to myself."

"I do not believe Lady Mitchelstown cared much for me. And I was jealous of her."

"Letty cared for life, and enjoyment, and beautiful things. But not so much for people. Of course you were jealous of her. She was rich, she had so many fine things she didn't appreciate."

"She had you. She was kind to me, but kinder when you were by."

"Then she knew me better than I knew myself, poor woman."

"I remember her in my prayers. But you were to tell me about the widow."

"Sally Possick. She was the daughter of the dairy-man on Jack Wickmere's father's estate. A widow of twenty-two with a little girl. Her husband was killed by a kick of his horse to his head when he went to see had she a shoe loose. That was in their first year together. So hard, to start a married life and then to be deprived of its pleasures and promise so soon."

"I would never want another man but you."

"Try not to be too hard on poor Sally. Jack and I were friends from babyhood. My father's cousin had estates then in Norfolk adjoining his father's, so we were much together. Then Jack's father died and we didn't see each other until we met at Charterhouse, and it was as if no time had passed. So I spent holidays with him near Thetford. We shared everything, did everything together."

"Including Sally."

"Including Sally, yes. Oh Mary, we were boys of seventeen. I am a man of nearly thirty years. There are no Sally Possicks in my life now."

"You smile at the memory."

"Mary, I would insult the lady if I didn't. Your pretty mouth trembles and your eyes fill. I am your husband, and now I have grieved you, when Benson told us all that you should be shown nothing but affection. I do want you to meet Jack though; you will like him, and his lady. He is a fine, honest fellow and the best friend a man could have. When you meet him, you will know all there is to know of me.'

"But what happened after, to Sally and her babby?"

"It ended well. When Jack and I departed on our Tour she went to live with an ensign in the East Norfolk Foot. We had hoped he might marry her—"

"So yous kept her for years then."

"On and off. We were in Oxford getting what is known as the education of a gentleman. And then I was here, and Jack met his Peg at the theatre and is with her still."

"Twould have been easier for you had the soldier married her, so."

"Well, yes. But he didn't. The little girl was brought up by her grandfather. In the end the ensign contracted gambling debts with an elderly half-pay captain of his own regiment, and made her over in lieu of his debt."

"He sold her!"

"The half-pay captain was in love with her, and married her, so now she has a name and some modest security; I heard there was another child. Her old husband was so pleased with his win that he forswore gambling ever after. He had all he wanted. But Mary, buying and selling is what happens in most marriages, more or less, amongst those who call themselves gentlemen. The ladies have a price and bring inducements they call dowries, and the bargain is struck."

'So are you not a gentleman, then?'

"I don't care if I am or not. All I care about is being your husband. I had not thought of poor Sally in years. Nor indeed had I questioned my conduct towards her until now. Mary, it is not the first who counts, but the last."

"You are my first. You count."

"Will I be your last?"

"Oh yes."

"Then can we cease talking Mary, and do again what we did just now?"

"What way, sir?"

"You choose, my darling."

Learning about *Ton* from Those Who Have It

London, July 1768

"Now that we have prevailed upon our men to leave us, we can talk freely, Mary."

Mary looked around at the door in a state of near-panic. It was the first time she had been left alone with any of James's friends and she wondered if she was being subjected to a test. How quickly could she with politeness excuse herself by a visit to the nursery?

"Fear not, they will not interrupt us for at least two hours," said Peg, deliberately misunderstanding Mary's gesture. "How old are you, Mary?' she continued.

"I am eighteen, I believe."

"And James is your first protector?"

"He is my—yes—only him."

"He seems most devoted to you, my dear. You are very fortunate, for there are many who have set their caps at him, not to mention his mother's attempts to marry him off."

Mary looked down at her hands.

"Even were she to succeed," Peg went on, "I don't believe it would make any difference, for it doesn't seem to for men. They go where they will anyway." Mary looked up, and Peg hastened to reassure. "His heart would still be yours, of that I am sure, even if he were married to another. And he dotes on that pretty baby. You took a risk there, my dear, but it seems to have turned out most felicitously."

Mary frowned. "A risk?"

"Well, yes, to be with child so precipitately. Most of us do what we can to avoid such trouble, you know, seeing as our men come to us for amusement, to be carefree. They want us to be brilliant, witty, beautiful more than domestic.'

Mary's shoulders drooped again. James was constantly telling her how beautiful she was, but witty? Brilliant? Reading for her was a joy and she learned fast, but here in London she felt so very far away from Mrs. Samuels's little parlour and her gentle voice. To enjoy what one read was one thing, but to have the confidence to speak aloud of it, with the glittering speed and verve that Peg and her friends had when they spoke of the latest French novel, the latest play, was quite another matter.

"But the babby came, so he did." She could have bitten her tongue for having slipped into the vernacular that James was so patiently coaching her out of.

"Mary, if I might give you some advice. Wait some time before you start another. Men do not amuse themselves as mothers do with their children. There is a very reliable lady in Pimlico, most discreet and very experienced. Her rates are reasonable. Should you ever need her assistance then do come to me—you look horrified, Mary. It is certainly painful but no more I am sure than childbed was, though that I have never experienced, and one does recover—of visits to Pimlico I mean."

"Reverend Mother said that I will never have no more. She despaired of me but she and Dr. Benson saved me even after the priest had to be called." Mary started to cry.

"Oh Mary, forgive me! Let us go up in a while and see how the dear little man does. Is that what they call the midwife in Ireland then, Reverend Mother?"

"Yes. I mean, she was a midwife in Limerick before… before she came to work by us."

Peg leaned forward and said in an altered tone: "I wonder if you know how fortunate you are, Mary. Many girls without husbands give birth alone. Favourites they may have been, but they are turned out when with child and nobody thinks to engage a midwife, let alone a doctor, for their lying-in. Another actress took me to Pimlico when I was sixteen after the theatre manager had threatened me with losing my place if I did not oblige him. It was better thus, for it is best not to dwell on the fate of the child who is born from such a liaison. But you weep at the prospect of having no more. Your protector brings you here to meet his friends and to show off his little son and is only with difficulty separated from either of you. I met Kilkeel first when he came back from the Tour and I was newly under the protection of Jack Wickmere, and he was full of the charms of Letty Mitchelstown."

"That is how I knew him first, with her. He made me her maid," said Mary quietly.

"And I would wager Letty was jealous of you, though she was too wise to let him see it. Goodness and innocence are considerable weapons, Mary. But he is different with you. He is devoted, not in thrall. If I didn't know better, I would say that he and you are not protector and mistress but man and wife."

"You are pensive, Peg. What did you make of Kilkeel's charming little maid-servant?"

"I think, Jack, that she might rather be a maidservant still than what she is, shown to the world as his latest possession."

"You see though how she hangs on his every word and gesture. She worships dear James. She lives for him and their boy."

"She does, but it's not a life that comes easily to her. She does not, I fear, relish her position of comfort. She dresses beautifully, but is almost austere in her man-ner, as though she were a professed nun made to get herself up in silks. You saw how she shrank back in the box last night and was astounded at seeing the pit and the stalls train their glasses on her; we go to the playhouse to be seen as much as to see, but she hates the gaze of others and will not raise her eyes."

"I had thought, Peg, that she might be an accomplished dissembler, but if she is, she has the powers of the most talented actress to keep it up for so long."

"No, I think not. I have tried today to give her some worldly advice that she might survive London the better and lengthen her career but I don't believe the astonishment she showed me was assumed. She is a poor innocent abroad, a little bird who may have longed for freedom outside her humdrum cage, but when she stretches her wings finds she is too terrified to fly. There is nothing worldly about her, just a longing for domesticity. I told her that I thought her manner more that of wife than mistress."

"And what did she say to that?"

"Nothing. She looked down at her hands so that I couldn't see her expression."

"Peg, it is because she believes she is a wife and is sworn to secrecy. I believe James went before some sham parson with her but she has no marriage lines."

"Oh, I think much less well of our friend James for that," Peg said. "He did wrong to profit of her in that way. That does vex me! She is left with no defences, a poor little crawling snail with a smashed shell. And she loves him so."

"If you can be her friend, then little by little you may help her learn to arm herself better. If it's a fine day tomorrow why don't we all take a turn through the Park in the phaeton? She can observe Society and be observed by it without being trapped in the crowds and the uproar of the theatre."

PART TWO: NEMESIS

Hell Hath No Fury?

8 Jockeys Fields
Clerkenwell
14th August 1776

My dear Niederer,

Our meeting yesterday was indeed fortuitous for us both. What a happy coincidence that you had just returned from serving another young Lordling and that I had come up from Ely on business of my master's: I have never forgotten that it was thanks to you that I obtained that post. Whilst there are the inevitable village Wat Tylers in Cambridgeshire too it is a relief to work for a God-fearing Englishman with tenants who know their place. They do not love me, naturally, for no one loves those who have the task of pointing out their failings, but it is my master I serve, not them.

I have made enquiries regarding that matter of interest to us both, and the Gowards do indeed reside still in Berkeley Square. Lord Goward shuffles about and shouts at the servants when the gout be particularly severe, but his Lady is as formidable as she always was and dotes as ever on her son, who has never thought to show his gratitude to his parents by doing his duty and marrying well but continues to be the protector of the Kearney girl. He has put his mother to some embarrassment by insisting on taking his demi-mondaine where respectable wives congregate, according to the footman they have engaged for this season (and have apparently under-recompensed for his trouble, or he might not have been so responsive as he was to the jingling of my pockets). Naturally they are not received in the very best houses but otherwise are welcomed by most and are to be seen regularly at Vauxhall and in their box at Drury Lane. They have a bastard boy, of some eight or nine years of age, for whom his father has engaged tutors for the season. The mother with her son regularly attends at the chapel of the Spanish ambassador, demurely veiled and apeing the lady though she is naught but a whore with nice manners. I have spied her, and see that she is still beautiful, the witch. She should be so, for she has had a soft life of it for ten years, and is not yet thirty, and the pleasure will thus be the greater for me when I take my opportunity to revenge myself on her for having baulked me. I appreciate your offer of help in that regard, the more so as you tell me you are immune to female charms. The suggestion that my aim will be better accomplished by throwing her skirts over her head and your holding them there has sense, but as I have reflected on that happy picture you paint for me I do think my pleasure might be all the greater were I to observe her face as she is made to learn her lesson. You might hold her down, or better still, we might bind her. Forgive me for this enticing phantasy of mine, Niederer, and let us move from talk to action.

Do you for your part spy when you have the opportunity on Lord Risborough's ménage and observe what you can of his youngest children for if in one of these you notice the lineaments of someone other than the child's declared father then I declare you and I have the opportunity to enrich ourselves, and when we have done so, then we can move to ruining Kilkeel. An action for Criminal Conversation might be the least of it; if as you say Risborough is of a choleric disposition then he may be prevailed upon to seek satisfaction in the more traditional way. Let us see how this perfect little family responds to such an earthquake. I doubt that Mary Kearney will find another noble protector; she may then be glad to accept another of more modest means though a gentleman born, but it will be on his terms. To arms, Niederer!

Yr. obdt. Servant

William Blanch

14 Berkeley Square
4th September 1776

Dear Jack,

I am in the most awful fix and need your help and counsel most urgently. I obtained an interview with Kitty Risborough, as you advised; she sent me word that Risborough was gone to the House and gave commissions to those servants she does not trust, to remove them for the afternoon. We must hope that those who remained are discreet and incorruptible, or my presence in his house was more grist to Risborough's mill.

I have not been face to face with Kitty for more than ten years and I found a woman much altered, more by grief than by time. You remember how glittering and gay she was when we dallied in Rome—how much dash she had. Rome suited her; she was Queen of our little world there and I was flattered, young as I was, by her attentions. We laughed so much at my escape from her house, wrapped in her maid's mantle, and her in her chamber dissembling her heat and hectic state as a fever— which it was but not of the kind she gave out to her husband. You remember my haughty manservant Niederer; 'twas he who saved the day with the greatest sang froid, when the cuckold decided to return home before his usual hour. I was vexed when he left my service after so many years, though circumstances demanded it, but you'll remember he took against my plans to have Mary educated. I might almost say that he was jealous, in the way a woman can be. We could laugh then, but not now. Kitty is threatened with Doctors Commons. For my part, I could weather an action for crim. con. though my mother and father would feel all the humiliation on my behalf, though it would grieve me to sell land that at last my excellent agent Mr. Andrews has started to get some returns on, in order to pay the husband's damages. But that is as nothing to Risborough's demand that he have satisfaction of me. Jack, I am asking you to be my second in the worst case, but see if you cannot mediate to avoid such an outcome. It is a delicate situation and poor exhausted Kitty has the worst of it. After three daughters she at last gave Risborough his longed-for heir. Young Arthur is easily his favoured child, but he is not his. Nor is he mine, Jack. I discovered today that it was Kitty that put me in the way of Letty Mitchelstown so that space could be made for a handsome priest attached to the French Legation. Risborough's heir is nothing more than the by-blow of her comely celibate (who died of the cholera at Naples four years ago). Risborough's unknown informant claims the child is mine, and I have no way to prove that the poor boy is not. Risborough is beside himself with rage and will not hear reason; if he had sense he would keep quiet and acknowledge his heir, as must a third of the husbands of England, but we do not know what else this scribbler wants. He has not demanded money. He wants to do me or Risborough or Kitty ill. I cannot think who this enemy may be nor what moves him. Risborough will not admit any doubt; the fact that the boy has dark hair is enough for him and he accuses his lady of inventing the priest to protect me and of having feelings for me still. I have none for her now, needless to say, but thoughts of pity, and anger that Letty came to me in that way. It makes me feel less of a man, even now.

I do not know how to begin to tell this tale to my poor faithful Mary. Jack, as my closest friend I want to entrust her to your care should the worst happen to me. I do not fear destitution for her and our boy, as I have already settled all I can on them both, everything but my name. You may call me foolish, Jack, but I have begged Mary to let me conduct her to St. George's, Hanover Square and make her before the world the honest woman I know her to be, but you know her obstinacy in matters of religion. Come quickly, dear Jack, for I am distracted beyond reason.

   Yr. faithful and needy friend,
   James Kilkeel

South Wood, Hampstead Heath

18th September 1776

"That's Risborough's groom," said Wickmere, nodding in the direction of a massive oak, where a youth held the reins of a large bay horse. "We must dismount here, and go on foot to the clearing."

The servant did not look at Kilkeel as he accepted the reins, acknowledging him only with a nod and a muttered, "Sir."

"Wait, don't lead him away just yet." James stroked his horse's nose and felt the animal push gently against the pressure of his hand. "He's yours, Jack, if I do not come back this way."

Wickmere held a box under one arm. With his free hand he took his friend's elbow.

"This is the path. Risborough is not the best of shots and rage will shake his aim."

"I hope you are right. This dawn promises a fine day, Jack. How beautiful the world is in this light."

"It's a day that you'll see, I am sure."

"Jack, I find I am not a man of courage; good enough to escape a lady's chamber but not to accept the consequences. I freely confess I'm frightened. I am not even man enough to have told Mary of today's business. She sleeps on; I got a servant to wake me without disturbing her."

"James!"

"You will take care of her, Jack, her and our boy?"

"God's providence today will select the winner, but yes, I have promised you."

They came out into the clearing where Risborough and his second were waiting.

"Who's that?" asked Kilkeel, catching sight of a man in a brown coat and hat standing under the trees.

"The surgeon. A capable man," answered Wickmere.

Risborough's second walked quickly over to them.

"Well, Pendleton?" said Wickmere.

"I have tried, sir, but he will not see reason."

"Very well. Let us get this over with."

Kilkeel and Wickmere followed the man back to where Risborough stood glowering, arms folded. He would not meet Kilkeel's eye anymore than had his groom, but watched attentively as the two seconds charged the pistols. Pendleton took a sovereign out of his pocket and placed it on the back of his left hand.

"His Majesty or St. George?" asked Pendleton, looking at Kilkeel.

"It's a matter of indifference to me."

"His Majesty," growled Risborough, speaking for the first time. The coin spun in the air.

"First shot to you, Lord Kilkeel. Your weapons." The curved stock fitted cool against his palm.

"Ten paces, gentlemen."

He turned, pointing the pistol towards the ground.

"Present!"

The barrel lined up neatly as if a natural extension of his arm. Kilkeel waited for the final command, and when it came, flicked his hand to the right and shot wide. Rooks tore up into the sky, protesting loudly.

"You need merely clip him, my Lord, sufficient to agitate the nerves, and honour will be satisfied," pleaded Pendleton. Risborough stared straight at Kilkeel, and fired.

42 Grosvenor Square
18th September 1776

Dear Madam,

I am grieved to have to bring you hard news, relieved only that it is not worse. I ask your pardon in writing to you, Lady Goward, in place of your husband, and do so only because I know that he is under his doctors and that there is great concern for his health. I therefore wish to spare him any shock I may until I have more news. That I do not spare you, Lady Goward, I trust you will take as my tribute to your strength of character. Your son, my dearest friend, fought a duel this morning on Hampstead Heath with Lord Risborough and has been wounded in the right shoulder. Risborough escaped unscathed for Viscount Kilkeel deliberately aimed wide. I will not trouble you here with the detail of how this unhappy state of affairs came about, as some of it you know already. I will call on you in person once I am certain I have given the surgeon in attendance all the assistance he requires. I write at speed now only with a view to giving you the truth of the matter, before gossip provides its own exaggerated version.

The ball was extracted within an hour. Kilkeel was duly strapped to my table and given a piece of wood to bite upon, but though he paled with the pain and strained against his bonds and his forehead sweated, he made little sound. I believe that he restrained himself so, knowing that Miss Kearney listened from the adjoining chamber. When I went to her afterwards I found her trembling on the floor in floods of tears, but when I raised her to bring her in to see her Lord, she recollected herself, dried her face and comported herself with all the dignity and fortitude of a Roman matron.

The wound is clean and has been dressed and though he is weakened from shock, the bleeding has been staunched and he now sleeps, his complexion a warmer hue. I witnessed a most affecting little scene between him and Miss Kearney that I am sure will move you as it did me, for that you love her too. He lay there pale as his bandages, but bright of eye. "Mary," says Kilkeel, "Do you have the ring I gave you?" whereupon she reached into her bosom and pulled out a little bag on a chain and drew from it a gold ring. "Put it in my right palm," he tells her, and she does this for his hand is lying open upon the sheet. Then he grasps for it with the fingers of his left, but is clumsy for that hand is not used to do the work of its stronger partner and in the end he tells her to put the ring on herself for he fears to drop it, but to remember always that it came from him. This touching episode does not end there, for he then tells her to put his ring on his hand, and she draws another little bag from around his neck and does as he says. "Now we will wear these always as a sign that we belong one to the other." Then his eyes closed and he fell asleep. No one in the chamber failed to shed tears and I declare that I have seen no marriage ceremony that moved me as much as did this private pledge of faith.

Expect me within the hour.

Yr. obt. Servant,

J. Wickmere

"It's you!"

"I didn't want to wake you."

"I could smell you in my dreams. Your hair tickled my face. What are you doing, Mary? Where's the surgeon?"

"He's downstairs at his dinner. He's shown me how to do this."

"How long have I been like this?"

"In this bed? Ten days."

"Why are you sniffing like that? You're like a cat round a mousehole."

"The surgeon said to do that. To see does your wound smell."

"All I can smell is turpentine."

"That's keeping it clean, so it is. Look." She held up a pad of cotton. "Just a bit of yellow. Can you feel this?"

"I feel nothing there. I know the arm's still there, but I feel nothing."

"Oh. But no pain?"

"No pain, because nothing. The surgeon says this is not a good sign for I may not regain sensation."

"Oh James."

"Ssh. As long as you are with me I can bear anything."

"The doctor says can I wash the rest of you. He wouldn't let me before."

He watched her turn away and lift a cloth from a pail and wring it out.

"Do you remember, Mary, when I came upon you washing my linen?"

She wiped his face carefully.

"Sure I do."

"I'm going to ask you again what I asked you that day, once I'm up from this bed."

She stopped, holding the cloth against the side of his neck.

"Go on, Mary. Your touch is so gentle, much gentler than the nurse."

"I am so angry with you," she said. "I could have been washing your corpse."

"I hope you do, one day. I wouldn't want to die after you."

"The dear knows you nearly succeeded. Could you not have told me what you were about? I woke up and no one could tell me where you'd gone, only that Jack had called early for you. Days that you hadn't been yourself."

"I was ashamed."

"Because of Lady Risborough? She matters little. Sally Possick was the better woman."

"You're right. Can you forgive me?"

"For the lady, yes. But James, I might never have been able to say good-bye to you."

"You've a coward for a husband, that's the long and the short of it. I hadn't the courage to tell you. I hadn't courage on that field either."

"You had so. Jack told me you wouldn't fire at that man. That was courage, knowing he could then fire back as it pleased him."

"I'm a poltroon."

"You're not. Now if I put my arm behind your good shoulder, and you hold me, can you rise?"

14 Berkeley Square
24th October 1776

Dear Jack,

I pray you write me a line to tell me when you may again be in town. I am loath to draw you away from your rural idyll when you had already stayed long beyond the season's end to see your friend out of danger, but I have need of you again. No duels this time! I have prevailed upon Mary at last to accept me. Her change of heart has come about in the oddest of ways, and I must be grateful to of all persons a Spanish Jesuit and an orphaned child.

My poor father is very ill and pain makes him delirious, but in a lucid moment I succeeded in telling him of my plans and was gratified that his eyes filled with tears and he exclaimed in what remains to him of his voice, "I only wish I had the strength to embrace you both." My father is dying, Jack, and I am maimed, but I have my darling son and his mother and we are to be married so I have many reasons to be happy. My mother had to be brought round, naturally, but her good sense tells her that I no longer

*have the makings of a desirable husband for any heiress, tainted as I am by the Ris-
borough episode. Did news reach you that he and Kitty are now apart? Risborough is
to move his mistress and their three children from their Camberwell cottage to a fine
house in Fitzrovia where they are to live with his three legal daughters whilst their
mother must comfort herself with that poor boy's company only when he is not away at
school.*

*I am to keep my arm in that it remains joined to my body and nourished by my
blood, but the doctors now despair of my regaining any sense in that limb; they say that
I may recover a little sensation in my finger ends over time, and with that some aware-
ness if someone will touch the limb. Mary cries as she helps me into my clothes of a
morning—for since my injury I want no one else so near to me—and pins the sleeve
with its useless contents to my breast so that it does not swing loose and make a nuisance
of itself. You see what a good hand my Mary writes? I shall sign this letter as best I can,
but educating my awkward crab of a left hand to hold a quill is a lengthy and frustrat-
ing process and as I have a good scribe I am inclined not to persist in what can only
have an indifferent outcome, and in any case there is nothing I wish to hide from Mary.*

*There is to be an addition to our little establishment of a Coram child by the name
of Elizabeth Norton; this little waif is owed my undying gratitude. You will remember
how Mary was much moved by the "poor motherless babbies" when we four went to
hear the Hospital Choir before your removal to Thetford. A subscription did not adequately meet her need to do something for them. Two days later I found her sitting in
the parlour window stitching infant clothes and weeping. She does not want to write
this down but I insist. What Mary desires is take in one of these children as her own.
At last she is to accept a maid, think I, and one though so very young already trained
in spinning, weaving and needlework. Nay, a little girl will also be company for Edward, she says, and his tutors can instruct her too. The Hospital's founder insisted girls
be lettered as much as boys, in order that they be better mothers, though the governors
have them taught mainly that they may read Scripture. I expressed some reluctance at
the idea of my son thrown into the society of an unknown child trained only for service,
at which my lady swiftly reminds me of where I keep company, at which I am ashamed
of myself for my want of sensibility. I went to make enquiries of the Governors, and
encountered an obstacle, or rather two. These fine sons of the Church of England were
sincerely grateful for my generous support of their charity, but explained as delicately as
they could that they were unable to grant my request as by their Statute they were not
enabled to release any child into the care of anyone who was living an irregular life—
who was "not legally joined" I think was their term—and furthermore, where the*

child's upbringing as a "God-fearing Protestant daughter of the Church of England"
might not be guaranteed, this last alluding to Mary's refusal to conform.

This news made Mary weep, but still did not shake her obstinacy. Then the follow-
ing day a priest from the Spanish Embassy chapel where she attends Mass came to call,
and finding her in such low spirits had the whole story out of her. This dark faced Jesuit
steeples his fingers and starts to talk of greater good and opportunities to bring others to
the path of righteousness, not giving scandal and so forth. I did not well follow his
arguments after a while for I grew so excited at the realisation that he was pleading my
cause. I never dreamed that I would find a champion in such a quarter. With his
blessing I accompanied an overjoyed Mary to the Hospital Governors. Here I feared a
terrible scene were Mary asked to choose a child, just as when little Eddie went to choose
his puppy, but fortunately the Governors themselves identified a suitable little girl, eight
years old and with her modest demeanour a small reflection of she who wishes to be her
mother. So Jack, write me when you and Peg might be able to come back to town that
this little family be made complete and your poor mutilated friend become the happiest
of men. I will then arrange all with the parson at St. George's, and an intimate little
feast with those whom I love best in all the world, after which I will take my wife home
to Ireland at last.

Yrs affectionately,

James Kilkeel

"I fear I try your patience. To think that unlacing you was one of my greatest
pleasures."

"You were getting along grand, so you were."

Kilkeel sat down on the bed and covered his face with his good hand, too distraught to try to correct the lapse in Mary's speech, but vaguely aware that such
lapses came when she was at her most tender with him.

"Please don't you cry, sir! I can take the oul' clothes off myself, so I can. And
when wee Bess joins us she can help me with my lacing herself." She turned away
to complete the task that Kilkeel's one hand had laboured over.

He looked up. "Don't go over there. Stand and face me. And unpin your hair.
Oh, my love."

"What's that you're reading, Mary?"

"Dr. Gregory's little book.[1] Your mother gave it me, now that everyone knows I am to be your wife. I think he is a kind man writing this for his motherless girls, and it will help me to behave like a lady."

"Let me see. Hmm. "One of the chief beauties in a female character, is that modest reserve, that retiring delicacy, which avoids the public eye, and is disconcerted even at the gaze of admiration." I hardly think you need this fellow. You are a lady already."

"There is something else, though."

"Oh?"

"He says that a lady should not show any learning she may have for she is made less desirable by it, yet you have insisted I be schooled and encourage me to read all I may lay my hands on. He says that even in marriage a lady should hold herself back, and not show her husband how much she loves him. But I always want to show you; I cannot help myself."

"My Mary. Come here. Promise me you will never hold back from me."

---

[1] John Gregory, *A Father's Legacy to his Daughters,* 1774.

A Warning

"Our plan failed, Niederer." Blanch nursed his brandy in a sullen fury. "Look at this announcement," he said, tapping the newspaper. "They are married. They have done the deed quietly enough but now they proclaim it to the world. What matter that the best houses won't receive her and that by the laws of England their brat was born a bastard and so will die one? We have succeeded only in bringing them closer."

"I told you we should have asked money, Blanch. At least that."

"And to think we so nearly succeeded," continued Blanch, as though he hadn't heard the valet. "Had the wound turned foul, or had he fallen dead upon the heath, then she was thrown upon the world's scant mercy."

Niederer stretched his mouth in a remote, joyless smile. "*Und ich würde ihn immer verlieren.*" he muttered.

"What's that you say?"

"Only that I would never be in his service again."

"I didn't understand why you had to leave it so precipitately. Or did one of them find you in the wash-house as I did, with your face buried in his dirty shirts?"

Niederer's face stiffened. "He showed more favour to a maid-servant than to me." Then his horrible smile appeared again. "It is comic, not so? You hate him because you wanted her, and he took her, and I hate her and so would further your aim with her, because I love him and *she* takes my place."

Blanch stared at him. Then he gulped back the rest of his brandy, pushed back his chair and stood up.

"Good-bye, sir." He grasped his tricorn and marched out, muttering to himself, "Wwe failed to destroy him. Now *I* must try her destruction, and this time I must not fail."

Niederer did not speak nor get up. For a few minutes he stared fixedly up at a dirty mark on the wall opposite. Then he motioned to the potboy and ordered another brandy, and paper and pen and sealing wax. He stared down at the creamy page for some time as though he read a sign there and then intently printed in the middle of the paper the words BLANSCH IS YHR ENNEMI.

It was a clear night with a full moon so Niederer had no difficulty finding his way to the house he had once known so well. The new terraces reared around him pearly-grey and sharp-edged. Lights glimmered behind heavy brocade curtains. Yes, *his* house was still lit. Niederer stared up at the windows. He could still walk all over that house in his thoughts, anticipate every creaking stair-tred, the rattle of the drawing-room door handle. Ah, but which servants were there now? He must not be recognised. Someone else must deliver this message. He willed his breathing to slow, then retraced his steps, turned two corners and came up to a young man he had passed earlier, lounging against some railings. He had been aware of the youth's stare then, but had not looked at him, being too intent on his task.

"I want you do something for me," he murmured.

"At your service sir," the youth said, detaching himself from the railings and straightening up.

"You will deliver this letter for me."

"That all?"

"I will reward you."

"Of course you will. Where to, sir?"

"Come with me."

"Gladly."

Niederer waited at the corner and watched as a line of light showed at the door of no. 14. He could not make out who the servant was. The door closed and the youth was making his way back.

"Here you are."

"Most generous, sir." The man looked Niederer slowly up and down, with a lopsided smile.

"Ain't there nuffink else I can do for you, sir?"

"Well… "

"You come along of me. I promise you'll not be sorry."

"This can only be Niederer," said James. "Those capitals could be anyone's hand but the spelling is unmistakable. The man that delivered it was a stranger; the footman would have recognised his old colleague. But what does he mean by writing it?"

"What it says, I fear," Mary said. "Blanch means you harm."

"Had he not fled I would have had him arrested. He would do well not to show his face anywhere near me. But clearly Niederer has seen him."

"Why did you send him away? You never said, then one day he was no longer there."

"An unfortunate business, which is why I never troubled you with it. There was an altercation with a young man in Mulholland's, one of Lord Moira's tenants; he accused Niederer of looking at him too long, and some blows were struck. Niederer came to me, his face all contusions, and told me a gentleman could no longer stay in such a place. I understand his adversary had many family members about, which would rather restrict his ability to wander abroad, something he did in his free hours, though he always complained about our landscape. The Mournes were mere hillocks, in his view, though large enough to hide men with cudgels. So I gave him a good character and I haven't heard from him since—until this."

"But he frequents Blanch."

"Frequents might be too strong a word. I expect they encountered each other in some drinking establishment and Blanch complained of me. Niederer in his own gloomy way was quite devoted to me; I wouldn't have got out of an awkward scrape in Rome had it not been for him. This note is probably only a clumsy profession of fealty to me. What harm could Blanch do us now?"

In which Mary becomes Lady Goward

Goward Hall, April 1777

"Aaaah! I am on fire, on fire in hell! Chittleborough, I cannot bear this."

"Lord Goward, I beg thee not to rouse thyself so. Dr. Benson expressly advised calm."

"Where is that damned quack? *He* doesn't have demons gnawing at his bones."

"Patrick has gone for him, sir. And Bridgie is up and has gone with my wife to the ice-house to fetch a big bag of it to ease your pain."

"Oh Chittleborough, I would I were dead than like this."

"Sir!"

"I do not deserve this pain."

Benson closed the door quietly and motioned with his head to Kilkeel and to Edwin Chittleborough that they should speak privately.

"I do not want Lady Goward to hear this, though I believe she knows it already," he said. "Your father, Kilkeel, has the strongest of constitutions. It is for this that he has been able to abuse his health for so long and still be with us. When word came that he was taken ill in London I didn't expect to see him again, especially after the shock of your wounding, sir. Yet he rallied and made the journey, and seemed to have some respite. You know that for years I've badgered him to drink less, to refrain from strong meat and cheese. We have tried, have we not, Chittleborough, to persuade him to change his ways?"

"That is so, Doctor, but my poor master was ever a stubborn man."

"It is also because he is stubborn that he is alive this long, but Lady Goward and you, sir, must be prepared for the worst. Chittleborough, forgive me my directness, but what can you tell me of his water?"

"Dark and cloudy, more so than usual."

"Has he also complained of the stones?"

"He has, but he tells me he does not even think of them now for this pain is so much the greater."

"It is his heart that will fail him now, for it must do so much more work when so much else does not function as it should," said the doctor. "The gout is cruel, gentlemen, for it inflicts exquisite pain yet will not in itself kill, though so intense is that pain that an apoplexy can follow, and thus the final blow is delivered."

Behind them the door opened. Lady Goward was pale but contained. "James, he is asking for Mary, and Eddie. Chittleborough, he begs that you come and hold his hand. He wants your forgiveness for all the times he has raised his voice to you, and swears you are the best of men."

"Tell them they do not need to seal up the vault so securely. I will join him before too long."

"Nonsense, Mother."

"It is time I got myself out of your way. He was a good man, your father, though I think you did not quite approve of his old-fashioned ways. It is a wise man, who does not seek to change what manifestly works. I do not know where you get your ideas from, James; I believe your Tour broadened your mind in more ways than your father could have foreseen. You are a cleverer man than he ever was. I do not disapprove, I am simply puzzled. Your father never questioned how the world was: the Lord in his drawing-room, the tenant in his cabin. That's how it has always been, and believe me when I say the tenants are happiest with that certainty. I fear you may confuse them, James. You ask them so many questions, and expect them to have an opinion when they want to look to you for direction. I do admire what you and Mr. Andrews are achieving—and I am so happy he is not the abominable Mr. Blanch—but I do ask myself if your tenants might not want to go back to their old, inefficient ways. I have no more education than I have ever needed, enough that I have been able to run this household in a reasonably ordered fashion, yet you will insist that your tenants' children be educated to a degree that will only put them at a disadvantage, or worse, brew discontent, when they grow up and consider the expectations life will place on them."

"Mother," said James gently. "You say the tenantry do not like change. But they do benefit from a better diet, which makes them stronger and more able for the work they do. And you talk as though Gowards have been here since time immemorial, whereas that vault goes back only about a century. There are no stone knights in that church with dogs at their feet. The Goward who built it was a Parliamentarian, yet every Sunday we say prayers for King George. I simply want to work with my tenants, for they are closest to the land and its vagaries, and understand how to make it profit them and myself. I need them, Mother, and they need me."

"So would you put Goward Hall and all your patrimony into their hands? Is this what marrying Mary Kearney was really about?"

"No. It was Mary who opened my eyes to what was possible, though I assure you that was never her intention; it was simply my astonishment at finding a woman of her qualities in such humble surroundings. Do you really see her as part of my experiment?"

"No."

"I think only that another Ireland might be possible, and that is what I want to prove here."

"You are Lord Goward now, James. You must do as you think fit. Believe me, I am more than reconciled to Mary as your wife. She has conquered us all, without setting out to do so. Her presence here as his daughter was one of the greatest joys of your father's last days. I shall relinquish the household keys to her when we return home and ask only that I remain beneath your roof and amuse myself with my needlework and with feeding the hens and the cats."

"Please don't do that. The very thought of taking those keys from you terrifies Mary. Can we not go on as before, with you as General, and Mrs. Chittleborough as your lieutenant? Do not ask this of Mary yet, but if you will, teach her."

"Gladly. But I doubt poor Janet will be there to support us long. Both she and Edwin have aged with this death. They feel your father's loss as much as we do. Chittleborough knew him for longer than I—"

"Mother?" Goward turned round to follow the direction of the widow's gaze.

"He's gone," she muttered.

"I know. He will be much mourned."

"Not him, James. There was a man watching us from the trees over there. As soon as he saw I'd seen him, he fled. Not a mourner. Not a tenant. I could have sworn it was that dreadful Mr. Blanch."

"Where's Mary?"

"Standing by that little obelisk, with Mrs. Samuels."

James hurried out the gate of the burial ground to look up and down the lane. There was no sign of the watcher, though the grass the far side of the low stone wall had been trampled and there was a fresh clod of horse dung. He resolved to say nothing to Mary, rather than trouble her. All the evidence was that Blanch was in London.

Neighbours

"A letter for me?"

"Yes, Mary, open it and read it."

"'Tis an invitation to us to visit Mountlyon. It is signed Lady Lyon. Why does she write to me? I do not know this lady."

"I do, and now she wants to make your acquaintance, too. That is the form, lady to lady. Her husband is a decent fellow, abominably rich, and Mountlyon has been much improved as a result. We will be taken around it and must say we admire it whether we do or not, and afterwards we will be rewarded with a good dinner when we will be lively in our reminiscences of the London season. And after a short interval has elapsed, you must invite them here."

"Here?"

"Yes, here to Goward Hall. Mary, you look like a rabbit transfixed by a stoat. There is nothing to fear except possibly boredom. You have joined the Quality and now the Quality wishes to know you."

One splendid room opened into another. Mary was exhorted by Lady Lyon, a thin, querulous woman in her fifties with a habit of peering down her nose, to admire the Zuccarelli landscapes. "So like the view across our demesne, don't you agree?"

"They are fine views all, both the painter's and yours, Lady Lyon. But yours have no pretty peasants, and his do not behave like peasants. They seem to have no work to do," replied Mary.

"Impertinent," thought Lady Lyon.

"Certainly I would not permit our tenants to pass across my view. For what use is a ha-ha otherwise? I do not imagine that you allow it either, Lady Goward, but perhaps I am mistaken. Are your ideas more democratic perhaps?"

Mary scented a coming insult, and chose her words carefully.

"Our tenantry approach the house by means of the Offices, Madam," she said truthfully. What she did not add was that the house servants now crossed before the house whenever it made sense to do so, and Mary did not believe that they spoilt the aspect. She would not tell her own brother and sister to stay out of her field of vision, and so would not instruct the other servants to do so.

"I am in any case usually too occupied to be looking out the windows," Mary added, and it was Lady Lyon's turn to be offended, though no offence had been intended. That lady simply stared, then drew Mary's attention to other acquisitions.

"This is Mr. Gainsborough's work." She pointed at a portrait of Lord Lyon looking like what he was, a genial middle-aged country gentleman, his spaniel at his feet and the plans of the new Mountlyon unfurled in his hands.

"And this is Mr. Reynolds's of myself, in his best Grand Manner. I am of course Hebe."

"Why did he show you as Hebe, Lady Lyon? Could you not just have been yourself?" blurted out Mary, mystified by the portrait's swirling draperies, sandalled feet and bare arms. "And why do you carry the pitcher, or is the big bird wanting to drink from it?"

"Oh my dear, you are so *droll*," tittered Lady Lyon. "Those of course are the attributes of the goddess of eternal youth, and I am cup-bearer to the gods."

"But Madam, you are so much younger than this goddess. Mr. Reynolds has not done full justice to the original," interjected James, dextrously guiding a mortified Mary towards Lord Lyon, who took Mary's hand and patted it.

"I shall take you to meet Skip, if you like? I think Mr. Gainsborough got a very good likeness, though the poor beast found the sitting—which was all about standing—as tedious as I did."

"Our son has a dog just like him," said Mary, looking up at him with tears of gratitude in her eyes.

At dinner, Mary's first mistake in Lady Lyon's eyes was when she glided round the table and cut up her husband's food.

"We have servants for that!" exclaimed the hostess, adding maliciously, "But of course it is a servant's work."

"We have simpler ways at Goward Hall," said James gallantly. "Mary knows without my saying what I have difficulty with and what I can manage with my left hand, for what I can still do, I prefer to do." This little exchange was repeated downstairs in the servants' hall, to universal approval.

Mary gradually brought out her little store of London observations: their visit to the newly-built Adelphi, and to Lord Burlington's villa at Chiswick. "Mountlyon is so much of their style," she added, eager to please. This earned a begrudging smile from Lady Lyon, who had been looking forward to further displays of Mary's ignorance, and who steered the talk towards painting, in the hope of seeing her blunder again.

But Mary was now on her guard. "James took me to the Academy at Somerset House, and to the gallery of the Foundling Hospital. This I liked more, and to think that the painters gave of their time and effort to raise funds for those poor children. At the Academy I thought Mr. Reynolds's picture of Mrs. Pelham with her hens enchanting, though I must confess he is not so good at the painting of the fowls. They were all so little. But Mrs. Pelham was so pretty and charming in her muslin."

"Yes, I expect you did find such a subject appealing—farmyard hens rather than eagles. You see, my dear," continued Lady Lyon, "people of Quality do not really go to look at the paintings. I believe that only the painters themselves do that. I know you are new to this world, Lady Goward, but you must understand that people of fashion go to these places to observe each other, and to be observed—"

"Damn'd tedious it is too," muttered her husband.

"Or at most, to decide which of these daubers is to have the honour of one's patronage with a portrait. You do not say that you have been painted, my dear? Mr. Gainsborough of course has done such charming pictures of simple country folk. I think he must prefer them to his fine ladies."

There was utter silence in the room. Mary looked down at her plate, crimson with humiliation, and pulled her lower lip under her teeth to hide its trembling. She breathed in hard, fearful that her nose was going to run. Instead, a fat tear splashed onto the remains of her dinner. She could not look up. Lyon spoke first, in a voice fractured with anger.

"I think, that is to say that it is my considered opinion, that *whoever* has the honour to paint Lady Goward will have the most difficult task to do her justice: the most limpid of complexions, the softest curling dark hair and most expressive liquid eyes, woodland pools in which a man might bathe and feel truly refreshed.

Harrumph! I get too poetical in my advancing years and I do not wish to embarrass you, my Lady, but Goward, you are a lucky dog. " Lord Lyon brought his fist down on the table for emphasis.

"Here," he cried to the footman standing behind Mary. "Bring Lady Goward a fresh napkin. I fear I have embarrassed her with my eulogies and she is fit to cry. A most becoming sensibility, I should say. I would that all womankind were possessed of it."

Mary took the proferred napkin gratefully and pressed it to her face.

Later, with the formalities got through, Lyon stood by his guests' coach. Patrick sat up front holding the reins, Bessie sat inside close to Mary, whispering excitedly about her evening in the servants' hall, and Goward, his foot on the step, uttered the words that custom dictated were Mary's responsibility.

"I do hope we shall see you and Lady Lyon at Goward Hall soon."

"Ah, well, you see, my boy, Lady Lyon goes so little abroad now. Says it unsettles her nerves. When that happens, she is not content but she must unsettle those of others, you see."

"Well, sir, I trust we will see *you*, if not your lady. You would be most welcome. We do not stand on formality. Whenever we are at home, we are happy to see our friends."

"You mean it, Goward? I should like nothing better."

"Then come, and bring Skip."

"Bless you. Bless you both!"

Lavinia Lyon met her husband's eyes in her dressing-table mirror. "Whatever is Goward thinking of? To be intimate with such a person, to marry her! Graceless in her manners, uncouth in her speech, infantile in her ideas."

"I thought her quite charming. An innocent, natural, artless."

"Artless indeed!" exclaimed Lady Lyon, vigorously rubbing away powder and rouge, and reducing her dark arched brows to mousy timidity. "Calculated."

"Goward clearly adores her. I told him he was a lucky rogue, and I meant it."

"Don't be absurd, Lyon. Just try to imagine what the world would come to, if every gentleman was to marry his kitchen wench."

"What *would* happen, Lavinia?" he asked mildly.

"You are being very trying this evening, Lyon. Will you please hurry yourself into your nightshirt and let us bring this benighted day to a close?"

"I enjoyed their company," he insisted, meek but obstinate.

In the rattling darkness of the coach Mary leaned over to the seat opposite and tucked a rug around Bessie.

"Does she sleep?"

"Yes."

"Come closer Mary."

"I could not bear another night like this, James."

"I am sorry, more than I know how to express. I wanted to show you to the world, to show all the chatterers how proud I am to have you on my arm. I had no inkling that polite society might be so impolite."

"We did wrong to go before that parson. We could have gone on as before. I was used to that pretence, and nobody minded if I was just your mistress."

"I minded."

"We knew who our friends were and that was enough, surely?"

"Well, we certainly know who they are now. That harpy's insults say more about her than about you. Do you not see that every barb she threw at you was sent by envy?"

"Lord Lyon was kind."

"He was, poor man. Him we shall see again. But may a man not choose where he loves, Mary? Has he not been granted free will? May *I* not choose?"

"Man has free will, that is so, woman perhaps less, but there are other men— and women—to consider. You will always be James Goward to them, and I a servant who doesn't know her place."

"Your place is by me. And without that parson, Bessie wouldn't be asleep over there."

"I did it for Bessie."

"Say you did it for me too."

"For you? I'd do anything for you."

"Then let us have one more tilt at the world. Let's leave London to manage without us this year and put Dublin to the test instead."

"Dublin might test *me*."

"What if Jack and Peggy came with us?"

Lord Lyon waited patiently until his wife stopped fidgeting and her breathing appeared regular. Then he slid gently off the bed and with the confidence of habit made his way to the door in total darkness. Lady Lyon's eyes snapped open and she dug her nails into her palms. Her husband moved through a succession of unshuttered rooms, silvered by moonlight, until he reached the main stairs. Reaching into a niche in which stood a marble Apollo, he pulled out a candlestick and tinder-box he was accustomed to keep there, lit his candle and began his ascent to the uppermost floor of the house. The corridor where his servants slept was low-ceilinged, carpeted with a strip of Brussels matting, the plain doors to each side spaced with the regularity of convent cells. He never mistook the one he wanted. As he expected, it wasn't locked.

He held up his candlestick. "Mrs. Laverty. I must compliment you on the sturgeon this evening. It was prepared to perfection, exquisite."

"Thank you, sir," said the woman, sitting up in the bed. "Pleased to oblige. Is there anything else I can do for you, my Lord?"

"Yes, Molly," he said in an altered tone. "Let me rest my old bones by you. I want only to be comforted."

"Sure you do, John. Isn't that why you gave me this grand big bed?"

Lord Lyon settled himself facing his cook's warm body. "Would you take this off, Molly?"

This done, he began to knead her ample breasts.

"Dear Dumpling," he said, "You are always kind to me. Now tell me the talk downstairs."

"Well, I didn't see the young Lady myself but all the rest of 'em did."

"So that was why there was such a changing of the guard at table, then?"

"Sure it was. They all wanted to see her as they'd want to see royalty. She is our royalty, you see. so we arranged it so everyone had a turn. They said she did not disappoint but that Lady Lyon was insolent to her and made the poor young lady to weep."

"She did too, damn her eyes."

"I'd to content myself with what they told me, and with their coachman and the little orphan servant. You know the coachman is her brother?"

"No!"

"And the wee girl was plucked from an orphanage to be her maid but lives more like her daughter. I think Goward Hall must be like no other gentleman's seat in Ireland."

"I envy Goward. I'd have his dead arm if I could live as happily as he does. Molly, will you bear with me while I tell you my little fantasy again? 'Tis all that keeps me alive."

"Of course, John." She knew the story would not change much; John Lyon was like the child who insists his bedtime fable is told the same way, on every occasion, for otherwise he does not feel safe. The location had changed from time to time, but for some while now he had fixed on one place in particular.

"Dundalk is a fine little town, is it not? You can see our beloved Mournes from there, Molly. A fine market square, well-laid out streets and a bustling linen trade. A little town house would suit us fine, and a small establishment; a grease-boots and a maid of all work should be sufficient for our needs. Your suppers would be the delight of all our neighbours. And whenever we walked out of an evening all respectable men would touch their hats to you."

"It would be grand, John," she said patiently.

"Oh Molly," he wept, "I would that I had half young Goward's courage."

Goward Hall
4th February 1778

My dear Wickmere,

You did warn me that her marriage lines might not be sufficient for Mary to be accepted into what goes for polite society. My attempts in this direction have not been an unqualified success. The London Mrs. Cracklethwaites did their worst and made Mary cry with their cruel insinuations that a crippled man can hope for no better than to marry his whore. But what the world is pleased to call an imprudent marriage—

meaning a marriage of love not interest—is a not uncommon event in the capital, and if the lady has the fame of a wit, or can otherwise defend herself, then she will find a way to survive opprobrium. I had hoped that amongst simpler people in Ireland matters might be easier, but find that the gentry stands on ceremony all the more because of their anxiety not to appear provincial. Thus the rules are more firmly enforced.

I find that for the most part Mary is welcomed by husbands, for what man could not admire her? But she is despised by their wives. To them she represents a threat, the embodiment of what they all fear, that their men if they could would choose a gentle helpmate from below stairs, and all their training be set at nought. She was treated abominably by Lady Lyon, to the chagrin of her husband and to my deep offence, for if she is my wife and is not accorded respect then no respect is shown to me. Lyon's mortification has been eased by the warmest entreaty to visit us when he will, and indeed he is now in the habit of riding over to us regularly from Dundrum, without his wife, and says he is never so happy but when he is in our company. On his last visit he brought his cook. That kindly female is the one who comforts him most in this life, and when they left us he thanked me with tears in his eyes for having accepted them both under our roof, for he dreams of such simple things often but knows that for the most part they are impossible. Mrs. Laverty is somewhat inclined to embonpoint *as all good cooks should be, and is as unlike Lyon's lawful lady as it is possible to be. That female is so excessively scrawny that I imagine (though I try not to) that her buttocks must be concave, and I thank Providence again for granting me unlimited and exclusive handling of the firm round whiteness of my dear Mary's bum, even if fate has left me with only one hand with which to caress it. Now she rails at me for making her write this down, but I see from the pinkness of her cheek and the brightening of her eye that she is secretly pleased at the compliment.*

We are inclined to make few further attempts on the fortress of gentility. With those at Gormanscourt I am now merely distantly civil, for Gorman showed dishonourable intentions towards my Mary when she was still my servant. Perhaps though I should be grateful to him, for his impertinence helped open my eyes to Mary's qualities when I was still in thrall to Lady Mitchelstown's memory. I would have liked her though to know Lord Rawdon at Moira, an enlightened and intelligent man and without a wife to be impertinent to mine, a champion of emancipation for Catholics, which must surely come by all that is fair, but he has lately sailed for the war in America. There are the Bangors at Castle Ward, but so eccentric are they that they could not even agree on the building of their house; it shows to the park a restrained Palladian face, and to the lough a Gothick visage. It is said that their heir shows signs of lunacy though until lately he took his seat in the House of Commons in Dublin, of all places probably the most fitting to hide a madman. No, we shall not attempt the Bangors; our demesne must be our domain. Where I see my Mary at her happiest is in the provision of a happy home for your friend and able support in all his schemes for the betterment of his lands, and in the commission of unostentatious good works, for there is much need hereabouts. She does not flaunt her charity like the hypocrite praying at the street corner, but works quietly with the Quakers of this district, for whom she has the highest regard. Little Edward continues to thrive and to do well in his lessons, and the orphan Bessie Norton has become for us a daughter. I am sensible of the debt I owe that child for my happiness. I fear Jack that you would find us very tedious in our contented life, but pray neverthe-less that we shall always have your love and esteem. You and Peg are always in our hearts. Our happiness would be complete were we to see you more often. Perhaps I may prevail upon Mary to see out a season in Dublin; she does not know that city well. Would you and Peg put aside the joys of London this year and sample instead the pleas-ures of our smaller capital?

Your aff. friend,

James Goward

Goward Hall
23rd April 1778

Dear Jack,

We are overjoyed that you and Peg are to join us in what we insist on calling a summer in Ireland, and will do our utmost to try to demonstrate to you that we are not so dull as we must seem from our correspondence.

Our little circle here has expanded to welcome a new curate (James, you are indeed tedious, I hear you say, if you must write to me of curates), a fine young fellow of open and cheerful aspect. Griffiths is his name, and I took him for a Welshman for he has that lilt in his speech, but he tells me he is an Englishman by five miles, being the son of a gentleman of Oswestry in the county of Shropshire, though he has the Welsh tongue as readily as he has English. He is greatly taken with Mary, as any man of sense should be. As you know, our rector continues to give us some concern, for he grows more moody by the day and more attached to his lonely glass. His wife is as much at the Hall as she is in the Rectory, for we have lost our dear Janet Chittleborough, who survived her lord, my father's old servant and companion, by a mere three months, and Mary thus relies much on Mrs. Samuels's society and her comfort for this loss of one who was as much a motherly friend as she was a servant. I had the honour to be invited to attend the funerals of both these good servants, and to say my few words in their praise. Their meeting house is aptly named; I might describe it as stripped to its bare essentials but that it has never been adorned in the first place. They have no celebrant, no pomp, no process but what each man or woman feels compelled to say and there is no forelock pulling to rank or status though they have what may be called elders and to run counter to their counsel is not wise; a Friend will be expelled from the community if he marries out for that is deemed to harm the whole body. A system of government based on their precepts might be a good thing indeed; as a system of worship there is much to admire but for me perhaps less to nourish. Yet they are excellent Christians. If they have a fault it is only that they do not laugh overmuch, and of course they drink nothing that intoxicates, not even small beer. By contrast Griffiths is an amiable fellow, quick to mirth and appreciative of a good grape. To tell the truth, I fear that he will not be let to do much, for the less able the Revd. Samuels becomes, the more jealously he guards his domain. I pressed Griffiths on his knowledge of farming, for you know well my hobby-horse, given that he hails from the depths of the country, but his enthusiasms lie elsewhere; his calling in life is as much to the primer and the slate as it is to the bands he wears. The man is a born teacher. Since Mrs. Samuels's little school is now not so little, he is most keen to work alongside this lady in their common endeavour of raising up the tenantry through the instruction of their children. He smiles and understands my intention when I tell him that he is simply to instruct them and not to proselytise them, that they may retain the religion of their parents without interference from ourselves. The numbers in the school-room will grow for a new family has recently arrived on our lands, in the most desperate condition, having been turned off in favour of sheep by their landlord in the county of Tyrone, and hence left to wander and beg their bread, with the vaguest of ideas of going towards Belfast. It was their good fortune that a tenant family had recently departed from here, bound for the Americas. They went with my heartfelt good wishes, having four strapping sons, to build their future in that new land that surely before long must succeed in breaking free of the King's domination. Such as they may be friends to Ireland when it is the turn of this country to come into its own (here my Mary frowns at me and reminds me that I am a father, and a farmer of sorts, and will that not satisfy me but that I must make noise about greater matters and cause only difficulty for myself?). Now this tatterdemalion family from Tyrone settle in the emigrants' cabin and wring my good hand with gratitude though I tell them not to for they are about to work for me and the benefit is all mine. Their name is Devlin, and I must confess their gabble is even worse than the English that is spoken hereabouts but my brothers-in-law happily can make more sense of their speech than I can.

I will stop here Jack or I swear you will decide not to come for fear of the tedium you will encounter here.

Our love as always to Peg.

Affectionately yours,

James Goward

The Dublin Bugle

19th June 1778

Great was the astonishment of all polite society in the capital at the flight of one of its less polite members from Lady C___r____d's ball in South W_____ Street on Saturday evening. The appearance at the ball of the lady in question, if she may rightly be described as such, had been much awaited, she and her Lord being of a retiring disposition much given to both improvements and good works on their estate in County D___, and not given much to appearing in fashionable circles. We assume that Lord G_____d had intended to provide his younger and reputedly most lovely wife with a little more diversion than was afforded in their Ulster Elysium, only to find that his good intentions, (as has happened to better men before him), have resulted in disappointment and the growth of a fetching ornament to displace his wig if he still wore one, namely a fine pair of horns. The lady, the fair M__y, began her career as his maidservant, and as we are led to believe it is quite usual for those of her class to serve under several masters in her life-time, in whatever position those masters should require her to assume, then she has merely moved to another lowly position this time beneath the standard of young Lord B__h, leaving her distraught husband to meditate on the folly of an imprudent marriage. As Lord B__h is not possessed of the same riches as the deserted husband, we assume that he is a young gentleman of altogether superior PARTS and he is of course fully-ARMED. The lovers came up with a most ingenious stratagem; the lady feinting a swoon when her husband was not in the room, whereupon she was borne out to a side-room to recover. By the time her husband was fetched to her side the bird had already fled the cage, but none of Lady C____r___d's servants say they attended her and so conveniently there are no witnesses. A service stair near to the chamber to which Lady G_____d was conveyed is thought to have been her means of escape, for a lady in a state of inebriation was observed being helped into a carriage by a rear door, which event being far from unusual excited no particular attention at the time. It is not known where the lovers are now, but we have had report of a gentleman and a lady in a state of some agitation acquiring passages at Dunleary, "for the earliest possible sailing."

"Jack, Mary would not fly! I cannot believe this. She's been taken. I am convinced of this but cannot convince the magistrates of it. One fellow even had the face to tell me that I should consider myself lucky, for few men can rid themselves of their wives so easily. If his colleagues had not restrained me, I would have done him violence even with this one arm and been taken in charge by now."

'Which would not help Mary.'

"What am I to do?"

"Stay here, James, for if there is news you must be in the one place to receive it. Comfort poor Bessie if you can, or let the child comfort you. Or else, damnation, cry together for I see no comfort here. I shall go directly to the publisher of this rag and beat his source out of him if necessary. We must also find out what we can of this Lord B whoever he may be."

"We have been *days* here, Jack, and always in company. She has had no opportunity to form any attachment. The very idea is preposterous."

"You do not have to convince me of that. But if we do not convince the magistrates then the yeomanry cannot be mobilised to search for her."

Trying to raise her hands to her throbbing head Mary found that they were tied, as were her ankles. As she regained consciousness she thought it was still dark, and that she was in the room in Dublin that the two servants had helped her to, but quickly realised from the motion of the carriage and the thud of hooves that she was being carried, blindfolded.

"Awake, your *ladyship?*" sneered a voice she did not recognise.

"Who are you?"

"No business of yours. I'm doing the job I was paid for, that's all."

"Your master?"

"Mr. White? You'll see him soon enough."

"I know no Mr. White."

"You will soon, I said. No more questions; I cannot abide female prattle." Mary felt hands around her head, gagging her.

Thus she spent the rest of the journey. With no way of measuring time it felt like hours. Mary had no idea where she was, nor which direction the coach took, but most frightening was not knowing why. In that muffled world there were no signs.

At last the timbre of the hooves changed, for now they slowed, and struck cobbles. By the echo they made they were no longer in open country, but in an enclosed space. An inn yard? The offices of a big house? They stopped. She heard and felt the shudder of the coach as the driver got down from his box, and opened the door.

"Who's this?" came a woman's voice.

"Mr. White's patient, for Dr. Ternan."

"The mad doctor?"

"That's the man."

"Well how long is she to be here then? Keep her well-tied, I want no lunatic running loose."

"She'll do you no harm. It's the usual delusion, the maid that thinks she's the mistress. More harm to herself than others."

"Robbed the mistress of her clothes, I see."

"But when she opens her mouth, the maid gets out."

"I don't want to hear her. Keep her gagged and get her moved on as quickly as you can."

"We just need to hand her over, collect our money, and we'll be gone."

Her ankles untied, they bundled Mary up a narrow staircase, to "Quick about it, I don't want my other guests seeing her," from the woman. A door opened, dragging on the stone threshold, and hands not too gently propelled her in. She stood there swaying, moving her head blindly from side to side, searching for light.

"Good work boys."

An Englishman. A voice not heard in years. There was a clink of coins, the shuffling of feet, "Thank you your Honour" and the door slammed. Mary turned in the direction of the sound in desperation. Anything but be left here with the owner of that voice. Was he still there? Oh yes, she heard his breathing. So quiet, just like that day when he'd crept up on her when she was preparing Viscount Kilkeel's room for his return, so long ago. But now she could not scream, and even if he removed the gag, who would come running this time? They knew her for a lunatic.

A step, and then the blindfold pulled off.

"Well, Mary, we meet again. Still lovely, I see."

Blanch lifted her chin, and smiled. She shook at his touch, whimpering into the gag.

"Lady Goward, indeed! Your husband believes you have eloped with a penniless squireen from Kilkenny."

Mary moaned and shook her head from side to side.

"By the time he finds out you haven't, you will have disappeared entirely. Even if he does find you, by the time he does he will not want to know you. Ternan will see to that. Stop making that noise and staring at me so. Those pretty eyes will start out of your head."

Mary started to cry.

"I shan't have you now. I have waited so long for this moment that I can wait a little longer; satisfaction deferred is the sweetest. You see, I want you to *want* to come to me, Mary. Tying you up each time would become wearisome. You will go to Ternan's madhouse, and I, and only I, shall decide when you'll leave. But by the time I do come for you, maybe in three months, maybe a year, whatever time it takes to break your spirit, you will be thankful to be with me rather than be in there. You would rather be handed over to one of the bawds in Temple Bar. Something to eat and drink will be brought here shortly. I suggest you finish all of it as Ternan's establishment is not known for the quality of the fare. And when I remove the gag I advise you not to make a sound. It will go worse for you if you do."

He took a handbell from the table behind him and opening the door for a moment, shook it vigorously.

"Sit, Mary," he said, and drew out a chair for her with mock solemnity. She lifted her bound wrists to him. When he had untied them, she sat clutching one hand in the other trying to stop them trembling.

Someone knocked, but Blanch's body blocked the door, and Mary's view. He muttered some instructions, then closed the door and turned the key. Then he sat down opposite Mary and stared at her so intently she had to look away.

Will no one come?

Ten minutes later a chop and some overboiled potatoes and a glass of beer were brought in by a slatternly middle-aged woman who studiously would not meet Mary's eye and who backed out of the room as soon as she had crashed down the tray.

"You see, Mary, it will be useless to attempt any signals to anyone. No one looks a lunatic in the face; it is as though they fear contagion." He went behind her and untied the gag. Then he lifted the glass of beer. "Now eat."

Mary clattered her knife and fork against the chipped plate. Could she do anything with these? No, they were so blunt they would probably make no in-roads even on the chop, which looked stiff, hard, and cold.

"I can't," she whispered.

"Never mind. Drink the beer." He put the glass down in front of her. Mary drank.

"All of it."

Blanch watched as Mary swayed forward, then sideways, then crumpled and slid to the floor. Two sleeping-draughts in a matter of hours was a risk, but one worth taking.

"Jack! What news? Who is this gentleman?"

"This is Captain Annesley, lately of the 18th foot. Until we can convince the magistrates to act, he has offered to help us."

"I am much obliged to you sir. Forgive me but I must use my left hand to shake yours. Allow me to introduce Mrs. Margaret Godwin, and my step-daughter, Bessie."

"Your right hand can keep company with my right leg, sir; since being wounded at Concord I am obliged to support myself with this stick, but on horseback can still go as far as any man. I shall help you as much as I can, Lord Goward, whether the magistrates shift themselves or no. I am mortified that such a thing should happen on your lady's first visit to our city. Perhaps, sir, before we talk further, it would be better if the little girl wasn't present."

"Of course. Peg, would you take her downstairs? We will acquaint you with all news as we have it. So, Jack, what did you discover at the *Bugle*?"

"An anonymous letter, pushed under their door some time on Sunday. They made no attempt to verify it, and were unapologetic. Nor would they let me see it, saying that it was their property. But I purchased the man's name of them: Burnchurch."

"Their seat is near Kilkenny town," said Annesley. "The family is somewhat decayed. A grandfather's gambling debts shrank a tidy patrimony considerably. I do not believe young Burnchurch moves in the circle that attended Saturday's assembly; he would not have the means. With your permission, sir, I will take two of my regiment as bodyguards and ride down to Kilkenny to enquire as to his whereabouts. I know my way there and it is best that Lord Wickmere remains with you."

"I will be forever in your debt, Annesley."

"It is the very least I can do. I have family in your part of the country."

Confused images swam before Mary's eyes, at last coalescing into a dark figure standing in front of her, appraising her. Then she became aware that she was dripping wet, and cold, and that the water must have been used to revive her. Daylight came in through a high, barred window, but she didn't know what time of day it was, nor what day. Her face was wet, but her hair... She shook her head a little. She had no hair anymore, her shorn head light without its weight. But why was she so cold? That man, squat, ill-shaven, she had never seen before in her life, but he looked her up and down with bold interest. She tried to move, and felt a bruising grip on each upper arm; two women held her fast. *Oh Mother of God, I am naked!*

"So you are the one who says she's Lady Goward," said the man, with a mock bow. "I am Mr. Ternan, and I am master of this establishment."

'I *am* Lady Goward,' she whispered.

"Sure you are. You sound so like a lady. You've a pretty face, even without your hair. Who doesn't come in here with a verminous head will get one within a week with hair such as you had. 'Tis a precaution."

He stepped forward, and without taking his eyes from her face, cupped her left breast in his hand, as though weighing it, and then deliberately ran the ball of his thumb across the nipple.

"Now don't shrink away from me, *your ladyship*. As you see we have left you your pretty pelt. We usually take that off too, because of the scabies, you see, but I'm partial to a pretty pelt, myself. Hold her still, ladies, for she shakes!" He bent over in front of her, and with both thumbnails parted the springy hair, his face so close to her body she could feel his hot breath.

"Dear little furred quim!" When did James say that to me? Years ago, or only ten days since? God help me, I do not know will I ever see him again.

"Healthy," he said, straightening up and smiling. Without changing his expression he pushed the fingers of one hand between her legs and cupped the heel of it proprietorially over her sex.

"Faugh!" He shook the drops from his fingers. "The bitch has piddled on me!" With his other hand he struck Mary so hard in the face that for a moment the world was dark, and she was helpless to halt the puddle forming around her feet.

"Clean her up!" shouted Ternan. "Restrain her in the cellar, in a shift."

There was no light in the cellar, none from the grille in the door unless someone came along the corridor with a light. The air was dead, damp and cold. The only furniture was a low wooden-slatted bedframe, fitted with iron cuffs at each corner. Onto this the two women attendants lowered Mary. "Cleaning her up" had consisted of a further pail of cold water flung at her lower body, followed by a sacking shift pulled over her head. "You need not lock me down. I shall not try to escape," she said timidly, but they fitted the cuffs around her wrists and ankles as though she hadn't spoken. Then they left her, in total darkness, but not in total silence. Distant cries and moans reached her, shouts and the crashing of doors, but she had no way of telling if they were in the next room or two floors above. Then, incredibly, she heard a sound that told her there was still a world outside, that she had not descended into an endless hell. It was a church bell, chiming four times, then a higher tone for the half hour. Half-past four in the morning or in the afternoon? She had no way of telling. All she could do was pray, and try to summon up in the darkness the faces she loved: James, Edward, Bessie, Peg, Jack, Mrs. Samuels. How would they find her here? But surely they would be looking? They wouldn't believe those things that Blanch had told her, would they?

Five o'clock rang out, followed by a light in the corridor. In a state of near delirium, from fear, fatigue, drugs and hunger, Mary thought, "They are here. Who will I see first?"

Ternan.

"Now let's see how much of a lady you are, shall we?" He put down his candle next the bedframe, and its flickering light cast monstrous shadows on a devil in charge of his own private hell. Before she could cry out, he had pulled up her shift, unbuttoned his breeches and forced his way into her. Mary thought she would faint with the pain, but with two or three thrusts he came.

"Damnation. That's no way to serve a lady, is it?"

His shadow reared up against the wall as he fumbled with himself.

"Please sir!" she cried, piteously.

"Make all the noise you like. They'll all hear you but no one will help you. And I like a woman's shrieks. There, that's better, standing to attention. Open your eyes and look, will you, or did they tell you ladies don't like to do that? Faith, I'll do you justice this time."

This was hell, for there seemed no end. Mary screamed until her throat ached, but Ternan went on and on, until with a groan and a belch, he heaved himself off her. Buttoning himself without turning aside, he picked up the candle, glanced at her once more, and said, "Cover yourself, whore," twitched down her shift, and was gone.

She lay in silent shock for some minutes, hearing something, Ternan's seed or her blood, drip through the slats onto the flagstones below. The pain between her legs was fading to a dull ache. Then the clock struck again. Half past five. It was then that Mary wept. The ordeal that had seemed an eternity had lasted less than half an hour.

"Burnchurch is in Killarney, sketching the lakes, according to his father," said Annesley. "He has been sent for, and if found and brought back here, he is likely innocent of all this. If he is not found, then we still have the task of convincing the magistrates that this is a kidnap, not a flight. He was a decent old fellow, the father, a poor half-mounted gentleman, shocked to his core. Apparently young Burnchurch is engaged to a Miss Atkinson, who from her future father-in-law's description seems worthy but dull, a little older than her groom, but possessed of a tidy portion that the old man was most anxious his boy should have. "I would have wanted him to make the Tour, but we have not the means," he told me, "so my boy must settle for sketching the Lakes in the rain. I could only permit him that because my agent has lately left us, and so I do not have to find his pay." To his knowledge, the family had never received an invitation to Saturday's entertainment."

"Annesley, you have been invaluable. But where can my wife be?"

"To my mind, that's no maid, Matilda."

"You heard what Ternan said: delusions."

"Look at her hands, though. They're no maid's hands. And for all she has that strange talk of the north, she's uncommon polite to us."

"Keep your nose out of it, Mag. The man is paying good money for to keep her here, so maid or not, she must be mad."

"Awfy fine clothes for a maid."

"Means nothing. Didn't your ladies give you their cast-offs when you were in service?"

"Not often enough," said Mag morosely.

"No jools on her, was there?"

"No, but who brought her would've torn them off her quick enough. She was out cold, remember. There was that ring, though. Ternan doesn't know about it, does he?"

"He does not."

"Well, so, you give it me and I'll get round to Flannery later and see how much he'll offer for it."

"All right, so."

"Lord Burnchurch is below, sir."

"Bring him up forthwith. Gentlemen, now we may know something, if it is only to discover what we do not know. I half-wish she *was* with him, only to end this agony and to know that at least she lives."

Paul Burnchurch was a fair, soft-faced young man of about twenty-two in a wig that looked older. He edged diffidently into the room, turning his hat in his hands. He looked nervously from one man to another, but it was Goward who spoke first.

"Damn you, where have you taken her?" he shouted, pushing the startled Burnchurch against the panelling, and holding him hard by the throat. "You're lucky I'm a cripple, or I'd be punching your fat face inside out by now!"

"James, let him be! Let him speak!" There was a tussle of some two or three minutes before Wickmere and Annesley could persuade Goward to drop his prey and subside panting into a chair.

"Sir, I have never seen your wife, nor knew nothing of this business until my father's messenger rode down for me. But I have come here as speedily as I could to tell you this myself, of my own volition. I have never heard of Lady Clanwhoever she is, let alone been at any of her routs. I don't move in such circles, sir."

Goward lent forward in his chair, covering his eyes with his good hand. Wickmere saw his shoulders shake, and patted him gently on the back.

"Forgive me, Burnchurch, I have been under such strain. But my behaviour is unexcusable. My wife has disappeared into thin air. I had so hoped to have news of her, any news. It's been five days now. Five days in which I have barely slept."

Annesley spoke up. "We should go again to the magistrates, at once, with Burnchurch here to swear his innocence. And then we must beat up the whole country round to find her."

Mary's days in the cellar began to take shape. In the mornings, for she assumed they must be such, she was released from her restraints and allowed to use the pail when her gaolers appeared with a cup of thin milk and a bowl of congealed porridge. But when the clock struck eight in the evening, they reappeared and she was again fastened hand and foot. By day she shuffled around the four corners of the cell on hands and knees, rubbing her chafed wrists and ankles, as images of her life played out in the darkness: her mother holding baby Packy and singing him a lullaby, a country lane where the grass grew so high between the cart tracks that it tickled her childish knees, a cow licking the sticky body of a staggering little calf, the bloody afterbirth lying in the grass, the shock and ultimate pleasure of Mrs. Chittleborough's hip-bath, James with his hand on her shoulder, looking down at her. When hours later she heard her gaolers shuffling along the corridor, Mary lay down and stretched feet and hands into position, desperate for those hard-faced women to see her as docile, tractable. Ternan came each night, lifted her by now filthy shift, raped her, pulled it down again, and left without a word. Mary saved the greatest efforts her imagination was capable of for when he was in her. She would count: the stooks of corn in September in her father's long field, the number of stitches in an intricately embroidered flower. It was a triumph of sorts for her when Ternan finished before she had completed the task she had set herself.

Then one morning one of the women, the one the other called Mag, spoke directly to her, not over her.

"You'll go upstairs in a few days. There's a new one coming soon, and if she's pretty enough, he'll go to her instead."

"Oh."

"You'll have to work though. Ruin your nice hands. If you're really a lady, you won't like that."

"I am not a lady, save my husband made me one."

Mag's hands stilled. Frowning, she stared at Mary, who started to gabble, not knowing what that look meant.

"It will be good to be with others. Will there be light upstairs? Will I know if it is day or night? Oh, to have something to do, anything."

"It'll be better than here, I give you that."

Once Mag had gone Mary wept quietly at the horrors she was discovering about herself. For the first time in her life she wished misfortune on another woman, as defenceless as herself. Mary hoped that the new inmate would indeed be pretty.

Mag turned the ring over in her hand and weighed it in her palm. It was a heavier gold than her "perquisites" usually were. What were these scratches inside it? Writing? Mag spat in the dirt and walked on towards Flannery's shop. He could read. She stopped again. The idea of Flannery knowing something she didn't displeased her. He might even claim that the scratches, or the writing, or whatever it was, meant the ring had less value. The prospect of immediate gain battled with a more nebulous idea of some greater future advantage. Who was the woman in the cellar anyway? Mag had seen plenty of inconvenient wives brought to Ternan's establishment, drugged and muffled in blankets, more than she had seen maids pretending to be mistresses, for all "Doctor" Ternan claimed this to be a common delusion. This one didn't talk quite like a lady, and she had that strange manner that was the Ulsterwoman's; Mag had never been further than Rathnew herself. Those ladies were as helpless as newborn babes and beatings and violations quickly reduced them to a state that prevented them ever going back into the world, even were Ternan's doors to be broken down and them all turned out into the street. The hands of the woman in the cellar were clean and fine, but strong. But there was something about her look that suggested some toughness in the face of adversity. Mag pondered those odd words she had said: "I am not a lady, save my husband made me one."

Mag turned back the way she'd come, but didn't go as far as Ternan's house. With a determined step she turned up Church Hill, where she knew she could find someone else who could read. No use going to Father; he'd only want to know why she hadn't been at Mass, but she was too busy and it wasn't good for her bones to be standing about in that draughty Mass-House catching her death (Mag was as strong as a horse as her less docile charges could testify). She'd go to the Protestant Reverend. He might give her something to slake her thirst on this warm day, which was more than Father would ever do.

"*Amor vincit omnia,*" said the rector. "Well, that's an obvious enough choice for a marriage ring. t could even be true for some. How did you come by this, Mrs... ?"

"Cullen, Margaret Cullen. I work for Dr. Ternan's establishment for the poor mad ladies."

"Ah, yes, the private madhouse," he said drily. "'I've never managed to gain admittance, though not for want of trying. So you'll have taken this from an inmate, a patient. Does she know you're here?"

"She does surely, your Reverence. She wanted to know how much would I get for it. Not knowing what it said there I was curious to know myself. It might give it more value, you see, and I want to get the best bargain I can for the poor lady."

"Naturally. Does this lady have a name?"

"She says she is Mary Goward, Lady Goward, but they told me that's her mistress and that she's her servant."

"There are initials in this ring too. M & J. Why would a servant have her mistress's wedding ring?"

"Sure, perhaps it's her own. She might be Margaret, like myself." Mag smiled ingratiatingly, displaying the wreckage of her teeth.

Reverend Kinkead stood up. "This is no servant's ring, Mrs. Cullen. It's too heavy. I see more marriage rings in my work than you have ever pulled from your poor madwomen. And I am an Antrim man, though Dublin educated. I know of the Gowards, and that the present Lord didn't make the marriage expected of him; he wed a servant girl instead, after keeping her for years. You turn pale, Mrs. Cullen. Why is that? I will keep this ring. No, protest all you wish but in this but you won't shake me. I would wager my last shirt that it is Lady Goward that Ternan is holding, whether her husband has put her there or no, though I can think of no reason why a husband would put aside a wife but leave her with a fine ring. I shall insist on seeing her myself. I shall not go alone. I'll give you something for your trouble, but say nothing about any of this to your master. If you do, I will ensure you're taken with him. As it is, you may have an opportunity to turn King's Evidence. I would strongly advise you to avail yourself of it."

The morning mail-coach brought from Dublin handbills to be posted in all market towns, urging anyone who knew anything of the mysterious disappearance of Mary, Lady Goward, from a Dublin ball-room to make himself known to the nearest constable, with a reward offered for information leading to her recovery. Dr. Kinkead called on Dr.Ternan in the company of Jenkins the magistrate and ten of Wicklow town's stoutest yeomen. He declined to accept his reward.

"I wonder are we right, Peg, to leave them now."

"Yes, Jack, they wish it. What they face now they must face alone. I only pray that after what Mary underwent today that the worst is truly over. Making her deposition was bad enough; I saw James put money in the clerk's hand, and I understand this was to ensure that it would not be published. The magistrate would not be moved on the question of an examination; I think because he had been so slow to act that he wanted to be sure that he had not been right all along about Mary's flight. The surgeon was a revolting figure—dirty linen and liberally sprinkled with snuff—a bird's nest of a wig, a loose underlip and fingers like sausages. I gave Mary that tincture before he got to work, that she be less mindful of what he did. The welts at her wrists and ankles should have been sufficient to demonstrate the restraint under which she was put, but he must needs lift her clothes and examine her poor bruised thighs and prod her like a cow at market. He marked her injuries on a little drawing, and would have proceeded to examine her most intimately had James not cried out, "Enough! Is this not sufficient evidence?" The fellow looked most offended at the interruption but contented himself with saying: "I see no signs of canker, though you will not let me look further, but I advise you to have your wife examined for disease none the less. As for this redness here, I advise fermented milk within, and cabbage leaves without."

"Good God."

"It was horrible, Jack. That doctor never addressed one word to poor Mary. He had the effrontery to ask James if he knew if his wife had had knowledge of other men besides Ternan. James looked as if he would run the fellow through, but mastered himself and said, "Until this outrage she has known no one but myself," which got a shrug and the words: "As you are a gentleman, we shall accept this as truth. Good day to you, sir." All this whilst Mary lay there. His receipt though has been followed and it has given her some comfort. You saw James afterwards, how pale he was."

"She is to see her own physician at home."

Benson knocked softly. He heard some muffled words, then Mrs. Samuels's voice: "Come in."

The room was in near darkness, heavy curtains drawn against the shuttered windows. There was a rustle near the bed, as the rector's wife rose and came towards him. He smelt vinegar, that homely disinfectant.

"How does she?" he whispered.

A thin, clear voice came from the bed.

"Dr. Benson. Good morning."

"My lady."

"Do not call me so. I am Mary Kearney."

He glanced at Mrs. Samuels but could not read her expression in the gloom. She laid a hand on his arm.

"Miss Kearney, then. I have come to examine you, if you will permit me."

"You want to know do I have the pox?"

Mrs. Samuels gasped. Shaken, Benson said, "I will need light."

"Would you oblige, dear Mrs. Samuels?" said Mary.

Benson approached, clutching his instrument bag in both hands.

"May I ask, Miss Kearney, do you suffer any discomfort? Pain, intimate pain? A grievous ache in the bones, perhaps, most particularly at night?"

The shutters swung back and pale light flooded the room. Benson bowed towards the thin white-capped face framed by the pillows. Were it not for the darkness of the eyes and the purplish mouth (he made a mental note to check for heart disease) it would have been hard to distinguish Mary from her bedlinen.

"I suffered much pain, Doctor, when those outrages were done to me. I thought I should die. But the pain grew less on each occasion; some tempering mercy at work in administering my punishment, no doubt. Now the pain I feel is in my thoughts, my dreams."

"I would not wish to cause you any more pain. If perhaps Mrs. Samuels could hold your hand, and talk to you."

Mrs. Samuels rustled over. "Dear Mary, do not talk of punishment. Of outrage, yes."

Benson turned down the bedclothes and lifted Mary's nightgown as though he feared waking a sleeping animal.

"Dear Master Edward thrives, does he not?" said Mrs. Samuels to Mary.

The doctor eased apart the thin white legs.

"Yes, he is the best of children though it is I who say so."

He inspected the yellow and green bruising that mottled her inner thighs.

"He showed me an anthill he had discovered behind the stables," said Mrs. Samuels. "He had tried to count the ants, he said, but that they would not stay in one place long enough."

The doctor knelt up on the bed, took a deep breath, and probed gently with the pads of his fingers.

"Oh!" cried Mary, squeezing Mrs. Samuels's hand.

"No swelling, no pustules, no reddening," he murmured to himself. He leaned closer, pushing his spectacles back as they slipped forward, and searched for sores. Mary clutched Mrs. Samuels so tightly now that the bones of her fingers ground together and that lady bit her lip not to cry out. Mary wept, and heard Goward call her name from behind the door.

Benson looked up at her, and said, "Forgive me," but it was Ternan she saw, Ternan's proprietorial hand she felt. The doctor pulled down the nightgown and said: "There is one test I must make, then I am finished, but I can say that I find no signs of disease, Madam."

He creaked off the bed and rummaged in his bag.

"This I fear will pain you, but it is the last indignity I will subject you to today."

He held up what looked like a spoon, its stem wound tightly round with a scrap of bleached linen. Benson knelt on the bed and again lifted the nightgown. Mrs. Samuels now held both Mary's hands and bent over her, kissing her cheek. Mary's body arched, and her cry was hot against the older woman's face. Then it was over, and Benson stood by the window, examining his instrument.

"Dear Lady, I detect no canker, no impurity. It seems that you have at least been spared that. To be absolutely certain, I should like with your permission to repeat my examination two weeks from now."

Dr. Benson came out of the bedchamber drying his hands.

"How does she?" asked James.

"She still bears signs of the violence she has suffered. It will take time, but she is young and strong and those wounds will heal." He paused. "I have examined her for signs of disease, and I find none."

"Thanks be to God."

"Since Ternan had a ready supply of virtuous women to his establishment he had little cause to frequent unclean ones. But I shall need to see her again to be sure. You must be patient with her, sir, for it is what happens here that causes me concern." The doctor tapped his forehead lightly. "Be alert to signs of that melancholy that gripped her after her child was born. How does she sleep?"

"Meg Samuels says she shivers as though she were cold, and starts awake at the slightest sound; a rook cawing is enough. She fears the dark where once she welcomed peace and rest, so a candle must burn in the room all night. If she wakes and it has guttered, she screams. And the nightmares—she shrieks that he is coming, that she is bound."

"Does she permit you to hold her, or does she pull away from your touch?"

"Oh yes, she cries to be held. It is the only way she will be comforted. She lets me stroke her poor shorn head, but allows no one but I and Meg Samuels see it uncovered. I tell her she looks to me like the most adorable of boys, a veritable Viola. And to think she kept those mob-caps she wore as a servant. When she wears them I tell her they bring back to me those early days of our love, and that I love her more for it, for this is true. I have not tried to lie beside her yet, but she lets me kiss her, though not insistently."

"That is a good sign."

"That monster used her, Benson, as though she were a rag-doll. *He* did not kiss her, nor use gentle words with her, so I may still. What she craves of me is affection, but not the embraces of a husband, not yet."

"No, she will feel an act of love as an act of violence still. How is she with the little fellow?"

"She wants him with her often, but when she has him wets his head with her tears. The poor child has asked Meg Samuels what he's done to make his mother so unhappy. And she has frightened Bessie with some wild words about the unhappy destiny of women. I have though encouraged the children to play before the house, so that she may hear their shouts and see them from the windows, for that brings smiles to her face that are not there when she has them in her arms."

'Hmm. Have the magistrates asked that she give evidence?"

"They know where to find us, but as yet we've not been called."

"It would be my advice, sir, even if it flies in the face of natural justice, that she should not be compelled to testify against her tormentor. They would try her as much as him. Or will you pursue him for damages?"

"No damages could lessen her suffering. Captain Annesley informs me there is already enough evidence to hang him several times over, for robbery, sequestration, impersonation. Mary has already given a deposition of sorts, though having to stammer out her ordeal to a lawyer was close to making her live it again. That, and being mauled by that dirty fellow who called himself a doctor. But one of Ternan's attendants has the lawyers filling their indictments as we speak, to save her own hide. The world will be the better when he dances upon air, though Blanch has escaped retribution again."

"Blanch?"

"All this was his doing, Doctor. It was not enough for him to leave me maimed. It was her he wanted destroyed, or bent to his will. He came back to Ireland in the service of young Burnchurch's father, and plotted. Being such a plain man, and a morose one, he astonished his employer with his predilection for the *Gazette* and all the scandal sheets that Dublin will support: tattle like the *Bugle,* which reported Mary's presumed elopement. He was a cat watching a mouse hole, waiting for us to peep out. The longer he waited, the greater his obsession. Burnchurch's harmless excursion to paint the lakes in Killarney was a boon to him, for Blanch had seen our names published as attending that ball, and having the young gentleman as his unwitting tool gave him more time to spirit Mary away, knowing we would start after Burnchurch first. All he had to do was to find villains happy to do his bidding for the right coin, and for them to then wait their moment in that crush. Jack Wickmere and I had gone to smoke our pipes on the balcony of the adjoining room; Mary objects to my smoking at home and I am well-used to puffing away outside. She was left alone for no more than five minutes, but that sufficed for a false footman to serve her a laced drink. If she had only stayed at home with Jack's lady, who was not invited of course. It was me who encouraged her to come. They delivered her to Blanch at an inn near Rathdrum, and he drugged her anew and took her to Ternan—who knew him as White—to break her for him, Benson, that she might thereafter bend wholly to his will. Had it not been for the greed of that attendant wanting to know what Mary's ring was worth, then she would be there still. Sometimes it is I who must restrain my cries at night. Annesley says that Ternan's establishment is now broken up, that such places are no longer legal only that reform is slow to penetrate here. I wonder will Ternan's death grant her some peace? I doubt there can be any for either of us unless Blanch too is taken."

"Curl in to me here, Mary. You won't crush my arm. He feels nothing, remember."

James stroked her head gently, felt the softness of her growing hair. Her denuded scalp had caused him unbearable sadness; now, each day, she became more like the woman he'd known, but he feared her sudden, abstracted silences.

"Tonight, Mary, I will kiss your little hand, like this, each finger in turn. Then I shall turn it over, and kiss the palm, like so. You laugh, my beloved."

"Too soft. It tickles."

"Then firmer, though I like your laugh. Like this?"

"Ye-es."

"Tomorrow, if you permit me I shall gently amble up to your elbow, starting here on the inside of your wrist, where these blue veins cross."

"And after?"

"And after, we shall see. We'll go together on this little expedition. You will not need to tell me if we go too fast, Mary, for if you flinch at anything I shall know to pause and not go further till you give me leave, for no matter how you try to hide that flinch from me I shall feel it and I shall not think ill of you for it. We have time, my darling, the rest of our lives."

Later, he watched her sleeping face, younger than it was when she was awake, the anxiety and watchfulness smoothed away, at least for a while. This was progress, surely? He remembered her as he had seen her in her dank prison, cowering from their lights, her arms over her head, making that terrible sound, like a wounded animal. He had crouched by her and spoken her name but she had recoiled and cried "No!" as he put his hand out to touch her face. Yet she had gone into Peg's arms like a child, and it was Peg who had got her to her feet. A collective groan of pity at the sight of her had risen from the little group crowded into the cellar. He had caught her when she staggered, for she could barely walk, but he would never forget that first flinch, her fear of his touch. Benson said it would take time. She could have all the time she wanted. But Goward wondered how long *he* would need.

Goward Hall
10ᵗʰ September 1778

My dear Jack,

That fiend Ternan is dead: hanged before his own door and his body thrown on a cart and taken to the anatomists in Dublin. But Blanch is still at large, and must have made good his escape to England by now. He has tried twice to destroy us; we must survive this or he has won. I say we, Jack, cognisant that the suffering has overwhelmingly been my Mary's, but because she suffers, I do also.

You will not recognise this letter's hand, and Mary will not know its contents. Our dear Mrs. Samuels, wife of our rector, who is much with us, takes down my words with tears in her eyes. I take the counsel of this kind and gentle lady as I would that of a loving mother, for such she is to us. Mary and I do not yet live again as man and wife.

The external signs of her suffering have healed and faded, but I must advance carefully; it is as though I should woo her again. Her physician advises patience, or the damage will be permanent, and Ternan's mangled remains would laugh at us from whatever circle of hell he now inhabits. When we discovered my poor Mary in that terrible place, my heart was full of rage and pity, and a determination that she should never be out of my sight again, even for a moment. Mrs. Samuels and I sit composing this in the chamber adjoining the one in which she sleeps. No one can enter without encountering us first. I guard her as if she were a princess in a fable, lest evil break in upon her, yet we are at home. If it is possible, I love her more now for having come so close to losing her. But—and it is here that I rely on Mrs. Samuels's counsel, and yours, dear Jack—if some magnetist were to put Mary into a state of trance such that all that occurred in Dublin and Wicklow might be erased from her memory, I do not know how I should be a husband to her. She is sinned against; she has not sinned. The fact remains however that the basest of men has broken into the temple that was my Mary's person, desecrating and befouling the place that was mine alone from the day Mary laid herself down for me. I cannot have Mary know these thoughts. She shrank from me there in her prison, for I was a man. There was relief at the end of her torment but not joy in her deliverance in the same measure; I am convinced that she feared my reaction to what had been done to her. What happened in there has changed her, and changed me. Believe me Jack when I say that she is not repugnant to me. She fills me with a tenderness I do not know how to express, and her face to me is more beautiful now for I had risked losing sight of it forever. But—and I beg Mrs. Samuels's forgiveness for my bluntness—I do not know how I am to make love to my wife.

Dr. Benson counsels patience with Mary, and mayhap that is all I need (I see Mrs. Samuels nodding as she writes this). If each day distances her from that dark time it should do the same for me. By the time you read this, I pray matters will have improved, and by the time your reply reaches me, even further. Forgive me for burdening you in this way, when you have already done so much for me.

I have heard from young Burnchurch and from Captain Annesley. I would lief have made their acquaintance in any other circumstances, but am honoured now to count them amongst my dearest friends. We expect Annesley here towards the end of this year, when he comes north on a familial visit. I only hope that the association of that good and courageous man with the worst experience of my Mary's life (and thus mine also) does not make for a setback in this slow progress when she does see him again. Burnchurch's Miss Atkinson has agreed that they may marry before Christmas, to the relief of his old father. It is what is considered a good bargain by both sides: her wealth and

*his title, but it is my impression that Burnchurch does not love her as he should a wife
and in fact somewhat fears her, though she treats him now as the hero of the hour.*

*As Mrs. Samuels writes these words I am brought face to face with my own obtuse-
ness, Jack. Burnchurch is about to contract a prudent and loveless marriage as do thousands the world over, all the time. My neighbour Lord Lyon is in love with his cook but
bound tight to a cold and elegant shrew of his own class, whilst he dreams of a small
house and a quiet life in a market town. Annesley mourns the wife he lost to consumption when he was at the American wars and warns me of the futility and pain of regret.
Here am I with a wife who loves me and I love her, restored to me when I thought her
lost. I will take time, and discover her anew. Ternan and Blanch have done their worst,
but they have failed, for I find (once more pardon me my plain-speaking, dear Mrs.
Samuels) that I want my wife. This discovery causes my patient scribe to cry anew.*

*Enough. Remember us to dear Peg, and know that I am grateful every day for your
friendship,*

James

Later, James glimpsed through a half-open door a motionless figure in a hip
bath, a tufted head in profile. Mrs. Samuels stood over Mary, gently sponging her
shoulders and back. Sensing his gaze, the rector's wife looked up and her eyes met
Goward's. A warning look, and the slightest shake of the head, told him "not yet."
Goward pulled the door softly closed, and walked away.

"You slept right through this night," said Mrs. Samuels. "You never cried out.
That is progress, Mary."

"I am glad for your sake for your watch must be weary. Is the door still locked?"

"Ever since you were brought home. It will remain so until you say otherwise."

"Against my husband."

"He is patient, Mary. He'll wait for you as long as you need him to."

"I'm afraid."

"You have no need. Ternan is dead. Oh Mary!" The older woman held the
younger tightly in an effort to curb her shaking.

"He was loathsome, loathsome. That fat greasy flesh fouling me. Fouling me for James. Blanch was right. He won't want me now."

"He will, Mary, he does. He has told me so. He'd feared never seeing you again."

"That's what I meant, when I said I was afraid. I am not the same person now and never will be again. When James comes near me that man will come between us. When he did those things to me, it was as if I sat apart and watched in horror as another woman suffered. I felt her pain. I heard her screaming. But only when he had gone and I was alone in the dark did I know it had been done to me. You tell me Ternan is dead but every time James reaches for me in the night, it will be that monster's hands on me. I can never be forgiven for that."

"Forgiven? What are *you* to be forgiven for?"

"I should never have fallen in love with James. I have dragged him down to my level and I have been punished; he has been punished. When I was his servant I used to gather little things of his that he had thrown away: scraps of his writing even when I couldn't read it, linen that was torn beyond mending that I kept without washing that it might smell of him for longer. I gathered them up never dreaming he would be mine. I still have those things though he doesn't know it. But in that cellar I told myself I should have yielded to Mr. Blanch that time all the family were in London. He would have had me and tired of me, and my Lord would not have wanted his leavings. But because I already loved James then, though could not speak of it to anyone, it would have been death to me if my brother and Mr. MacNamara had not stopped Blanch in time. He was stopped, and so he took his revenge first on my husband, who was left with his poor dead arm, and then on me. Blanch wanted to drag me down so far that I would be grateful to be with him. I will be fearful as long as he lives. I do not know if Ternan knew who I really was: he knew I wasn't really a lady, sane or mad, and so fair game for him. If I had been a lady, Mrs. Samuels, Lady Lyon would never have insulted me as she did."

"All that means is that *she* is no lady."

"It was after that time that James thought to take me to Dublin, and it's true, I did see people there who accepted me and professed to like my company, but it were better I'd not gone there. This is what I thought of, round and round and round like a dog going after his own tail, when I was tied up in that place, waiting for that man to come back. They put out there that I was a poor mad servant who thought she was her mistress. They were right. I have done the man I love only harm by being his wife. It were better that I died bringing Edward into the world than the trouble I have made for James."

"You should not refuse life, Mary. It is not yours to refuse. Nor should you refuse a child his mother. Remember too that James freely made you his wife because he wanted to show the world that you were his."

"I have always been his wife, before God."

"I've always suspected it. This being so, would you see the priest? He has called on you several times and we have told him you were not ready to see anyone. He has spent hours closeted with your husband, counselling patience, as I have. I am a daughter of my church, so I have been taught that one should not confess to another mortal but only to God, yet I see how it might grant you some peace."

"We confess only to God, Mrs. Samuels. A priest is merely His instrument."

"Well, would you speak to Fr. O'Dowd? He knows that you are sinned against, not sinning. If you sin at all it is in permitting the forces of evil to prevail against a truly Christian marriage. May I send for him?"

"If he will see one who has been abandoned by God, yes."

"Mary!"

"I tried to pray in that place, Mrs. Samuels. When I was in that darkness I saw myself at the foot of the Cross."

"This was hope, surely?"

"No, anything but. I was alone, in a barren, rocky place, a field of sparse grass that could not take the plough. Pale moonlight lit me where I knelt, but made me fearful of looking about, that those stones might not be stones but skulls. I could not raise my eyes to Him."

"Why, Mary? His comfort never fails."

"I thought I might see our Blessed Lord as a rotting corpse exposed on a gibbet, Mrs. Samuels, and that all I had ever believed was naught, that evil triumphed over good. I thought that if this was so, then that if ever I was to leave that place then I must set my husband free on the point of a dagger, like poor Lucrece in the story."

"That lady was a pagan, if a noble one. If you think that way, then you do let evil triumph. You were not being punished, Mary. Let us say you were being tried, you and James, not by God but by the devil with those wicked men as his instruments."

"Husband?"

"What is it, my love? How long have you been awake?"

"A while. I wanted to watch you sleeping, but the candle had gone out."

"Come closer. There is some light to see me by now, so if you wish I will oblige you and fain sleep. So you woke in the dark, but there were no terrors this time? Oh Mary mine."

"No. I listened to this old house creak, and to your breathing, and I was not afraid, not like before. I knew myself to be at home. It is not the darkness I fear now."

"What, then?"

"Do you love me any less than you did before?"

"I love you more each day, because I thought I'd lost you. A little more each day, even if neither of us sees love grow, and yet it does, quietly, like your pretty hair."

"But, can you love my person, as you did before?"

"Oh Mary, what a question. Don't you think our little expeditions go well? See, our intrepid little mountaineer sets off up the incline again for the summit he conquered last night," he said, as his fingers walked softly up her bare arm to the lace on her shoulder.

"Wait." She took his fingers in hers and kissed them before putting his hand gently away. He groaned inwardly; he had gone too fast for her. But her next action took him quite by surprise.

"What are you doing, Mary? You don't have to do this yet."

She was pulling her nightgown over her head. Then she lay back on the heaped pillows, her arms covering her face.

"I was thinking of that first night you brought me here, husband, and what you asked me to do," she said, from behind her hands.

"Oh Mary, how could I not love your person?" With relief he realised he meant it.

"Will you let me kiss your dear self? I promise not to do more, unless you wish it."

She nodded.

"Don't cover your face. Touch me instead."

With infinite gentleness he began to kiss her: mouth, neck, shoulder, the hollows of her collarbone, all his senses sharp to the slightest tremor of withdrawal. Each kiss was ground retaken. "Now this, and this, and this," he said to himself as he moved stealthily across the terrain of her body. Then, by heaven, he felt her hands timidly stroking his hair, followed by the gentle insistence of her fingertips, guiding him, until the last lost cry escaped her. He gazed down on her, her skin flushed and glowing. He covered her, and glided home. Her arms around him, he wept into her shoulder.

"My love, my Mary." He wanted to shout his love to the world.

Later, as they lay sated and entwined, he said, "I should like to lie beside you in a great green meadow, with only the sky to cover us and the clouds to witness our love. And when you'd had enough of me, I should go gathering bog cotton, naked as I was, and weave it into a diadem for your hair."

"What if you stood in a cow-pat?"

"Ha! I could rely on Irish rain to wash it off."

"What if I was scratched by the whin bush where I should not be scratched?"

"Then I should examine your dear little white bum for the marks, most attentively, so that I might kiss them better. That reminds me, Mary, do me the pleasure of rolling over so that I may reacquaint myself… No scratches. I see you have not been sitting in the fields without me, but I would be happy for your sake to get the scratches on *my* bum, if by doing so I might look up at the sky, and at you."

"When I was a child the place I most liked to lie to stare at the sky was in the bracken. It was the best place to play in autumn when were were childer, for it was brown and dry and crackled. We made nests where no one could see us, with just the sky above us."

"Mary, what a capital idea. Let me see what the day promises us."

She watched him as he pushed aside the bed curtains and went over to the window, folding back a shutter.

"Don't let anyone see you."

What a fine looking man he was. Even the poor limp shrivelled arm for her only served to accentuate the beauty of the rest of him. Better, far better, than those naked marbles they had all over Mountlyon. He turned back, smiling.

"It's a fine day. Would you show me where the best bracken nests are to be found?"

"I would."

"Somewhere we can gather bog cotton on the way?"

"Yes, but with your clothes on, James, or you'll frighten the cows."

"What do they say of me, Mrs. Samuels?"

"They, Mary?"

"The world."

"I am not much in it, to be able to say, if you intend what goes by the name of polite society. Mr. Griffiths has spoken from the pulpit, giving thanks for your deliverance."

"I have searched Scripture myself for comfort, Mrs. Samuels, as you suggested, but find little to comfort a woman who has suffered the outrage I have. Nay, if she is a maiden she is to hold her tongue and wed her ravisher. James should be putting me aside that I may marry Blanch, for Ternan was merely his catspaw."

"You do your husband a disservice to say such a thing."

"I know, but—"

"That, Mary, is all that should count now. Griffiths spoke instead of the damsel in the field, betrothed to another, who cried out and no one came to save her. Scripture says that the man who dishonours her must be stoned but that the poor lady not be punished for she is without fault. He struggled to master himself two or three times, describing you in broken tones as the noblest of women and the most chaste of wives. I swear that in the congregation too eyes were wet and sword-hands clenched."

"But if that damsel were not another's, then he might profit from his violence and wed her, to enjoy her poor flesh for the rest of her life whether she would or no."

Mrs. Samuels opened her hands, surrendering. "Different days, Mary. We must be thankful that we did not live then, before the coming of our Lord. Look less at the prophets, for they were not yet enlightened, and seek answers in the Gospels. My husband was once a good scholar, Mary. It was he who showed me how Our Lord was merciful whilst the Old Testament fathers sought simply to be just. Theirs was the easier task, I've no doubt, for reason and conscience do not need to be questioned where there is an infallible rule. It is men, and what goes for polite society, that judge us, though I see no right for them to do so, and who show little mercy and often little justice either."

"Then heaven must look down on us in dismay."

"I am sure of it. But you were delivered, Mary. Ask yourself what you will do with this mercy, you and your husband."

"He loves me still, Mrs. Samuels."

"He has never ceased to. May I ask you, child, are you again man and wife?"

"Yes."

"Thanks be to God."

"It is just that I don't know how to face everyone else."

"Then don't, not yet."

"So I must stay behind these demesne walls, and let no one breach them, at the mercy of my own thoughts."

"In the company of those who love you."

"Without that I should be dead by now. Mrs. Samuels, when first I could read, I sought to divert myself with those novels Lady Mitchelstown left behind."

"I'm really not sure that—"

"—I looked at them because by reading what a lady reads I thought I could become more like one, because I hadn't the Latin and all then. I thought I might know from them how to please my husband better, so I could try to be a better wife."

"Letty Mitchelstown's example was hardly the one to follow."

"I know that now. I had no mother to guide me, and I didn't know what questions to ask you about matters I knew nothing of. But I've thought of those books since my kidnap, and the pretty, tormenting pictures in them. Now when I read those words again I find only darkness and despair. There are girls in them served like me, and it never turns out well for them. They tempt their ravishers, though they protest they do not. I tempted Blanch, that's what the world will say of me. I tempted James, and now he has the one arm."

"Mary, stop this. You are neither a Roman matron nor a personage in a doubtful novel that must surely have been penned by a Frenchwoman."

Goward Hall
21ˢᵗ December 1778

Dear Mr. Ingham,

You know, as do all, that I have lately been delivered from incarceration in a place for poor women considered mad. It has taken some time for me to recover from the sufferings, the indignities I was forced to undergo there, and indeed I do not believe I will ever again be the person I was before those insults offered to my person, my soul, and to my husband. Whatever I may say the gossips will supply all the salacious detail they wish in speaking of me. I dare not venture into Society again, though to be truthful I was often loath to do so, mindful that Ladies always talked of me behind their fans and Gentlemen stared at me as though I were exposed upon a stage. There are those who will say I got what I deserved for my presumption, and I have no energy to confound them, for if I make the attempt, they will merely say of me, as they did of that unhappy lady in the play, that she doth protest too much. In my darkest moments I was inclined to believe that indeed I was deserving of my fate, but those that love me, wiser counsellors than I, have patiently persuaded me that what happened to me was the Devil's work and that I malign our Creator if I continue to think that way. I was freed; I might well not have been. I must consider how best to use the liberty that has been restored to me. I wish to be useful, Mr. Ingram; I feel I am not. My husband reads that he may learn how the world may be changed; as I am a woman, my sphere is perforce narrower, so I may seek only to better the lot of my immediate neighbours. I have prayed for direction and think I may be able to comfort in some way those unfortunate women who languish behind bars, be they those of the madhouse or the prison, in a way that a masculine hand or voice may not. To ransom the captive is a Work of Mercy in the faith my mother taught me, and though it may not fall to me to free anyone who was captive as I was, I hope my presence may show that they are not forgot. We women cannot make the laws by which unfortunate members of my sex may be confined, nor may we defend ourselves against them. My husband counsels caution, for he fears a relapse into the melancholy that has governed me these last months should I go in a place where there are bars and chains, but I am thrown too much upon my own thoughts if I do nothing, and have reassured him that if I am in the company of good Quaker people then I can come to no harm.

The memory of your father's kindness stays with me always.

Your humble svnt. and friend,

Mary Goward

"Mary, you look pale. You have been quiet all through our meal."

"I am quite well, James."

"Speak to me, then."

"I went with Mr. Ingham to the gaol after breakfast."

"You see—I feared those visits would tire you."

"They do not tire me; they are necessary to me, perhaps more than to those poor souls I see."

"But you come back whey-faced and silent."

"So let me speak then."

"Forgive me."

"There was a woman there who had not yet stood her trial, but never will now. It was for the theft of a petticoat from her employer. When the constables came to arrest her, she was behind the house pegging washing, and put up a struggle, falling against a wall. Her hand caught on an old nail and tore it. This morning she was in the last agonies of lockjaw."

"You saw this?"

"Her head was thrust back and she was raised in an arch on her elbows and heels. Her mouth was held in a terrible fixed grin. Her eyes bulged from their sockets."

"Good God. As though she had been hanged."

"We could offer her no comfort but kind words but I don't know if she could hear us above her groaning, a terrible sound like metal dragged across cobbles. The comforts of religion were denied her. A priest was anointing her as best he might, forcing himself into an acrobatic performance to do so, but the sacrament could not have passed her lips, and nor could she have swallowed it."

Mary started to cry, but when he got up, intending to come round to where she sat, she motioned him to stay where he was, and reached for her own handkerchief.

"Have you not suffered enough that you must also witness the sufferings of others?" he asked.

"All this for a petticoat, James. She probably thought it would not be missed; perhaps her mistress has many. That lady will sleep tonight between linen sheets that the poor wretch washed and dried and stretched upon the bed, whilst the servant's corpse lies in a sack tossed into a lime pit."

"I must speak to Matthew Ingham. He must not expose you again to such sights."

"No. I have been tried, husband. Reviled, debased, chained, violated. I have gone from despair to guilt to rage. I cannot leave others to suffer alone if there is something, anything, I may do, even for just one of them. I am no longer that child you married."

"You mean I treat you as one?" He stared in bewilderment.

"I mean I was an innocent; a "natural human" I heard you say to Lady Mitchelstown, though the philosopher who spoke those words first I now know for an unnatural wretch who gave up his own children to an orphanage."

"Monsieur Rousseau, another of my youthful enthusiasms. Forgive me."

"I was an ignorant girl out of a cabin. By my reverses I am innocent no longer, and I have been educated out of my class, but you try to protect me from the world as though I were still that girl."

"That stings. You say that to me, who did not protect you well enough."

"I have never accused you of that, nor even thought it. I mean that my eyes have been opened, my conscience awakened. You took a girl, James, and loved her, and shaped her, and dressed her in fine clothes, and led her about on your arm that others might admire her."

"I loved to do it. I still remember the look on your dear face when you had shoes for the first time, made to fit your pretty feet. I love to do it still, when you let me, though it is your restraint in matters of dress that makes you more charming still to my eye."

"You dressed me well and so others look at me."

"Do you know how much you hurt me? I could have bought any pretty girl that way, and have tired of her as quickly."

"In your world, the world of the Quality I mean, a woman is praised for her person. That and her witty tongue. She must do all to captivate and thus to keep."

"Don't you see, Mary, that you have none of the silly coquetries I used to be offered? You were—you are—simply yourself. Your sweet face, were it not the bearer of your qualities, would be nothing else; it would turn simpering, or hard. That face made you easy to love, Mary, but consider your kindness, your steadfastness, your tenderness as a mother, your stubbornness even. Or should we call it wisdom? These are what adds esteem to that love, for those who know you, not only for me. These are the same qualities that inspire hate and rage, and vengeance, in those who see the world through a jaundiced eye: that of Lady Lyon, or Blanch."

His eyes were wet.

"Mary, let me try to protect you. Yours is the weaker sex, though I would never call *you* weak."

"A girl born in a cabin must work as hard as her brothers. I do not see that we are the weaker sex, though I see that *ladies* are brought up to be so. We cannot be if we are to carry life within us, and to bring it into the world, in the pain God lays down for us. Not weak, no."

"Yet I have seen you fearful. I have watched you when you didn't know I was there, going out to the Offices, peeping round corners where anyone else would have gone confidently on. It tears my heart to see you so."

The Education of a Gentleman?

"Griffiths is very impressed with how our boy progresses with his lessons, Mary."

"We must be grateful he can spare the time, as Mr. Samuels is so demanding of him."

"Yet snarls his resentment of the help Griffiths gives him," said James.

"Mrs. Samuels fears for her husband," said Mary. "He gets ever stranger in his ways and so red in the face that she expects him any moment to explode with the heat that is in his head. She tells me that some of his flock are already gone to Dr. Breen's church though it be a longer journey for them because what he says from the pulpit sometimes puts the fear of God into them."

"That news does not surprise me. He stands up there beneath the canopy with his wig askew, shaking his fist as though it held a thunderbolt, fulminating like a prophet on the mountain. Before long we will find ourselves lying in the aisles and foretelling damnation in strange tongues. Certainly one cannot sleep through his sermons now."

"No, husband, before long we will be burying poor Mr. Samuels. I fear what will happen then to our dear Meg."

"Let her come here. There's enough room in this great barn that we can find a chamber and a sitting-room for her, surely? You'd like that, would you not?"

"Indeed I would. She could have the use of the school-room when Mr. Griffiths isn't there, and learn Bessie—"

"Teach Bessie. I have been thinking about Mr. Griffiths's future too, for when I appointed that cheerful young man to teach Edward I was also thinking about this incumbency. You know he is a Balliol man as is Mr. Samuels?"

"You mean he studied where did Mr. Samuels?"

"Precisely so, though Mr. Samuels has I note ever been most reluctant to talk of Oxford with him. Well, the living here must go to a Balliol man. It is in their gift just as a father gives his name to his son."

"If he be not a bastard."

"Yes, if he be not a bastard. I have the choosing of that Balliol man, which if they knew it in Oxford would make them spill their claret. A Catholic Lord choosing a parson of the Church of England. We shall have Methodists choosing the archbishop of Canterbury next. See Mary, there is some fun to be had out of our strange situation."

"But if Mr. Griffiths is to be the parson, then who is to teach Edward?"

"Ah, here you arrive at the sticking point. It's time to consider how our boy's education best be continued. He needs the society of boys of his own age. I know he has that of the tenants' children, Mary, for I see your mouth open to tell me so, and that he is often outdoors as a boy of his age should be, fishing with them or out on his pony. He is ruddy, sturdy, and his resemblance to his uncles who have grown straight and strong pleases me nearly as much as does his resemblance to you. But he is a gentleman's son even if he may never sit in the House in either Dublin or London—not that I would describe all those who do as gentlemen, by any means."

"You would send him to Charterhouse," said Mary faintly. "You would send him to London."

"To Charterhouse, no. I could not even if I wished it. For the world he is your son, Mary, and my by-blow; St. George's Hanover Square can't change that, but at least that means we have been able to bring him up in our religion. As a Catholic he is barred from Charterhouse, from the universities, for always. We cannot ask him to pretend, as I pretend daily that I am a Protestant. When I went to Oxford I had to swear to all manner of things too absurd to take seriously. I think not one man in twenty did, though many of them were destined for the Church. It was just one of those things to be got through. But a Catholic cannot swear that "Romish doctrine is repugnant to the Word of God" or discard all but two of the sacraments and mean it, and if he does swear without meaning it, must perjure himself. If we look though beyond the shores of these damp islands, Mary, the Church reigns supreme and there are men well able to instruct our child. There are Catholic Englishmen, Mary, of the highest quality, though obliged to practise their religion with the greatest of discretion. In the north of their country there are gentlemen of distinction, in Lancashire, in Durham, who in manners and learning are the envy of their Protestant neighbours. Their sons go to Douai—"

"Where would *that* be?'

"France. I have been there on my way south, though I never dreamed I might visit it again with this end in view. It is a neat little town, healthy and clean, and the college is run by English and Irish priests for the education of boys and for the training of priests to return to these islands—"

"So Edward might become a priest?"

"Oh, ah, yes… I suppose he might." For the first time Goward faltered in urging his case; he had not considered this possible outcome, and his upbringing fought to reassert itself against the man who had knelt and vowed before Father O'Dowd. *My son a popish priest?* All he said was, "I can see that prospect pleases you, Mary. But he is not yet twelve. He is clever and strong-willed already—he will decide his course."

"It does not please me, James. He is our only child and I would lief see him married and a father, and you trying to run after grandchildren out in that there park."

"Don't cry, Mary."

"It is not that. You have always spoken hard against them Charter Schools."

"*Those* Charter Schools—"

"Those," she said, with an impatient movement. "You said it was unnatural to take children from their cabins and the only life they knew and to make them work for their keep and take away the religion of their fathers. Well, so, is it not wrong to take a child from his mother's arms and his father's love and all the things he cares about, even if his religion is left in peace, and put him in a place where he does not have the words to tell them there that he is lonely?"

"Mary, my education fitted me to be little other than a gentleman about town. What I learned that was useful came to me mostly from Abercrumble on our Tour."

"Well, can't you take him on the Tour yourself? Couldn't we all go?"

"That's a capital idea—when he's older. What I meant to say, is that my education did little for me but Edward's must do more for him. He will need to fight his way in the world more than I ever did. He doesn't have my name, though he will have as much wealth as I can leave him. He is openly Catholic, while I disguise that fact."

"Not well enough, I fear."

"You think so? Well, it seems not to have troubled anyone overmuch. What I hope is that Edward will carry on in a wider sphere the work I've started here. I hope he will one day do great things in Ireland—for Ireland. For that he must have accomplishments he cannot attain here."

"And Bessie?"

"What about Bessie?"

"Will you send her away too?"

"I'd never thought to. She does well enough here with you and Mrs. Samuels, does she not?"

"Should a girl not be educated as well as a man, if she is to be a fit companion for him?"

"Mary, if you allude to your old idea that you are not a fit companion for me, I beg you not to. Of course, Bessie must be educated to the degree that she may be a man's greatest help and support."

"Indeed, it's the only path open to her, unless she is to serve as Coram intended she should."

The Education of an Orphan

Wash off my foul offence
And cleanse me from my Sin;
For I confess my crime, and see
How great my Guilt has been.

In Guilt each part was form'd
Of all this sinful frame;
In Guilt I was conceiv'd and born
The Heir of Sin and Shame.

"God love you child, but what is that you're singing?"

"Oh Ma'am, 'tis just the hymn I learned at Coram. We'd to sing it at morning prayers."

"Did they tell you what it meant?" asked Mary.

"Only that every one of us is born in Original Sin and that our Saviour died for us that we might have eternal life."

"And what sins did you commit?"

"Wanting another apple. Wishing my hair was as pretty as Harriet's. Being cross with Lucy for talking in her sleep. Wanting to stay in my cot when I should be up for prayers. Looking blackly at the instructress when she made me take out my stitching and do it again."

"Well, perhaps she was right," said Mary gently. "She has made a fine needle-woman of you."

The child smiled and bent forward over her embroidery.

"These seem such small things, Bessie. Not much for a little girl to want."

"But not what I wanted most of all. I dreamed of my mother coming for me. Lucy's came. She was called from the sewing room and did not come back. One of the monitors told me afterwards that she had gone out holding her mother's hand, along with the gentleman that had married the lady, and that she would have again the name she came into the Hospital with. So there is no Lucy Jenkins now; she lived only seven years. I did so envy her, a mother to love her, a mother all her own. I wanted to run outside and find them and tell Lucy's mother that I would be a good daughter and not talk in my sleep and to take me in her place. But I couldn't. So I wondered how long I would be Bessie Norton for, and would it be my turn next. But no other mother ever came for any of us in that big room. Then you came."

"Do you want to be Bessie Norton still?"

"Yes, begging pardon. If my mother was to come one day and I was not there and they told her I was in Ireland and she came over here on the boat to look for me but there was no one of that name here then she might never find me."

"Do you miss the other wee girls?"

"I do. But I don't want to be there. It was the happiest day of my life when you took me away. The people were kind, mostly, but all we really had was our own companionship. I did love my nurse, Mrs. Wilkinson at Camberwell. I stayed with her until I was five years old and then a carriage was sent for me. I cried for I thought my heart would break and she wept also and begged that she might keep me as one of her own but such a thing was not to be allowed. But at least she knew I loved her. When you came, like Lucy, they didn't let me say good-bye to my companions."

"They let me keep you," said Mary, thinking about poor Mrs. Wilkinson.

"That's because you are a fine lady and Mrs. Wilkinson was a carman's wife, with four children of her own," said Bessie, in a matter-of-fact tone. "And you have taken me as a servant, not as your child."

"No, Bessie, as my child, but we didn't say that to the Governors."

Mary pondered whether the Governors might be prevailed upon to let Bessie see her friends again were they to be in London again, but as quickly rejected the idea. Would those children want to see Bessie, or would they resent her good fortune, as she had resented Lucy's? Or worse, might Bessie with a child's careless insensitivity boast of her new life and thus provoke resentment where none might have existed? Mrs. Wilkinson however might be found. She wanted to defend the poor wet-nurse, for it did not feel right that Bessie should see the woman as less the lady, when she, Mary, was merely a maid-servant who had been extraordinarily fortunate.

Bessie said: "I know what I shall do when I'm grown."

"What's that, Bessie?"

"I shall go into service in a Big House like this one, and I will marry the young Master there, just as you did. Then I shall go back to the orphanage and choose me a little girl of my own."

"Oh Bessie, not all young masters are as kind to servant girls as Lord Goward is to me." Mrs. Samuels's warning dinned again in her ears, advice *she* would want to give to this little girl not five years from now. Mary's hands rested on her work as she contemplated Bessie's bent head and listened to her contented humming.

I shall bring her up as though for service, as the Governors intended. There is no shame in that. I will teach her how to run a household, how to manage her accounts, how to furnish a home with the work of her hands—all things to comfort and support a husband, be he a servant, an innkeeper, a grocer, a parson or a Lord.

The Gentleman's Magazine

*for January 1779, containing more in Quantity and greater Variety,
than any Book of the Kind and Price*

Deaths

Nov.. *The Rev. W. Boote, D.D.*

*The Rev. Dr. McCartin, Titular Bishop of Down and Connor, at Loughan Island,
near Downpatrick, in Ireland.*

*Dr. William Murray, Vicar of Gainsborough and Prebend of Corringham and
Stow, in Lincoln Cathedral.*

*Mr. John Reynolds, at Lambeth, one of the Gentlemen of the Chapel Royal, and of
the Choir of Westminster-Abbey.*

The Lady of Lord Deerhurst, at Ledbury, in Herefordshire, in child-birth.

Dec. *The Rev. Dr. George Samuels, of Balliol, Rector of Kilkeel, near Newry, in
Ireland.*

"Well, Mary, our poor Mr. Samuels outlived the bishop in the end."

"I think that's why he is gone. It was the last object of his life. Once obtained,
he had nothing else to strive for."

"Poor faithful Mrs. Meg, after all her devotion. How does she now, do you
think?"

"She is content. She likes her rooms, and the aspect from the windows. Her
little dog has had more difficulty settling than she. He and Springer have had to
be separated."

"Oh dear. But the demesne is big enough for even Springer to admit an elderly
pug to encroach upon it."

"I was so afraid of Mr. Samuels once, James. I did not understand how unhappy
he was."

"You and he were both victims to another of my early enthusiasms—your education—more evidence of my belief that I could move mountains just by telling

others what a capital idea it would be to do so. You may blame me; I am sure he did."

"An enthusiasm, was it?"

"To begin with. Then I saw what fruit it bore. But I must confess something, Mary. I made myself do something for you, rather than to you. I am ashamed to admit it now, but my intentions were not the most honourable. Making you the Reverend's pupil made you safer. I could not treat you as thoughtlessly as I might have done. Forgive me."

"You are forgiven. You were long ago."

"Will you forgive me for sending Edward to France?"

"I do. He is so excited at the prospect. I mustn't let him see how it grieves me."

Le jeune monsieur irlandais

Irish College
Douai
3rd September 1779

Dear Mother,

Father left me yesterday to go home and I do not know if you will receive this letter or him first. He slept here three nights and I am very pleased that he did for now I can think of him here with me and the place is not so strange. I have a good plain chamber, Father says, and it has a fireplace so I will be warm when the weather turns colder. A Servant attends me and four other boys and he smiles a lot and I think his name is Jong. I think he understands me but is instructed to speak only in French that I and my companions may learn that tongue. We are obliged to observe Silence in this college after 9 of the evening. This is a marvel for there are so many under this roof yet this rule is respected. However I know not why they have it for there are so many bells in this town that make such a noise without, and in particular a big belfry with a won-drous number of bells in it that can play a tune, which altogether make such a sound tolling the hours all through the night that at first I wondered would I ever sleep here—yet after three nights I find I note them much less though the sound of a mouse scratching in the wainscoting will wake me. No animal may enter this building apart from the kitchen cats and this is as well or the mice would be without number but I cannot have Springer here and I miss him sleeping at my feet. Please tell him not to forget me and remind McNamara for me to throw sticks for him if he has time, or let him go ratting with my uncles. But mind and keep him away from Sally's pen for he has always looked on her in a hungry way and he must not for she is a very dear rabbit to me and I miss them both. Tell Bessie I miss her and mostly that I will not be there to play hide and seek in the bracken on the cashel as we did last year; it was a capital place Father found for us. I miss you too Mother and I remember you and Father and dear Bessie, Aunt Bridgie, Uncle Robert, Uncle Patrick, Mrs. Samuels, Mr. Griffiths, Mr. Andrews and McNamara in my prayers.

Your loving son,
Edward Kilkeel

Irish College
Douai
16th September 1779

Dear Sir,

I shall endeavour to write you regularly with news of your boy Edward Kilkeel. He is a child of a sunny disposition, given to enthusiasms and often in search of new amusements, but we will endeavour here as he settles to the discipline of this school to teach him the value of application and attainment. He is still young, in some respects younger than his fellows of a similar age, given that he has grown up in circumstances where he is the centre of his own world and where he may have lacked companionship of young gentlemen of his own age. Being of an affectionate and open nature, he speaks easily and artlessly of those dearest to him and is still moved quickly to tears when he thinks not only of his parents, but also of a child called Bessie, two men he describes as uncles though they appear to be farm labourers, and a variety of servants one of whom he similarly claims as his aunt. I am very pleased to say that his study of the Classics has clearly been of the highest standard, so much so that his tutors in these languages already intend that he should help teach some of his less advanced companions. Edward himself has taken kindly to this suggestion and in his willingness he shows a maturity that in other regards he has yet to learn to demonstrate, or have confidence in so demonstrating. I beg that you will pass my compliments to whoever has had the teaching of the boy, for he is evidently a man of no mean ability.

His aptitude for the dead languages is clearly a gift though, and not simply the result of hard application, for he proves already to have a good ear for the French language though less interest in understanding its structure and grammatical forms, though in this last he differs from no other normal boy of his age. His religious instruction though shews signs of some confusion in his ideas, but this you were kind enough to intimate to me might be the case given some of the peculiarities of the situation currently pertaining in Ireland. Indeed we have found this often in ways we do not with some of our English pupils for whom the practice of the faith is not always easy but is not so fraught with difficulty as it is for our Irish ones. He shows signs not of having been proselytised by Protestants so much as having been much in their society.

He is also taught Geography and Natural Philosophy; looking at the globe he marvels still at how small a place he has occupied in the world when he feels he has travelled so far.

If you wish it Edward can also acquire some of the gentler accomplishments which would fit his station in life, such as drawing, fencing or dancing. These activities would naturally attract an additional charge, but we have found them to be useful pursuits for such of our young gentlemen as demonstrate aptitude in them. Edward is still a mere boy, but it is my considered opinion that boys who develop such interests are less likely later to fall prey to less useful pastimes. I beg you will instruct me either directly or by word to our agent Mr. Corey.

I remain yr. obedient servant,

Dom Anthony Turner

Irish College
Douai
30ᵗʰ September 1779

Dear Mother,

Today I received your letter and I have put it under my pillow and will keep it always there close to me except when Jean comes to change the bedlinen. As you see he has told me how to say and spell his name but mine makes him laugh and he calls me Monsieur Ed Wad. Please I beg you write me again when Father is once more home for he has two seas to cross one after the other and much land in-between, but the sailing from Kent to France was for me a much easier one than we have ever had going from Ireland to England.

I am kept at books in the classroom with eleven other boys each at his own desk and they are mostly sons of gentlemen from England, only three others from Ireland though the monks who teach us are mostly Irishmen. Please tell Mr. Griffiths they are very pleased with my Latin and Greek and the merit is all his. The monks wish us to converse in Latin or in French but this is still hard for us but harder still is when we eat for then we must be as silent as they.

You would marvel at the number of priests and monks there are in this town, and they all dress as if they were in a grand play so I know they are priests not like at home or in London where only his plain clothes and solemn face hint at what the man really is. Our teachers are Benedictines and Jesuits and also Friars who in wintertime must suffer in their feet on account of not wearing stockings and indeed their robes look to me to be comfortless being rough and scratchy.

We go to Mass every day in the chapel here but on Sundays to Notch Dam this being the biggest church I have ever seen and the finest more so than any in London and full of pictures and coloured glass and the ceiling high up has ribs across it just like the skeleton of a beast. There is an organ which makes such a wondrous loud sound that I think I must be in heaven and such a throng of people there that they must be the heavenly host though some do dress in the plainest way so they cannot yet be risen to heaven.

Please remember me in your prayers as I do you and everyone at home and I hope Father is with you again by now.

Your loving son,

Edward Kilkeel

"He starts to grow away from us, James."

"So he must. But it is less that he grows away from us, and more that he grows."

Capital Crime

14 Berkeley Square
16th July 1780

Dear Jack,

I have engaged a lawyer's clerk to write this for me, for reasons you will soon understand. Our sojourn in the capital was somewhat overdue. Mary was taken by the idea of looking up a lady who had had care of Bessie but sadly the poor woman has since died. By contrast I have had the most extraordinary encounter today—one that I sought myself, though I still question why I did, and you will probably say and not for the first time that your poor friend has taken leave of his senses. Niederer is to hang; I read the account of his trial in the court returns and resolved to see him. You might with reason say "good riddance" and that he deserves his fate, but it has nothing to do with his plot and Blanch's against my person. My former servant is to swing for b-gg—y, a crime for which no rich man ever has to pay, and with him a seventeen year-old pressed sailor, an unlettered Cornishman. I have been to Newgate, Jack, and I think I would not wish such a place on anyone save Blanch. My request to see Niederer was looked upon with some suspicion by the turnkeys, but apparently it is not an unusual one. Those who wish to gawp at the condemned can usually have their desire satisfied if they dress it up as Christian charity and accompany it with coin, but such strollers usually come in twos and threes, as though to give each other courage. Single gentlemen are rather rarer, and our meeting was observed from beginning to end by two gaolers through an opening grille in the door.

Never have I seen such surprise on the face of any living soul. "The last man I thought to see," he exclaims, and then in mockery he bows most formally and says he is at my service, and apologises for the poor state of his apartment. I pulled out that paper you have seen but did not need to ask for confirmation that it is his work; I saw it in his face. Have I seen Blanch, he asks. No, I return, and ask if it was he who was behind that business of poor silly Lady Risborough and her hapless boy. We both, he replies, "He made me do it or it would go bad for me. But it has gone bad for me all the same. I only see him once again, and then I write you the note." But I would know why Niederer meant me such harm back then. He smiles and mutters something about "das schöne Mädchen" but says it with such venom that clearly he intends no compliment. He tells me of Blanch's obsession, of how he felt slighted first by my father who preferred the company of a popish priest to a freeborn Englishman and child of the vicarage, of his loathing for the poor Catholicks over whom he held sway in my father's name, that their women no matter how poor would not think to ease their trials and those of their children by lifting their skirts when Blanch so desired. When Mary came to work at the House and he saw her clean and fed and loved by all, he wanted nothing else but to trample that beauty and in his words, "teach her a lesson." He berated me for not using Mary as Blanch wanted to do, "Then you tried mind-easement by sending her to learning," he cried, for the more heated he became the more Germanic also. "What really happened at Mulholland's?" I ask, at which he laughs like the very devil and waves his arm at the other figure in the room, who all this time has been crouched in a corner facing the wall, like a catatonic lunatic. "I must have him, and others also, as I cannot have you," he cries. At this I almost have to sit down on the cold flags, for I feel as though the breath has been knocked out of me and I cannot get air back in my lungs. I have the presence of mind to ask one of the gaolers to step in for it occurs to me that I am in a position now to be compromised. The fellow comes in willingly enough as for such an entertainment he wants the best seat in the house. Then I remember Mary telling me of a reprimand her sister Bridget had of Mrs. Chittleborough for some vulgar name she gave Niederer once. Mary pretended not to remember what it was, but Bridgie is not one to mince words and I wonder what life Mr. Andrews will have with her if she finally accepts him. To think that Mary was the object of one fixation whilst I was the other. "What did you hope to gain?" I ask, when I have at last recovered myself a little. At this the bluster goes out of him and he weeps. "Nothing. If you are not for me, not for her either. Blanch did not even give to me money. If he had been giving to me money it would be better; maybe a little." Only now at the sound of this sobbing does his companion look round and I see a face of such hopelessness that no painter showing the damned going down into hell could conceive of it. A boy, a wretched starveling boy. It was not even a vicious face, merely a beaten one. Did he want what Niederer offered him, or did he accept for the weight of a chop and a glass of ale in his empty innards? I could not bear the fetid air of that cell any longer, and so pressing more money into the gaoler's hand I say, "Get them food— whatever they need—both of them," and I turn to go. As I follow the man on my uncertain legs down the tunnel where I will take the turning that will lead me at last to light and air, where they must tomorrow take that which leads them to the drop, I hear Niederer screaming, "Master, I have writ you, Blanch is your enemy! It is not to forget!" and I realise that his note is the nearest he came to regret. For as long as Blanch is alive I will need to be on my guard against him, for I did not give enough import to Niederer's message then, and Mary paid the price, though when Niederer has been choked tomorrow there will be no one but myself to testify to how long it is he has plotted vendetta against me. Dearest Jack, come here quickly if you can. Mary is out with Bessie engaged on works of mercy and I would work this afternoon's events out of me properly before I trouble her with any of it.

Your friend once more in need,

James Goward

Sorry for Your Trouble

Goward Hall
14ᵗʰ September 1780

Dear Eddie,

I have news both joyful and sad. Your aunt Bridget is Mrs Andrews by a fortnight, married by Mr Griffiths in the Protestant Church. Bridgie was always of a practical turn of mind but I do not believe she turned, for she had permission of Fr. Hanlon— the priest we have now after poor Fr. O'Dowd died of the consumption—and she says it was on condition their children were brought up in the faith. I think they are like to go to England as Mr Andrews says there are places where it will be easier for them.

I wish I could tell you my other news in person, Eddie. Dadda gave Bridgie away of course, but it was one of the last things he did. A week ago your uncle Robert found him lying by the pump when he had not come down to the fields where the others were scything. His face was all darkened and Fr. Hanlon when he came said a great vein would have burst in his neck what he named an apoplexy but that Dadda would have known little for it makes for a great swoon and death comes swiftly after. When they laid him out they painted his poor purple face with china clay and a fine corpse he made for the wake, like a statue with his white face and hair and all the cares smoothed away. I could see Patrick and Robert and you, my Eddie, in that face which I could not so well when Dadda was alive.

Fr. Hanlon said the Mass in the house, the fine new one with the fanlight over the door and the staircase and all and I am glad Dadda accepted it from your father for at least he lived out his life in more comfort than in the cabin. All those years he had fretted about the land that was taken from the Kearneys but when it is yours one day it will be Kearney land again as that is the name you bear.

Your father though in his goodness takes more risks than is good for any of us. The Mass was just we Kearneys with your father and Mr. Andrews. He stood back respectfully from the sacrament but saw the Host laid upon your father's tongue but I am sure Mr. Andrews can be trusted to say nothing of it.

So with your two uncles there were four men there. Packy went to call two more from the long field so that the coffin could be closed over Dadda and him make his last journey. '

Your father insisted he carry Dadda too, even with only one good arm. So he unpinned the maimed arm and stood at the left side of the coffin and it was lifted onto his right shoulder with Mr. Andrews to balance him on the other side, and him steadying himself above with his left hand. He said he barely felt the weight of it, for as you know he has so little sensibility in that shoulder. With Patrick in front of him and another man behind and all six proceeding carefully nothing unseemly occurred. You know how our burials are here, they did not have to bear Dadda for long, for as they moved down the path and all the way to the burial ground, with Bessie and Bridget and I walking behind, the men in the fields one by one laid down their scythes and pulled off their hats and came over gates and walls and ditches each man to take his turn. So with stops and starts that journey is always a long one, but the longer it is the better the burying, for so many men wanted to show that last respect to my father by carrying him some way on their shoulders, and so most of the way your father and Mr. Andrews were able to walk with us.

At the burial ground your father said the responses as clear as any man present, and if the company there had not noted this then they cannot have failed to see him make the sign of the cross for he went to such trouble to do so, lifting his poor dead arm up and holding the fingers of his right hand in his left as though one part of him led the other in a dance, so that he should cross himself with his right hand as we all do who are not so afflicted.

I know your father wanted only to show respect to his goodfather but he thinks too much good of other people and ought to be more prudent.

Your loving mother,

Mary Goward

Going for a Soldier

École Militaire
Grenelle
4th September 1784

Dear Father,

I am safely arrived at Paris after a journey of some tedium but without mishap. I know that you do not wholeheartedly share the direction I have chosen in life but that it is typical of your generosity that not only did you not stand in my way but you have supported my decision in the belief that a man, whatever his station, must strive to better himself in the way his gifts would lead him. I am not so bold as to make great claims as to my own talents for a life in uniform, but if I do possess them, then I am convinced that this academy is the place where they may be discovered. If they are not there to be discovered, I will be the first to admit it and to return home for your better counsel, and to dry my mother's tears.

I know Mother wondered if my education might lead me to become a priest. I still hold in the greatest esteem and affection the men who taught me in Douai. Yet it is that very esteem which prevents me following their path, for I would make a poor priest beside them and do them no honour. It is though thanks to their care of me that I have made my choice; the moment my tutors recommended I also learn to fence was I believe the moment when I began to discern my future.

I hope you can forgive me for not sharing the love you have for the husbanding of your land though this in no manner diminishes my humble admiration for the changes that you and Mr. Andrews and my uncles have wrought, not least because I owe to you and them the freedom I have to follow my chosen path. If I have any good sense at all, I owe it to both you and my mother, though it shows itself in quite a different sphere. Thus in my own way I hope to put my efforts to good use in the study of military stratagems and in the leading of men. I will judge the success of this undertaking if I am able to save as many lives as I can of those who are entrusted to my command, for the best won battles must be those where a commander can bring back alive from the field as many as he can. On this matter I know we shall argue for as long as we are both alive, for I hear you asking me, as clearly as if you were sitting by me here, why those men should be brought onto a battlefield in the first place. I hope in any case that I shall acquit myself well in the next two years and that you will find reason to be proud of me. You would I am certain have the greatest respect for those who have the shaping of me as an officer, veterans of the American wars who fought for that new republic against a common enemy. Forgive me, but in France I have learned to be more candid than might be wise in Ireland.

I have commissioned a likeness of myself in uniform, a miniature that will not show my entire person but will provide some sense of the splendour of our uniforms: a blue cutaway coat edged with silver braid, a red waistcoat. I shall send with it an engraving of the Academy itself, a building as fine as anything London or Dublin can boast and of a greater scale, with vast long corridors and a chapel with the finest organ I have ever seen and all of the newest most classical design, and before it a champ de Mars for our exercises and drills that extends almost as far as the eye can see. I cannot describe to you how full my heart is when we are amassed there for manoeuvres—the blaze of colour, the glitter of our weaponry—the sound when hundreds of men present arms in the same moment, the discipline and precision of it. I hope and pray that what I learn here may one day be of benefit to Ireland. On this we may talk when next we meet.

With all my gratitude, affection and esteem,

Your loving son,

Edward Kilkeel

Goward Hall
18th October 1784

My dear boy,

I enclose this note with your mother's letter but without her knowledge. Griffiths writes it for me; he may wear his parson's bands but this makes him no less a man of the world and one of good sense. This though is an occasion which I would have spared Mr. Griffiths. Of course he smiles at me and tells me gently I may go on with whatever I want to say.

Given your determination I have no intention of standing in the way of your desire for a military career, despite your mother's pleadings. I would though repeat a father's warning to fulfil your ambitions in ways that will do least harm to others and to yourself. I know well, as you do, that cannon and musketry must by their purpose encompass the ending of human life. What I refer to though is what armies will do off the field.

You describe to me the pomp and discipline of the life in the Academy in ways that I can begin to see and share your admiration. I ask you only to remember that each man who will be under your command is a unique being, with his own hopes, fears, aspirations and loves, who has others who love him. At the same time a man will go along with his fellows if urged enough to do what he might not do if he listened only to the promptings of his own conscience. Therefore remember that a victorious army should be congratulated, but the true sign of its discipline is that murder and rapine are not its reward and any wretch in regimental colours who commits an outrage of this kind should be punished as would any other man be. I hope that the Academy will teach you also this. Every woman you come across, Edward, of whatever station she is, I impress on you to treat with the respect you would offer your mother or our dear Bessie.

You are to be an officer and I hope and pray you will distinguish yourself for your humanity and wisdom. Do not roll your eyes sir and shake your head (I know you as myself) but store up this advice for the future and let it guide you. When you are off the field I urge you also to behave with prudence, for remember that you are all your mother and I have. Remember that little package I pressed into your hand when your mother was not looking, before you departed for France that last time? When you and your friends go seeking amatory bayonet-practice (as you will, I do not doubt) I urge you to go armed, just as you would wear a visor for fencing lessons. That sheep-gut will protect you. You will have friends who may tell you that with it the pleasure is lessened. They would be right. They may not remind you however that the bedlams and poor wards are filled with poor wretches in the delirium and paralysis which is the last stage of the pox. Nor will they be there when the foundling wheel swings round in the dead of night and some poor scrap of humanity is consigned to who knows what future whilst the mother walks away weeping; not all such children are as fortunate as our Bessie. Treat Colonel Cundum, then, with the same care and attention with which you would treat your spurs and your ceremonial sword, and abandon this friend only when you one day present to your mother and I the woman you wish to marry. If the faithful Colonel is worn out by the rigours of battle, obtain another officer just as steadfast, or write me and I shall go to Belfast to where I acquired that package. I would not have you come home via Clapham.

I have been prolix, as usual, but Mr. Griffiths has been patient. Remember your father loves you with all his heart and wishes you only well in whatever you do.

Affectionately yours,

James Goward

A Death Less Mourned

Thetford
28th November 1786

My dear Goward,

I hasten to give you this news for it will bring to a close an unhappy chapter in your life and Mary's. Blanch is dead, and the manner of his death such that he was punished far more severely than had he been brought to justice for his plotting against you both.

I had read in the Norwich Courant the announcement of the death of a W. Blanch at the Norwich Bethel, noteworthy because some five years before this date this same inmate had attacked one of the warders with a scythe. This Blanch had been employed to maintain the hospital grounds as part of his treatment, being judged to be delusional but not believed dangerous; he had formerly been a bailiff to a gentleman near Diss which role he had fulfilled with a relentlessness which his employer first saw as conscientiousness but later as harshness. His increasingly erratic behaviour, obsessions with being slighted and finally unwanted advances towards the gentleman's wife led to his being forcibly admitted to the Bethel. The hospital governors had resisted having their patient brought to trial for the injury done to their man on the grounds that the patient was incapable of reason; swift intervention meant the warder made a full recovery and is still employed there, whilst Blanch was ever after kept under physical restraint. I had to know if this was your Blanch, and so travelled up to Norwich and requested an interview with the Governors. They run a model establishment, I must say, and can boast that upwards of half of their patients quit the place fully cured and able to lead useful lives. Blanch was not one of them, though, and whilst he lived the rest of his life manacled after that attack, it was clear that before long he was capable of no more harm to anyone. He died in an atrophied and catatonic state, of what they termed General Paresis of the Insane; the pox, in other words. His attendants reported that for as long as he was capable he raved about revenge on all of the female sex, but in his delirium two women were repeatedly named. One appears to be an officer's wife, and the other, oh James, our beloved Mary, though there was no love in the epithets he gave to her. Blanch believed himself to be immortal, to be possessed of extraordinary powers and untold wealth, and that when the spell put on him that kept him in that place was lifted he was to seek vengeance on all who had slighted him, but the punishment he would mete out to her would be nothing less than enslavement and abasement to his most peverted desires. As the Warden told me, "Here we hear all manner of things, and at present under this roof if they are to be believed reside Julius Caesar, St. Paul and Queen Boadicea, for the lunatic will seldom choose to be someone as ordinary as his true self. However the words of Mr. Blanch would turn a sturdy man's blood to ice." He said though there were signs that Blanch's upbringing had been that of a gentleman, but disease and deep-seated obsession and a natural predilection for cruelty had stealthily tipped him into madness. No one ever visited him and his body was not claimed; it lies in the common lime-pit.

I have made a subscription to the Bethel; I do not do this in memory of Blanch as he does not deserve such a memorial, but those who run this hospital in this most neglected field of medicine are humane and selfless men. The contrast with what we discovered in that terrible place in Wicklow could not be more marked. You told me however that Dublin now boasts a hospital for the care of the mentally afflicted that is the envy of the world, so let us hope that the dark days of the private madhouse are truly at an end, in your part of the world at least.

Please remember me to Mary and to your boy when you see him next. Peg sends all her love, but I will not let her see this letter, for I am contemplating an action that will not please her nor be in her interests, and about which I would like your counsel. I will say no more now but will acquaint you with my plans when we next meet.

Yr. aff. friend,

Jack Wickmere

"Let's sit a moment, Mary."

"You are tired, husband? Yet the frost has made the going easier today."

"It's not that. I need to tell you something."

"I thought so. There was something in Jack's last letter or you would have showed it to me."

"I think he wishes to marry."

"Oh my poor Peg."

"He wants an heir. It doesn't necessarily mean that he'll put Peg aside."

"What else could it mean? A young wife wouldn't tolerate an old mistress."

"Jack won't let Peggy starve."

"So easy for men to say these things." Mary pulled out her handkerchief. "Try to imagine her now, James, in front of her mirror in the bedroom they have shared all these years, gathering up her brushes and creams. Reaching her slippers out from under the bed and her nightdress from under the pillow she rested her head on whilst she watched him sleeping. Emptying the press of her gowns and remembering all the happy occasions she wore them. She knows the sound every door makes in that house, and now they will close behind her forever."

"I'm sure he does not take this step lightly."

"No, but he does as the world does, husband. He will be praised as a grey-haired man who takes a girl as a bride, and a pretty dowry with her, no doubt—like the one you were meant to have."

He slipped the glove from the hand he held and kissed her fingers.

"I've not regretted for a moment marrying you. God willing, we at least shall have a sweet old age, you and I. I wish only that our boy was not so far away, that is all."

"I too. I miss him every waking minute."

"There was something else in Jack's letter, Mary."

"Go on."

"Blanch is dead."

Her hand gripped his.

"Where?"

"In an English bedlam. He died raving—the last stage of the pox. Oh God, you're shivering. Let's go in and drink some brandy."

"I'm not cold. I walked barefoot on days sharper than this. God forgive me, James, but I have prayed for this news."

"We are free of him at last. Nothing and no one can harm us now."

PART THREE: REBELLION

The Courtship of an Orphan

1787

"Bessie! Wait for me, will you?"

Bessie turned reluctantly, and clutched the basket of eggs closer.

"Ah, it's you, Joe Devlin," she said, glancing over the drystone wall to see if anyone else was in sight. The sturdy young man caught up with her and stood close to her—too close—cold blue eyes fixing her from beneath sandy brows.

"Who else would it be, so? Are you not glad to see me?"

"I'm going to the Rectory," said Bessie, ignoring his question.

"I shall go with you then. I've an appointment there myself."

"Oh"

"Give me the basket."

"I don't—"

"Give me the oul' basket. I can deliver it for you. No need for you to go, so there isn't."

Bessie bit her lip and handed it over.

"Well, come with me anyway. There's something I want to say to you, Bessie. Then I can ask the Reverend something else besides what I'm going for."

"What were you going for, Joe?" she asked, walking a little faster.

"The Reverend Griffiths is instructing me, so he is."

"Is our schooling not finished?"

"In the Book of Common Prayer. In the thirty-nine articles. I am to be as much a Protestant as yourself."

"Whatever for?' she exclaimed, her hand going to her mouth.

"You don't seem very happy at this news. I thought it might please you."

"Please *me?*"

"Lord Goward explained it to me. A Catholic and a Protestant cannot wed, he says, for it is against the law, although the justices often look the other way and not hang the priest which they are meant to do. So one or the other must turn. Lord Goward says it is the first thing he would change if he had charge of Ireland. But I have been thinking a lot on this for myself. The Quality are all Protestants, like yourself, Bessie, and if a man is to succeed he must seek to emulate his betters as best he may. Even if the law were different it makes for a happier home life, I think, if husband and wife can agree—"

"Stop, Joe, I beg you. You have been talking to my guardian about *me?*"

"Sure but I have. Who else should I speak to? Your father?"

"Oh, that's cruel of you, Joe."

"Take no notice, 'tis only my jest."

"So what did Lord Goward say to you?'

"He gave me his blessing, so he did."

"I don't believe you."

"He said I'd to speak to you of course, but you'll agree what a good thing this is. I've a good tenancy, the land yields well, a fine sound house as you know. As we'd be in a manner of speaking related, then Lord Goward would look well on me and my advancement would not be long in coming. Now we can make whatever arrangements we need with the Reverend and we could be wed in September."

"*No!*"

"Aw, come on with you now—"

"No, Joe. I do not love you. I do not *like* you enough—"

"Sure you do. We were at school together—"

"I remember. You brought that poor mouse in that time and were teasing the poor creature until Mrs. Samuels took it from you. Then it died, you had frightened it so much."

"You take against me for a *mouse?*" He stared, incredulous.

"Whoever frightens the humblest of God's creatures and takes pleasure from their fear as you did, Joe, can only progress in his cruelty. I'll not be your mouse."

"They've made you soft at the Big House, so they have. You, who have no name, whose mother was—"

"Stop, Joe!"

"Or what? You'll tell on me, will you?"

"Leave me now, Joe. We will speak no more of this."

"But you'll go blabbing to the Reverend. It's him you're sweet on, then? Only a gentleman is good enough for you… you… charity child!" He crashed down the basket.

"Please go, Joe, I can see the Reverend another time. Go. He's expecting you."

"I will, so. But you'll get no better offer than you've had today."

Bessie watched his retreating back, the stiff set of his shoulders, and sank back against a gate for support. Then, "*Oh!*" Someone had pulled at her skirt. She turned round and stared down into the curly black face of a curious sheep.

"What an afternoon I've had of it, sheep. Let's see how many of these eggs he's broken."

Later, a pensive Bessie was sitting close to the window to get the last of the light for her mending, when Goward entered the drawing-room.

"Hello, Bessie. Don't let me disturb you. I'm only looking for the book I was reading."

"I'll help you look," she said, putting aside her work.

"Don't go to that trouble; it'll be here somewhere. Oh, did I tell you? The quaintest thing imaginable. You have an admirer, Bessie, and he came asking me for your hand."

"In fact he has spoken to me."

"You refused him, I expect?" said Goward, hunting behind the cushions.

"I did."

"Thought you might. He's a good tenant, but too serious. He's perhaps a better opinion of his abilities than other men would have of them. But I told him that he must speak to you, not me. You're my ward, my daughter, not a dairy cow with no mind of her own. Ah, here it is! Don't sit there long, my dear, the light is fading. You'll hurt your eyes."

His blessing, was it? Bessie sighed with relief, and picked up her work.

The Courtship of a Lady

Paris
2nd September 1788

Dear Father,

My adopted country appears to be bankrupt; the bars of the gilded cage in which the French king has lived for so long are broken and twisted, but he does not leave it, for fear of what lies outside. For if his coffers are empty, he at least has some fat about him still, both on himself and in his possessions, but the condition of his subjects, both peasantry and townspeople of the more modest sort, is indeed parlous. If the situation does not improve Frenchmen will make even Connaught men look prosperous. It may be that my own stipend will be withheld for some time, but I expect I and my regiment will continue to be fed at least, and so I do not complain. I do not tell you this in a plea for funds, Father, or at least not yet. A meeting of the Estates General has been called, for the nobility that goes for a parliament here will not bankroll the country any longer unless the King relinquish some of his most absolute powers. It is the common people who as always carry the burden for all, including Mother Church who should be the champion of the dispossessed and the downtrodden and not a beneficiary of their labour, but who thrives on tithes. Not different, you might say, from what keeps good Mr. Griffiths in his rectory, but a source of sadness to one who knows the simplicity with which Fr. Hanlon lives. This cannot continue; the country rumbles and the air is heavy, as though a storm would break at any moment. I am an officer in a French regiment; the prospect of being called to active service against Frenchmen is a real one, and fills me with horror. My fellow officers are almost to a man loyal to the King. To those whose allegiance is not so obvious I dare not speak, but in conscience I do not know how I should defend this King.

But I also write with other news, and suspect it may please you even less. I am in love, Father, and with the most delightful, amusing and handsome of women (but what man in love would not say this of his adored one?). So I must try for a better description, or find a miniaturist, for I do not know when or ever I shall be able to bring my fair one for your approval. She has a profusion of brown curls, her own, un-powdered, and tumbled upon her head in the way you like Mother to wear hers. She is a little above

the middle height, has merry brown eyes and a nose that is in the slightest degree re-
troussé. She is well-read, and speaks easily Italian and English, the latter with the most
appealing of accents, takes an interest in the affairs of this country and others which in
those of her sex are seldom encouraged, but on which she can debate as well as any man.
She dresses with restraint, in what they call the democratic fashion, which serves only
to accentuate the liveliness of her face and manner. Her name is Cécile, and appropri-
ately to her name, she is accomplished at the harpsichord and has a voice to rival a
nightingale. My adored one is the daughter of a noble in somewhat reduced circum-
stances—and the wife of another rather richer than her father but not much younger
than he. I see you, Father, with your head in your hands, groaning. I do not know what
you will want to say to my mother. It is no defence, I know, but I can at least reassure
you that her husband the Marquis is what they call complaisant, *and indeed behaves*
towards me with the greatest of civility, receiving me into his home and at his table.
Indeed, I resent a little his forbearance, for it suggests that others may have eaten his
fare and shared his wife's embraces before me. About this I do not yet have the courage
to enquire further. He loves elsewhere, a lady spoken for. He and Cécile have three
charming children and in all of them I see his lineaments, but now that his young wife
has provided him with enough heirs he graciously allows her to do as he pleases, on the
understanding that he may do the same. So there will be no pistols fired in this case, yet
my sense of adventure is such that I could almost wish he put some obstacles in my way
rather than generously wish me a good night.

    Your wayward but ever loving son,

    Edward Kilkeel

Goward Hall
20ᵗʰ October 1788

My dear boy,

    As you will recognise Mr. Griffiths's hand you will already have some idea of the
import of this letter. As your father I can only wish you happiness in anything you do.
As the father that you have and the man I have been, I am in no position to counsel
you in this affair of the heart, partly because you are inevitably in a state of mind in
which you would not listen (or what kind of love would it be that could be so readily
swayed?), and partly because I confess at your age I had a similar tail—forgive my
mischievousness—TALE to tell. I paid for my indiscretion dearly in the end, yet it led

to St. George's, Hanover Square and your mother at last appearing before the world as a respectable woman (which of course she always was). This French noble is accommodating, and this is to his credit even if it simply suits his purpose. I ask you to consider only one thing, and to reflect on the circumstances of your own birth. When I married your mother before God, it was in secret. I married as a Catholic—ah, now it is out, but my dear friend Griffiths maintains his impassive look, and scratches on. However if this were known, I could not have inherited and I could be pitched out of Goward Hall by the britches by cousin Timothy if he so desired. So for the law, you will never be any more than my natural son. I have always recognised you and for me you bear my name no matter what the lawyers have to say about it. What would your feelings be, my boy, if your dear Cécile were to conceive (as she is clearly able), for I suspect that for her you leave poor Colonel Cundum fretting his time away in your valise? Would her most civilised husband still be so accommodating if he had to feed and clothe a boy with your eyes and smile and give him his name? Many husbands do this, and some may even find the little cuckoo to be the child they love the most. If that were the case, might he then resent your presence, as he wishes to have the affection of the adored infant for himself? And how might you feel to see a child with your glance, your little ways, mannerisms your mother would recognise, with another man's name? Or this most gracious of men might take himself to a better place, for you tell me he is older than his wife but not by how much, nor how hale a man he is. Would you then wed your Cécile? I would hope that you would, but as a father (and as a man who once was young and enjoyed the opportunities the world presented him with) I must ask you if part of her allure is the fact that for the world she belongs to another man. Do forgive me this unworthy reflection, but I would not be a dutiful father if I did not express it.

I am happy for your happiness, Edward, but harbour a little resentment of the Marquise only because we will see less of you, and with it some fear that if matters take a worse turn in France, as it seems they must do, that you will remain there to be at her side when as a father I would rather you kept your own self safe by coming back to Ireland to avoid the storm. I can hear you say that an officer of the French army will not renege on his duty, but I say this only because you are my son, and as your father I have I believe a greater claim than that of duty, that of affection.

Remember that we love you, unconditionally,

Your proud father,

James Goward

"What is the Third Estate? Everything. What is it now? Nothing. What does it want to be? Something!"

– Abbé Sieyès

17th July 1789
Paris

Dear Father,

Perhaps all young men dream of being present when history is made, when they kick against a school-room desk or hear the pipes and drums of a regiment. Yet when they see it being made all around them at last, or find themselves a part of it, the sensation remains dreamlike, for that state of exhilaration and fear does not seem quite real.

History for the little Dauphin ended last month; he was seven years of age. His four-year-old brother the Duke of Normandy will succeed his father—if he does. The King snubs the deputies of the Third Estate, the nobility will not talk with them, and the clergy hesitates. The old prison was stormed and a handful of inmates set free, but its governor and the provost of the city were beaten to death by the mob and their heads paraded on poles. Twenty-five workers die in street battles with the police, but did not know quite what they fought for except that there be change.

Lives end well or badly and other lives begin. Cécile is with child. You are to be a grandfather.

Your loving son,
Edward Kilkeel

The Gentleman's Magazine

and

Historical Chronicle

For the Year MDCCXC

Volume LX

Dec. 13 1789 at Dorking, Surr., aged 72, Mrs. Eliz. Dallowes, relict of Dr. D. of Epsom, and the only surviving daughter of the late Sir John Hartopp, bart. Her death was occasioned by her shawl taking fire whilst sealing a letter.

15 at Goward Hall, in the County Down in Ireland, aged 76, Dowager Lady Emma Goward, relict of Lord John Goward and daughter of the late Sir Toby Fielding of Castle Acre, Norfolk, mother of Lord James Goward, of an apoplexy.

18 In his seventy-third year, his serene Highness Prince Christopher, of Baden Dourlach, field-marshall and master-general of the ordnance in the Austrian service...

"Thank you, Griffiths, for your kind words."

"Your mother deserved better than my feeble efforts. She will be much missed."

"A lady of the old school; she found the world around her less recognisable by the day. She warned me, you know, the day that my father was buried, against my meddling and my ideals. She believed that they did not serve."

"One cannot help but meddle, Lord Goward. It is impossible to stand to one side in the game of life as it is now played."

"That is my view, indeed. Will you come and dine with us, Griffiths?"

"Gladly. If I may just arrange the sealing of the vault, sir?"

"By all means. Mary and I intend to stay outside that quiet little chamber for a little longer, do we not, dearest?"

"Do not talk so. It does not fall to us to know the times or the seasons."

"But I am sure we can influence it. You weep for my mother, so let us not add fear to our sadness. I spoke only in jest, and this is not a day for jesting."

" What is it they call what I must be now? Like the lady that has all the keys at her belt. Shatty?"

"Châtelaine, Mary, or as the Italians have it, castellana."

"Castellana is easier on my tongue. I've never understood why the French eat half their words nor where they put the letters they have chewed off."

"Ask Edward."

"I cannot. I fear him a little when he speaks the French. His face and his manner changes, and he seems less my son, though a fine man in either tongue. So I must be this castellana."

"Not if you don't wish it. I am not sure that I do either. I want you as my companion, the lady who takes my hand in hers when we walk the lanes, who shows me I am still loved behind the curtains and does not berate me because my sap does not rise as readily as once it did, and who smiles at me over the breakfast board as if we were married a mere two months and not upwards of twenty years."

17th January 1790
Paris

Dear Father,

Forgive my brevity. For a matter of hours I knew what it was to be a father. I had a daughter but my poor little scrap of humanity did not hold to life even a day. Tell Mother she was baptised, with the name Marie, and so sings with the angels. Cécile is distraught but will live, the Marquis grave and kind. I did not know such grief was possible. I shall strive to be a better son.

With love and sorrow,

Edward Kilkeel

4th September 1790
Nancy

Dear Father,

I have been an unwilling witness to an execution of such brutality and horror that its means could only have been conceived in an innermost circle of Hell. My fellow officers remain loyal, but the common soldier chafes and in desperation reacts knowing that he cannot succeed in overturning his servitude but he cannot fail to try. Three regiments in this city mutinied, one of them composed of Swiss mercenaries, in normal times the most docile of all the infantry, and the National Assembly's retribution has been swift and merciless. So much for declaring the rights of man and of the citizen; the poor soldier it seems is made the exception, and so also, the African slave. People riot for bread while others protest the measures taken against Church property, though so often the Church is not their friend but their oppressor. The King loses power by the day and is not free even to decide where he may live. A revolution that began with the declared aim of freedom of creed and conscience for all men—so much to be wished for in Ireland also—has now made the ordination of a priest or the taking of religious vows an offence. Whoever had retreated behind the walls of monastery or convent is now turned out upon the world as undefended as a fledgling fallen too early from the nest; what freedom of conscience is this if one is only really free to have none at all?

Here at Nancy this mutiny might have ended quietly had a stray shot fired by a panicking foot soldier not killed an officer who sought to negotiate, for pandemonium followed and some five hundred men are now dead. A score or more of the rebels twist in clusters from the gallows, like polony sausages hung up to cure, and still more will spend the rest of their lives in hard labour, but their ringleader was broken on the wheel in the public square. I shall hear the poor wretch's shrieks forever, Father, for they smashed every bone, every joint in his body with a hammer before delivering the coup de grâce to his head. I am afraid I disgraced myself as an officer, by behaving as a man, vomiting my breakfast over the cobbles, and was laughed at. I believe I must be more circumspect in what I write. I pray you not be anxious if you do not hear regularly from me.

Your loving son,
Edward Kilkeel

"Mary, I didn't want you to read that. I meant to spare you."

"Doesn't he know that I think of him in every waking moment, whatever I am about? I'm a tougher woman than he thinks, James, but not to know the horrors he sees, the risks he runs, is worse still. You took an awful long time, James, to tell me about the poor wee babby, but I saw your pain in your face and your silences and in everything you did. Don't shut me out, husband, trust me as you trust so many that perhaps you should not."

"Mary? I know you do not sleep; I sense your wakefulness on your very skin. Will you hold me? No, not out of obedience, I beg you. I need your comfort. Hold me close, as if you would never let me leave you. I can promise you no fireworks; your poor bull is tired and sad, but he wants to know he is loved."

"What are the rights of man, and how came man by them originally?"

– Thomas Paine

14 Berkeley Square
2nd September 1791

Dear Wickmere,

I hope my godson knows how very attached I am to him; young Charles is a lively little boy with a quick wit and an affectionate nature. He is his father's son in more than just name. When he is older I pray that we may at last welcome you both to Goward Hall. However, I do not hold out hope that this will be soon, for from what you tell me Lady Wickmere grows fretful at the time she is obliged to spend in Norfolk and is happy only when she glitters here in town— and glitter she does, Jack, for I have never denied your lady is a handsome woman— and thus she would be loath to accompany you to what she would with reason declare a hopelessly rustic situation.

Speaking of Norfolk, yesterday I made the acquaintance of a most singular man, much travelled (to the Americas and to France) but who hails from Thetford and I believe to be of quite humble beginnings. He is an agitator and a pamphleteer: Tom Paine, the same who worked so tirelessly that America might no longer bow to our indisposed sovereign. He has a most direct gaze, with what I took to be the slightest mocking smile but which is simply the natural arrangement of his features, and when he talks he holds his head a little to one side, which taken with the brightness of his eye reminds one of a raven. He is radical not only in politics but in creed, or rather the lack of one, yet will quote scriptural arguments to reinforce his own. It was young Fitzgerald who introduced him to me at the house of a firebrand of a bookseller where he is paid court to by a veritable swarm of radicals, writers, freethinkers and the occasional blue-stocking. Naturally he showed great interest in events in Ireland, though has the wit to understand that we are not merely a smaller edition of the Americas. and in your humble correspondent (the more so, Fitzgerald murmured to me, because I am married to my former servant). Fitzgerald himself invites either suspicion or admiration depending on whoever expresses an opinion, for his wife is a Frenchwoman and his ebony servant a freed slave. Mary did not accompany me there, for though she has enough native wit and good sense to hold her own with any of them, she prefers not to be what she would term forward (and she of course frowns at me now as she puts my words down).

Of my son in France I did not speak with them; I do not hear from him enough but he has the wisdom now to be discreet when he does write, and I for my part would not put down anything that would place him at any risk. It is easier for some to be enthusiastic with their words in the name of a greater good, when that good may be of little benefit to those others who are directly caught up in such a turbulent reality. But come with me, Jack, the next time I pay a visit to this lively circle in Marylebone, and let me know what you make of these idealists. Your little son is merry, but I do not find you so. I do not complain of this or demand that you paint a smile on your face; it grieves me not to see you in your usual good spirits. I am as always your affectionate friend as you have ever been to me,

    James Goward

14 Berkeley Square
7th September 1791

Dear Jack,

    I can conceive of no hell worse than an ill-combined marriage, though with yours you have done only what polite society expected of you, and married "well." It pains me to witness the price you have to pay for this. Hold to what you have gained from it, Jack; you have your heir and the little lad would be the envy of any man, and your wife's wealth has secured your land for him and with it the livelihood of all that labour thereon. This peace of mind, to say nothing of your grip on immortality on earth in the only way permitted us, is worth much.

You have behaved in what the world calls an honourable way by poor Peg. There are few in her position who could aspire to a simple home, a pension, and a life of quiet retirement. Is it easy though for you to cancel decades of companionship and shared experience? Jack, from what you say you do your duty by Lady Honoria. She has the title and standing she craved, and has thus neatly cancelled out her grandfather's modest origins (though I incline to admire a man who proved his worth as he did in the Indian service). You have fulfilled your part of the bargain, Jack, and so has she. You owe each other nothing now but appearances, so I beg you, leave your wife to her salons and journey out to Norfolk and call on that lady in her cottage whom I would wager loves you still despite your faults. When you do, tell Peg that we love her also and that Mary misses her greatly, for when she left her world and joined ours, Peg was her first friend and remains the closest to her heart. We have both seen how Honoria regards Mary; she would cut her directly were she not my wife and as it is will honour her only with the most distant nod when their paths happen to cross. But know Jack that you are always welcome under our roof here or in Ireland, whether you come alone or with whoever you choose to bring with you.

I could not but notice your reserve at our little soirée in Marylebone which I put down to your heaviness of heart, but when you said afterwards "Honoria would not approve" you said it with some of your old merriment and I saw again for a moment the happy Jack I have always known.

You will rightly though tell me I am an old fool to be so taken up with the ideas of this Norfolk stay-maker and that England is not France. But Ireland is neither, and it is there that his words appeal to me. You are used to the sturdy Norfolk yeomen and hale peasants on your land. Our Irish tenantry are but miserable specimens besides them. As a boy I saw them only when they crept round to the back of the Hall to pay their rents, when Mother would occasionally waylay the most desperate looking of them and press their rents into their hands—unbeknownst to my father, and later done to spite Blanch whom she could not abide. It was a most singular proceeding but one she justified to me by saying that she had brought my father wealth and she would have the spending of it as she saw fit whatever the law said. But until I met Mary I did not know how the tenants were compelled to live. Had you seen the poverty of her father's cabin, you would wonder like me at how such a graceful and beautiful creature as my

Mary could have ever have issued from such a place. Our dogs were better kennelled and better nourished. Mary's family were clothed thanks to Quaker charity, but this we did not know nor cared to in the Big House though it was my father's manservant who had drawn the attention of his co-religionists to their need. Yet it is the fashionable belief amongst those Irish landowners who throng London in the season that these people bring their misery on themselves, through poor self-management, superstitious religion, profligacy and that fire-water they distil from the few potatoes they do not consume themselves. Yet with the right instruction I have seen them achieve much and gain much satisfaction and comfort thereby. Andrews before he returned to England man-aged great things, and did so with tact and patience which Blanch lacked entirely, and his successor as my agent is an Irishman. Their priests, at least those whom I have met, have struck me as able men who achieve much in their way in the most difficult of circumstances. They are forced to be trained abroad for the most part, and return with a learning superior to anything taught by Cam or Cherwell, to labour in the most meagre of vineyards. Am I about an apologia for Catholicks? No, Jack, though my son has been educated as one, for to bring him up for Rome is something I can do for my wife. Yet though freeborn this means he cannot cast his vote. My neighbour Lord Moira is vociferous in the House on the subject of Catholick empancipation, but is regularly shouted down. Do I wish that the priests hold sway in Ireland in affairs of state? Again no, for I have seen what power can do to good men and would not want to see in Dublin or Belfast any of the pomp and show you and I have seen in Rome. Yet our Anglican bishops in Ireland as in England live in near-papal splendour, though in Ireland they tend very small flocks for the most part. There is something in Paine's disdain for the trappings of religion that is attractive to me, yet such thoughts frighten me. Edward tells me what happens in France, for there they vie with King Henry's greed and the Protector's zeal for who can do their worst when men are told they may not worship according to the dictates of their conscience. But at the base of all my mus-ings, Jack, is the question that leaves me more perplexed than about anything else: am I an Irishman, or an Englishman? Must one always be profited from, and the other profit? I would fain see you again soon, Jack. What say you to our usual place in the back room of The Ensign? Send me word and we can meet there for supper tonight.

Your affectionate friend,

James Goward

16th December 1791

Paris

Dear Father and Mother,

My regiment is to be deployed in a new army to defend France's borders. For reasons of discretion I will say no more here, but I am glad of this order, for it is proper soldier's work. The King is in effect a puppet for he must accept what the Assembly direct him to do, and change does happen, though stealthily. A Jew is now a citizen of France, as is any man living here, no matter what his hue. But priests must swear loyalty to government above that of loyalty to Rome, and slavery can persist unchecked in French dominions beyond our borders. Is what we cannot see to be our yardstick, not that of conscience?

My Cécile believes that the person of the King is safe, for no one would risk making a martyr of him, yet he becomes less regal by the day. My adored Champ de Mars where I first strutted as a boy officer so proudly, was theatre of a brutal put-down of unarmed citizens who went there to sign a petition for his removal. The thought that the National Guard should be deployed on such a barbaric and unsoldierly task utterly revolts me.

I cannot ask a blessing of either of you on my continued union with Cécile but I hope that the comfort and tranquillity she offers me in these difficult times will raise your opinion of her a little. To my sorrow I fear that there will be no tiny occupant of the cradle prepared for our poor Marie. Cécile has been with child twice since we lost our daughter, but God has willed it that each budding soul should sigh and die within her. Perhaps it is better thus; these are uncertain days. I shall miss Cécile sorely when I join the regiment on this latest undertaking—the Marquis too, for he has gone from being merely complaisant *to being the firmest of friends. Naturally, I miss you both, every day I live, and you and all whom I love at home are ever in my prayers.*

Your loving son,

Edward Kilkeel

"What is a mother to think, James? It grieves me to think of him with another man's wife. But am I to be glad that he is to be taken from her side only for him to go marching into battle?"

"There is no battle as yet, they go only to defend France's border."

"I am not a man, and don't know anything about military matters. But when my father put up walls on his few acres—Goward acres, I should say— it was not only for to keep his beasts in, it was to keep his neighbour's beasts from trampling all over. There'll be good reasons for this defence, so there will; they fear something."

"We can only hope and pray. But if he is glad of this turn of events, perhaps we should be too. Would you humour me in something? For once it is not friend bull who speaks. Christmas is almost upon us and again Edward won't be with us. If the sky does not threaten us too much ill tomorrow, let us quietly go as an old married couple should, on a little pious outing and say a quiet prayer for our boy. That is if you could bear to?"

"You want us to go to Struell?"

"I do. Have we let enough time elapse?"

"I mind not what anyone may remember of that day now. Even with all the badness that happened then, what I remember most and treasure in my heart is Edward quickening in my belly; he protested at the shock of that cold water. I should be glad to go. We may remember both our mothers there."

"I am not suggesting either of us take the baths this time."

"In December, no. But we could do the penance."

"Penance?"

"Seven times around St. Patrick's chair on a path of sharp stones."

'What, *barefoot*?"

"Ah, no. On your knees."

"Have we really been so wicked?"

"O Liberté, que de crimes on commet en ton nom!"

– Madame Roland, on her way to the guillotine

The Gentleman's Magazine

and

Historical Chronicle

For the Year MDCCXCIII

Europe, since the period when it was overrun by the Goths and Vandals, has never experienced more alarm and danger than at the present moment—Religion, Manners, Literature and the Arts, are all equally menaced by a foe, whose characterisk is a compound of impetuosity, ignorance and crime... what would even the magnanimity of Britons avail against the venom of poison mysteriously prepared, and communicated with the malignant silence of assassins? Yet such is the natural operation of these new-fangled doctrines, this strange and heterogeneous philosophy, which has deluged France with blood...

– Sylvanus Urban

"The French king is dead, Mary."

"And his lady?"

"They hold her, and their children. I do not see that she will survive; they are too many who bay for her blood."

"The poor weans."

"There are some who will take heart from this terrible news, and push for revolution here. They look to France's declaration of war on England and long for their success. Patrick tells me that liberty, equality, fraternity, are words often spoken in the rudest of cabins. Don't look so frightened, Mary, for those few of our own tenants who might talk in this way would expect me to join them more than be overthrown by them."

"That troubles me more."

"Mary, if a man is treated honestly and kindly he will not think of revolution; if he is not, then it is my belief he will think of little else. The priests though look at France with dread and would swear allegiance to any Protestant king to not see the Mass-houses, so hardly won, desecrated, nor the religious turned out of their poor convents."

"Surely nobody would turn out Mother Catherine?"

"Why would they? She and her daughters have nothing to steal and do great service. They don't have fine buildings or wealth for others to covet. I fear though for those silent men who welcomed Jack and I and Abercrumbly all those years ago; I can only pray the remoteness of their home saves them. There is so little news; Edward's letters are ever more brief. I fear what he does *not* tell us."

!If we didn't have those, I don't know how I should still live."

"But we do have them. And all governments need an army, little though we might like that fact. His uniform protects him so long as he does what his government expects and doesn't set himself against it. What he saw in Nancy was a message for him too."

Goward Hall
14th January 1794

Dear Jack,

Our son has been restored to us, but not as yet to himself. It is all too extraordinary to believe; I half fear that I shall retire tonight and wake in the morning and find that I have dreamt his presence, that he has never been back under our roof. The entire household was asleep when some time in the smallest hours a mighty knocking at the main door roused us all. Patrick was first on the scene bearing an ancient arquebus that must have come over here with the Dutchman, and which he proceeded to fire through the fanlight above our front door, "For to show himself out there we can defend ourselves." We await the glazier this afternoon. He then roared to the intruder to "Get away out of there!" I urged caution, for had our visitor wished to murder us all in our beds he would not have been announcing the fact by hammering at the front door but would have crept in around the back. Hugh (the spaniel) soon added his contribution to the mayhem, so that it was impossible to hear anything from the other side of the door, only that someone was there, crying out. Finally I threw caution to the winds and opened the door. A tall man stood there alone, trembling with cold or fear I am not sure which, though with Packy's firing and the fact he was wrapped in a heavy cloak I think the latter. He raised his hands above his head and beseeched us, "Do not shoot, for the love of God!" My son, my poor boy, with a voice I barely recognised, for it was weary and hopeless, the voice of a much older man. I clasped him to me, and pitifully thin he felt. Our Edward, from whom we had heard so little for so long, letters on which we felt a censor's gaze, and for whom we feared who knows what fate. I held him for a moment only, for I had to bring his mother to him, and so exhorting Patrick to find him some rapid restorative, I thundered up the staircase only to find Mary already coming down, candle in hand, though I had begged her to stay abed.

"It is he," said she, "I knew he would come. St. Anthony never fails."

Jack, our boy is much altered. He has been in hiding. The woman he loved is dead—guillotined. They took her husband first and then came for her, on the charge that she had attempted to hide him. If she had, then she made a poor job of it, for they arrested him at home without hindrance. She was taken instead most probably to prevent her from communicating with others deemed conspirators. Edward was at this time stationed at Wissembourg with his regiment. His commanding officer had got wind of the arrests of all the Girondin faction, of which the Marquis and his wife were a part, and urged Edward to flee, officially granting him leave of absence to attend to French business in Ireland. Edward raged about going to Paris and liberating his lady, and would not see reason until his superior coolly pulled rank and told Edward that if he did not control himself he would find himself on a charge of insubordination. Once Edward had mastered himself this enterprising man arranged for false papers with which our son made his way into Germany, north to Hamburg and hence to a passage from Cuxhaven.

Not only was Edward gaunt from poor nourishment, but dirty, dishevelled and utterly exhausted in body and spirit. Yet he bears himself well, like a Frenchman indeed, and moreover, like a French officer and nobleman. His hair is long and curling, in the French style, free of powder, but not free of grey though he is not yet thirty.

He had need of all his wits about him on his journey, for were he taken for an emigré by the wrong persons then his life was surely in danger. If he were taken for an Englishman then he would be believed to be an enemy spy. So much of the time he posed as an Irishman, which he is, and a merchant of Belfast, which he has never been, caught up in events that had prevented his return home to his linen business. Yet the most testing part of his journey he tells me was that last crossing of the Irish Sea, delayed by inclement weather as it was, because he was by then so close to home and so impatient to be here. I have asked him why he did not warn us of his arrival. I shudder when I think of his uncle's zeal with that antique fire-arm (I must ask Packy how he came by it) and he grows pale again and says that he has learned to trust no one. I, on the other hand, trust everyone, which no doubt one day will land me in trouble, and to hear him talk so makes me think him the father and I the son for his experience has aged him beyond his years.

Mary, however, is become a girl again (though for me she always was). She sits by him and hangs on his every word and will not let go his hand (though I see that when he is in this way chained to his better parent, he becomes calmer). He asked to be put in his old room, just as he did when he was a little boy still, back from his schooling in Picardy, and then asked though that a second bed be prepared there for he fears to sleep alone. His uncle Patrick will keep him company; he will do better than I, for he will ask fewer questions. Edward has cried on all our necks: Bessie's and Meg Samuels's too. Tomorrow I will ask Griffiths to call but for today I think Edward has had enough to think on. When he gets up from his chair and relinquishes his mother's hand, it is to touch restlessly everything in the house that he remembers, as if to ensure himself of their continued existence, or his own. If there is anything moved, then he wants to know why, and puts it back where it sat in his memory.

I am a father, Jack, and you know the joy that brings.

Your affectionate friend,

James Goward

Goward Hall
21ˢᵗ June 1794

Dear Jack,

Our son becomes more like his old self by the day, but I do not believe he will ever be quite as he was before: he has seen too much. He is given to spending more time alone than ever used to be his wont, going for long rambles, or sometimes calling on Griffiths at the Rectory and engaging him in long arguments about what our purpose on earth might be. He has taken up again a pastime which was favoured by him as a boy at school. Not fencing this time, but sketching. We intend to cross to England soon and pass a short and retired season in London and whilst Edward will accompany us on the crossing he asks leave to take his sketch book and etching plates and see what he can find of the sublime in Wales. Griffiths has arranged for him to visit his brother's seat in Shropshire before he sets off on his little tour so we will have some report of how he fares in normal society beyond the family hearth. His mother is anxious that he should be so much alone on this tour; first she feared that he would fall too much into melancholy, but now she fears his increasing restlessness, as do I. Now we pause and look at each other as Mary writes this for me; with all our hearts we would have him contemplate the making of history from a prudent distance rather than again play an active rôle in it. For my part, I consider history has already caused him enough suffering. You will have read of the death of the journalist Desmoulins; Edward had no love for him for he blamed him for the deaths of his Cécile and her husband. Now he too has gone under the blade, screaming and struggling at the end when told his wife had been arrested. If this diabolical Robespierre can thus order the death of the friend of his infancy, the father of his own godson—now an orphan entirely—then what future has anyone in France? This tyrant champions freedom for slaves in French colonies but kills Frenchmen by the hundred if he suspects them of either moderation or radicalism. No one is safe; we must hold fast to Edward as long as we can. What of Ireland looking on at these events? I observe how this island is governed, by men who take what it yields yet seldom set foot in it. The Presbyterians who by their probity and industry have brought prosperity to towns where there was little, often suffer the same disabilities as their Catholic neighbours. The breath of liberty reaches them from across the Atlantic, and a stronger revolutionary wind blows from France. Greater men than I will emerge to demand rights for them, yet I will look at them and wonder if any may prove to be an Irish Robespierre, for whom all that counts is power at any cost. What I am not permitted to be is indifferent; I could pin my hopes on whoever I think may be victorious in any coming fight, or pin my hopes on whomever I believe in my heart to be right. Edward murmurs that his place is with his regiment, for France is not only menaced from Flanders by England but also in the east by Prussia and Austria. Mary was right of course: no army is sent to defend a border unless an attack is feared. I beg him though to remember what is also due to his parents and to restrain his ardour a little longer, at least until the action of that deadly blade slows. I wish most that he might fall in love in Wales, and want no more to leave, but see that he will not or cannot turn his poor murdered Cécile out from his heart just yet.

What news, Jack? Shall we see you next month in town?

Your troubled but always affectionate friend,

James Goward

Recalled to Arms

18th November 1795

"Father, I am come to bid you farewell."

"I know. I've known it since that letter came ten days ago. All your thoughts have been elsewhere. I have been expecting this news since Robespierre's fall. There were moments when I wished even that devil with all his works longer life, for as long as he lived, you might go on living here. But every man must have a purpose, Edward, and you're as recovered as you will ever be, though you will never be the same as once you were."

"I have been asked to return. I am told I am needed. I have been given to understand that their plans for me include Ireland."

"I don't think your correspondents intend merely to flatter you. But if you know any more I beg of you not to tell me, for what I don't know, I cannot be prevailed upon to repeat."

"Then all I will say is that I believe Bonaparte is the coming man. We were boys together at Grenelle, when we were both still shaving for a beard. I could not shine beside him, the most able pupil of our year. France won't be enough for him."

"Do not play Danton to his Robespierre, Edward."

"I am a soldier, not a statesman. Nor am I a farmer. I fret."

"Then God go with you. Let us go and tell your mother. She will weep but not stand in your way."

Goward Hall
9ᵗʰ January 1796

Dearest Peg,

This Christmastide has been a bleak one for me. I think often of you in your cottage and pray that you are not too much alone and that you want for nothing except of course Jack's company which I wish he had never taken from you—and which I am sure he regrets but does not know how to frame this in words.

Edward has gone from us back to France. James did all he could to interest our son in his projects but although he is Thomas Kearney's grandson he does not feel the same tie to the earth of we Kearneys but longs to be back in uniform. Though he looks an Irishman I believe he thinks and feels like a Frenchman. When he was first home he couldn't sleep well for the horrors he had seen and whenever he did would talk and sometimes shout but always in French. In his way he is as much the idealist as his father. I fear for both of them, the one in his uniform and the other in his study with those pamphlets he reads and those men he meets up in Belfast, from where he returns with a look on his face that frightens me.

I do not live alone, but sometimes I feel alone, dear Peg, and I pray you forgive me because I write this to one who now unwillingly leads a solitary life. Three days ago our dear Meg Samuels left us forever, and though I think I will never leave off crying for her it was a merciful release. She was eaten up by a canker which began in her womb, says Dr. Benson. The poor lady had always longed for a child who never came. I wonder if we poor women in reflecting upon how our frail bodies fail us do in dwelling on our infirmities feed them. Her suffering was cruel though Dr. Benson did not stint her in opiates. He gave her so much in her last days that there was nothing could be done but hold her hand and listen to the space between each breath get wider and wider for she could not speak but I pray she knew we were with her. I loved her as I loved my mother, God rest her also, Peg. I think her the kindest and most generous woman I've known. Her life was not an easy one: a husband often angry and more wedded to his bottle, an empty cradle. But instead of kicking against her lot she gave all that was in her to the instruction of the poorest children no matter what religion their mothers and fathers professed. The Governors of the Charter School came after her more than once saying she should be making Protestants of those children that were not. James supported her in every way and the school will go on. Some of the teachers are children she had the instructing of herself. James says that the new Ireland will depend on the work of such as they. He talks much about the new Ireland.

So they are all gone now, my good-mother Lady Goward, Mrs. Chittleborough and now Meg Samuels. I do not know what I should do without your friendship, Peg, though we are countries apart. I think of you daily and fall eagerly on your letters hungry for another budget of the news of you and your neighbours in Methwold. It must be a dear quiet place from the way you talk of it, more dear as you are in it. You pray my patience, saying you are tedious, but indeed your letters are anything but. They give me relief in anxious times for I fret about the tales I hear from beyond the demesne walls though blessedly all within it and all who work the Goward fields would seem to lead peaceful and contented lives. With your words I am also able for a wee while to divert James from some other matters that occupy him, and which I wish did not.

Yours affectionately,
Mary Goward

Goward Hall
4th April 1796

Dearest Peg,

Belfast comes to us now. There are men who ride up to the Offices by the back roads and gather in our kitchens to talk and bang their cups on the table. James takes my hands when I ask about them and tell me that they are educated men, many of them, lawyers and doctors, and reminds me that when he went to Fr. O'Dowd to ask for me, he vowed he would fight that nevermore should anyone live as we did in that cabin, and that they will fight with him. There are times when I think it was better I should have committed a mortal sin and let him put his hands on me so he'd never have thought of marrying me after, but could have gone on living as he did behind the wall of the Big House without a care for what happened beyond it.

I have never been so frightened.

A Protestant Wind

"The wind continues right ahead, so that is it absolutely impossible to work up to the landing-place, and God knows when it will change... Had we been able to land the first day and march directly to Cork, we should have infallibly carried it by a coup de main, and then we should have a footing in the country; but as it is—if we are taken, my fate will not be a mild one...'

– Diary of Theobald Wolfe Tone, off Bantry Bay, Christmas Day, 1796

4th January 1797

"Mary, he lives! Our boy lives! Look, all this time he was in this place called Kehl. He was never with the French fleet, never near Ireland. He writes in high dudgeon, saying that this was the least successful engagement of his career. I can almost see him scowl, the way he does when he looks most like a Kearney: *"The siege has ended,"* he writes, *"though we came so close to twitting our besiegers. In the end all we could tell our men to do was to make a Carthage of the fortress so that we would cede the Austrians nothing but rubble and a fistful of flies. All our military skill engaged in seeing how much we could blow up, how quickly. This is not what I call soldiering."* Oh, Mary, hold me—yes, cry, my darling. Edward is alive. You have been so strong but now we can be as weak as kittens if we want. Our son breathes, and walks, and gets angry."

"May God forgive me for rejoicing when so many mothers' sons are drowned, only he was not one of them."

"That fleet came so close; had the winds blown differently then French boots would be marching through Dublin by now. I take heart that the Directory were pleased to look so favourably on Ireland's request and might do so again."

"Ireland's request? You talk as one who knows more than he's been saying."

"Forgive me, Mary, I am probably talking nonsense again, merely musing aloud on matters that concern greater men than I. But even if this invasion has failed utterly, the conditions that make it necessary have not." He grasped her upper arms. "Ireland interests revolutionary France, Mary, whether we like it or no. The French see us as the little boy who can squeeze through the bars of the kitchen window and open the front door to his confederates whilst the household sleeps. Take Ireland and they can overcome England next. Ireland's reward will be her liberty at last."

"Do you know this? Or will one empire be replaced by another?"

"I'm no soothsayer, but we must look for the next favourable wind or stay as we are. Mary, before we married, Fr. O'Dowd, God rest him, spared me no detail of the risk I would run in turning, and in uniting myself to you. It's true that things are changing: a Catholic may set up a school these days, even without the gracious permission of the Protestant bishop. In Kildare they have a seminary now. I may ride as good a horse as Lord Bangor or any other Protestant neighbour. Patrick can take a lease of an unreclaimed bog, if he so desires. Robert could go to the bar, if he were so minded. And at last a man may ask a woman to make him happy without one of them having to renounce what a mother and father had taught their child in good conscience."

"Then should we not be content?"

"You know we cannot be. Those measures were very successful in their purpose, of making an Irishman poor, unlettered, unable to resist whatever his oppressors had in mind for him. That changes have been made at all has been due in part to enlightened and merciful Englishmen. But there are many who are not, and who may haunt gaming tables and bordels and never do a hand's turn for another man because Irish tenantry do it all for him. Until a Catholic has a voice—a vote—then matters stand still or must wait on Protestant men of principle. Remember when Fitwilliam was recalled to London leaving all Dublin decked in mourning, for insisting that nothing less than Catholic emancipation could prevent unrest? He was right, and so was regarded as too dangerous to be Lord Lieutenant by all the vested interests that hold Ireland down. By failing to act I believe it is London brings the French army to these shores. I see the fear in your eyes, Mary, and your wish that I would confine myself to the betterment of our little corner of this island and its inhabitants, and leave the pamphletting and speeches to younger men who have the full use of their limbs. But I cannot. There are too many wrongs to be righted for me to hide behind my demesne wall, when your brothers have more right to this land than I."

"I am fearful. I fear those things you read and those gentlemen who come here."

"Remember Orr!"

Goward Hall
19th October 1797

Dear Jack,

My faithful scribe tells me I should not disturb you with these matters, yet her real meaning is that she wishes I would let them alone myself. Three days ago in a neighbouring county a man was hanged for administering an oath, for such can be a capital offence in this country. I took sufficient interest in his case to ride up and attend his trial last month and that there was some time between sentence and execution led many to believe that clemency might be shown.

This Orr was a towering and impressive figure of a man, of most handsome aspect, a Presbyterian farmer's son, dressed to restrained perfection, but the sobriety of his attire relieved by a green cravat proclaiming where his sympathies lay. He stood accused of administering the oath of allegiance of the United Irishmen to a soldier in a Scotch regiment. He was most ably defended by a gentleman whom I would want on my side were I ever to face such an awful test, a Trinity man by the name of Curran whose occasional fault of a stammer only forces his hearers to pay him greater attention. This Curran argued that the entire proceedings were not of proper legal form and thus by their very nature conspired against justice. It was so evident to anyone who wished to open eyes and ears that the chief witness was forsworn and the jury, when they returned their verdict, in drink. Though proclaiming his guilt, they recommended mercy, but the Judge, weeping profusely, pronounced sentence of death all the same. Furthermore, it is reported that two jurymen came forward later and on oath swore that their foreman made threats to both their persons and their property, claiming that only a disloyal man could fail to find Orr guilty. To see the machinery of the law which should protect all men of whatever confession used in the most foul way, to hang a man and to hear any voice of dissent called "disloyal" is not something a gentleman, be he an Irishman or an Englishman, can ignore. Here poor Mary urges me to contain myself as she claims I am fairly shouting in my indignation. Pressure was brought to bear on this Orr in his confinement to make confession of the crime he was found guilty of, with the induce-

ment that his life might thus be spared, but he was steadfast in his profession of inno-
cence and in his accusations of a forsworn witness and a packed jury, and so he is made
a martyr. Ireland forments, Jack, and Mary trembles. I urge her to take comfort from
the fact that I am no longer a young man, and am furthermore crippled, and so may
not take arms in my enthusiasm and indignation, as I might once have done, but I see
her look at me askance. She knows me well. I will send word to Edward that he stay in
France longer; by now he has passed more time in that country than he has in his own
and must be wholly the Frenchman in speech and manners. Write me Jack of the doings
of young Charles, and when you see our dear Peg pass to her all our love. Has Lady
Honoria returned from town or are you free to do as you please for a little longer? Here
Mary frowns at me for my levity.

    Your affectionate friend always,

    James Goward

Protection

"What is it, Packy?"

"There's three men to see you."

"What appearance have they?"

"One of them is armed. I don't know them but don't like the look o' them. If I'd met them on the road I'd take them for foot-pads. I have left them out the back for they came through the Offices."

"You did right. Leave them there and tell them I will be with them directly, but look for Robert and old McNamara's new boy, whatever he's called, and have one of these pistols. I'll take the other."

"My name is Lamont, sir, and I'm a loyal servant of the king."

"I'm sure you are, Mr. Lamont. And your colleagues? Gentlemen, will you not also be seated?"

"Begging your pardon, sir," said Lamont, "they will stay standing. At the ready, as you might say."

"In my agent's office? As you wish. Now could you please state your business?"

"We have come to offer you our services." Lamont smiled, and Goward recoiled at the odour of rotting teeth. "Our peace is threatened, sir, by those they call United Irishmen, who even find Presbyterians in their ranks but we know them for Jacobin traitors who look to France and revolution. They ferment the people against their proper place and would bring down the rule of law. My men and I—we are numerous, each man of a size with Mr. Warnock here," and he indicated with a movement of his head the ox of a man standing at his right shoulder— "we aid the yeomanry in their work of searching for arms."

"You'll find none here, Lamont."

"Ah, no sir, you misunderstand me. That's not what we're here for at all, not in the house of a gentleman. But yesterday we discovered thirty pikes in a barn behind Bryansford, such as would be used against you, sir, and your honourable wife, for the Papists are awful roused up by their priests and these gentleman agitators who would have this island invaded by Frenchmen and us all murdered in our beds."

"My wife is what you call a Papist."

"Begging your pardon, sir, for I do get carried away when I think of the threat to us all. Of course she is, sir, we know that, but married to a Protestant gentleman as she is we were inclined to forget it. An uncommon fine lady she is—"

"Please get to your business."

"It being of the utmost importance to you, sir, to protect the lady and your property in these lawless days when you can trust no one, least of all Catholic tenantry or servants beneath your own roof, we wish to offer you our protection. The magistrates rely on us brave Orange boys for there are none other that can keep order hereabouts. All we ask is a small consideration, paid regularly, towards our expenses, that will allow you to sleep soundly at night."

Goward stood up.

"Thank you, Lamont, for coming to the point. I will give your suggestion every consideration. I bid you good-day."

"Good-day your Lordship. I beg leave to call on you again when you have had time to think on it."

"They've gone, Goward. You don't consider paying them?"

"No, Robert, I do not. But what the consequences of not doing so are I know not. Do any of you know of this story of the barn and the pikes?"

"I do, sir," spoke up the young stablehand. "They fired the barn and killed the two men they found there with their own pikes and threw the bodies in the flames."

Principles have their Price

In the room above the stable McNamara sat bolt upright. The creak of the door opening below had entered his dreams but not his consciousness, and so for some minutes he had shifted uneasily in his sleep. It was a cry of pain that brought him fully awake.

Make sure the boy is out of harm first.

Barefoot, he reached for the blunderbuss he had taken to keeping under the bed. McNamara was no shot but he knew it would make enough noise. But first he tiptoed into the adjoining room where his apprentice slept, being careful to cover the boy's mouth before shaking him awake.

"Mmnugh."

"Be quiet, it's myself. There's someone down in the stable. Get yourself into the press and quickly. Don't come out unless I tell you and you're sure I'm alone."

McNamara did not have the opportunity to use the blunderbuss. It was later used to kill a family accused of concealing a fugitive rebel, granting them a quick death after long and futile pleading for their lives. The intruder's lantern had rolled away behind him and lay sputtering on the flagstones, but he still lay behind the horse clutching at his thigh. Until the day he died he would bear the mark of the seventeen-hand horse's shoe, and would boast to his grandchildren that he had received it gloriously in battle fighting the rebels.

"Come away out of that, now," growled McNamara, convinced all he had to deal with was a horse-thief. Too late he heard a step behind him, felt a breath on the back of his neck, and then a rifle butt cracked his skull. McNamara crumpled without a sound.

Upstairs the boy tried to work out how long he had lain in the press. He tried counting the way Mrs. Samuels had taught him. Sixty was meant to be a minute, but how long a gap between each number? He couldn't remember. *Best count slowly.* It was getting stuffy in there, though there was something comforting about the smell of the familiar clothes, old great coats and heavy coachman's capes, and the reek of horses and old human sweat and tobacco. That was twenty times sixty, so what was the old man doing? *A bit longer, maybe.* He eased towards the door of the press, where there was a bit more air. The heaped up clothes were softer than a bed. He curled up, his nose against the door, and shut his eyes. All was quiet. McNamara must have scared whoever it was away and was just quieting the horses. Sure he'd call him when it was safe to come out. The boy slept.

The male servants and representatives of the tenantry sat in silence in the servants' hall, Goward himself next to McNamara's empty chair. He was the first to speak.

"We must remember how much we loved him."

Some of them shifted in their chairs. Nobody spoke, and nobody met his eye. "Lamont was there, looking on when we buried him," said MacElhone, dressed as a footman but known to everyone there as Goward's chaplain.

"I know. He will be here tomorrow to condole with us and to renew his offer. I don't know what I should do. I must give him an answer or there will be other outrages. He is the last man I would give a farthing to but I cannot risk your lives."

"He killed McNamara," muttered one.

"Yes, or his men did. I don't doubt it. Once he has them posted here he will know everyone who calls at the House, whom we see, how often we meet like this in domiciliary committee. They will be able to intercept any correspondence that comes here, and we have no efficient way of warning all our friends not to put down in good faith words that could hang us all. I do not know how we can get letters from here without they are intercepted in the town or on the road. If we go to Downpatrick or Ballynahinch and ask others to help us we risk their lives too. I had thought of Ingham the chandler but I cannot bring trouble to his door more than he has already. But if I do not pay Lamont to put us under this siege then we will one by one be murdered in our beds, though not in our sleep for we can have little enough of that in these circumstances. There is only one other way open to us, and it's risky. It is that we all fly, one by one, disperse and leave this place to them. I would not stop any man who wished to take that course. I trust each and every one of you not to betray his fellows who remain behind."

"That means no part in the rebellion at all, sir."

"I know, unless we link with other United men elsewhere, but it is so hard to trust others that they are what they seem, or for them to trust us."

"There are desertions all over Ulster, my Lord."

"You're right. If we do not rise soon, then this province is lost. I don't know how as yet, but I must get word to Munro. I will go at dawn, and hope to complete my commission before Lamont comes here. Then I will accept his offer. I do not believe we have a choice."

'We're rats in a trap, sir. What will you do with your wife?'

"She stays here. I begged her to go to Bridget and Mr. Andrews in England but she refused outright."

"Mr. Griffiths. What a pleasure it is to see a friend's face in days like these."

"The pleasure is mine, though you may not care for my errand, Lady Goward."

"My husband has sent you."

"Yes, but I came willingly."

"You too urge me to flee."

"I do. I urge you to obey him, as a wife should. As you have promised him."

"I also promised him that I should be with him in bad times as well as good, and that I should never be parted by him but by death, Mr. Griffiths, not by the Irish Sea."

"It would only be temporary."

'Would it?"

"Please do not be so short with me. I am your friend and his, if I do not presume too much, not merely your rector. I ask you as a mere man, Lady Goward, one who has great affection for you. There will be more work like the loss of poor McNamara before this business is finished. If you were safe in England James would have a weight taken off his mind."

"That is your strongest argument yet, but I reject it for reasons purely selfish. I don't know how *I* should bear it, not knowing what he is doing."

Aftermath

"The men of Ballynahinch... chose rather to retire to Slieve-croob, and the other adjoining mountains, rather than hazard their lives in that cause, in which, before the frowning front of war presented its terrors, many of them had embarked with as much show of ardour, and as much courage, as their neighbours... the chief injury sustained by the rebels... consisted in the gradual desertion of a great part of their army...in the dusk of the evening, and during the night... "

– 'Recollections of the Battle of Ballynahinch [12th June 1798], by an eye-witness', *The Belfast Magazine and Literary Journal,* February 1825.

"Throw water over him—the coward has fainted again."

One of the soldiers pulled their prisoner's head up by the hair. Patrick Kearney's face was unrecognisable, a mask of blood and pus, his nose broken, his eyes swollen. The flash of water washed the worst of the red away, revealing a mass of purple and yellow bruising, for he had been beaten intermittently for some days before being brought out here to the flogging tripod for the purposes of "helping him remember." Eight hundred lashes was the sentence; hanging would have been a more merciful end, but they'd been unable to obtain the rope, and there'd been an instruction for no piking, in order that it be seen by the populace as the method favoured only by the rebels. A quarter of the sentence had been carried out, and the ground around the frame was a welter of gore. The little crowd had assembled first in curiosity when they saw the strange contraption assembled in front of the barracks, but now the soldiers prevented them from leaving. Patrick's back was a mass of raw meat, through which the white of two ribs was visible.

A white-haired but still straight and tall old man then stepped forward. "You have him killed, for the love of God, now leave off his corpse," he said.

"Who's that?" asked the soldier with the pail.

The man holding the whip eased back his right shoulder and with his left hand smeared Patrick's blood across his own face.

"Old Benson, the doctor," he said, looking round.

"Would you give me the corpse, gentlemen? I've a mind to give an apprentice of mine some practice with his dissection. If you go on like that there'll be nothing left for him to put his knife into."

"What's it worth to you, Sawbones?" asked the soldier, laughing.

"Gentlemen, I see we can negotiate in the interests of Science." Benson rattled some coins.

"Fetch a door, would ye's?" roared the other soldier, finally letting go of Patrick's hair. The head hung limp, dripping water and blood.

"I'll untie him myself," said the doctor, hastening forward. "I don't want any more damage to my purchase."

Firstly he lifted the head and professionally pushed up a eyelid, then lent in towards it as though to make a closer examination and hissed "If there's any life left in you, Packy, make not a sound."

"Ah, that'll do fine," he said, as not a door but the top of a mess table appeared. "Now if you gentleman would just lift the corpse as carefully as you can, and lay it down as it is, on its stomach. That's it. You two boys, there, you can carry him for me. It's not far."

Benson watched his patient's burst lips move, but struggled to make out his words.

"'Tis a pity you've had to wake now, Packy, for I was about to stitch you up. You could have been spared that pain."

"Cannot be worse than the pain I have now," said Patrick, faintly but clearly.

"Ah, but it can. The boy is going to gag you and then we'll strap you down. I can't have you letting on that you're not a corpse."

"Not yet, but in a fair way."

"Now you hold on, Packy. What I do now will hurt but the worst is over for you."

Benson muttered to his awed and silent assistant as he prepared his needle and gut, "Pray the shock doesn't kill him, nor the gangrene get him after. But the Kearneys that last beyond infancy are made of strong stuff."

Strong indeed, thought the assistant, as he struggled white-faced to hold his patient still, slippery and slick as an eel even in his bounds.

"I'm an old man, but I've done what I can," said Benson, wiping his hands on a rag. "I hope you've learned something from me today, Daniel, for to be sure there'll be many calls for your skill in the days to come."

"C-could you not have got to him earlier?" stammered Daniel.

Benson looked hard at him from under his shaggy brows.

"Now that, you see was the most difficult bit of it all—judging the moment. They wanted him dead after they saw he wouldn't, or couldn't speak, and he'd have been swinging by now in front of the court-house if they'd got hold of the rope to do it. But Matthew Ingham stood his ground and wouldn't give them any. He risked them breaking into the shop and taking the entire chandlery for their foul purposes, and being hanged himself with his own goods. I don't know what else stopped them were it not that the Quakers are thought well of here and they didn't want to rouse the people up any further. His father was a good and charitable man and Matthew is like him."

"But sure there is no rebellion left here," said Daniel sombrely.

"No, and to my mind they never had a hope. South of the country has all gone awry, with their fine declaration thrown aside by those who would have a religious war and a bloodbath on both sides. Here in Ulster they were deserting in droves even before the fight, the Presbyterians saying they'd want an English yoke now before a French one after Bonaparte served the Americans so ill."

"Do they know where Goward is, so?" whispered Daniel.

"They do not, but that's what they wanted out of *him*." Benson leant over the bed where Patrick lay prone, his battered face turned to one side.

"Make the report on our patient, Daniel."

The younger man gingerly lifted the dressings and inspected the staining, and the stitching in the living flesh. Then he bent near Patrick's head and placed the back of his fingers momentarily against his forehead.

"He's cooler, and the bleeding has stopped."

"So he could be dead, then. What else should you be checking?"

Daniel bent down again.

"His breathing is shallow, but it's regular."

"We'll make a doctor of you yet. Now it's up to more able hands than ours, God and Nature and their handmaid Sleep. I never held with this rebellion, but I like what comes now even less. Goward's ideas are too French for me, but he's always been a gentleman, a man of principle, and as far as was possible he has done whatever he could to curb rebel excesses; more than can be said for those brutes in the barracks."

"Goward is a hero."

"You'd be advised not to say that again to anyone, Daniel. Look at this man's back again and have sense."

"They say Edward Kilkeel is in France, but that he will be back with an army."

"Too late now. Hush, won't you, or it would be better you were in France too. Now you get away home to your mother and say nothing of this. If anyone asks you, tell them you'll be doing your dissection tomorrow. If Kearney survives, we'll have to think about how to get him out of here."

Daniel saddled his horse and took his bag of instruments with him in case he was stopped on the road. Five miles beyond the town he took a path across fields, leading his horse for the last half-mile. Before the cabin he tethered his horse, looked around him once more but saw and heard nothing but sheep, then knocked in the way he had been taught. Goward opened the half-door, nodded, and let him in.

"It's Daniel, Mary."

"I've bad news, and good," said Daniel, and recounted Patrick's ordeal. Weeping, Mary sank to her knees and murmured a prayer. Daniel stood irresolute, until Goward said to him: "There's something else, Daniel, is there not?"

Daniel swallowed. "Munro is taken—betrayed. They took him back to Lisburn and hanged him before his own house; he threw himself off the ladder. Nugent has put out a declaration: all rebels will be spared if they lay down their arms. But if their leaders don't give themselves up, then Killinchy, Killyleagh, Ballynahinch and Saintfield are to be destroyed utterly and every cottage or farm around fired and all livestock carried off. Upwards of sixty houses are already fired in Ballynahinch and there is no restraining the militia."

"I must say good-bye to my wife, then. If, God willing, Patrick lives, then one day when it is safe to do so bid him farewell from me. But if you see me when I come to give myself up in the morning, make no sign."

Drear dusk was falling as Daniel led his horse away. "Thank God no one can hear her in this lonely place," he thought. Mary's shrieks grew fainter as he drew away, but he knew he would never forget them.

The Spoils of War

Kilcoo Rectory
19th September 1798

Dear Lord Wickmere,

I ask your forbearance in reading these few lines from a complete stranger. It may be some weeks hence, if not longer, before you can read them, for I have sent this by the hand of a brother clergyman for fear that my correspondence be opened and that I become the tool of others' misfortune.

I am the rector of the parish of Kilcoo, in the gift of Lord Goward, and I also had the honour to be the first tutor to Viscount Kilkeel though I swear to you and anyone who asks me, even on pain of death, that I know nothing as to his whereabouts beyond a rumour that he is in France. If this is so, it would be better for him that he stayed there for here he has lost everything and if he were to return would lose his life also. In happier days my patron Lord Goward spoke often of you in the warmest terms and as his oldest and dearest friend. I have had some trouble though finding an address for you as I cannot despite all my efforts make any communication with either Goward himself nor Lady Goward. You will doubtless know of his arrest after a rout at Ballynahinch; the truth is that he gave himself up in order to spare others, which is of a piece with the noble and honest nature of the man. I have not been able to see him. I applied at the gaol here and after the administration of some bribes ascertained that he had been taken to Belfast in company with other rebels. So I made for the city the earliest I could, and thankfully arrived safely which is not to be taken for granted in these difficult times for though the rebels here are now cowed, no man is safe from the reprisals of the militia, much dominated by the Orange and Peep o' Day boys. A Protestant gentleman of my acquaintance was taken and flogged for having in his possession some lines of poetry written in French; I am thankful that I was able to intervene and have him conveyed home where he slowly recovers from his injuries. My journey to Belfast though was in vain for there after much insistence (I was obliged to lodge there three nights before I was answered) I was told that Lord Goward had already been taken under military escort to the Newgate in Dublin. His captors' plan, it would seem, is to turn him informer and thus save the difficulty of hanging a nobleman; since Fitzgerald died of his wounds in June he is like to become a martyr and there is no appetite to create another such. But if I know Goward at all I do not see that he would enter into any barter of this kind. I was advised that it would be of no use to me to travel to Dublin for I would not be permitted to see him so I have sought to employ myself as usefully as I may here in alleviating suffering and my hands are thus fully occupied. I have though written those two friends who were of great assistance in the matter of Lady Goward's kidnap; I mean Lord Burnchurch and Captain Annesley. Goward's poor lady is herself taken, clapped in a cell when she asked if she might see her husband, and though she be not ten miles from here I am not permitted to see her either. I applied to the magistrate who is a decent man but utterly powerless against the militia. He fears to carry out his tasks fairly as reprisals may be taken against him or his family. I have sought an audience with the governor of the gaol and reminded him that he owes his position to the word of Lord Goward along with that of other gentlemen hereabout, who like him contributed to the building of the new prison which now holds Lady Goward, along with many more wretched souls than it was designed to accommodate. He had the grace to blush but like Orde the magistrate lives in fear though he thinks something may be accomplished. He told me he would send his wife to see Lady Goward for in earlier days both were active together in good works. My inability to gain admittance to her pains me as much as my failure to see him.

If you have any contact at all with Kilkeel you must urge him not to come home. I was given to understand that his mother is held as bait for him. Her companion Bessie Norton I have brought to my own house in the guise of a servant and indeed she insists that she be my housekeeper for having that responsibility she says helps her survive these dark days, so we strive to keep each others' spirits up and to hope for better times.

A further outrage, as if what has happened to their persons were not enough, has been committed against their house. It was Lady Goward's brother Robert who lived at the Big House, continuing the work of Andrews, who came running to me to say the house was overrun with militia destroying whatever they did not carry away with them. Her other brother Patrick had been lately their footman, for this was indeed a house like none other in Ireland. I saddled my horse and with Robert Kearney mounted behind me went there at all speed (I pleaded with him to stay with Bessie and not risk his life by returning there, for whilst the militia might not lay hands on me they would certainly bear him away with them—if not worse—but he would not hear of it).

By the time we arrived they had done their worst and fled. What they had not carried away they had systematically wrecked or befouled. Drapes torn from the windows which were all smashed; not a pane was spared. Upholstery and bedding disembowelled— all china smashed from the finest Meissen to the most humble kitchen Delph. The worked fire-screens and other pretty items which I have seen Lady Goward and Bessie embroider by the hour—ripped to shreds. The great Batoni portrait of James for which he sat in Rome that hung in the drawing-room was slashed beyond repair. But one object was I able to save from the wreckage of their bedroom—a likeness of Lord Goward when Viscount done by a pastellist in Venice after the manner of Rosalba—wearing a domino and a look of mischief (you will remember both likenesses, sir, for doubtless you were with him when they were made). The glass was smashed and the frame cracked, but in their hurry to wreak havoc elsewhere the likeness itself is more or less intact. This I will keep safe in the hope that I can restore it one day to Lady Goward.

When we had gone all over the wasteland of the house we proceeded to the Offices, and there found the worst horror. They had caught a stablehand of not more than thirteen years of age, who lay in a pool of his congealing blood, holding hopelessly to a terrible rent in his belly. They had bayonetted him and left him for dead, but with his last breath he told me they had threatened him with all manner of tortures if he did not tell who beneath that roof was Lady Goward's priest (and his Lordship's too). Word had reached the Orange boys that Goward was as much a papist as his wife, and if he and she did not go to the Mass-House of a Sunday and Fr. Hanlon who is the priest in these parts called but rarely, then there must be a priest beneath his roof. The poor lad at last gave them a name; Mr. MacElhone who always appeared in the figure of a manservant and yet also, being a lettered man, had that air of a personal secretary. When they had the name they thrust the bayonet into the boy anyway. I held him and strove to give him what comfort I could, for having delivered his message and begged forgiveness he shortly after resigned himself to his Maker. Robert searched the Offices— all the horses were taken—but he found poor MacElhone strung from a beam above the hay and there was nothing more could be done for him.

I have only one more piece of this sorry tale to relate and then I am done. Patrick Kearney the quondam footman was taken after Ballynahinch and flogged they thought to death, but his corpse was taken by the old doctor who had attended the Gowards all his life, before they did it any more damage, on the pretence of wanting it to teach dissection to an apprentice. Patrick proved not to be a corpse and now I have him in hiding.

Sir, I beg your pardon for my prolixity but beg your help in anything you can do to assist poor Lady Goward for I fear that good man her husband is beyond our aid and we can only pray for him in whatever words we have been taught. I will only say that in all the years of my poor attempts to till God's vineyard I have seen no two people better joined than they, though many have frowned on their union. I thank you for reading thus far, for strange as it may seem, the opportunity to relate these dreadful events on paper has brought me a degree of comfort. There can be no war so terrible than that which leaves no witnesses.

I am your obedient servant,

Revd. Nathaniel Griffiths

Citoyen Bonnaire

Mail Coach Hotel, Dawson Street, Dublin
30ᵗʰ September 1798

"Humbert! Humbert! *Vive la France! Liberté, egalité, fraternité!*' clamoured the voices from the street.

"They are calling me to the balcony, again, *cher Edouard,* but stay behind the shutters for we don't know who may see you," cautioned General Humbert.

"*Mon général,* may I again express how sensible I am to the risk I place you under—"

"Enough. They have conducted too many of my best officers to a dishonoura-ble death, though they wore the colours of France, simply because they were Irish-men. You are too valuable to me and too valuable to the Republic—the French Republic, *bien entendu,* though if Bonaparte continues on his course I fear it will be no republic at all before too long. Give me the satisfaction of stealing you away from under their noses that we may mock them from afar and come back again to menace *les Anglais* another day."

"But I have cheated death by a ruse."

"You are my adjutant and are obeying orders."

"Very well, General."

"Let me acknowledge our well-wishers, Kilkee—Bonnaire I mean—and then tell me more about my dear *Douaisien.* If there is any doubt in our captors' minds as to who you are, I must be able to second anything you say."

"I am Jean Bonnaire, native of Douai and before taking arms was servant at the Irish College in my native city. I had the care of English and Irish gentlemen's children sent to the school. For this I speak middlingly good English. My father was a cobbler in that city but I was educated by the priests in order that I might serve them. My sister entered the Benedictine house at Dunkerque and when it was suppressed went into service also, but she has been dead these past two years. My mother died when I was a child of seven."

"Ha, this is good, Monsieur Bonnaire. It reeks of authenticity."

"Because it's true. I am not so imaginative, sir, as to be able to invent such a story. Jean Bonnaire, God rest him, was my servant when I was first sent away from home at barely twelve years old. I corresponded with him until his death; my father has always encouraged me to hold dear all those who had shown me a kindness, whether they were to be considered gentlemen or no. You know that my mother was a servant when my father wed her. Bonnaire could speak English but would not, for his task besides caring for my material needs was also to ensure that I spoke the French tongue as if it was my own."

"As if it was *his* own, my dear Bonnaire. You are quite the *Picard* whenever you open your mouth."

"In this he has saved my life."

"So do not waste his gift. Take this advice, Bonnaire. Had you never set foot in France, your face would proclaim you to the world an Irishman. That it does not is not only due to the darker cast of skin that a kinder climate than Ireland's has given you; you also have the attitude and manners of a Frenchman. And I have noticed that when you speak French your expression changes; in repose you are more the Irishman. So I urge you not only to speak French always, but to think it. Until we have safely left these shores, speak no English and show no signs of understanding it."

Grenelle
10th November 1798

My dear Lord Wickmere,

It may be the case that by the time you receive this letter events have moved on considerably. I do not even know when you may be reading this, for I have sent this by the hand of a trusted friend, a man of business travelling to London, asking him to consign it to the mail coach for Norwich at his convenience. I would not expose you, sir, to any risk were it not that I were desperate for news; the very least I could do is to ensure you do not receive correspondence of evidently French origin. To write to Ireland is impossible. If my letters were to reach their intended destination, it would not be without their having been read by spies beforehand. I must not put any friend there in any greater danger than he faces already.

I had set foot in Ireland again as a French officer. Had the wind blown differently two years ago the bloody events of this year in my homeland might never have taken place. Though our army succeeded in landing this time, we were already too late, and despite the fact we were to begin with victorious, we were obliged to bend to superior numbers at Ballinamuck and were taken prisoner. My general and his French officers were treated with every courtesy, but every Irish officer, no matter that he wore the uniform of France, hanged. I escaped Ireland only by assuming the name of a French servant of my youth; please understand that I did not act from mere cowardice but was ordered to make this pretence. I was billeted in some comfort in a Dublin hotel with General Humbert and other officers. Humbert by the office he holds is the enemy of England and thus you would be within your rights to decry him, yet I serve under him and admire him as a strategist, a soldier, and as a gentleman. I also owe him my life because of information he kept from me until we were safely landed once more on French soil. Your dearest friend and my most dear father was being held in a prison cell not a mile from where I dined with Humbert and where he waved to adoring crowds from the drawing-room windows. Humbert knew, but did not tell me. I raged at him when I later discovered this—an offence which merited a dishonourable discharge—but with great forbearance he let me rage, for in doing so he showed me how impossible it would have been for me to have contained my feelings had I known this in Dublin. My subterfuge would have been immediately discovered.

I do not know my father's current condition, nor if he yet lives. I am powerless to change it, for in Ireland I am a wanted man. I do not know where or how my mother fares, though I tremble less for her only because I believe she is surrounded by friends. I beg of you, insofar as you can, dear Wickmere, to let me have news of them, any news, even the worst. Not knowing is the worst kind of helplessness.

Respectfully yours,

Edward Kilkeel

Dublin
21ˢᵗ December 1799

Dear Wickmere,

I was most grateful for your last letter and am relieved to be able to tell you that as a minister of religion I have at last been able to see Lord Goward in person and to convey to him the love you bear him and your anxiety for his current unhappy situation; this is a small mercy but one I must be grateful for.

Your friend and my patron was long kept without visitors, excepting his lawyer, in the hope of convincing him to turn King's evidence and convict other oath-takers. Goward refused them, saying he had nothing to tell them beyond what he has already re-counted in Mr. Curran's presence—his lawyer, a decent man fighting with a child's hammer to make way through a wall of deceit. After some weeks of this, it was put to him that the prosecutors instead would provide him with the evidence to which he should swear, and being the man he is, he naturally turned down this offer. So he is to stand his trial. Curran tells me that the jury will be packed, as with all the rebel trials, but that he will make as many objections as he may.

Lord Goward has good friends in this part of the country who have asked to be remembered to you: Captain Annesley and Lord Burnchurch. It is they who have de-frayed Curran's expenses and ensured that our friend has not died of starvation in his confinement. I have to tell you that Lord Goward is thin and pale and wasted, for he is seldom let to leave the apartment assigned to him, but he attempts to live in as dig-nified a manner as any man may in these circumstances. Other prisoners not considered dangerous may wander the stairs and corridors of this gaol, and so visit Lord Goward for what he laughingly calls his "salon." Typically for him, he has made of his regular gaoler a firm friend who guards him less as a gaoler and more as a faithful hound. This letter I have entrusted to this man, for he is not searched whilst I am despite my cloth. Lord Goward may have books and newspapers brought him, and receive letters though these are always read by the governor first. What weighs on Goward most is that he not only cannot see his wife but until recent days did not know how she fared. At least in this I have been able to give him some scant comfort, that she lodges not in the prison but in the Governor's House at Downpatrick Gaol, though she is not allowed any cor-respondence. I thus traffic up and down this island between these two gaols and my parish and wish that my face could take the imprint of husband to wife and back again. Goward makes a Herculean effort not to betray his fear that he may never see her again, but instead hangs on every word I relate of her, and of his ward Bessie whom I shelter and who he thus may see on those occasions when she accompanies me to Dublin—which is not every time for I refuse to inflict the fatigues and dangers of that journey on her overmuch. Bessie is also assiduous in her visits to Lady Goward in the company of the family's physician. Goward's thin face shines with pride when we talk of Viscount Kilkeel, but here we are obliged to be very circumspect, for he is a wanted man. That young man's talents will be lost to Ireland forever but France will have the benefit of them.

I will keep you appraised of any changes in Lord Goward's circumstances, and in particular when he may stand his trial.

Your obt. Servant,

Nathaniel Griffiths

Green Street Court House, Dublin

June 1800

"Lord Goward, you have been put upon this trial upon a charge of High Treason. There are two counts to this indictment, one charging you with compassing the death of the King, and the other with adhering to his enemies. In support of each of these counts, the following twelve overt acts of Treason are specified: firstly, that of assembling and conspiring with other traitors to stir up rebellion, and procure arms and ammunition and men for that purpose, secondly, that of conspiring with other traitors to depose the King, thirdly, that of conspiring with these same traitors to overturn the Government, fourth, conspiring and consorting with the aforementioned traitors about the means of raising rebellion, procuring arms and armed men to overturn the Government and Constitution by force, fifth, by conspiring with said traitors to depose the King by an armed force, sixth, becoming a member of the Society of Traitors, called United Irishmen, with design to raise rebellion and overturn the Government by force, seventh, with such design keeping and receiving accounts and returns of arms, men and money for the purposes of rebellion. Eighth, in collaboration with the executed traitor Henry Munro, causing and procuring armed men to the number of four thousand to assemble at Ballynahinch to levy war against the King, ninth, assembling to receive returns of armed men, tenth, providing a chamber in your own dwelling Goward Hall in order that certain traitors might meet for those purposes, eleventh, giving notice of such meeting and summoning diverse traitors to attend the same, twelfth, collecting money to purchase arms for rebels."

The court clerk cleared his throat and looked up at the Bench.

"Lord Goward, how do you plead to this indictment?" asked the judge.

"It has never been my intention in thought or deed to encompass the death of the King. I took the oath of the United Irishmen in the sincere belief in the right of all Irishmen, whether of the Established, Catholic, Presbyterian or other dissenting persuasion, to full emancipation and the right to govern themselves, and this I did in accord with the dictates of my conscience."

"Your conscience, Lord Goward, is a matter for a higher court than this one. I asked you how you intend to plead and would be glad if you would answer either guilty or not guilty."

"Not guilty."

"Mr. Stewart, you may call your first witness."

"Please state your name and occupation."

"I am Joseph Devlin, tenant farmer to Lord Goward there, in Moneyscalp townland in the County of Down."

"And your age?"

"Thirty-four, sir."

"How long have you been a tenant of Lord Goward's?"

"My father brought us to Goward's, sir, when I was about twelve years old and we had been turned off our last place. So when my father died I assumed the tenancy."

"Are you a United Irishman, Devlin?"

"I am, sir. Lord Goward administered the oath to me and to all his servants and others near the end of 1797. It was after Mr. Orr was hanged in Carrickfergus and Lord Goward said this was a crime that cried out for vengeance."

"Are you aware that the administration of this oath is a capital offence?"

"I am sir."

"Do you have an order for protection, Devlin?"

"I have, sir. I have it of the magistrate in Downpatrick."

"You say that all the servants at Goward Hall were sworn?"

"Yes. I do not think it was a question of choice, sir, and so may they be dealt with mercifully."

"Now will you describe what you saw occur at Goward Hall and in the demesne with regard to rebellion."

"Goward Hall had its own domiciliary committee. It met in the servant's hall."

"The prisoner was always present?"

"Oh yes, sir, it was Lord Goward who would give notice of the meetings."

"Who else was there besides the household?"

"To begin with there would be delegates also from the neighbouring barony committees, from Downpatrick or Ballynahinch mostly. Then when the Orange boys came to protect the estate they came no more but messages were taken to them."

"Messages taken by whom?"

"By myself, sir, on pretext of going for goods, sir, or sometimes by Lord Goward himself."

"In whose hand were these messages written?"

"By any one of us, sir. Not in Lord Goward's hand but by his dictation."

"What did you do with the messages?"

"I went first to the magistrate so he had the copying of them and on his instructions I then took them to whoever Lord Goward said."

"Amongst the charges made against the prisoner is that of procurement of arms for the purposes of rebellion. What did you observe in this regard?"

"That in the Offices there were stores of pikes, muskets and bayonets hidden beneath the straw. Some of these arms were of new make—French, I believe, while others were much older—going back to the Lord Protector's time."

"There is another matter I wish to explore with you. From your observations as his tenant is the prisoner in your view a member of the Established Church? I see my learned colleague is getting to his feet to object but I can assure you My Lord that my question is a pertinent one."

"Devlin, you should answer his question," said the judge.

"Lord Goward attends services in the parish church with his chaplain Mr. Griffiths, as we all do—did. But I believe him to be of a the Romish persuasion, in secret, as is his wife. They were never to be seen at the Mass Rock, nor latterly the Mass House in Newry, but the suspicion was planted when his father-in-law was buried and Lord Goward showed himself conversant with all that happened—I mean that he knew all the responses as well as any Catholic born and insisted on making the sign of the cross though he had to lift his dead hand in his live one to do so. In his house it was common knowledge that Mr. McElhone was not a secretary as he was presented but a priest. Lord Goward said that in the new Ireland divisions of belief and practice would not matter anymore, for all should have liberty of conscience and that effort to divide Irishmen served only the ends of the King and his government."

"We hear much of the promptings of conscience in this court today. Tell the court what nature of a man was this father-in-law of Lord Goward's?"

"Thomas Kearney was a tenant like myself, but he being of the place for some generations he had pretensions that the land he farmed for Lord Goward would one day return to him or to his sons. When Lord Goward took Thomas's daughter for his mistress, and then married her after he lost use of his arm—"

"As long as he lost use of no other part of him, then!" came a shout from the gallery, accompanied by laughter.

"Silence, or the constables will clear the court," retorted the judge. "Please continue, Devlin."

"When Mary Kearney as she was became his mistress, Lord Goward had a decent house built for Kearney, and his family were given special favour."

"Please go on."

"There was another daughter already in service but she is gone away married to Lord Goward's agent that was. One son became head footman and another his agent when Mr. Andrews went to England. In the Big House the Kearneys were more family than servant."

"*Fraternité, egalité*, indeed. We have seen the harvest such ideas have reaped in France. Thank you, Devlin, I will not trouble you with further questions, but I believe my learned colleague has something more to ask."

"You are not a Downshire man, I believe, Mr. Devlin?"

"No, sir, I was born in Gortalowry townland in the county of Tyrone.'

"And you say your father was turned away there."

"Yes, for being behind in the rent. I was but a little fellow but I remember the hardship and the places my father tried until we came to Lord Goward and he took us."

"Was he a good landlord?"

"Yes, I cannot deny that. He worked hard with Mr. Andrews to make the land more profitable not that he might turn out tenants but that they might lead a decenter life."

"These letters you claim Lord Goward dictated; you say that any one of the servants could write them. Does that include yourself?"

"That is so."

"So Lord Goward's entire establishment could read and write? An uncommon situation, I believe?"

"Lord Goward insisted on it. He said Ireland would have need of educated men of all classes, that growth and prosperity depended on it. Mrs. Samuels, the old rector's widow, got up a school where the children of the tenantry and such of the tenantry themselves as wished it could be taught. All of them in the Big House had lessons there."

"So this man whom you describe as the best of landlords, who took your family in when faced with starvation, and who had you taught to read and write at his own expense that you might forge letters and say they were by his dictation, is repaid by you with testimony that may send him to the gallows?"

"Curran, you will refrain from making such insinuations against the character of the witness. No one has accused him of forgery."

"I beg forgiveness My Lord. As regards forgery, I believe he has no stain on his character. Mr. Devlin, when Mr. Andrews sailed for England and Lord Goward was in want of an agent, did you present yourself for the position?"

"I did, sir, but a Kearney was to have it."

"I see. You have told us, Mr. Devlin, that Lord Goward wanted an Ireland where there was to be toleration of a man's beliefs. May I ask what are your own?'

"I am a professed member of the Established Church, sir."

"Since birth?"

"No, sir, by conviction. I turned, and was instructed by Lord Goward's chaplain Mr. Griffiths."

"When was this?"

"Twelve or thirteen years ago."

"Lord Goward has a ward, I believe, a London foundling by the name of Elizabeth Norton."

"That is so."

"Does this Miss Norton profess what you claim is the creed of her guardian?"

"She does not, sir. Lord Goward said as it was probable that her parents, whoever they may have been, were of the Established Church, and that she had been brought up to it from her earliest days in the orphanage, then she should follow that path until such time as she might decide herself to do otherwise."

"A most generous and enlightened stance on the part of Lord Goward, I would say."

"Mr. Curran," interrupted the judge. "Do bring us back to the indictment we are meant to be examining today. I do not see the relevance of this line of questioning."

"It is relevant to understand what has moved the witness to be here today, My Lord. I am almost finished. So, what were your feelings towards this Miss Norton, Devlin?"

"I... I had thoughts of marrying her. I sought out Lord Goward to ask his consent, and he laughed and said it was not his that counted but Miss Norton's. In his view marriage should be a love match, and therefore a girl should consult her emotions, not her father. He also pointed out that a Protestant and a Catholic might not lawfully marry, and to be aware that Miss Norton had been brought up to be a Protestant."

"So you "turned," Mr. Devlin."

"I did."

"And what did the lady say?"

"She refused me."

"I see. So you admit that Lord Goward gave your family refuge and a livelihood when there was sore need for both. You state that he was an excellent landlord, when so many of his class barely even set foot in Ireland. He educated you when few men of your station can hope for that, yet when you were disappointed in ambition and in love, you chose to betray the trust of this man who had only ever sought to benefit you and whose eyes I note you refuse to meet across this courtroom. I have no further questions for you, for all I am curious to know what your future intentions are."

"I shall depart for England, once the court has defrayed the expense I have had in coming here, and have made good the loss of my livelihood."

"Indeed, it would be amiss if you were not to claim your "expenses" sir, and your swift departure from this island would I think be prudent."

"Mr.Curran! I have had to warn you against these insinuations already," shouted the judge. "If you have no further questions of the Crown's witness, I would have you let that gentleman go about his lawful business."

"I am Nathaniel Griffiths, Rector of Kilkeel, and lately tutor to Lord Goward's son Edward."

"Your living is in the gift of Lord Goward, then."

"Yes, Mr. Curran. I was first appointed as tutor and then when the living fell vacant due to the indisposition and then death of the last incumbent, it was conferred on me."

"Do you consider your patron a faithful son of the Established Church?"

"Lord Goward was—that is to say, is—faithful in his observance of the requirements of the Protestant faith. He was married according to its rites although not perhaps according to the dictates of fashionable society, and he has proved most active as Christian gentleman should be in the betterment of his tenants, in the provision of instruction for their children and in the establishment of model methods of farming that if imitated could do much to raise this country from the poverty and misery in which much of it now languishes."

"We have heard the Crown's chief witness declare him to be a Papist."

"Lord Goward is an enlightened man who has spoken often of the need for emancipation for our Catholic brethren, and indeed for all dissenters. His pew was never empty of a Sunday but as our Church does not encompass the individual confession of sins I cannot say what was in his heart as it is not for me to look into a man's conscience."

"Are you acquainted with Mr. Joseph Devlin, Mr. Griffiths?"

"I am."

"Did he, as he has asserted in this court, attend on you with a view to conversion to the Established Church?"

"Yes… he did."

"You hesitate, Mr. Griffiths. Why?"

"I thought he did not treat the matter with the solemnity that it deserved. For whilst there shall be joy in heaven over one sinner that repenteth, more than over ninety and nine just persons, and such a one has often more zeal than those who are born in their faith and instructed as children, I divined no real sense of repentence or zeal in Mr. Devlin so much as a hurry to advance the process. He told me he would swear to fifty-nine articles rather than thirty-nine if it would help his case. The interest he showed in scriptural arguments or doctrines seemed done only to satisfy me, rather than as the quest of a soul for enlightenment."

"Is it the case that Mr. Devlin had hopes of becoming Lord Goward's agent on the departure of Mr. Andrews for England?"

"It is, but Lord Goward appointed his brother-in-law Robert Kearney as he had been trained by Andrews as soon as he was able for it. I do believe that decision was the right one also as Mr. Devlin's is a rather directive nature and not the more accommodating one that Lord Goward sought, and indeed Mr. Kearney's appointment was greeted with approval by the larger number of the tenantry."

"Mr. Curran," interposed the judge, "I would remind you that there are other witnesses we must hear today."

"I have just one more question to put to my witness, My Lord. Mr. Griffiths, were you aware that Mr. Devlin sought the hand of Lord Goward's ward, Miss Elizabeth Norton?"

"Certainly. They had grown up together, for Lord Goward did not encourage separation of children by rank or religion. He said there was time enough for them to do battle with such prejudice later, but not in infancy. Miss Norton told me she refused her suitor because she already knew him too well."

"Hold your peace in the gallery! This is a capital trial not a Smock Alley farce."

Curran continued. "Miss Norton is an orphan, sheltered by Lord Goward out of the kindness of his heart. As we understand Lady Goward is at present imprisoned, what is the current condition of this young woman?"

"She is my house-keeper, sir. It was the least I could do for this unhappy family."

Laughter erupted in the public gallery once more. As it died down, Griffiths began to weep.

"Mr. Griffiths, I am sensible of the distress these questions cause you. Do you need time to compose yourself? I will not disturb you much longer."

"No... no. Lord Goward was my patron but I am prouder to call him my friend. Seldom does one discover a man in whom kindness, generosity, wit and principle are so happily combined. It grieves me beyond measure to see him a prisoner in this court, as it grieved me to have to see him in a prison cell, where his privations however never prevented him from attempting to raise the spirits of his visitors and to be concerned instead with whatever troubled them."

"One more question, so that the jury may be satisfied of your disinterest. Are you a United Irishman, sir?"

"No, sir, nor have I been pressed to be one. That I have always abjured violence or the possibility of it in any form is known to anyone of my acquaintance. I was asked however by the yeomanry to join them and they were not pleased at my refusal."

"Quite the Quaker," muttered the judge, audibly, then more loudly, "Mr. Curran, if you have finished with your witness you might let him step down and search for his handkerchief."

"I am Captain Thomas Annesley, lately of the 18th Regiment of Foot."

"Would you tell the court where you have seen service, sir?"

"My last engagements were at Lexington and Concord, where I was wounded, and thus invalided out of my regiment."

"And in the late rebellion?"

"I was long retired by then, but served as a volunteer with the Wexford yeomanry, insofar as I was able."

"How long have you known the prisoner?"

"Upwards of twenty years."

"How did you meet?"

"His friend Lord Wickmere enlisted my help in tracing Lord Goward's wife, who had been kidnapped from a levée here in Dublin—a notorious case. I assisted in the first instance because the honour of this city was at stake, and then because Goward became my friend."

"Did you know him as a United Irishman?"

"No, though I knew where his sympathies lay. I did not share them but I respect him as a man of principle and integrity. I believe that he would have been a moderating influence on those who would otherwise have committed outrages in the name of their cause."

"I am Paul, Lord Burnchurch. Yes, I have known Lord Goward for as long as Captain Annesley, since the occasion of the kidnap of Lady Goward.

"I am not a United Irishman nor did I enlist in the Government's forces, though a regiment was raised in my county. During the rebellion I sheltered fugitives from both sides and believe that those occasions were the only ones in my entire existence when I have acted with real courage and principle.

"I came today to testify to the good character of James Goward, as a man who wanted nothing other than what was fair and just for all Irishmen, and who, if events had turned out differently might have been a great leader in Ireland. I have long been grateful for his friendship and for the interest he has shown in a dull fellow like myself."

Two broadsheet scribblers were whispering in the public gallery.

"You were too young to remember it, but that kidnap was in 1775 or thereabouts. Goward's lady was drugged and seized by an agent he had dismissed and was locked away by him in a madhouse in Wicklow. By the time Goward got her back she was somewhat soiled, by all accounts. Now she's locked up again, but in the gaol in Downpatrick."

"What hope would you give him for seeing her again?"

"Ah, i'faith, none at all this side of Judgement."

"Twill be another good spice to add to our account of him to sell at his execution, though."

"Indeed. I'll write the part of the kidnapped wife, while you get up his last confession. You know the form."

"Alright, so."

"I now wish to call the final witness for the prosecution: Mr. Samuel Warnock.'

"Mr. Warnock, will you tell the court in what capacity you know the prisoner?"

"I and others had the task of protecting his property, following the murder of his ostler."

"And you and your colleagues are?"

"We are the loyal order of Orange boys of the Kilkeel Lodge."

"The court has heard from a witness that the prisoner convened a domiciliary council of the Society of Traitors, otherwise known as United Irishmen, within the walls of Goward Hall, and corresponded with other domiciliary and baronial committees to further the ends of rebellion in this country."

"He may have done. Twas his own house."

"I beg your pardon, Mr. Warnock."

"I didn't sleep under his roof, sir, none of us did, though we were welcome at his table. "For I was an hungred, and ye gave me meat: I was thirsty, and ye gave me drink"—Matthew twenty-five verse thirty-five, sir. So you see, I couldn't rightly swear to any assembly."

"I see... but in your perambulation of his park and offices, you discovered a sizeable cache of firearms and pike-heads, did you not?"

"Now who would have told you that, sir? No, I did not—"

"Mr. Warnock, may I remind you that you are on oath and this is not—"

"Not what, Mr. Stewart? Not what we agreed? I am indeed on oath and know it, and know that I am answerable to Him as I swore that oath to for "thou shalt not bear false witness against thy neighbour"—that would be Exodus twenty verse sixteen—with respect, sir."

"Thank you, Mr. Warnock, now with regard to the arms—"

"Sure, what arms would you be talking about? I never saw any and it would be a foolish man indeed who'd keep them there under the eyes of the Orange boys— and after when the yeomanry were stationed there on free quarters."

Flustered, the prosecuting barrister appealed to the judge.

"Mr. Warnock did not see these arms which doubtless were well hidden, but we have the evidence of a reliable witness that they were there—"

"I can hazard a guess as to who your reliable witness is, Mr. Stewart," rolled on Warnock before the judge could respond. A murmur swept the public gallery, and distracted, the judge shouted again for silence, forgetting that the greater danger was from Warnock, who now addressed him directly, leaving Stewart to wave his papers ineffectually in an attempt to regain control of his witness.

"It's written in the first of book of Timothy that "The love of money is the root of all evil." Chapter six, verse ten as I'm sure your Honour knows, and so it is. Money to hit the poor ostler over his head so that Lord Goward would pay the protection and be spied on. Money to come here and talk of muskets and pikes where there were none. Money for a safe passage to England under another name."

"You've no proof of any of this, Warnock!" squealed Stewart.

"You may be right there, Mr. Stewart. Twas Lamont, Master of our Lodge found the spy, but our poor Mr. Lamont fell at Ballynahinch."

"I have no further questions."

"Whatever you the jury may think of the character of Mr. Devlin and his motivation in giving his evidence today, I would remind you all that here we do not deal in matters of conscience—a term much mouthed in this trial—but in facts. The witness Mr. Warnock has denied the presence of arms on Lord Goward's land, but all he has told us when we regard the facts, is that he did not see these arms with his own eyes. This does not mean they did not exist. Mr. Warnock has further sought to blacken the character of his fellow crown witness—for what reasons I cannot fathom but no doubt he too will claim conscience, and find words in Scripture to suit his case—by imputing to him involvement in the murder of Lord Goward's ostler, but again he cannot find anyone to corroborate his story. The man he accuses is conveniently dead—dead I might add in defence of his King and Government—and unable to defend himself against this calumny. In Lord Goward's defence we have heard the testimony of his good character from men of undoubted good character themselves, including in the person of Captain Annesley, one who has been active himself in resisting the rebels in Wexford where insurrection was arguably at its most powerful. The Reverend Griffiths is no doubt sincere but his livelihood depends on the patronage of Lord Goward. None of these witnesses has provided any evidence to counter that presented by King's counsel though we commend them for coming here today and for conducting themselves in a way that befits gentlemen. It would seem that Lord Goward has more loyal friends amongst the class to which he belongs and wished to overthrow than amongst those whose lot he mistakenly thought to better. Gentlemen, please retire and consider your verdict."

Annesley mouths at me and clenches and unclenches both fists. A good soldier, he is urging me to have courage. Burnchurch is the picture of dejection, his head in his hands, whilst Griffiths prays, and I am in need of a good man's prayers, for the jury is returning already, though a scant three minutes have gone by. They do not look at me. It is over.

Mary Talks to Mr. Ingham in the Governor's House

"I cannot tell you how grateful I am for bringing me here."

"I hope at least you may sleep better here."

"I should. I am not in the danger I was there. But not knowing where James is means I cannot rest."

"Dear Madam—"

'I can barely describe how we passed that last night. It is too painful to tell, and too private, so I will leave his words lying quiet in my heart. At dawn he put me before him on his horse and took me to the Sisters though it was I took the reins. Mother Anne put me in the room where I slept all that time ago when I went there for my confinement. That's where we said good-bye. I wonder will I ever see him again. I could see the Sisters were anxious at my presence there though they said nothing, and he was too distracted to see it. So within an hour of his quitting me, I told them I too would leave for I had to see him wherever he was. I was very wet and cold by the time I arrived at the court-house for on foot it was a journey of some three hours. I asked to see my husband. The officers smiled and said, "Certainly my lady" though I knew they mocked me. They led me up the stone stairs and locked me in a cell and there I was—how long was it?"

"A year or more."

"I'd be there still if you hadn't petitioned the governor on my behalf. The place was full of unhappy souls that I heard crying in the night. When the soldiers had drink taken there were screams, for they made free with any poor woman they wanted, and I know how a woman may be made to suffer. I believe I was let alone only as there were many younger than I. The worst times for me I will confess were when the bell tolled for that meant a poor soul was being taken out to be hanged by the gate, and every time I prayed it was not him but I did not know, until after some weeks the Governor's wife got admittance to me and told me, swearing me to secrecy, that James had been taken on a car with other prisoners to Belfast three days after he had given himself up. I cried much at this for then I thought I would never seen him again and it had been a meagre comfort to me that I might one day see him if we were in the same building. She could give me no other news for there were so many locked up that there would be trials and executions and flog-gings and transportations for a long time to come, and what she called habby's corpse was put aside so that anyone under suspicion could lie in gaol for as long as was needed and not see his trial. I knew the Governor's lady from earlier days for she was much given to good works and since she came to see me my material condition improved but I was always sore at heart. She told me that Mr. Griffiths and yourself had applied on diverse occasions to see me but been refused, and this news did give me some comfort for you are both kind and good gentlemen and I was happy you had not forgot me. What is it, Mr. Ingham? Have you news?"

"A deputation has been got up to get you moved from here into our keeping, so that you might live in the house built for your father, and we vouch for your keeping to it, Lady Goward. Dr. Benson and I are standing surety. Goward Hall, I am afraid, is open to the crows. The lead has already gone from the roof."

'Oh! My home… our home. I expected this. There is no reason why it should have been spared. But I would be happy if I could go to the house that was my father's. It is a kind place."

"Lord Rawdon's man also came to see me on confidential instructions from his Lordship that you might be taken to live quietly in his dower-house. He also has lent his support to getting you released."

"I am surrounded by kindness," said Mary. "I would be happy anywhere pro-vided James join me there."

Ingham inclined his head towards her and reached for her hand.

"I have other news. Your husband stood his trial in Dublin."

Viaticum

"What's the matter, O'Byrne?"

"Galvin is here to see you, sir."

"Good evening, Lord Goward. I have come to take the measurements of you. This will not take long, if you'll pardon my jest, sir."

"I am at your service, Mr. Galvin."

"'Tis an advance on the old methods, sir. With an accurate calculation it's all over in an instant. I position the knot just here, and with your weight and the right length of the rope, your neck breaks and you go to a better place without so much as a sigh."

"I should thank you, then, Mr. Galvin, for such expertise."

"We will meet again the day after tomorrow, my Lord. You will have much to do and think on before then, so I will not trouble you further."

"Please drink the brandy, sir. 'Tis the best thing for the circumstances, though no remedy. No one will know that you weep, only Francie O'Byrne here and he is your friend though your gaoler."

"God help me, O'Byrne. I am so frightened."

"They'd have you die the traitor's death but you will do so as a hero and a gentleman."

"My poor wife. My boy."

"Your boy is safe, sir. He knows not to come back to Ireland. He'll be proud of you, and so will his childer, and his childer's childer. You heard what the Captain said, and Lord Burnchurch. They will look to your lady. You've been so strong, sir, you've kept all of us in here in good spirits, and I don't know how you have managed it. Weep, sir, there is no shame on it. 'Tis only you and I and our Lord who sees all that sees your tears."

"I would find this much easier to bear if it were not public, O'Byrne. A death agony should be a private suffering, not a spectacle."

O'Byrne looked at him in horror.

"If 'tis Mr. Tone's example you are thinking of then I shall stop you for you'll be risking your immortal soul."

"No, O'Byrne, you need not fear that."

"I'd be happier all the same, if you'd let me take away your razor, except for when you need it of a morning."

"Take it."

"I shall give it to your friends, sir, with your other effects."

"My friends were unsure what they should do, O'Byrne, but Annesley has decided at last to take a window opposite the gaol so that he and Burnchurch and Griffiths can attend me as nearly as they could were I to be dying quietly in my bed at home."

"Mr. Griffiths could attend you with the priest, sir."

"He must not, O'Byrne. His life will be difficult enough for his association with a rebel; I will not have it made any worse. He is too dear to me for that."

"You have some rare friends, sir. 'Tisn't always I see such faithfulness here."

"I count you one of them."

"You do me too much honour. But I am thinking I shall not do this work much longer."

"I would wish no one had to do it, but you have brought me much comfort."

Passing by Smithfield on his way home, on cobbles already slick with rain, Galvin slipped on manure left behind by the monthly horse fair, and fell heavily on his right side. Cursing, he hauled himself to his feet, pulled a grubby handkerchief out of his pocket and tried to brush the worst of the dung from the skirts of his coat. The following morning when he reached into this pocket to find the scrap of paper on which he had scribbled Lord Goward's measurements he found only the handkerchief. He swore and spat at the annoyance of having to repeat his visit to the condemned man, then shrugged. "Ah, sure, can't I remember the shape of him well enough?"

Newgate
Dublin
13ᵗʰ June 1800

My beloved Mary,

I write this by the hand of the priest who has come to hear my last confession, and who, God willing, will accompany me when I leave this cell tomorrow morning on my last and most important journey in life. This will have reached you by other hands, for there is someone here I can trust who has sworn to bring you this, but for his sake I will not name him. He is not the priest for his person is always searched on entering and leaving this place. My friend is not to blame for how long it has taken for this to reach your hands.

I will not see you or Edward again this side of Judgement Day. It is my greatest comfort to know that he has reached France and so is safe and my greatest sorrow that I know not where you are or how you fare. I beg you only as my last demand of you as a husband—and I know that I have always asked much of you in all ways—that you apply to dear Jack Wickmere for aid and shelter for he has always loved me as the best of friends and thus loved and admired you also. My Mary, oh my Mary, my life. My love, my wife. Esteem for you was for me the prelude to love, and became love's foundation. Without your steadfastness, our story would have been a commonplace tale of master and servant-maid, begun and ended near thirty-five years ago. Without what then seemed to me your blind faith, your acceptance of both the unknown and the inexplicable as part of a plan greater than ours, I would never have come safely into harbour as I have now, in the hands of this priest. I am dead, my Mary; the man who loved you body and soul lies in some dishonorable grave. Better men than I have died as traitors in the eyes of the world but history may grant them a different reputation. I am privileged, for many good men have fallen in battle on both sides in this rising and innocents have perished, without being granted the opportunity to prepare for death that I have been given here. Profiteers thrived on either side, and the basest of men with weapons in their hands have indulged their most cruel instincts without principle or restraint. It is only God now who will call all of them to account. "The rules of fair play do not apply in love and war" it is said, but that does not mean that we must accept this, Mary. I fought for fairness and failed, and will not be the last in the history of this island. I took my oath to bring liberty and equality to all Irishmen, of whatever creed. We might have succeeded, and we could not have failed to make the attempt. I dreamed of an Ireland in which those divisions of creed might no longer provide those who would exploit this island with the means they needed to divide and rule—and then saw even within our own ranks the Hydra head of bigotry raise its loathsome head—but forgive me my Mary, for I see you now shake your head again at my enthusiasms: for French ideas, planting turnips, theories of education. You urge me to have sense and remember that I am a father and that if I am going out would I remember that the dog needs an airing.

I have presumed on this good priest's patience for too long, though he shakes his head and denies it, and I must let him put his stole about his neck and confess me so that I am ready when the hemp goes around mine. Mary, remember me to all those I have loved and have loved me even when I did not deserve their love. Tell Jack—again I recommend you to his care—that he is the truest and kindest of friends, and that he must not reproach himself for not being here, for he could have done nothing against the forces ranged against me, and his place was with my godson; God willing the little fellow is now fully restored to health. Annesley and Burnchurch have been faithful to me and will be so to you also. Tell Bessie that I love her as my daughter and remind her that it was by her agency that I at last convinced my wife to be my wife before the whole world. Trust to Griffiths for his counsel and support and tell him I have always been grateful to him, and to remember me in his prayers; I ask the same of your dear brothers and of Bridget. Tell our beloved Edward that his face has sustained me with yours in my dreams and that I am proud of him and love him and believe him a far greater man than I ever was. You, Mary, you made me the happiest man alive and I love you, my dear wife.

Farewell,

Your loving husband,

"Wait a moment, Father. I should like to try to sign my name this time, though I am sure to make a mull of it. I barely know how to hold the pen in this hand. There, it is not done well, but 'tis done."

– James Goward

Hanging Platform

Dublin
14ᵗʰ June 1800

"'Tis time my Lord, and I pray you to forgive me."

"Don't kneel before *me,* O'Byrne. No freeborn Irishman should do that."

"We are not free, sir, or we would have none of today's work," said O'Byrne, scrambling to his feet. "I brought you a hood, sir. They do not permit it, but I shall put it on you at the last moment, and not give 'em time to fight about it. I am sorry that mine should be the last face you shall look upon."

"Thank you for your kindness. I should like to tell you that I shall remember it for ever, though my forever this side will be somewhat short."

The gaoler looked perplexed. "But sure, sir, all men of goodwill—and women too—shall live always. He hung on the cross that this might be so."

"Your kindness will be remembered by He who is more powerful than any of my captors or your employers, O'Byrne. Who dies as I do shall live long in memory of living men, certainly. You will need to tie me, I believe. Have they let the priest come?"

"They have. He waits outside. If you would just put your arms behind you sir. Ah yes, I am after forgetting your poor sword-arm sir that will not do as you tell it. I will pull it back meself. There, it's done."

The fingers of Goward's left hand felt for their mute companions on his right, and once more he marvelled that his dead hand felt nothing, could do nothing, and yet was warm. It belonged to him.

Outside the cell with O'Byrne's help he clumsily knelt before the priest. Goward felt the warm pressure of the man's hand on his head and the splash of holy water on his face. Then he was helped to his feet and the priest moved ahead of him along the whitewashed corridor, O'Byrne and another guard following behind him. The prison bell tolled its dirge and between its strike the muffled tumult of shouting and banging on doors reached them from deep in the building, as the prisoners bade farewell. Then suddenly they were out on the platform with the light of a fine June morning dazzling Goward's eyes. He had not breathed anything but the stale fug of the prison for months and gulped the fresh spring air. A great swell of sound reached him as thousands of faces turned upwards.

He felt the scratch of the hemp as Galvin slipped the noose around his neck, pulling his shirt clear. Then O'Byrne's ugly kind face appeared before him with a murmured "Good-bye, sir," and the dark cloth smelling of other men's fear cancelled out all but the noise. "Mary," he whispered into the darkness. With a rush of sound and air the ground gave way.

The rope was too short.

Those few seconds lasted centuries. His good arm jerked upwards, pulling its useless companion with it as his legs thrashed in hopeless quest of a foothold. An intolerable rushing pain tore up his body as he gasped and fought to get air into his collapsing lungs. A burst of blinding light filled the inside of the hood but illuminated nothing. He was conscious, far off, that his breeches were wet, but not conscious enough to know why. Above the blare in his head he heard O'Byrne shouting: "You oul' eejit! You've the wrong length of him."

Then as Goward struggled, the little gaoler, agile as an ape, swung himself hand over hand along the iron balustrade, and to the gasps of the crowd, hung by both hands as he kicked backwards and downwards searching for the jerking man. A foot on each shoulder, a push, and O'Byrne felt the crack of Goward's neck and his body relax. Weeping and drenched with sweat, O'Byrne pulled his feet up and pushed them between the bars, and clung there too exhausted to move, hunched and folded like a bat. Below him and the gently-swaying figure of the dead man the crowd screamed and cheered and wept.

"No family vault for this one then," said Sullivan, peering at the corpse's neck. "Where'll he be going?"

"To the Croppies' Acre," growled O'Byrne, who had quite other ideas.

"Well, that might be what his Lordship wanted, him and his French ideas—washed away on the tide side by side with the common people."

"Don't mock, Sullivan."

"When would I do that? Galvin made a mess of the work, I see," said Sullivan, noting the blue lips drawn back from the teeth, the fixed glare of the protruding brown eyes, the dried blood around their rims, the burn of the rope.

"That's why you have the cutting of him, Sullivan. You know the pride that's in Galvin. He'd not easily forego the pleasure of holding up a head and proclaiming it that of a traitor. When he made a mull of the drop and I'd to finish the poor man off, he strode off the platform and back into the prison shouting "You hoors finish the work, 'tis obvious you know it better than I." This was a good man, Sullivan, and I couldn't have left him to thrash there, for all Galvin's rage."

"You've taken this one hard, O'Byrne. I just do the work I'm paid for. Hmm… Some of them teeth look good for a feller his age. His friends must have kept him in charcoal and vinegar all the time he was in here. I'll get my pincers. It's easier managed now than after I have the head off him. They'll do someone else nicely, and our pockets too."

"You will not."

"All right so! He can keep his teeth. I'm in a hurry in any case. Help me with his clothes, will you, before he stiffens on us. That's a fine pair of shoes he has on him. Not big enough for me though, but they'll fit you well enough. You'll need to sell the shirt and the breeks for they'll not go round me and you'd lose yourself in them."

"I won't walk in hanged men's shoes, you know that."

"Who you sell 'em to won't need to know."

They stripped the corpse in silence, O'Byrne folding the stained garments away into a jute bag, as carefully as though they were holy relics. Sullivan reached for his cleaver.

O'Byrne closed his eyes as his companion raised it above each limb in turn, administering a swift gouge to each; the flesh parted like mouths opening but no blood seeped from the wounds.

"Sure it's not like the old days, when they spilled their tripe for them and had their manhood stripped away, and then quartered them for real. Then the birds got a rare ould feast off them. They'll have to make do with what they can pick off his head, though I don't know where they'll spike it. This Greek temple of a courthouse has nowhere it could go."

"Stop there a moment. I'll close his eyes first."

"Ach, O'Byrne, you'll have a hard time of it—they've come too far out. What use would that be? 'Tis what the birds go for first."

"Well I'll not have it made easy for them."

Sullivan watched as O'Byrne struggled ineffectually with his thumbs to push the eyeballs back.

"Stop there, now, will ye, or you'll have them out of his head altogether. This is how to do it."

Sullivan rummaged in the pockets of a greasy brown coat lying across a chair and brought out a filthy rag.

"Tis best wetted," he said, and damped it in the bowl of water provided for him to wash in afterwards. He laid the rag across Goward's eyes and with a quick manipulation of thumb and index finger pushed each eyeball back.

"That's a grand job is it not? The surgeon and the butcher are not so far apart, are they, O'Byrne? Only there's them as have fine manners and big bills and them whose patients don't squirm. You can have the closing of his eyes now."

"Thank ye, Sullivan."

"Right, so. But it's a useless bit of work this all the same. Will you hold his head still whilst I take it off?"

"He'll not be moving on you."

"No, but it's more cleanly done if you hold him," said Sullivan patiently.

O'Byrne placed his fingers gently just above Goward's ears. Sullivan brought down the cleaver twice more.

O'Byrne put his head down and scuttled along the Quays like a determined crab, eyes fixed in the dusk on the logs rattling and jumping in his barrow as it passed over the uneven cobbles. Steep Fishamble Street at last, darker here amongst the tall houses—*that's better*. He braced himself against the incline and heaved the barrow forward. A gust of voices reached him from the Bull's Head but he didn't turn his head. "Later, O'Byrne,", he told himself, "You can get Burnchurch to stand you a drink though by the look of the feller he'll be needing it more than you." At last he reached the squat façade of St. John's, and paused to catch his breath. He turned down the flank of the church, seeking the side door with his right hand for he could now see nothing in the narrow alley but looming shapes in the gloom; it was going to be a cloudy night, no stars nor moon. A log rolled off the cart and onto his foot. He swore, and kicked it away. Something squeaked and skittered behind him. Yes, here must be the door, the wall giving way to an embrasure, then the smoother touch of wood. *What time is it?* Nothing to do but wait. He leaned against the door and closed his eyes. "Not long now, sir," he muttered. "I'm sorry you've had such a rough journey of it."

Half-dozing, propped up against the door-frame, he was shaken awake by the bells tolling the hour. Ten o'clock. Yes, he was right. He was on time. But what the devil was he to do if the other didn't show himself? He looked in the direction of Fishamble Street and the occasional flash of light and clop and rumble of carriages. None of them stopped, and no figure entered the alley. O'Byrne swore softly; in that moment heard a rattling at his back and the door opened, then his name, whispered. "Will you help me move the wood, sir?" O'Byrne said. "I have him in the sack underneath."

"I've the crypt open. We must be quick."

With rapid fumbling movements the two emptied the barrow of the blocks of wood, carefully placing them on the cobbles so they made little noise.

"Now, sir, you take this end. Them's his feet you can feel there. I'll take him under the arms. I'll manage the little bag too."

"We'll lie him down inside a moment," said Burnchurch. "Then I'll bolt the door and bring the light up."

After some grunting and heaving their burden was brought in and laid upon the flagstones. As Burnchurch barred the door, O'Byrne looked around the looming space of the church. He saw a wavering light at floor level, casting vast shadows of the high pulpit, the galleries and the box pews, flickering across the pipes of the vast organ as though it was playing its own silent music. But where was the light coming from? As if Burnchurch read O'Byrne's thoughts, the younger man said, "I've left the lamp on the steps to the crypt. I couldn't stay down there myself for I would have died of fright, though I have made all ready. I suppose though it might be a better death than dying of a surfeit of Sunday Schools at home."

"No, leave the light on the stairs. We can see well enough now, and you cannot carry him and it. We don't want it seen from outside if we can manage it, or we'll be taken for resurrectionists."

Despite the musty air O'Byrne breathed more easily once they had got their burden down the steep, clammy steps.

"In here," said Burnchurch, backing into a smaller chamber. "Let's rest him and I'll bring the lamp through." O'Byrne kept his grip on Goward's armpits through the tied sack, his torso resting against his knees. The smaller bag he had slung around his neck by its strings; its contents rested against his chest. Burnchurch came back quickly with the lamp and as he held it up O'Byrne saw a veritable store-room of ancient lead coffins, some split or cracked or stained with unnameable fluids, ranged haphazardly on stone shelves. A dusty heap of leg bones and upturned skulls in one corner suggested an abandoned attempt to bring some order to this forgotten chamber and its nameless occupants.

"You did well to manage this, sir. A connection of Mr. Griffiths, was it? No, best not tell me."

"I don't know that he can stay here long," murmured Burnchurch. "There's so little space for dead Dubliners now that these poor bones will be cleared out to make room for new ones sooner or later."

"Better here than the Croppies' Acre."

'Yes, the tide would have taken him from there before we'd have had time to move him. This coffin down here was already empty, thank God. I don't know what I would have done if I had had to clear one out myself. This place rattles me as it is."

"Ready to lift him again, sir?"

"Yes," but O'Byrne saw Burnchurch struggle to conquer his nerves.

"Our job's almost over, sir. Take his feet as before. That's it, let him down gently. Good, that's him safely in. Let's see will he straighten out a bit. God bless you, sir."

Burnchurch didn't know if O'Byrne was addressing him or the huddled form in the sack.

"Just a moment, sir," and O'Byrne leaned over. He loosened the tie at the top of the sack and drawing a knife from his pocket, he slit one side of Goward's improvised shroud, exposing the torso in its torn, dirty shirt, and the ragged curled edges of flesh where Sullivan had sliced through the neck. Burnchurch turned away and vomited over his shoes, but O'Byrne went on talking as though he wasn't there.

"I'm just going to move your arms, sir, so that you lie as a Christian should. You're a bit stiff on me, so forgive me if I use a bit of force. I'm sorry you've no better grave clothes than your own shirt, but if you travel with this you'll want for nothing," and he reached into another capacious pocket and pulled out a rosary which he wound around the now crossed hands.

"I've your head here, sir." He lifted the strings of the bag over his head, and cradled it. After a moment's thought he turned to Burnchurch and said, "Best you not look at him. Death changes a man's face so you'd not know him sometimes, and it's that way with him. Remember him when he was live and laughing."

"Thank you," croaked Burnchurch, turning to face the far wall. O'Byrne rested the bag on the body and with both hands gently lifted its contents.

"There now," he said, placing the head in the space above the neck, only for it to tip back, leaving a gaping space. O'Byrne swore softly, pulling the grubby stock from his own neck, and arranging it over the terrible wound. Finally he tugged the cut ends of the sack around the corpse.

"Help me now with this coffin lid, and then we'll say some prayers over him. You've had a mighty courage to do what you did this night, sir."

Burnchurch turned, white-faced and trembling still. "I think you mock me."

"I do not. You're not used to sights such as these. You could have washed your hands of him and all this, and stayed at home."

"I couldn't watch, at the end," said Burnchurch, starting to cry. "I was at a window opposite with Captain Annesley and Mr. Griffiths, and I had to turn my face away. I could hear the crowd roaring and cheering. I cursed them all, but Annesley told me afterwards what you'd done, and that they were cheering you. You were a better friend to him than I, O'Byrne, and you are now."

"It's his wife will need friendship now, sir. I had made a promise to him, regarding her, and I shall need you to help me in it."

Dublin Evening Post

20th June 1800

It is to be applauded that the fine new building that is Green Street Court House lacks the spikes that adorn some provincial seats of justice for the purpose of displaying the heads of executed criminals. Thus we have been spared the sight of the face of James, Lord Goward, who paid the ultimate price for treason on 14th June inst., frozen in his last agony. It is our considered view that as this ostensibly enlightened century draws to its close such medieval manifestations of the workings of justice no longer have their place, but there are those who point to continued foment in the North in particular and argue that the example of a severed head therefore serves its just purpose. We have been told that on occasion in other parts of the country where justice has been so served, that faithful servants of the deceased, with the agility of a cat and the head for heights of the alpinist, have effected the removal of a master's head.

It remains the view of this paper that Lord Goward was dealt with hardly. That he was guilty of convening a domiciliary committee of rebels under his own roof seems not to be in doubt, nor the offence of administering the oath of the insurrectionists on more than one occasion, and both are sufficient for a man to hang. Yet others have escaped with a lesser penalty. Lord Goward gave himself up to the authorities willingly, to avoid the reprisals promised by Lord Nugent in the aftermath of Ballynahinch (reprisals which to some degree occurred in any case as that gentleman was unable or unwilling to adequately control those under his command). The jury was presented with the unedifying spectacle of a witness who was openly bought but despite the dramatic unmasking of this gentleman's interest by a fellow Crown witness, the twelve good men and true—true to those who carefully selected them—decided a man's fate in less time than it takes another to fill and light his pipe. Lord Goward was regarded by many of his own class as suspect even without the charges brought against him. His religion seems to have been in doubt, from the start of his long liaison with the Papist mistress whom he later made his wife, to the education in France of his natural son Edward Kearney, sometimes styled Viscount Kilkeel. It was his habit to fraternise with his servants, a number of whom were relations of his wife. The son is now in exile, an officer in Bonaparte's army. He is believed to have been of Humbert's band but was sent back with him as he was taken for a Frenchman, but if he sets foot on his native soil again he will be tried under the same indictment as his father. Indeed, it is our considered opinion that the father had to hang because the son had not been taken; a humiliating failure that demanded vengeance. Once the news reached Dublin that the son had escaped, his father's fate was sealed.

So Lord Goward has been made an example of, a man no longer in the prime of life, and furthermore unable to shoulder a musket or handle a sword, due to a duelling injury that deprived him of the use of his right arm. He will become the subject of ballads and broadsheets extolling his virtues, just as have Lord Edward Fitzgerald and Mr. Theobald Wolfe Tone, and if the Union now debated so hotly is eventually achieved, it will do nothing to prevent his attaining such heroic status—a status which, by all accounts, he never sought in life.

Whereas the said Lord Goward died before he was attainted, be it enacted by the authority of the present parliament that the said James Goward, commonly called Lord James Goward, deceased, as from the fourteenth day of June, one thousand eight hundred, shall by virtue of this act be adjudged to be convicted and attainted of high treason, to all intents and purposes, as if he had been attainted during his life, and that all and every manors, messuages, lands, tenements, rents, reversions, remains, possessions, rights, conditions, interests, offices, fees, annuities and all other the hereditaments, leases for years, chattels real, and other appurtenances of what nature whatsoever they be, of him the said James Goward, which he, or any person to their or any of their use, or in trust for him, had on the said day on which the said James Goward, is hereby adjudged to be attainted as aforesaid or at any time since, shall stand and be forfeited to his Majesty, his heirs and successors, and shall be deemed vested and adjudged to be in the actual real seizure and possession of his Majesty, his heirs and successors, without any inquisition or office hereafter to be taken or found; and also that all and every other the goods and debts, and other the chattels personal whatsoever of him the said James Goward, whereof upon the day of the death of him the said James Goward, or any person in trust for him, stood possessed, either in law or equity, shall be deemed and adjudged to be forfeited unto, and are thereby vested in his Majesty, without any inquisition or office to be found hereafter.

"So I am destitute, gentlemen." said Mary. "If they free me I have nothing but the clothes on my back and what I may henceforth earn by the labour of my own hands."

Matthew Ingham glanced at Dr. Benson before answering. The older man gave an almost imperceptible nod.

"That is so, Lady Goward. Where lawyers are prolix you are admirably concise."

"I don't care that goods and chattels and leases and impertinences or whatever they call them are no longer mine. They have taken him and so I have nothing left but those still living whom I love and who truly love me."

"I fear there is more."

"Let me see."

Be it also enacted that any dignities and honours, right or title, conferred by marriage duly solemnised or which might have descended to any lawful issue of Lord James Goward prior to this Act of attainment are hereby extinguished. Specifically he who goes unlawfully by the name of Edward, Viscount Kilkeel, being the natural son of the said James, Lord Goward by an invalid marriage has no right to that title and henceforth shall be known as Mr. Edward Kearney as the lawful marriage of his parents contracted subsequent to his birth does not expunge the fact of his bastardy. The right or title of Lord Goward shall now be conferred on Timothy Hartsmere, Esq. of Diss in the County of Norfolk, distant cousin of the aforementioned James, Lord Goward, deceased.

"I beg that you will call me Mrs. Goward, just as though I were a member of your Society, Mr. Ingham, for I know you reject all titles. I have seen that in the Quaker burial ground Edwin and Janet Chittleborough that were the dearest of friends to me lie in graves of utmost simplicity equal to all their companions who await Judgement Day with them there, and this to me is right for we are equal in the eyes of our Lord were we rich or poor in life. So I ask that you will both do your utmost to put it about for me that I wish only his name, for there were plenty who begrudged me his title. Know that I was his wife from when I was seventeen years old but had to appear to the world in a far less honourable light though the good Lord knew differently and that our marriage was lawful so not as they say, for my husband was a Catholic when he married me and for the rest of his life after, but had he declared it he would be no Lord Goward. So now he is no Lord Goward but a Catholic gentleman who was my husband and now is dead. I loved him and that with God's blessing was enough for me."

"Dear lady, there is yet another page," said Ingham. "Benson, would you read it to Mrs. Goward? I don't know that I can, and the poor lady weeps too much to do so herself."

Furthermore, whereas the said Mr. Edward Kearney has been notoriously engaged in the rebellion, by taking up arms and levying war against his Majesty, and by having corresponded with, and adhered to his enemies, and by otherwise fomenting and promoting the same and acting therein, and being conscious of his guilt has fled from justice, this same Mr. Edward Kearney late of Goward Hall in the County of Down but now, or lately, resident at Paris and in the pay of the army of the French Republic, is ordered to surrender himself and abide his Trial on Pain of being attainted of High Treason.

"I shall never see my boy again. Forgive me gentlemen but I—"

Benson caught her as she slumped forward in the chair. He gently eased the limp body backwards.

"Chafe her hands, Ingham, until I find the hartshorn."

"You did well to think of it."

"There is a limit to what poor humanity can stand. She is so weakened by incarceration that I had thought the shock of Goward's death would have carried her off."

"Tis a pity to put the hartshorn to her so soon. If she is insensible then she is granted some fleeting escape from sorrow."

"Which is why she swooned. Nature knows what can be borne and when a moment's blessed release is needed. I shall physick her that she sleeps, and if Patrick will take turns with me to sit by her and follow my instructions then we can save her."

"Save her for what? What will her life be now?"

Griffiths slipped twice on his way to the Kearney house, on a path greasy with rain. He was trying to get the worst of the mud off on the boot scraper when the door opened.

"I thought I heard something," said Patrick. "If anyone wished me ill he wouldn't have been scraping his shoes, though. Come away in."

"I'll walk half the road through your house, Patrick."

"So leave the shoes in the passage along of my boots. Sure you can get about in your stockinged feet well enough."

"Thank you."

"It'll be my sister you're wanting to see?'"

"Well, yes. But how goes it with you?"

"I manage. I've a back as tough as pig skin now. Tis herself that troubles me more. She won't talk much but insists on doing the work of three men. I'll put you in the parlour till I find her."

The furniture in the little panelled room looked to Griffiths to have the forlorn look of people made ready for a party but for whom the carriage never called. Goward's gifts, surely? The space was dominated by a circular oak table, but the ladderback chairs were ranged against the walls; sitting on one, Griffiths wondered if the Kearneys ever ate there. A fine long-case clock however was clearly kept wound, though the fireplace was swept out and the log basket empty. A burst of rain spattered against the window. He sighed and looked down at his muddied stockings, and wiggled his toes. This was not how he'd wished to appear.

He stood up at the sound of the door-handle turning.

"Mr. Griffiths." Smiling, Mary held out both hands.

He took both in his, and awkward, he dropped to one knee, kissing the fingers of the right.

"Please don't, sir," she said, gently pulling his hands upwards. He faced her. "How do you keep?"

"I am as you see me. I have food in my belly and clothes to my back, but my heart is raw. I sleep better now for I make myself work so hard and long that I can do nothing else. Thankfully I dream less now."

"Work?"

She held out her hands, scrubbed, clean, but roughened.

"You see? A countrywoman once more."

The contours of her face had softened, that pure youthful oval gone, but her skin was clear, the blue eyes bright and kind. Her still plentiful hair was pinned under a spotless white mob-cap, but a grey tendril had escaped and curled against her collar-bone. He remembered then that it had always done that. Griffiths wanted to wind it around his finger. She was wearing a plain brown dress, the sleeves folded back to the elbow. Her only jewellery was her wedding ring.

"Wickmere has written me that he would like to bring you to England. You would want for nothing and would be a companion to Mrs. Godwin."

"Dear Peg. That's impossible, though. My husband's bones lie somewhere in Ireland and though I can put no monument over them I must walk the same earth until I am buried in it myself. Please be seated, Nathaniel, we may talk better."

"Would he want you to live like this? Your poor hands… "

"I am useful. I am with those who love me."

"I love you."

'Don't."

"Don't love you or don't say so? I'm sorry. I didn't want to declare myself so abruptly—nor to offend you, as I see I have. I would take it back except that it's true. I had rehearsed my words so carefully, but find now that I have lost my place. So being the clumsiest suitor a woman ever had to bear with, I shall stumble on in the hope that you will at least appreciate my sincerity if not my wit. I confess that I have always admired you, Mrs. Goward. I now ask that after whatever you consider to be a decent interval, you will allow me to protect you. In sum, will you marry me?"

She took his hands. "I wondered when this question would come. You do me great honour, Nathaniel, but I do not need to consider. I cannot marry you. I cannot marry anyone."

"I wouldn't expect you to give me an answer all at once. You would not have to leave Ireland, or leave here. I have my new patron's lethargy to thank for my still being here. It is too much effort for him to replace me with one of his own choosing, when he has so little interest in this place."

"That might change, but that's not why I refuse you. I do not love you as you deserve to be loved, Nathaniel. My heart lies in an unmarked grave."

"I have been too precipitate—"

"No. You were one of my husband's dearest friends. You were with him in his last days when I could not be. You saw him die. You brought me his last letter. It is I who cannot consent; I do not believe he would object to your suit."

"Then please consider. Let me return, even six months from now."

"I cannot bear you children, Nathaniel, and that rectory has had need of their presence for many years now. You are a young man still, you would find yourself in your prime burdened with an old woman—a laughing stock—and without a dowry to excuse her."

"Where one loves does age matter? I would become a better man in your embrace."

"I am sorry, Nathaniel." She paused. "Does Bessie know your errand?"

"Bessie? No. But would you not be happier beneath the same roof as your daughter?"

"The cruellest thing I could do to her."

He stared.

"Did you not know, Nathaniel? She has adored you for years."

"Bessie? She has never indicated this, by word or sign."

"How could she? A woman has enough difficulty saying what she does not want, let alone what she does. Who was there to speak for her?"

"I never considered—"

"Does she eat at your table?"

"Yes. I don't consider her a servant. She is furthermore of great help to me in my work; she is thorough and conscientious, and knows also when I should be left alone."

"You have also said how much a help she is at the school. Nathaniel, I educated her for such a station in life. She does all that a good wife should do excepting that she makes your bed for you but does not lie in it. You are a man, with all man's impulses, are you not? To intrigue with another man's wife I do not think is in your nature, so—"

"Indeed, not."

"So I imagine that when you have need of release you go away from here. Belfast I expect."

He flushed.

"Forgive me if I do not speak as a lady, nor as would the humblest drudge in the meanest cabin. As a woman I have had to submit to the most unspeakable treatment which the most degraded drab would not deserve. I have been so tried that I find I have little inclination to feminine niceties, and in any case, I must speak as a man only because Bessie's father cannot."

"As you speak as a man I shall answer you as though you were one. I don't know how you divined it, but it's true, I do go to Belfast. My congress is with the owner of an establishment, not with her stable. She is an accomplished and astute woman, and her salon is peopled with judges, writers, men of commerce. That I can be intimate with a lady I do not even like overmuch, though she has many admirable qualities, only shows me with utter clarity how far I have fallen away from God's plan. I had hoped that in uniting myself with you I might recover my better nature."

"Your candour does you honour, Nathaniel, and I wish I could answer you as you deserve. I cannot. I can only be practical, and urge that in Bessie you might find all you need if you could but see it, and the most innocent affection if you wanted it in the place of purchased smiles and caresses. I cannot command my own heart, much less expect to direct yours, Nathaniel, but could you not try to make my child happy?"

"I do not love her as I do her mother, Mary."

"Even if I loved you as a wife should, I could not make her miserable."

"Oh Mary."

He lifted both her hands and kissed them repeatedly, then pressed her knuckles to his eyes.

"Nathaniel, I'm sorry."

"There is one other matter I must speak to you of, but you must keep this in your heart, or it will harm braver men than I. I know now where he lies, Mary. His bones. His head."

Methwold

24th June 1804

Although Jack owned the little flint and ragstone cottage, as he did all of its fellows in the village, and paid for the upkeep of its one inhabitant, he always paused before knocking on the door. He would never have dreamed of walking in unannounced, even though Peg longed to tell him she wanted him to.

"No fool like an old fool," he repeated to himself, as he had at least once a week since his marriage.

The door opened as he raised his fist to knock. "Come in, dear Jack. I was out in the garden, but I heard your horse. I know his hooves by now. You have a way of riding him which is yours alone."

He stooped under the low lintel.

"Mrs. Greene's daughter is here with the laundry. I will ask her to prepare some tea for us. Take this chair by the hearth and I'll be back directly."

Jack stretched out his long legs and stared discontentedly at the fire-irons. There was little here that did not have some utility. The china dogs on the rough beam that formed the mantelpiece and a glass vase of flowers on the windowsill were the only ornaments. He thought about his own fireplace in the Long Gallery at the Hall, darkened oak in which the Wickmere arms had been carved by a Royalist ancestor. That gentleman had lavished funds and attention on the old Hall in celebration of the Restoration, but now all was at risk from a determined younger wife with not enough to keep her busy but a Grenadier and a preoccupation with modernising.

"How is Lady Honoria?" asked Peg.

"She has a lover."

"Oh Jack! Will you challenge him?"

"No, Peg, with neither pistol nor summons. I don't care enough. It is my indifference to what she does with him that perturbs me more. She is set on rebuilding the Hall—*that* I care about. I shall have nowhere I recognise as home soon."

"My poor Jack. How does the young fellow?"

"I hardly see him. He is forever in the hands of tutors. Honoria is already talking about schools. I want to take him for walks, or to punt on the lake, or to go with the gamekeeper and shoot something for the pot, but she will not have it—— calls it vulgar and tells me I am too old to be good company for a boy."

Peg lent across and held his hand.

"Perhaps school will be no bad thing. It will free him of petticoat government, teach him friendships and help him grow up. Then when he comes home he may himself insist on doing all those things with his father. Or you go yourself up to Charterhouse or wherever it is Honoria is thinking of and take him around town with you, just the two of you."

"At Charterhouse I had the dearest friend of my life, Peg."

He turned his face up to the low white-washed ceiling, blinking.

"James counselled me against my marriage, Peg. I have had barely a day's happiness since I sent you here. My only delight is the boy and that delight is severely rationed by his mother."

"You'd counselled him against his," she said smiling. "He took no notice of you either."

"When they did marry, it was utterly the right thing to do."

"Ah, Jack, they were already married."

"In some sham way. Surely she must have realised."

"No sham, Jack, but a Catholic marriage and thus a secret one. James outwardly conformed but there was always a chaplain in that house. All you saw was a servant."

"Good God, Peg, James Goward a papist! You will be telling me you are a Methodist next."

"No, but think how hard it must have been for them, and for her to play the dishonoured role all those years."

"Not nearly so hard as it is now."

"You've had news?"

"Only that she is definitely under her brother's roof, a house about the size of this one, caring for his children and trying to be useful. An old doctor who delivered Edward apparently paid her way out of the gaol or she might be there still.

Not that *I* did anything to help her." He kicked savagely at the fire-irons, clattering them over. "I don't know how they fare there, for a traitor's estates are confiscated. Edward has tried to get her to join him in France but she will not leave Ireland for James's poor bones are there.'"

"If only he were at rest in the little churchyard here and her a widow under this roof with me."

Jack contemplated his shoes in silence. Peg sipped her tea and watched him.

"It would be a dangerous undertaking even now," he said eventually. "But perhaps not an impossible one. I shall start with Griffiths. I believe he knows more than he thinks prudent to say."

"I didn't seriously want to suggest—"

"Hush, Peg, you have given an old man a sense of purpose. Thank you for that, my dear, as for so much else."

Le Comte

My dear Mother,

I write once more to plead with you in the face of your obstinacy, to leave your difficult situation and let me bring you here, where you would also be a comfort to me. I fear I plead in vain, for you would rather rely on your own strength than be beholden to anyone, even if he be your son. There is room too for my uncle Patrick and his family. I can get them land to till, and it would be honestly got—and it would be theirs.

It is a fine place, this France, though you might pronounce it godless. My dear school in Douai is no more, closed by the revolution. Its work continues, though, on English soil. How matters, change, Mother. An English gentleman who is also a Catholic may educate his children in his own land if he not make too much noise about it, and my old school, now in the north country, is endowed by a number of landed families who for all those years have kept the faith. If change is wrought so in England then may it also reach Ireland one day. But the dwindling band who fought for Ireland—and may fight no more now that Emmet and Russell are dead—is honoured here. Our enterprise failed, but it had to be undertaken. I shall never forget the rout of Castlebar, the astuteness of Humbert to listen to those who knew. The poorest peasants of Connaught told him to take the path by night through the wild country by Lough Conn and thus take the militia by surprise. So many joined our side that day and those that followed— a glimpse of what a victory over our enemies might have been—and paid with their lives when hope died at Ballinamuck. I so longed to tell Father of those last days of glory but all that time he was locked up defenceless against the forces ranged against him— and you also, utterly without protection. He was hanged because they couldn't take me, mother, and when I wake in the darkest hours, as I do often, I ask myself again and again what I have done to deserve so rich a gift as the life he sacrificed for me, for I spend it so unworthily.

I meet members of the Irish Directory here in Paris from time to time, the men who might have been our leaders now: O'Connor I have recently seen and he changes little,

but that he is now resigned to dying a Frenchman. He is otherwise the same opinion-
ated, exasperating and argumentative O'Connor of earlier days, always in search of
emoluments and now embarked on a mission to marry both a fair face and money.
Though he now enters middle-age he is still considered a handsome man and a charm-
ing one when he wishes to be, so I expect he will be successful in his mission. He has
though been of great support to me in my military career: there is now less glory in it
but there is honour. It will not fall to us to raise Ireland from her knees. I have not seen
active service since Hohenlinden but I am much respected for my teaching here at my
old Academy, and I am regularly in the company of Cécile's children, who have been
raised by an aunt and uncle in straitened circumstances, from whom they have learned
prudence as well as unassuming good manners. They see me as an affectionate elder
cousin, and I do not tell them the joy and sorrow combined it gives me to glimpse in
their lineaments, their gestures, their glances, my lost Cécile and their father, my friend.
I do not know that I shall ever marry, Mother, though not for want of O'Connor's
encouragement to keep him company in his quest. It is your company I miss, the more
because I believe I did not appreciate it sufficiently when I had it in plenty. Here in
this country I shall always be "le comte", years of revolution notwithstanding, and you
would also have the title my father gave you, though everything else that was his, his
life included, was taken from us. I beg you to let me do whatever I am able in order
that I might support you, for his sake.

Your loving son,
Edward Goward

March 1805

The horses plodded patiently onwards, over the crest of the long field and downwards, the earth peeling open its rich dark flesh in their wake. Mary followed as Patrick whistled to the mares, hearing the rhythmic slap and suck of the plough turns, without looking up from her work. With her right hand she reached into the bag wedged against her left hip, drawing out a fistful of dung and pressing it into the furrow. With her left she took a seed potato from the basket carried on her right elbow and pressed it into the manure, releasing its rich aroma. In one deft movement of a little stick, she measured an unvarying distance from potato to potato. What Mary had lost of youth's suppleness she made up for, in contrast to her companions, in method and patience. But all the splashing and scrubbing at the icy pump would not remove the black half-moons from those finger nails that had darted over lace bobbins and embroidered fire screens, things destroyed or in use in other hands. She and the other women worked fast, for as soon as the ploughing finished, the horses would be turned to the bottom of the field and the work of covering the troughs commence. Thus did the Kearneys always sow now. Mary thought of her father and mother scrabbling in the stony earth, and felt again for them a burst of pride at this new method introduced by their son-in-law. The land though had never been theirs, and now it was no longer his.

Bones: September 1805

There was something familiar in the gait of the figure Mary saw coming in at the gate, and in the still boyish enthusiasm with which this grey-headed man started to run towards her, calling her name.

"Jack, is it you?"

He embraced her. "I have him. I have his poor bones."

"I am almost ready, Jack."

Wickmere looked up. What a pretty woman she still was, as dignified in her country-woman's garb and stout boots as she had been as a lady. Those dark blue eyes had not faded and her face was warmed but not weatherbeaten by its exposure to soft winds and rain.

"I have said farewell to them all: Dr. Benson, Mr. Ingham… " The blue eyes filled. "And to all those who were dear to me and who sleep in the burial ground."

"And what does Patrick say?"

"He wants longer to think on Mr. Andrews's offer, and thanks him for it. I think he fears the sea voyage more than what he might find beyond it. But with me there, he believes he will eventually be persuaded."

"Let us call on Griffiths, then, and speak with Bessie."

"I am thinking that Bessie will stay wherever he is."

"Ah."

"She is all a man in his position could look for if he does not look for wealth. She has loved him long and silently. Without my distracting presence, and with their continued respectable proximity I hope his eyes will be opened to her virtues. He seeks preferment back in England now but it will be hard for him—perhaps not so hard there as here—for he is tainted by his connection to a traitor."

"He regrets nothing, Mary. The circle is closing, then. I have written to Peg to expect you; this is a happiness she has long dreamed of. Your chair is waiting at her hearth, and the quiet corner in the churchyard for him whom we both loved. When spring comes we will make that journey into France."

"I have just one more task here."

"I was wondering what you did with that sack, Mary. Can no one else do this for you?"

"No, this I must do alone. I will nevermore see the place. It is a cashel. The bracken grows thick upon it, brown and dry as a nest at this time of year. I will line my husband's grave with it, so that he may lie soft upon it and turn his face up to the sky."

Historical Background

In 1795, on Cave Hill overlooking Belfast, a group of United Irishmen took an oath "never to desist in our efforts to until we subvert the authority of England over our country and assert our independence." Amongst them were the Dublin barrister Theobald Wolfe Tone, the Belfast linen merchant, Henry Joy McCracken, Samuel Neilson and Thomas Russell. Tone and Russell were Anglicans, the other two Presbyterians. The society of the United Irishmen had been founded in a Belfast tavern in 1791 but proscribed in May 1794; the republic the movement sought to establish was inspired by the revolutionary principles which had convulsed France since 1789 and encompassed equal rights for and enfranchisement of all Irishmen regardless of religious persuasion (the emancipation of women was still far off). Indeed, the United Irishmen looked to France for practical as well as ideological support for their aims. Accordingly the French Directory sent a fleet in 1796, with which Tone sailed, but which due to a series of miscalculations and adverse weather had to turn back in disarray without a single French soldier landing in Ireland. A further French invasion in August 1798 led by General Jean Joseph Amable Humbert met with initial success at Ballina and notably Castlebar and but had to eventually surrender to superior numbers at Ballinamuck. Escorted to Dublin, the French officers were exchanged for British prisoners held by France, but those officers of Irish origin were hanged for treason; Wolfe Tone was captured at Buncrana when the French ship he was on surrendered, and he committed suicide in prison.

That invasion came too late. From May to October 1798 rebellion gripped Ireland. An estimated 30-50,000 lost their lives, of which only a relatively small proportion died in battle, greater numbers being accounted for by atrocities and reprisals committed by both sides, of which the New Ross and Scullabogue barn massacres (to give an example from each) are amongst the most notorious, and characterised not just by killing but by acts of torture apparently peculiar to Ireland at that time, such as pitch-capping and half-hanging. From the beginning the United Irishmen movement was infiltrated by spies in Ireland and where members were active on the continent, notably in Paris and Hamburg. The final battle of the rebellion in Ulster took place at Ballynahinch in County Down in June.

I first heard mention of the United Irishmen aged about ten in a (state) primary school in Belfast in the 1970s. What caught my curiosity then was that here was a rebellion led predominantly by Protestants, in which Irishmen were apparently *united*. It felt to me then, growing up in a city in the grip of apparently intractable sectarian violence, as though it had been Ulster's last chance, an "if only." What was not mentioned in this glancing school-room look at the rebellion was that dissenters of any kind were then subject to certain penalties. There were penal laws in place against Catholics, designed primarily to legally deprive them of land, including for instance the requirement that a Catholic landowner had to divide his estate equally between all his children (which might sound fair but in fact was aimed at the break-up of major estates) and the right of a Protestant neighbour to "discover," i.e. appropriate, Catholic-owned land. It was illegal to set up a Catholic school (which led to the phenomenon of the "hedge school-master"), or to be guardian of a child (so a dying Catholic would not be able to nominate a co-religionist to take care of his children). Catholics could not follow a military or legal career, or hold public office, though they could be doctors. Catholics could be whipped for refusing to work on a holy day, or for making a pilgrimage to a holy well, were not allowed to carry arms or to own a horse costing more than five pounds. This list is by no means exhaustive, and does not include the restrictions placed on Catholic clergy. Until 1793 it was illegal for a Protestant and a Catholic to marry, and the priest who performed such a marriage could be hanged. These laws, developed to keep or reduce Catholics to a state of poverty and ignorance, were introduced following the Cromwellite and Williamite settlements of the seventeenth century. The English agricultural reformer Arthur Young was shocked at their severity, but was reassured that they were frequently not enforced, though whether they were or not would depend entirely on the zeal or otherwise of local magistrates. The Protestant Peep o' Day Boys however justified their own outrages against Catholics by saying that they were enforcing the Penal Laws when the magistrates failed to do so. In 1792 an off-shoot of the Peep o'Day Boys developed into what is now known as the Orange Order. What is less well-known is the fact that Protestant dissenters (so in Ulster predominantly Presbyterians) had some common cause with Catholics. Presbyterian marriages, for instance, were not legalised until 1782. The inspiration of events initially in America, and latterly in

France on this common cause was both positive and negative. Deepening Directory-sponsored violence frightened not only London but also those who would otherwise have supported rebellion in Ireland. Napoleon's increasingly imperialistic tendencies and French hostile reaction to Anglo-American trade agreements alienated numbers of northern Protestants who looked across the Atlantic and admired what they saw, and in increasing numbers emigrated there.

Post 1798 rebellion flickered again, notably in the abortive Dublin uprising of 1803 for which Robert Emmet was hanged, but was considered to have been crushed decisively with the death in ambush of James Corcoran at Enniscorthy in 1804.

Catholic emancipation did not finally come until 1829 thanks primarily to the efforts of Daniel O'Connell and the Dublin-born Prime Minister the Duke of Wellington, but shades of the penal laws persisted much longer. In 1854 a parish priest in County Fermanagh had to flee to America to avoid arrest for having married a Miss Ann Jones to a Mr. Pat Teague; he was able to return in 1859 only due to the intervention of the local landowner, the Earl of Erne. When my mother trained as a school-teacher at Stranmillis College in Belfast in the late 1960s she was obliged to obtain a reference from a Protestant minister before she could teach in the state school system. A fellow student who refused on principle to do this never taught. It would take some time to list the inequalities in employment opportunities, council house allocation and all the rest which lay behind the Civil Rights marches of the late 1960s and their aftermath.

The love story of James Goward and Mary Kearney has a different geographical inspiration. In 1820, the 10th Earl of Strathmore, John Bowes, married Mary Milner, his former servant, at St. George's Hanover Square, a few hours before he died. He had lived with her for years and they had one son, John Bowes, founder of the Bowes Museum at Barnard Castle. The 10th earl's mother's matrimonial misadventures had already found their way into fiction, as the inspiration for Thackeray's *The Luck of Barry Lyndon*. Prior to his liaison with Mary Milner, the Earl had had as a mistress a married woman, Sarah Hussey Delaval, Countess Tyrconnell. When she died, the distraught Strathmore himself made up her face to make her as lifelike as possible.

Real People in the Novel

Theobald Wolfe Tone (1763-98), a barrister and founder member of the United Irishmen, born in Dublin, a descendent of Huguenots from Gascony, he persuaded the French government in 1796 to send an expedition to Ireland under General Hoche and was made an adjutant-general in the French army. Tone was unable to persuade Napoleon, distracted by the Egyptian campaign, to repeat an invasion until 1798, when Tone accompanied General Humbert. When that invasion was crushed, Tone was taken prisoner and court-martialled. Refused a soldier's death by firing-squad, he cut his throat in prison.

Francis Rawdon-Hastings (1754-1826) from 1793 known as Lord Moira and from 1816 as Marquess of Hastings, politician, army officer, landowner and champion of Catholic emancipation, served with the British in the American and French revolutionary wars, and later was Governor-General of India. Wolfe Tone described him as 'the Irish Lafayette'; Thackeray gave his name to the character Rawdon Crawley in *Vanity Fair*.

Bernard Ward, 1ˢᵗ Viscount Bangor (1719-1781), MP for Down in the Irish House of Commons and builder with his wife Lady Ann Bligh of Castle Ward by Strangford Lough. Bangor favoured the Palladian style and his wife the Gothic, so the house has two contrasting façades and the stylistic split is reflected internally. Their eldest son the second Viscount was considered an irredeemable lunatic from 1785.

John Philpot Curran (1750-1817), lawyer, politician, orator, champion of Catholic Emancipation, Master of the Rolls in Ireland and fighter of duels (five in all) born in County Cork, an Anglican. He eloquently defended a number of United Irishmen, including William Orr, Wolfe Tone, Napper Tandy, the Sheares brothers, Lord Edward Fitzgerald and William Drennan. He disowned his daughter Sarah for her relationship with Robert Emmet (executed 1803).

William Orr (1766-1797), a prosperous Presbyterian farmer from County Antrim was hanged for administering the oath of the United Irishmen to a soldier in a Scottish regiment. He was rousingly defended by Curran, but the chief prosecution witness gave perjured evidence, the jury was apparently under the influence, and it was believed that Orr was to be made an example of to discourage others from joining the United Irishmen. In the rebellion of the following year "Remember Orr" was a rallying cry in Ulster.

Lord Edward Fitzgerald (1763-1798), the fifth son of the Duke of Leinster, officer with the British army in America under Rawdon, New World explorer, politician in the Irish parliament, and United Irishman who negotiated Hoche's Irish expedition of 1796 and was colonel of the Kildare contingent of the rebels. He was betrayed by an informer and shot whilst resisting arrest in Dublin, and died in prison of his wounds. Stella Tillyard's biography of Lord Edward (see below) is as gripping as any novel.

Thomas Paine (1737-1809), son of a Thetford staymaker, political theorist, activist, philosopher, anti-slavery campaigner, journalist, revolutionary and one of the Founding Fathers of the United States. He was elected to the French National Convention in 1792: his *Rights of Man* (1791) is in some respects a defence of the French Revolution and was in effect required reading for leaders and adherents of the United Irishmen. Arrested in 1793 as an ally of the Girondins, he narrowly escaped the guillotine. Paine met Lord Edward Fitzgerald in London, a meeting into which I introduce James Goward.

Henry Munro (1758-98) was a Presbyterian linen merchant from Lisburn who commanded the United Irish forces at the battle of Ballynahinch, having taken over from the Presbyterian minister William Steel Dickson when the latter was arrested. Munro refused to carry out an attack on Nugent's forces by night, on the grounds that this was unchivalrous. Many of Munro's men deserted as a result, and the battle was lost. Munro was betrayed by the farmer paid to hide him and was hanged before his own house.

William Wentworth-Fitzwilliam, 4th Earl Fitzwilliam (1748-1833), landowner, mine- owner, politician, was known for his generosity as a landlord, cancelling rents or arrears in hard times. Appointed Lord Lieutenant of Ireland in August 1794 he was convinced that Catholic emancipation was the only way to stop unrest but under pressure from Ascendancy interests he was recalled by Pitt's government in February 1795.

Jean Joseph Amable Humbert (1755-1823), French general and commander of the 1798 invasion of Ireland. As a convinced republican, he was critical of Napoleon's imperial ambitions and was relieved of his post, emigrated to America, supported rebellion in Spanish Mexico and in Argentina, and fought the British again in 1812 at the battle of New Orleans. He ended his life peacefully in America as a school-teacher. He was said to have been a lover of Pauline Bonaparte whilst she was married to his commanding officer.

Thomas Galvin was hangman for Dublin City and County from 1787 to 1831 and thus executed a number of significant United Irishmen. The long-drop hanging technique in which the condemned person's neck is broken, rather than slowly strangling, was not adopted officially until 1872, but was in use earlier in Paris and Ireland. There are accounts of executions where death was instantaneous which suggest that the rope, whether by accident or design, was of the appropriate length. The cutting of the arms and legs of the corpse, as performed by Sullivan, was a nod to quartering as the final part of an execution for treason, and is described by Jonah Barrington (see contemporary sources, below).

Arthur O'Connor (1763-1852) a Protestant landowner from Bandon, County Cork, was a United Irishman who together with Lord Edward Fitzgerald sought France's support for an Irish revolution. He was arrested on his way to France in 1798, acquitted, but gaoled in Scotland until 1802 when he was released on condition of banishment. He became a general in Napoleon's army, married the daughter of the Marquis de Condorcet (she was about half his age), became a French citizen and ultimately the mayor of Le Bignon-Mirabeau.

Robert Emmet (1778-1803), born in Dublin to a wealthy Protestant family, expelled from Trinity College for United Irish activity, fled to France to avoid arrest and tried with Thomas Russell to enlist Napoleon's support for a further invasion of Ireland. Returning to Ireland, he led an abortive rising in Dublin in 1803 but might have escaped to France had he not gone to say good-bye to his betrothed Sarah Curran. He was hanged and decapitated by Thomas Galvin.

Thomas Russell (1767-1803), from County Cork, served in the British Army, but became a United Irishman at its foundation in 1791. He was author of the pamphlet 'Letter to the People of Ireland', outlining social and economic reform, and championed religious freedom and the abolition of slavery. Imprisoned from 1796 to 1802 and then banished to Hamburg, he met with Robert Emmet in Paris and planned a further, failed rising in 1803, for which he was hanged outside Downpatrick Gaol (where Mary was imprisoned).

At the time of writing the Rev. Jack Kinkead is priest-in-charge at Wicklow Parish Church (Church of Ireland). He is indeed 'an Antrim man, though Dublin trained.' I hope he will forgive an Antrim woman for using his name in the novel; he has an entirely positive part to play.

Sources

Contemporary Sources

John Killen (ed.), *The Decade of the United Irishmen: contemporary accounts 1791-1801*, Belfast, 1997.

"A brief account of the Trial of William Orr of Farranshane in the County of Antrim to which are annexed several interesting facts and documents connected therewith," Dublin, 1797.

"The trial of Mr. John McCann, for high treason: Dublin, 17th July, 1798," Cork, 1798. The wording of the indictment against James Goward is based on that in McCann's trial.

Statute 38 George III, c.77, "Act for the Attainder of Edward Fitzgerald, commonly called Lord Edward Fitzgerald, Cornelius Grogan and Beauchamp Bagenal Harvey, deceased, of high treason," Dublin, 1798. This was in fact the last use of attainder in British legal history, but I have used its text as the basis of the document read to Mary by Dr. Benson and Matthew Ingham.

The Autobiography of Wolfe Tone, edited by Sean O'Faolain, London, 1937.

Mary Leadbeater, *The Leadbeater Papers: The Annals of Ballintore*, London, 1862.

Arthur Young, *A Tour in Ireland*, 1780. I am indebted to this pioneer agriculturist for, amongst other things, the description of Mary's method of planting potatoes. Young particularly admired as a model landowner the Robert Andrews of Suffolk, subject of Gainsborough's portrait "Mr. and Mrs. Andrews" in the National Gallery, London; it seemed appropriate then to use his surname for Blanch's successor.

Jonah Barrington, *Personal Sketches of his own times*, London, 1827-1832.

Walter Harris and Charles Smith, *The Antient and Present State of the County of Down*, Dublin, 1744.

All excerpts from *The Gentleman's Magazine* are actual, with my characters added.

Selected Secondary Sources

Richard Robert Madden, *Antrim and Down in '98,* London, 1900, excerpt from his seven volume *The United Irishmen, their lives and times,* London, 1843.

William Edward Hartpole Lecky, *A History of Ireland in the Eighteenth Century,* five volumes, London, 1892.

Helena Walsh Concannon, *Women of Ninety-Eight,* Dublin, 1919.

Constantia Maxwell, *Country and Town in Ireland under the Georges,* Dundalk, 1949.

Thomas Pakenham, *The Year of Liberty: History of the Great Irish Rebellion of 1798,* London, 1969.

J.F. Heyes, 'Roman Catholic Education in County Durham', unpublished M.Ed. thesis, University of Durham, 1969.

R.F. Foster, *Modern Ireland, 1600-1972,* London, 1988.

Stella Tillyard, *Citizen Lord,* London, 1998.

Acknowledgements:

The late Dr Brian Trainor, formerly the Director of the Public Record Office of Northern Ireland, advised on and encouraged the writing of this book in its earliest days. He was the first person to address me (in writing) as 'Katie – author.' I have also been supported selflessly by my friends in the Irish Writers Union and the Irish Chapter of the Historical Novel Society. These notably include Conor Kostick, Catherine Kullmann, Maria McDonald, Derville Murphy, Patricia O'Reilly and Maybelle Wallis, but there are many more.

I would like to thank my husband Carmine Mezzacappa and our two sons, Antonio and Tommaso, for putting up with research trips thinly disguised as family vacations. I would like to thank my agent, Annette Green and all the dedicated team at Histria Books, especially Amna Majid, Diana Livesay, Dana Ungureanu, Emily Lane Schlick, and Kurt Brackob.

HISTRIA BOOKS

HISTRIA ROMANCE

Look for these other oustanding Romance titles

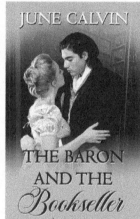

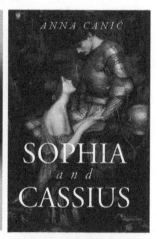

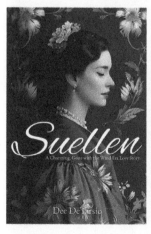

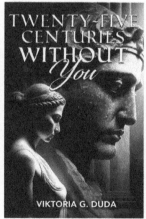